Kerry takes a vacation.
Will Europe ever recover?

It's not easy coming to terms with life, love, sex,
and a diminishing supply of traveler's checks . . .
but it's loads of fun through the eyes of this brash
and genuine American wit.

> *"Hitchhiking was a piece of cake in
> France. I was a young girl, alone. All I
> had to do was point my thumb and
> smile into the windshields of the ap-
> proaching cars. When they saw my out-
> stretched female arm, Frenchmen pulled
> over so fast I never even had a chance
> to pee between rides."*

"High-spirited . . . truly hilarious."
Cleveland Plain Dealer

Spend It Foolishly

Mary Gallagher

AVON
PUBLISHERS OF BARD, CAMELOT AND DISCUS BOOKS

AVON BOOKS
A division of
The Hearst Corporation
959 Eighth Avenue
New York, New York 10019
Copyright © 1978 by Mary Gallagher
Published by arrangement with Atheneum Publishers.
Library of Congress Catalog Card Number: 77-23661
ISBN: 0-380-46011-4

First Avon Printing, September, 1979
Second Printing

AVON TRADEMARK REG. U.S. PAT. OFF. AND IN
OTHER COUNTRIES, MARCA REGISTRADA,
HECHO EN U.S.A.

Printed in the U.S.A.

*To my family
and especially to Peggy,
my fearless reader.*

PART ONE

The Whirlwind Tour

Yurrup and Grace

I decided to take Grace with me to Europe for one reason: cowardice. I had to get out of Cleveland. I had to go somewhere and have adventures, or I would burst. I was afraid to go alone. Grace was the only person I knew who had the money and the time to go with me.

Grace and I had adjacent desks in the Coding Department of the Occidental Insurance Company. We were relatively kindred spirits. She was the only person in Coding, besides me, who laughed. Neither of us fit the Occidental mold: we didn't bring the same lunch every day, and we were under forty. But Grace didn't hate Occidental with a passion equal to mine. I considered myself a captive in transit, a prisoner of war who had started a tunnel the first night in camp.

I broke the dress every Friday, partly on principle, and partly because I only had two dresses. I wore them on alternate days, Monday through Thursday. Friday, I wore pants. I called the dresses "Julie" and "Tricia." I'd bought them on sale for student teaching, my last year of college. In my role as teacher, I'd worn them on alternate days for ten weeks, tossing a coin on Fridays. My supervising teacher hadn't seemed to notice. But after graduation, the only teaching job I'd been offered had been the seventh grade dumb track at Split Rail Middle School in Dogtrack, Ohio.

The Monday morning after graduation, I wore "Julie" (navy with white collar and cuffs) to an employment agency. Except for babysitting and coaching softball every summer, I'd never had a job in my life. I flunked the typing test. But I got fifty for fifty on General Skills, which was just like the tests I'd been giving my kids in student teaching, "plus and take away." Dixie, my patron at Elite Office Aides, had symmetrical teeth and the charm of a

3

metronome. She was very earnest, as if she were explaining where babies come from. When I told her I had a teaching degree, she was sympathetic. She was a failed stewardess.

"See, Kerry, the difficulty is going to be, you're overqualified," Dixie said. She sent me to interviews for Mail Sorter, Salad Girl, and Parking Lot Attendant. I wore "Julie" to all of them. I told my father, "I'm never going to change this dress till I get a decent job."

"Is that for luck?" said my father. "Or are you making a statement?"

"If I'm going to work in an office, I'd better get used to monotony," I said. My father worked in an office—he was a vice president—but he also played sax in a band. He didn't mind slurs on nine-to-five. I said, "Four years of pinching myself in lectures so I could get a good job! 'If You Can Teach, You Can Always Eat'—that was engraved on the forks in the college dining room. Now I've got my certification, and I can't get hired as a locker room guard in a health spa. I'm sick of being on the auction block. They look at my teeth. I've quit brushing them."

"I hope you get a job before you're a health hazard," my father said.

Between interviews for menial positions, I spent the days of summer after graduation lolling on the beach, inhaling Coppertone and eating Fritos. I watched Lake Erie yield to the encroach of sludge. At night, I went with my best friend, Randy, to triple horror bills at the drive-in or sat drinking beer at the Churchkey, the local low-rent lounge, with some boy I'd known forever as escort and all of our buddies as entourage. One pal from the Churchkey offered to get me a job just like his. He had an M.A. in Asian Studies from Stanford. He was a gluer in a Roman collar factory. "It's not too bad," he told me. "They let us play the radio."

My father gave me money. All my life, at college, at camp, he'd sent me money before I'd asked, with a note: "Spend it foolishly!" Now, as always, I obliged. I saw myself at fifty, still on the paternal dole, painting tea cups and annotating my journals.

My mother consoled me. "You wouldn't like working for someone else anyway. I know you," she said.

"You think I should start my own company?" I said. "Kerry, Inc.?"

"You could do anything you set your mind to," my mother said. "Look at how well you did with Girl Scout cookies."

I was almost ready to open a Kool-Aid stand when I got a job. I was hired at $2.30 an hour as a coding clerk at Occidental Insurance. I had my very own desk and my very own red leather manual. Every day from eight-thirty to five, less half an hour for lunch, I verified the rates that the agents had used to write the policies. I looked up numbers in charts, and multiplied. I checked the agents' figures. If we agreed, I marked *O.K.* and chucked the thing in the OUT box. If we disagreed, I wrote the agent a terse rebuke. I had to do the math on paper because the only adding machine in the Coding Department rested silent and dusty, a disconnected electric shrine, on the supervisor's desk, while ten clerks scrabbled with pencils and crumbly erasers. When the erasers were worn to nubs, we turned them in to the supervisor, who doled out new ones. The supervisor had a flattop hair-do and wore a bumpy knit tie. On my first day as a coder, he had reassured me. He'd thought I was a sweet little girl because I'd been wearing "Tricia" (white chintz, pink flowers). He'd said, "If anybody ever tells you he knows everything there is to know about the insurance game you just met Jesus Christ walking down the street."

Apart from an occasional prickly rebuttal from an agent who had an adding machine, my only diversion was Grace. She didn't share my interests. I had a library card. Grace read only the *TV Guide,* cover to cover, before the TV week began. Her evenings were spent before the television in the rec room, with one of her boyfriends, who alternated, like my dresses. Richie and Timmy were an indistinguishably oafish pair who worked side by side, loading a banana truck. Their friendship dated back to stealing doughnuts out of milkchutes in nursery school. Now they were rivals for Grace's love. They told her awful tales of each other's bestialities. The subject of Grace's conversation, apart from TV and her dog, was which of her swains was the Rat.

"Maybe they're both lying," I said, daily.

"No, there has to be a Rat," said Grace, daily. Tracking

the Rat through the sewers of Richie and Timmy's small talk was the central quest of Grace's life. She'd been coding for five years. She tried to enlist me as a spy. "I'll fix you up with Timmy" (to double with Grace and Richie) "or Richie" (to double with Timmy and Grace). I declined. But Grace pursued the Rat Hunt, on Friday nights with Timmy at the Demolition Derby; on Saturday nights, when Richie played the bells in a band called The Polka Chips. On Mondays, in the ladies' room, we raked over clues.

Grace's brain was fuzzy, and droned, like a test pattern. But she had the vivacity of Bert Parks compared to the lifers around us.

Gloria sat at the desk in front of mine, square in my sights, the specter of the nightmare future. She was stringy, with hair the color of her stapler. Her skin had a green tinge, as if the metallic green of her desk had seeped through her pores and saturated her body. Her black skirt was worn away in patches to the meshed threads, windows on her skinny ass. When it looked like rain, she wore see-through plastic snap-on galoshes. She carried her lunch in a limp, weightless bag, the same lunch every day: a liverwurst sandwich on Lite-Diet bread, and two Lorna Doones. Sometimes when her stars danced, she went mad and bought a brownie from the vending machine. The brownie was wrapped in cellophane, square, stale, stamped out of one inch-thick factory-rendered ersatz chocolate sheet the size of a football field. When Gloria bought a brownie for lunch, everybody teased her. She giggled about it all day, as if she'd hidden a rubber in with her liverwurst. The first time it happened, it depressed me so much I went into the ladies' room and lay down on the floor. Grace had to come in and get me.

"What's wrong?" she said.

"I can't stand it," I said.

"You have to come out. The supervisor wants to know if you're sick."

"Tell him I'm languishing. Only his adding machine will ease me."

"Come on. He keeps looking at his watch," she said.

After lunch, Gloria folded up her bag and put it in her purse. I knew she'd been carrying that same bag every day for twelve years. The bag was magic, like the pitcher in the fairy tale. Every night, Gloria put the bag in the icebox and went to sleep. Every morning, when she took it out, it held a slab of liverwurst-and-bread and two air-flavored cookies.

Genevieve was a dumpy, kindly grandmother whose lumpy print dresses smelled sour and powdery. She brought in a banquet every day: half a pie, a whole chicken, a pound of grapes, fudge "for the department," which the file girls stole. She swilled quarts of Tab. She toted her provisions in a plastic flowered bag, tucked beneath an afghan, which she crocheted in the last ten minutes of lunch. Crocheting ten minutes a day, five days a week, Genevieve had churned out an afghan for every member of her family, every member of the Coding Department, most of the underwriters, half the Mail Room. She had crocheted the county with afghans. She had a fiercely loyal relationship with her pencil sharpener, which she refused to lend. I didn't blame her. She'd had it since before I was born.

Shuttling in the Slot A Tab B repartee of Genevieve and Gloria, I pounced on Grace with hysterical relief. We read each other agents' reports of highway accidents. Our favorite catastrophes featured tractor-trailers. The star cataclysm of my term at Occidental was a nine-vehicle chain collision. It had begun with a motorcycle that skidded, and involved two cars, two police cars, an ambulance, an air-port limo, a Good n' Plenty truck, and a Trailways bus. We laughed about it for weeks.

But we had to be sly. The supervisor frowned on the rustling of papers. The first month, I outcoded even Gloria, the champion drone of the department. To keep my mind hovering above the morass, like a bird on quicksand, I whizzed through months of backlog. I inherited most of Grace's work. Grace divided her day into thirds: working; talking to Richie and Timmy on the phone, as if they were agents; and going to the ladies', where I joined her for the Rat Hunt. The whole time, she was eating irredeem-able crap—hard crullers, cheese corn—which she hid in a drawer with the rubber bands and catsup tubes. We weren't allowed to eat at our desks. But the supervisor could have followed the Hansel and Gretel trail of crumbs from the john to Grace's desk.

Sharing Grace's snacks and Genevieve's fudge, I gained

five pounds. "Julie" was splitting at the seams. "Tricia"
was rotten under the arms. I could see my skin turning
the color of the booths in the john. By August, I was
plowing through November policies. I caught myself re-
buking agents—"No, you flaming fool!" The file girls who
had to burrow in back drawers to fill the maw of my IN
box staged a slowdown. Idle, I fell asleep at my desk.
I made Grace talk to keep me awake, as if we were
truckers on a haul across Nebraska. We chattered across
the aisle, ignoring the swivel-orbed reproach of Gloria.
The supervisor confronted me.

"Are you bored?" he said.

I prayed to be fired. But the speed of my multiplica-
tion saved me. I couldn't quit the only job I'd ever had.
But my days, like my dreams, were numbered.

I had an escape fund. My father, predictably, refused
my offer to pay my room and board. "Save it," he said. "I
don't think you're going to make a killing in insurance."
To speed up my exit and pass the time, I followed a budget. I allotted each workday fifty cents for morning and
afternoon liquid from the boiled-chestnut machine; fifty
cents for busfare, which I was permitted to squander if
I walked; and thirty-five cents for a can of pop at lunch.
Weekday expenses came to six dollars and seventy-five
cents a week. Ten dollars covered the weekend. In Cleveland, there was nothing to spend it on. Every Friday, I
went to the bank with a check for $75.87. I deposited
$59.00. I blew the twelve cents extra on mints at Howard
Johnson's on the way home.

Spending money foolishly had been easy, when it was
my father's money. The novelty of making my own gave
zest to hoarding.

In mid-September, ten weeks into my coding career,
when I was chastised by the high priest of the adding
machine, I marched into the ladies' and opened my bank
book to compose myself.

I had five hundred and ninety dollars.

I decided to go to Europe.

My best friend, Randy, had spent her junior year in college in Rome. While I'd been attending curling matches in
an ice rink in the middle of a cornfield, Randy had been
sleeping on beaches and living on bread and eye-squint

wine. I'd been deflowered on a golf course between a catsup plant and a sewage ditch, by a blind date who'd been rendered even more inert than I was after six hours of swilling tomato-beer. My major sensual recollection of the event, apart from the golf tees biting into my back, had been the mingled odors of orange peels and offal from the ditch, and stewing tomatoes. I'd been careful to avoid the boy ever after, and annoyed to notice that he avoided me. But Randy had become a woman in a sleeping bag on a Sicilian hillside, in a tryst with a shepherd who, Randy swore, looked exactly like a younger Marcello Mastroianni.

I wanted equal time!

But school was out. I couldn't go to Europe as Randy had—with a claque of twenty-year-old hedonists to play with, and school as an excuse for frittering. I was a grownup. My friends were being paid to make felt boards in country day schools. They were engaged to former track stars who worked for Addressograph-Multigraph. Randy was pushing fudgies for Kraft. She couldn't quit. She'd bought a car and eleven pairs of shoes.

"Do you want to stay in Cleveland all your life?" I badgered her.

"Just till I pay off my National Defense loan," she said. "Anyway, I like Cleveland."

I told her she'd wake up in twenty years and find herself living in Warrensville Heights with six kids and a husband who played third base for the Plain Dealer "A" League, when he wasn't selling hardware. She said, "So I'll take the kids to the baseball games and let 'em eat candy apples while they watch their old man play. Then they won't want dinner, and me and my hubby can go to the drive-in and neck."

Equilibrium perched like a smiley bird on Randy's shoulder. The things that drove me crazy, that I labeled CLEVELAND, didn't bother Randy. She'd had a fine time in Italy. Now she was content to molder in Ohio. Once I'd made friends with life outside, I'd never set foot in Cleveland again unless a band was waiting.

What I needed was a fellow traveler. I tried to enlist any one of the boys who bought my beer at the Churchkey. But it was hopeless. They didn't see me in terms of elopement. I'd had one or two candidates in mind for a summer romance—they seemed to be the only boys in Cleveland that I hadn't, at some time, beaten in spelling bees. But they'd known me, or girls who looked like me, since grade school. They thought I was too pure to kiss. I still had straight hair and freckles. My WASP buddies thought I looked like a milkmaid. The Catholics thought I looked like their first-grade nun. I'd had to go to college in the farm belt to meet boys accustomed to humping the wholesome. And the three boys I'd slept with in four years at college had married their childhood sweethearts and were hip-deep in corn and manure. (I'd had a brief reign as queen of the Agriculture School.)

But I tried. I scouted the local talent, casting discreetly desperate glances up and down the bar. Once I'd zeroed in on a prospect, I proceeded cautiously. First I bought a pitcher of draft and split it with the target. Randy would distract the target's buddy—all of us traveled in pairs, as if yoked—at the bowling machine. I'd have a shot of Jack Daniels, for nerve. Finally, in the bleary death of the juke box, I'd mutter in the target's neck, "Let's go to Europe. You and me, no kidding, come on. I can't stand this, I gotta get outta Cleveland. Just for a month, even. I've got money. Let's go."

"Yurrup, goddamn, wouldn't that be fantastic? But Christ, I can't quit E and E. It took me eight months to get hired."

Or: "Yeah, yeah, let's do it. Only you know what? . . . Not right now. See, I gotta stand up for my roommate, he's gettin' married in Buffalo—"

Or: "Are you outta yore gourd? Marlene would kill me!"

"For God's sake! I haven't got the hots on you! I've known you since Junior Olympics!" I'd say.

They were wary. Nice girls who offered to hitchhike in Latin countries with men had blackmail in mind. Me in my sleeping bag—him in his sleeping bag—God knew what could happen to those proximate zippers! Italians would be eager to avenge my pallid honor. An accordion wedding loomed. I got a lot of free drinks and some sleepy groping. But I got no takers.

I threatened to go alone. "What could happen?" I demanded at the dinner table. My brothers didn't answer. They were arguing over who had emptied the milk. But my father suggested some consequences: smarmy gigolos, chloroform. My mother was opposed to solitary travel because, she said, it wasn't any fun. Her idea of a perfect vacation was loading the family and some friends and cousins and a three-month supply of peanut butter and gin and 6-12 in a bus, and driving through every national park in America, camping at every campsite, clambering out at every scenic overlook, feeding every bear, pushing every button on every trailside speaker, and listening rapt to every taped description of the reproduction of the yucca. Since my father's ideal of a perfect vacation was lying in a hammock playing the saxophone while everybody else in Cleveland was stuck in a car on the freeway trying to get to the beach, my mother had to make her Conestoga treks with scout troops, in which my brothers and I were draftees. Milk plants, soap box derbies, air shows, open-air markets, planetariums, antique car museums. . . . Years of being my mother's hostage on buses crammed with sweaty little girls hoarsely bawling, "The ants go marching one by one, hurrah! . . . hurray! . . ." had instilled me with a vicious animosity toward group maneuvers.

Mother, in her giddy youth, had "done" Italy with fellow debutantes from Miss Dilworth's Academy in Sioux Falls. She hauled out the snapshots: there she was, round-faced and unaccountably young, one of fifteen laughing girls in monogrammed cinch belts and saddle shoes, drinking Cokes at little tables in the sun in the Piazza San Marco. The treble cacophony must have driven the pigeons berserk. Wanting me to have a similar magical experience, Mom was pushing the Alumni Tour of the Low Countries sponsored by my alma mater.

"That would be keen," I said. "Most of the people who went to that school think Luxembourg is in southern Ohio. I can see us now, the class of '76, four thousand strong, trampling through the tulip beds of Holland while the former football players make up dike jokes. I'd rather tar a road in Alabama with a chain gang."

"You'll never get any fun out of life if you take that attitude," said my mother.

October pounced upon us. I was desperate. After four months as Tillie the Toiler, I wanted nothing more than

to resign and be kept. Work was worse than school. Even
under socialism, who'd get a kick out of coding?

Providence gave me its Mona Lisa smile. Grace got
the boot. She goofed off more than I did, and she couldn't
add. Gravely, the supervisor informed her that she wasn't
Occidental material. We spent the afternoon in the ladies',
as a protest. "What are you going to do?" I said.

"I'm going to buy myself a big goopy maplenut sundae
on the way home," said Grace, picking her cuticles with
a bent staple.

"Yeah, but . . . you know . . . where will you get another job?"

"Oh, I don't care anyway. Poop on everybody. Mom and
Dad won't care if I just sit around for a while. And
Sparky will be so happy that I don't have to go away
every morning! You should see—"

Sparky was a peekapoo, a breed of dog whose name
speaks for itself. Sight unseen, I hated his guts. I cut her
off. "Have you got any money saved?"

"Oh yes, lots and lots, but it's for when I get married."
Like the girls in the ads, Grace wasn't engaged, but she
was thinking about becoming engaged.

"You mean for five years you've been saving just for
when you get married?"

"Oh no. I've been saving ever since I was a little girl.
Not just plain old money—everything, you know."

"You mean . . . a hope chest?"

"Well, not exactly a chest. I mean most of it's in cartons.
Linens . . . Corning Ware . . . ordinary china, you know,
for every day. . . . I picked out my crystal and silver
patterns when I was twelve, and every birthday and
Christmas, Dad gives me a fork or a spoon or a knife,
and Mom gives me a goblet."

"Just think, by the time you're a hundred and seven,
you'll have the whole set. What does Sparky give you—
fingerbowls?"

"Just you laugh! *I'm* planning for the future."

"How do Richie and Timmy feel about all this?"

"Oh, I'd never tell them about it! All they know about
is the vacuum cleaner. They checked out the brand and
all, you know, before I said I'd buy it. They were just so
cute, the two of them—"

"You bought a vacuum cleaner?"

"Well, it was such a bargain, I thought I'd just do it now. I got it for half price, when I bought the complete set of stainless steel cookware."

"Now let me get this straight. You mean that, for instance, any Saturday, you just set off for Sears and pick out your complete set of—"

"Oh no, I bought that from a salesman who came to the house! Craig, his name was—He looked like Robert Wagner! I would've bought just anything! But Mom asked him a lot of questions—you know, she knows about all this stuff, like what pressure to cook corn and all. And my Aunt Linda was there, and my cousins. We had chips and dip and RC—and Sparky ate the velvet cloth that Craig used to polish his samples! It was lots of fun."

"And you bought the complete set of stainless steel cookware and a vacuum cleaner."

"The vacuum cleaner was later. After Ritchie and Timmy—"

"Right. Do you keep all this stuff in your bedroom? Where do you sleep, on the loading dock?"

"I know, Dad just gets livid every time another carton comes! No, we keep them in the rec room. Ritchie and Timmy are always asking, 'What's in all those boxes?' I say, 'Oh, just tools.' "

I studied her.

"But I do keep my files in the bedroom. Because sometimes, you know, I look at them before I go to sleep."

"Files?" Of candidates? Could there be more banana loaders I hadn't heard about?

"Files of rooms for my dream house, silly. That you cut out of magazines. I've got a whole little cabinet Dad made. It's just cunning."

"Grace, I've got the job for you," I said. "Mail order bride."

Grace giggled. "Well, I just guess I'm ready."

"Ready? Aren't you packed?" Then it came to me. Doubt leaped, but I sapped it behind the ear. "Exactly how much money have you got in the bank?"

"Two thousand seven hundred dollars," said Grace.

I braced myself on the sink.

"Grace," I said, "how about a honeymoon . . . dry run?"

She was easy to persuade. She must have been trapped

in her living room five nights out of seven, mesmerized by the Mandrake passes of Melmac vendors. Her only qualm was that Richie and Timmy—and Sparky of course—would miss her. "It'll do them good," I said. "They'll pop the question the day you get back."

"Oh, I hope not," Grace giggled. "Then I'd have to figure out which one is the Rat!"

Apprehension twinkled up my neck. What if Grace took the Rat Hunt to Europe? I had to chance it. Escape with Grace was better than a slow green death by Coding. I didn't care if she brought Richie and Timmy along, in identical garment bags.

It was scarey. For a month, I'd been railing that I couldn't go to Europe alone. My inert friends were stones in my path. Now I'd dislodged a boulder. Grace roared downhill; I was a pebble in her wake. Once I'd won a three-week leave from Coding, and told my family and the crowd at the Churchkey, I had to go through with it. Grace and I fell upon Europe like an avalanche.

I found the Flights of Fancy Travel Bureau in the Yellow Pages. The agent assigned to me over the phone was Alma. She referred to herself as my "contact," as if I were smuggling out files. Alma thought it would be nice if Grace and I took a bus tour, which included meals, hotels, sightseeing stops, free postcards, discounts on souvenirs, and announcements of scenic points for those with cameras.

"Who takes pictures from a bus?" I said.

"I've gotten some of my nicest pictures from the window of a bus," said Alma.

I didn't let Alma communicate with Grace. She could have sold Grace three weeks in a Winnebago with fifty members (and their wives) of the Van Wert, Ohio, Peony Growers.

We planned our trip with surgical caution, prepared to amputate at symptoms of extravagance. Grace wanted to go to Switzerland. The only book she'd ever read cover to cover, when she'd had the chicken pox, was *Heidi*. I wanted to go everywhere. But it became apparent that every time we took a train, I would be hauling a gibbering Grace, who wouldn't take a bus downtown without her mother. For the sake of peace, I settled for two weeks in Switzerland. But I held out for one mad week in the land of art and depravity: France. "Just Paris, and we'll do it last," I promised. We'd have to fly to New York to pick up the cheapo flight that lasted nineteen hours. Grace had never heard of the airline. She was a little nervous. I said, "Look, they only have two planes. They can't afford to crash, they'd lose half their business." Alma, our contact, had booked us into poverty pocket hotels. Grace had wanted rooms with baths. I'd shamed her into taking hotels with a tub on every floor.

We applied for passports. In the pictures, I looked like Margaret O'Brien in *Meet Me in St. Louis.* Grace looked stolid and corrupt, like the mistress of a Nazi general. Processing would take three weeks. We made our reservations for November first.

Grace bought the current volume of *The Book,* the Bible of the marginal tourist. She adored it. She even read the chapter on Prague. Her favorite nuggets of wisdom were "Tips from Our Readers." Our Readers were so cheery, so spartan, and so tight with a buck, they made me feel like the Widow Onassis. An image had formed in my mind's eye of Our Reader, an icon of pragmatism, hygiene, and thrift. She wore a drip-dry polyester suit and crepe-soled shoes. She carried one plaid cloth ziplock suitcase, small enough to fit inside a baggage locker, but large enough to hold two changes of underwear, three wrinkle-free ensembles, and a folded inflatable tent, in case an act of God demolished the cheap hotels. The champion Reader had traveled in Europe all summer without a suitcase. Grace called me one morning at seven-fifteen to read me her story. Every day, the Reader had worn the same navy linen suit. (I pictured a bunch of cherries at the lapel and a matching hat with veil.) She'd washed out her only pair of underpants every night in the hotel basin using a bar of soap which she'd carried in a Baggie in her purse.

"What if the Baggie leaked?" I said. "She'd be breeding tadpoles in her wallet."

Like a firm nanny, Grace continued reading. Our Reader's handbag had also contained her nightgown, her toothbrush, and of course, *The Book.* She'd covered ten cities in three months.

"She was wise to keep moving," I said, thinking of the

gradual erosion of the cherries at her bosom, not to speak of her underpants. "I hope this has inspired you to leave your steamer trunk at home."

Grace had bought a set of matched luggage, and cut a swathe through the city's Young Matron departments. After a two-day wrangle, I persuaded her to jam her new wardrobe into two of the massive suitcases. Packed, the larger suitcase was as easy to lift as an upright piano. She also had a train case to tote her cosmetics and bubblebath mitts. Knowing I'd be Grace's porter, I folded up my spare jeans and Wendy nightgown and three sweaters, and tucked them into a small canvas bag. The bag was a compromise between a knapsack and a Reader plaid cloth suitcase. I didn't want to backpack, like what Alma, our contact, referred to as "hippie-type travelers." A hippie in trail boots in Paris would look like Rip Van Winkle, down from the hills. On the other hand, I didn't want to go as Our Reader, a crepe-soled, drip-dry closet nun. I wanted to sneak up on Europe, and belong.

October 31, I was awake all night. Already I was homesick. I'd have only Grace to talk to for the next three weeks. I was rotten at making friends. The only summer I'd agreed to go to camp, my parents had had to pry my hand from the handle of the door of the car. I'd never spoken to the kid in the bunk below me till I'd stepped on her. I'd gone to the same state college as half the kids in my high school class. I was twenty-one and I still didn't speak to strangers. Who was I kidding?

Or else I would become a different person. Everything could change in three weeks, including me.

In the morning, I ate a peanut butter sandwich to soothe me. It had the definitive taste of home. Randy came to take me to the airport. My mother cried when I kissed her goodbye. "Come on, Mom, I'll be okay," I said. "I know," she said, "I want to go!" My father gave me a hundred dollars. "If you feel it violates your independence, you can throw it out the window of the car on Route 71," he said.

Randy gave me a lira for luck, a souvenir of her sleeping bag days in Trieste. I hugged her hard. She let me out at the airport gate.

In the airport lounge, Grace was hidden in the moist

bosom of her family till the plane was loaded. I'd dragged her halfway across the runway before I noticed that she was clutching an enormous stuffed turtle. "What's that?" I said.

"This is Turkle," said Grace. Suddenly a croaky voice issued from her middle, as if from a walkie-talkie. "Is her coming wiv us to Yuwwup?" said the croak. "Now be nice," said Grace in her own voice, in hot-fudge tones of whimsy. The croak said, "Hewwo, Kewwy."

I looked Grace in the eye. She had the same button-blind gaze as the turtle. I said to the turtle, guardedly, "How are you?"

Grace held the turtle in her lap on the plane. In the cocktail lounge at Kennedy Airport, the turtle ordered a sloe gin fizz. On the transatlantic flight, Grace introduced the turtle to the stewardess, a six-foot quadrilingual ice queen. "Charming," said the stewardess, placing a tray of poached veal on the turtle. I tried to look crusty but reliable, as if I were Grace's highly paid nurse.

All around us, bushy-headed vagabonds were rapping on the Real Yurrup Tourists Never Dig. Passengers who weren't hippies were spry, greying ladies in crepe-soled shoes. The plane's hold must have been bulging with backpacks and plaid cloth ziplock suitcases, copies of *The Book,* like dope, concealed in every parcel.

The passengers deplaned in Luxembourg in clumps: quartets of wholesome freaks in sixty-dollar boots; trios of ladies in hairnets. In clumps, we boarded the airport bus. In clumps, we disembarked at the first stop, the train station. Luxembourg, to most tourists, was an extended depot. One lone teenaged boy remained on the bus. "This is the train station," someone informed him as the crowd fled. "I know," he said, abashed. "I'm staying in Luxembourg." The bus door closed before him, like the stone that seals the tomb.

In Yurrup, I ordered *The Book* and Turkle quarantined in the hotel room. But Grace didn't need props to perform. In the marzipan mountains of Lucerne, Grace was chased across a fourteenth-century covered bridge by a swan as big as a pony. A mad Swiss doctor must have been breeding monster swans to swoop down from the Alps when Switzerland took over. The mutant swan was after Grace's pastry.

"Drop the cream puff! Drop the cream puff!" I kept yelling. But, galloping, Grace pressed the gloppy lump to her breast. I had to throw snowballs at the swan to chase it off.

In Zurich, where every other building was a bank, and the bells ringing in the frosty air were cash registers, Grace let an English-speaking female in combat boots talk her into changing our hotel. We wound up in a females' hostel, a tiled and steamy incubator of Calvinist repression. Hearty maidens kept bursting into our room to "check the beds." Most of the residents wore their boots in the shower. Schussing down the hall in fuzzy pink slippers, Grace remarked, "Those girls in the boots are so friendly! Every time I go to the ladies', one of them asks me to Indian wrestle."

In a ski club in Leysin, blond Australian men with snow between their ears bought me beer, till Grace joined us at the bar. Soon there was a two-stool gap on either side of us. Even girls wouldn't talk to Grace, fearing the contagion of her gaucherie. Americans backed away, all but ringing bells and crying, "Unclean!" European girls spoke only to flat-assed Americans, trying to buy their jeans. My jeans were so old I had to fasten the waistband with a safety pin. French and German girls kept backing me against the bunks and offering me sex with their boyfriends as barter for my jeans. I refused. My jeans were all that stood between me and European contempt. Poor Grace! In her lime-green ski pants and Sandra Dee bubble cut! Nobody wanted anything from her. All those girls with big boobs and small butts were sleeping with skiers— the dormitory was a tomb at night—and Grace was sleeping with Turkle. Condemned to keep her company, I was sleeping with blighted hopes.

Entering Paris with Grace, I felt like Dorian Gray with his portrait taped to his back. She was a cartoon of the American tourist. She declared the scenery, the paintings, and the natives "cunning." She bought pink plastic reproductions of the Eiffel Tower. She took off her shoes in the Palace of Versailles, and walked barefoot, throwing the guard into apoplexy. She made me ask baronial waiters in cafés where the toilet was. Then she emerged announcing in tones of brass, "It's just a hole in the floor! How can they live like this?"

She took up the dime-size café table writing postcards, and read them aloud: "Dear Mom and Dad, This is the famous Notre Dame, but it sure is a funny place to play football, ha ha!"

I sipped at the foul but cheap espresso, and made up News from Grace:

"Dear Mom and Dad, Here we are at Notre Dame Cathedral. The gargoyle on the left is me. I just love the cunning little nuns who tear your traveler's checks out of your hands. So French! We rented sackcloth and ashes, and the ravishment by Quasimodo was so cheap, I went back twice! He looks just like Jean-Claude Killy!"

The only time Grace's complacency was shatttered was the day we saw the flasher at the Louvre.

We spent three squinting hours in that cultural cafeteria, hunting for pâté among the succotash. I told Grace I wanted to wander by myself, and "soak it up." But everywhere I turned, there was another Rubens and an odor of mold. I was marauded by platoons of Germans, goose-stepping in double lines. They backed up onto my ankles, as if I were an observation deck. When I rendezvoused with Grace in the lobby, her raptures on the *Mona Lisa* were drowned by the bellowing of French, English, Italian, Spanish, Russian, and Rumanian guides, and the oblivious babbling of their charges. We escaped into the beige damp of the Tuileries.

The gravel of the garden was squishy with settled mist. The trees were picked clean, and huddled scrawny and ashamed before the wind.

Grace clutched my arm. "Ow," I said. My nerves were so tightly clenched, I would have screamed in pain if someone had kissed me. In the shadow of a sand-colored arch, we confronted a frieze: an open raincoat, and a red, raw penis, chafing in the wind. I'd never seen one outdoors in the daylight. It looked like the nozzle of a garden hose.

I looked at the man's face. His eyes were scared, but eager, seeking mine, as if for verification. I wondered what he hoped I'd do. Probably what Grace was doing—she was turning orange. I said to him, "Congratulations." He bobbed his head. The mud-colored raincoat scuttled off around the fountain and vanished in the mist.

Grace was gasping for breath. I thought I'd have to give her heart massage. But she came around to hysterics. "He had his thing hanging out!" she kept yelling. Skinny women with fat blue baby buggies fixed us with snaky eyes. "Shut up," I said, hauling her toward the street. "Think of it as a postcard. 'Dear Mom and Dad, today at the Louvre we saw a private exhibition.' "

In private, Grace was even more embarrassing. Mom and Dad had stuffed her train case with twenty little gifts and twenty little notes, one for each morning of the trip. Every breakfast was Christmas morning. Grace opened her present—for instance, a pamphlet of *Sonnets from Shakespeare.* Cheeks streaked with jelly and tears, she read me her note: " 'Just some immortal words to go with the immortal sights of Europe. We miss you already. Love, Mom and Dad. Me too! Sparky!' Isn't that cunning?"

Knowing Grace's penchant for whimsy, it figured that she'd be a tinkle announcer. She tinkled constantly, proclaiming her intentions (sometimes numerically) to intimates and crowds. She was as gleeful as a toddler who's finally grasped the concept of toilet training. "Kerry, I'm going to tinkle now," she'd say, as if I were supposed to say, "Good girl!" Paris was heaven for Grace. She found a toilet right in the hotel room. It was like tinkling on the *Johnny Carson Show.* Five minutes after we'd arrived, she was doing her business. "Isn't this just super? I can tinkle whenever I feel like it!"

Grace might have a vocation to tinkle, but I had not been called to witness. I said, "There ought to be a screen around that thing."

Grace said, "Oh, you know how the French are about bodies and things."

It seemed unlikely that the nation of liaisons would put the bed and the toilet in the same room. What of romance?

Grace heaved herself around. She said, "There's no toilet paper. Honestly, these people are so *cheap.* Would you hand me the Kleenex in my suitcase?"

I gave her the box, averting my eyes. Grace dropped wads of purple Kleenex into the curiously oblong toilet. She pushed the flusher. "That's funny," she said. "It doesn't go down."

I observed the contents of the toilet. She was right.

The drain was a sink trap, with a metal knob that opened only enough to let the water out. I said, "Grace . . . I have a feeling that this is not a toilet."

"Of course it's a toilet," said Grace, annoyed. "What else could it be?"

There should have been a chapter in *The Book* called, "Le Bidet: Why a Low-Slung Sink?" I refused to help Grace scoop it out. "Use *The Book*," I said. She ripped out the Balkan section and used it to transfer the mess to the wastepaper basket. We'd seen the chambermaid, haggard and rouged, hanging around with an armload of unlikely towels. She'd looked at us with envy and contempt, the look reserved for oil-rich Arabs. Wait till she emptied the wastebasket.

I cherished the bidet for that dent in Grace's chrome. I made it the tool of my revenge.

Every night, Grace and her turtle would climb under the covers before I turned out the light. Shortly after I'd bashed my knee on the blind voyage to the bed, she'd croak, "Kewwy, tew me a stowy." The first night, I was stunned. I fell asleep before I'd recovered. The second night, I said I didn't know any stories. "You're mean," said Grace. The third night, I told her "The Pit and the Pendulum." She had nightmares. The fourth night, I said, "Oh, get bent." She was only temporarily squelched.

Our fifth day in Paris was wretched, like every day in Switzerland, but with lusher orchestration. We visited the Panthéon, since we'd heard of the Roman one from which it was copied. It was stuffed like a Franco-Roman mushroom with Readers of *The Book*: gym teachers, sneaking slides; AmEx hippies; children whose parents were straining to be cheery. We couldn't see the murals, or even the walls. Grace had to stand on my hands to take a picture. All at once the old crone who stood watch on the shrine descended on us, shrieking, and snatched Grace's camera. "You can't do that!" I said. I snatched it back. The crone chased us into the street.

That night I dragged Grace through every cobbled alley in the Latin Quarter, eyeing doorways for glimpses of the Real Paris. We ate dinner twice and drank three coffees, smiling hopefully at glacial natives. We beat away a total of fifteen Moroccans and a junkie from Santa Barbara. We took the wrong train, and wound up in the graveyard of the Métro, screaming and pounding on the sealed door of the car. A man in a blue smock came to hurl abuse at us before he let us out. We walked home miles in freezing rain, through streets anonymous and terrible with night. It was almost light when we found our hotel. The whorey chambermaid was lying in a pool of brandy outside our room.

As I lay my battered body down, cursing Paris and all who'd lied about her, Turkle's croaking came to my incredulous ears. "Kewwy, tew me a stowy."

I ripped off the bedclothes, leaped up, fumbled in a whimpering heap of nylon, grabbed the turtle, ran to the bidet, dropped the turtle in, and pushed the flusher. I held Grace off with both arms while I shoved Turkle under with my foot. Grace sobbed and pleaded. Finally I went back to bed. Grace rescued Turkle, sodden, but not extinct. Stuffed pets are hardy.

Drifting to sleep, I thought, "Next time I'll use a razor."

Who Are You Calling a Tourist?

Switzerland had failed me. The whole country smelled like Lysol. The only bar in Zurich open after ten was at the airport, an hour outside of town. The desk clerks charged me half a franc to rent the alarm clock. In a world where overhanging grey peaks, etched with fir trees, vanished into one white sheen when the snow mist rose, Switzerland responded with the cuckoo clock.

And Paris had broken my heart. Paris—the City of Light, the city of Cézanne and Baudelaire and Joyce and Scaramouche and Louis XV and Charles Darnay and Sidney Carton . . . Paris!—where Hemingway had sat in cafés, eating potato salad and writing *The Sun Also Rises* . . . Paris!—where Gene Kelly had shuffled off to Buffalo with charming urchins in streets of Technicolor sun. . . . Paris was dirt, crowds, assassins armed with taxicabs, snooty chi-chi females, lonely Algerians, pumped-up prices, bad manners, cold churches, sad old guys with their flies unzipped, and what seemed to be a convocation of the two hundred thousand most obnoxious of my countrymen. The cafés were pinball parlors. The corrugated beetles of the French were driven from the cobblestones by buses emblazoned, PARIS BY NIGHT—AMERICAN EXPRESS. My own language mocked me. "Le snack," said Paris. "Le drugstore. Le hot dog. Le film."

My savings were gone. I couldn't even bring my brothers a bar of Toblerone chocolate apiece. At least I'd bought myself a pair of boots in Switzerland. I had nothing else to prove I'd ever escaped from Ohio.

In the hotel room, fourteen hours before we'd start the journey home, I was wishing I'd died of staple wounds before I'd ever come to Europe.

Grace was lolling in the tinny trough of her bed. She wore her peach nylon nightie and fuzzy pink slippers.

Brushing off the flakes of her third "milles feuilles" of the day—the Countess of Tip Top had discovered real pastry —she mused, "Just think, it'll be so neat when my pictures are developed! We can just relive this whole fantastic trip! I hope they all come out, otherwise I might forget the most memorable stuff. I'm going to take them to Occidental and show everybody. The girls'll just die!"

"Disruptive to office procedure," I said, stirring my raspberry yogurt. "You'll have to sneak in while the supervisor's in the stock room, counting erasers. You can hide in the ladies', and have the girls come in one at a time. Make them swap you something for a peek. Get Gloria's brownie."

"Pooh, what do I care if he doesn't like it? I don't work there any more! You're the one who has to go back to work on Monday, ha ha!" Grace always giggled to mitigate offensive remarks. "Anyway, I'll make copies of all my pictures for you, poor you with no camera!"

"You don't have to do that," I said. I envisioned a stream of dim grey towers and dim grey hills against dim grey skies, with a foreground pattern of multiplying Grace and diminishing me. My face would be contorted in grimaces meant to hide growing rebellion: the first week, scant tolerance; the second week, sullenness, outrage, revolt. After two weeks, I'd refused to pose. Nothing is more scarring to an American than standing beside a European Sight while a countryman bleats in loud, flat accents, "Move over, I can't get the street sign in!" But I had to take pictures of Grace. She loved to pose, beaming, clutching the sleeve of some mystified native, a human illustration of her rapport with the Continent. Pictures of Paris would be stamped with the complaisant smirk of Grace, Grace, Grace . . . I couldn't face it.

"Well, I don't mean I'd pay for the copies or anything, ha ha," said Grace. "I mean, that would cost a fortune. And of course you wouldn't want the ones of just me. . . ."

She wanted reassurance. She was drawing on a dry well. I propped the yogurt against the bars of my bed and opened my book.

"Whatever I don't spend in the hotel in Luxembourg, I'm gonna blow in the airport duty-free store," Grace announced, bouncing her turtle on the peach nylon mound of her belly. "I want to be able to say I spent every cent on my vacation!" Grace had wrested eleven hundred dollars from the groaning coffers of her dowry. She had eighty dollars left. "Maybe I'll buy a pipe for Timmy. What do you think?"

I pictured Timmy of the ducktail haircut, smoking a pipe as he heaved another load of bananas on the truck. I said, "You've bought him three presents already." Grace put on the brakes and pulled out her wallet at the sight of a souvenir stand. She thought anything sold in the open air was cheap. I had to drag her away from winos whose blankets had caught her attention. She thought they were selling jewelry.

She croaked, "Her has bought fwee fo' Wichie, but her has on'y bought two fo' Timmy!"

From the corner of my rigidly focused left eye, I saw Turkle's waving arms. I turned the page and stirred the yogurt. One more day, I told myself. And the plane ride. Nineteen hours. God.

Grace was sliding across the bed, fuzzy pink slippers coming at me like headlights, croaking, "Her needsa buy the same numbew pwesinks fo' Wichie an' fo' Timmy, 'cause her wuvsem bof! But guess which one her wuvsa mos'?" The green felt nose of the turtle prodded my neck. Grace's hyacinth talc settled over my yogurt.

"Turkle, kiss off!" I smacked it away with my arm. The turtle fell to the pitted linoleum. Grace stood still for a moment. Then she picked the turtle up and sat on her bed. The tin slats squawked. "I certainly don't know what you're so grouchy about all of a sudden," said Grace.

"All of the sudden!" I said. Then I was ashamed. Why should I spoil poor Grace's vacation just because mine was a bust? "Don't mind me. I'm in a lousy mood. I'd better go for a walk." I got up and put on my coat and mittens and fleece-lined new Swiss boots. Paris in November was dank, rank and drizzling: meaner than cat shit.

"Maybe I should get dressed and come with you. I mean this is Paris, and it's our last night."

Hastily I said, "You mean for safety, what with all the white slavers? I'm safer alone. They like to take women in groups, they can fill their quotas faster."

"Very funny. You just better be careful."

Leaving her a mass of yeasty grievance on the bed, I marched down the clammy hall and plastic-treaded stairs.

I passed the desk. The concierge gave me a bleak look. He had the eyes of a depraved raccoon. Like all Parisians, he made me feel hulking: the primitive, trampling out the cultural vineyards. He wouldn't speak to Grace at all. When he spoke to me, it sounded like gargling. A hotel keeper in Paris might have been expected to recognize key words like "room" and "breakfast." But he shook his head impatiently at the drop of a hard-T "toilet." His regard for pronunciation was fierce. We had even ceased to nod. I was convinced that he and the whorey, chicken-breasted chambermaid ravaged our effects while we were out. I could see them, dressing up in Grace's plastic hat and galoshes, rubbing each other with Grace's Wash'n Dri towelettes, engaging in foreplay with Turkle, reading each other portions of Paris by *The Book.* As I came in from the street, I always listened for the echo of their fiendish French laughter.

I went out into the bleak chill of the square. In a thin, nagging drizzle, I walked down the Rue St. Jacques, past the cafés, the open booths where crepes were sold, the chestnut wagons, the frames hung with purses and belts, the lone wet hippie, strumming at the rain-beaded strings of a grubby guitar. "I've seen fire and I've seen rain," he sang, eyes closed. Parisian students whose socks cost more than his guitar were stepping over his outstretched legs. His sneakers were knotted with string and ragged with holes, as if he'd been pursued through the gutters by dogs insatiable for canvas. His naked ankles were gritty, the bones crowned with scabs. His floppy leather hat was inverted on the sidewalk, its crown spilling over like a dog's dish. In its depths, the lone franc was a hint not taken.

I dropped another franc in the hat. There's one born every minute.

Another freak was skulking in the stone arch of a doorway. He was dressed for skulking, in a green stocking hat, dark glasses, and a full blond beard. His beard cracked in a grin. He raised a harmonica and gave one mournful blast, in honor of my franc. He wasn't pulling his weight in the combo.

The dripping hippie on the sidewalk opened his eyes. He looked in his hat. "Hey, thanks," he said. "Where ya from?"

"Cleveland," I said, walking.

"Hey, I'm from Dayton!"

It figured. The only male in Paris who was willing to converse with me had to be from Ohio. Even in Cleveland, hippies were passé. But in Paris, American hippies were everywhere, swarming the Latin Quarter. They hung out at the fountain in the Place St. Michel, swapping dope and saying, "Paris sucks." The black jagged wings of the fountain sculpture were splotched with khaki bodies, like the droppings of diseased birds. In the next two blocks, three hippies approached me and asked for "spare change." I said, "There's no such thing." When the last one fixed me with his boiled-grape gaze, I said, "Go sit on the Eiffel Tower."

I turned down the Rue de la Huchette. The cobblestones were slick and bumpy, like river stones under my boots. The road was made of sleek black lumps, burnished with yellow light from open doorways, with shadow rainbows from neon signs. Girls in pairs bobbed along the sidewalk, arm in arm. Their pants billowed around the knees of glossy high boots, and strained across their hips. Men wore their trenchcoats and heavy patterned sweaters open to the rain. They stood smoking under lamp posts, tossing frizzled, mousy hair. Their eyes drooped. French students seemed to live in frenzied sleep. Black men stood isolated under umbrellas like multicolored parachutes, calling softly to every woman, "Mademoiselle . . . mademoiselle . . ." The pastry shops were closing, the shelves emptied of flaky crescents and sculptured glaze and cream, the bins that held the long baguettes of bread scoured silver. But the Algerian bakeries were jammed, dispensing flat, dry cookies of green and pink, and baklava dripping with honey to Parisians who never spoke to Algerians except to say, "How much?"

It was eight o'clock. In the cafés de Viet Nam, students were slurping bamboo shoots and wine. Viet Nam was still the rage among the Left Bank Left. They liked to remind themselves of America's faux pas, by eating what Ho ate. Lucky for them we hadn't lost a war with England. The French would have held a national fast before they would have eaten boiled peas and custard.

Watching diners mass in doorways, I felt aggrieved. I couldn't afford to eat again just for company. No one would have talked to me anyway. I was lonely. I was American. I didn't need a third strike; I was out.

French girls were hurrying to meet their lovers. The sad, dry voices of black men hissed in the rain: "Mademoiselle . . . mademoiselle . . ." They echoed my own yearning, helpless and dumb: "I'm here . . . I'm ready . . . I'm going home tomorrow. This is Paris! Where is it?" I walked.

Something slammed into the back of my leg. I fell forward, twisting with the force of the blow. Nose to the slimy stones, I lay still. My right leg was shaking with impact and pain. My jeans and mittens were soaked. A voice said, "Ça va?"

I turned, vertebrae cracking. I looked at the wheel of a minibike. Above the handlebars, a boy's face hovered. He watched, one foot on the pedal, as I groped to my knees. He wore a leather jacket and elaborate boots. His pants were so tight I could count the keys in his pocket. Beneath a mop of curls, his small eyes were distracted. He was probably thinking of his pinball date. "Ça va?" he said again: you okay, lady?

"Oh, sure, ça va," I said. I started to cry. I knew I'd lose whatever shred of self-esteem still clung if I cried in France. But my face had puckered up from desolation. I could have been a kid knocked off my trike. The boy extended a hand to help me up.

"Never mind," I blubbered, on my feet. My leg was twanging like a loose guitar string. "Just never mind . . . stinking French creep." I wiped my nose with a mitten, spreading slime.

His absent eyes were taken by surprise. He said, "You should not 'ave been walking in za strit." He sounded like Peppy LePew, the skunk on Saturday morning cartoons. "French girls do not walk in za strit. Amurrican girls don' know 'ow to be'ave." He kicked the accelerator.

"Americans don't run people over and then blame it on the people's bad manners!" I yelled. "I guess if I died of ptomaine in one of your lousy cafés, you'd say nobody else but an American would have eaten there!"

The minibike rolled past me, revving effetely. "You are talking too fast," the boy said. "I do not un'erstan' you."

Skinny-ass girls and fancy-ass boys had gathered on the sidewalk. There was sniggering and clucking. A female voice cooed, "Ooh, là là!" It was the dinner show, "Taunting the Barbarian." But I didn't care. I was out for blood.

"You French kids make me sick," I said. "French, big rockin' deal! Taking American money and then pretending you can't speak English! Riding some farty little motorcycle, like you're Marlon Brando. Well, here's the news— he's an American! And he didn't ride a motorcycle made out of tinfoil!"

"Qu'est-ce qu'elle a dit de Marlon Brando?" said the female voice.

"You think you're so political, and what's your big protest? Eating Ho chow mein! Ha! I've seen you eating hot dogs! You even *call* them hot dogs!"

"You are crazy Amurrican." The mini minced away. The crowd dispersed to restaurants, their fluty laughter floating back. Even the Algerians ducked under their umbrellas. They were untouchables, but I was a pariah. Up ahead where the alley turned, a pair of slick red humps with silver bars bounced away. Backpacking Yanks were escaping from the plague of my disgrace. "You should talk! You're the ones who wrecked it for the rest of us!" I hollered: "Buy a suitcase!"

The street gleamed empty. I stood in a brackish puddle on a riverbed of stones. I stared up at the clogged sky, fringed with gables. I had to laugh. "Dear Mom and Dad, Paris has really had an impact on me."

"Hey . . . are you okay?"

It was the hippie, the one I'd chucked a franc to. Water trickled down his face and neck from the soaked crown of his hat. He clutched the slippery neck of his guitar. Not even odors from the restaurant kitchens open to the damp air—scorching crepes, bitter coffee, chocolate, floury baking, garlic, cheesy crusts and frying onions, lamb and thyme—could overwhelm the odor of human, unwashed. His pale eyes were fleetingly focused on mine. But they were filled with a dope-riddled kindness. Hippies drove me nuts with their amoebic goodness. I wanted to put sugar in their underwear, if they had any. But this time, I was grateful.

"Want to have coffee or something?" He gestured vaguely up the street.

"Where?" I said.

"In a café. St. André-des-Arts."

I hesitated. I was lonely, but hippies weren't company.
"It's okay. I'll give you back your franc," he said.

I went, limping. He was even slower. He seemed to be walking in his sleep. We crawled across St. Michel. He wakened as I grabbed him from imminent puréeing by a taxi. "They can tell we're broke, so they want to bump us off," I said. "You better watch where you're going."

"Oh yeah . . . I keep walking into trees. . . ."

"My name's Kerry," I said.

He looked mildly interested, as if I'd said, "I bite my nails." He didn't speak again.

The door of the café gave him pause.

"Uh . . . should we go in?" I said.

"Oh . . . yeah . . . sure . . ."

I opened the door. If his friends were as fuzzy-minded as he was, I wouldn't last long.

The Americans were easy to spot, adrift at the center of a windswept, unpopulated sea. Three of them huddled around a tiny table, holding cups and ashtrays in their hands. Satellite tables, like life rafts on tow lines, were piled with their flotsam: peacoats, army jackets, scarves, long socks, gloves, hats, trousers. Ballast on one raft included a harmonica, a tambourine, a dulcimer, and drumsticks—no drum. A khaki knapsack, an Air France bag with a broken strap, and two straw bags of fruit, bread, and lettuce bobbed independently, like life preservers. In a small café in Paris, the Americans had recreated Ellis Island.

The French had retreated to the pier of tables along the wall. Girls and boys in the garb of swish Cossacks made supercilious eyes at the invaders.

As we approached, I knew why the refugees were quarantined. Apart from their equipage and bizarre appearance, they stank. They must have come to Ellis Island in steerage, with goats. Despite the drifting rummage, all three of them wore several sweaters each. The atmosphere inside the circle of laundry was post-football-scrimmage.

My escort said, "She's American."

"Who ain't?" said a flash of teeth in a thicket of blond beard. I recognized the doorway skulker with the harmonica. "Have a seat," he said, hooking a chair with his ankle. I sat beside him. The girl on my right had greasy hair that hung in strands, like Raggedy Ann's. She wore a full cotton skirt striped green and orange; yellow and red checked kneesocks; black wool knickers; a green cardigan; a purple turtleneck; a T-shirt that said, GIRLS' SOFTBALL LEAGUE; and a black chiffon scarf, knotted like a garotte. Her wrists were decked with bangles and encrusted with dirt. Her fingernails were symmetrically black. She had ghastly white skin and eyes like cigarette burns in a sheet. She must have run away to join a circus in 1956, and never adjusted. She smiled at my cowlick and offered me a piece of the pomegranate she was wrenching asunder with her grubby fingers.

"No thanks," I said.

The waiter cracked the kitchen door. Spying reinforcements to the Hun, he tried to retreat. "Uh, excuse me," my escort called. "Sir?"

"Quelque chose?" said the waiter through the crack in the door.

"Coffee. Two coffees. Deux," said the boy. He shrugged out of his jacket, releasing malodorous gusts. The atmosphere intensified: football scrimmage, August, noon. Three français made tracks. The kitchen door slammed. I leaned on my hand and inhaled in my palm. I'd seen hippies swabbing their armpits in the basins of powder rooms in hotels. They shaved their legs and washed their ankles. They left a rubble of soap chips, hair, and sludge. They lost the public to the cause of peace and love. But these gypsies, under their layers, were festering. In their desperation, they should have stormed our embassy and used the tub.

I smiled at the three faces, trying not to gag. The third male, across from me, was bearded too, but grizzled and fat. His black rubber poncho was flung back over his shoulders. His jersey seemed to be woven of seaweed. His eyes were almost hidden by the brim of his captain's hat. He looked like he'd been washed overboard while playing a concertina. He said, "How long you been over?"

"Three weeks," I said.

Everyone looked bored. I had nothing to contribute. Just to be perverse, I added, "And I'm going home tomorrow." Everyone looked sick.

"Dan's been out of the States three years," said the matey one, nodding at the beard on my left. Everyone looked humble except the beard, who flashed his wide-lens grin.

"The grand old man of bums," he said.

"Your name is Dan?" I said. "Mine's Kerry."

Dan looked mildly amused, as if I'd said, "I'm from Wapakoneta, Ohio, home of Neil Armstrong's Moon Museum." But I said to the circus girl, "What's your name?"

She gazed at me over the pomegranate pulp. Her filthy palm spilled seeds and spit. "Duse," she said. Nobody laughed.

My escort was plunking one guitar string, spattering drops of water on the table. The string bonged with a full fathom echo. He didn't look up. I said, "Um . . ."

The mate replied for him. "His name's Dwight. Dwight D. E. Clanski. Hails from Farmersville, just outside of Dayton. Pop, twelve hundred fifty-six souls. He's nineteen years old, has two brothers and one sister and a dog. Useta have a turtle, but she died. His father sells shoes. He's in Paris on a cultural mission. Want to see his passport?"

This time they all laughed, even Dwight, who had listened with detached good humor, like a terrier at a dog show hearing himself described as best of breed. The mate added, "I don't have a name. Names are for tourists." They laughed again.

Dwight said, smiling hazily, "The Captain's just kidding. He doesn't mean you."

"I'm a tourist, all of us are. At least I admit it," I said.

Everyone looked affronted. The Captain, Dwight, and Duse regarded me exactly the way the French regarded them. Dan leaned over and whispered, "It's like a black man sayin' 'nigger.' You can say it about yourself, but can't nobody else say it about you."

Dwight said, "She's from Cleveland."

"Cleveland! Home o' the burnin' river!" said Dan.

"All anybody remembers about Cleveland is that once, the river caught on fire," I said. "Everyone remembers the oily Cuyahoga, but nobody remembers George Szell, or the Browns, or Carl Stokes—"

"Cleveland! I'll bet you teach first grade," said the Captain, smirking.

"Kindergarten," I said. "I was a clay major."

Dan burst into demonic laughter that rattled the ashtrays behind French lines. His teeth must have graduated summa from the Crest School at Indiana U. His fingernails weren't clean, but neither were mine. It's hard to scrub your nails in the lukewarm stream of a bidet. He smelled like rain and tobacco and must—as if he lived in a linen closet—but he didn't seem to contribute to the pack effluvium. His hair was thick and honey blond, Breck ad hair. His eyes were Delft blue. The folksy accent completed the picture. He only needed a Rocky Mountain backdrop and a box of Alpen. Why was he in Paris, inhaling carbon monoxide and decadence, instead of sittin' on a Colorado hilltop, pickin' and singin' to the little woodland critters?

The Captain said, "Only someone from Cleveland would come to Paris for just three weeks."

"I spent the first two in Switzerland," I said loudly.

"Sounds like the whirlwind tour," said Dan. "Did you climb the Jungfrau?"

"I bought it. I'm having it shipped to Cedar Point for a sno-cone booth. Listen, spare me your jaded expatriate routine. I had the money to come for three weeks. I came, I spent the money, and I'm going home."

The waiter edged among us with coffee, placing the cups with delicate repugnance.

"Was the trip worth the bread?" said Dan.

"No. I've had a rotten time and it cost me eight hundred dollars."

The silence was thicker than the stink—or I was adapting. The gypsy spoke. Her chin was red with pomegranate juice. "Eight hundred dollars," she said in a scrapy alto.

"Wow," said Dwight. With his pinky eyes and wispy hair, he looked like a rabbit hiding in a pile of leaves. "I could live for a year on eight hundred dollars," he said.

"Oh, come off it," I said. "My travel agent laughed when I said I had eight hundred dollars."

"Travel agent!" said the Captain. " 'Paris by Night!' "

"Do you carry more than fifty dollars in cash?" said Dan.

"No, I carry it in pomegranates. Listen, I've slept in cheesy hotels, I've eaten in crummy restaurants—"

"You eat in restaurants?" said Dwight. "What's it like?"

Dan gave his demon laugh at my expression. "No use, little lady. We live like junkyard rats—"

"Wharf rats," said the Captain.

"In your case," said Dan. To me he said, "These three live on a barge near Point Royal. No heat, no runnin' water —have to tote it in a bucket. Have to scrounge wood and make fires in a rusty ole stove—"

Dwight said with pride, "I've been cold for seven months. I don't even notice any more. Central heating saps your energy." Like the Captain and the gypsy, he was sitting on his chilblained hands, vibrating with every drafty flap of the café door. He said, "We scrounge food, too. We beg or we steal—"

"We fish in the Seine," said the Captain.

"But we don't catch anything," said Dwight.

"And here you are with a travel agent," said Dan. "You do seem a little like a poodle at a rodeo."

"But I worked in an insurance office for four months to pay for this trip!" I said. "Why the hell shouldn't I blow the money?"

" 'Cause now, you have to go home," said Dan.

"Yeah, wow," said Dwight. "You have to go home." The circus girl gave me a sad-eyed smile.

The Captain's smile was smug. "I don't even know who's in the White House," he said.

"Patty Hearst," I said. "We call her Miss Tanya." I pushed back my chair. The waiter bounded out of the kitchen. He had me pegged as the one with the wallet. I hadn't drunk the coffee—it tasted like sandbox mud. Dwight, all dreamy-eyed, was plunking his guitar. Like Banquo's ghost at the table of Macbeth, the waiter was only visible to me. "That figures," I said, paying for two coffees. The waiter barely restrained himself from sterilizing the coins with a match. I didn't blame him. I must stink too, by now. Grace of the hyacinth talc and flowered bath mitt would have me boiled and my clothes burned.

"Sorry you're goin' so soon," said Dan. He looked like he meant it, but I didn't trust him. He reminded me of a boy I'd known in college, who asked everyone, every vacation, "How's school?" and then went into gales of laughter when they told him.

I said, "I have to see if the maid has packed the trunks in the Rolls."

"I'll give ya the three steps of decency," said Dan, pulling on sweaters.

"Is that the custom in Paris?" I said snidely.

"Nope, in Tuba City, Arizona." What with his thicket of hair, a stocking hat, and the high-rolled collar of his sweater, Dan was nothing but nose. He took up his harmonica and followed me out. I wished he'd stay with his noisome companions. If these were cosmopolitans, I'd take tourists.

I thought of the dear blue-haired lady with the Instamatic who'd stood beside me as both of us gazed at the Eiffel Tower. Gazing, and clicking the shutter, she'd said to her guide, "How did they ever get the top on that?"

She'd meant well, and she'd smelled nice. What more could an invaded country ask?

Paris by Night

Out on the street, we gulped air.

"I didn't think it was you," I said. "How do you stand it?"

"The stink?"

"That, and the conversation."

"Oh, they're all right. You know, poor ole Dwight . . . he's kind of a dim bulb. And I guess the brine has pickled the Captain's brain. He doesn't mean to give offense."

"Yes, he does. He thinks if he's really offensive, no one will know he's American. We're all so pathetically eager to please."

We walked up the crooked street toward St. Michel, passing an apothecary shop. Blackened stone framed the window display of medical journals in peeling leather bindings, moldering between a mortar-and-pestle and a skull. A girl in a trenchcoat drooped by the window. Her reflection was a specter, displaced in time.

"She's in the wrong century," said Dan.

"That's what I was thinking," I said. He was folksy, but he wasn't a clod. A couple jostled us. They were striding, his arm hooked over her neck. We passed another café. The glass box on the sidewalk was dark. Inside, two men in grey coats, humped like moles, stood drinking under a lamp at the bar. A boy at a corner table lit a cigarette, looking up eager from a book as we passed. We approached the carny clamor of St. Michel.

"Let's walk this way," said Dan, turning. We plunged down a hole of wet brick. The lane kinked down to the quay. Wet gusts drew the moss across the corners. Shadows rode on our backs. The rugged stones were sprinkled with the dandelion heads of window lights. The century wandered, bereft, in convoluted passages, in rows of low stone. Houses hunched under chimney pots, deep behind crossed casements. Boxes of laurel foamed richly with night. Shutters clattered like bones, and stoops were scooped to fit the bellies of cats.

"I love this," I said.

Dan nodded.

We crossed the bridge just west of St. Michel, the Pont Neuf. The ivory icicles of Notre Dame pierced the watery sky. The Right Bank swept upon us like a cavalry of light: bridges crowned with knights for chess; monuments of sandy grandeur, each one shining in the floodlight dawn like the embassy of heaven. A milky nimbus muffled the stars. Black water clucked and slapped the stone below. Its snaky rivulets were crested silver. Mist sifted up from the water and settled, glistening, in our hair. A vessel draped with fairy lights roamed the eastern stream.

"What's that boat?" I said.

"Tourists. High class. Instead of a bus and a megaphone, it's artichokes . . . champagne . . . violins playing 'La Vie en Rose' . . ."

I noticed that his accent was less shackled by cactus. "I don't think that's hokey. I'd do that," I said.

"You're all defensive now. Hokier than thou. You'd sign up for the boat tour of the Paris sewers."

"Ha! I bet it's sponsored by Disney. I bet the rats have motors and wear sweaters and berets."

"And sing "Frère Jacques,' " said Dan. "In rounds."

"Who else but Americans would pay to take movies of some other country's turds?"

"Intimate look at the culture."

"The French look constipated to me. Pursed up. Like that nitwit who ran me over with his Tinker Toy motorcycle."

"Is that why you're limping?" Dan had slowed his pace. My leg was aching, and stiff from the river damp. "You tired? Want to go home?"

"Oh no! This is the first decent conversation I've had in three weeks. Besides . . . this is wonderful. I've hardly been out at night."

"In Paris? Hell. Things don't start churnin' up till midnight."

"I guess. But the girl I'm traveling with writes letters at night."

"Every night?"

"She bought a lot of stamps." I didn't feel like going into the Richie and Timmy papers. "And alone . . . I wouldn't feel safe."

"That's half the fun."

"No. If I'm not at home in a city, I might as well stay in my room. I don't know where to go. The places *The Book* recommends are jammed with Our Readers—I feel like I'm still on the plane. And I'm scared to stick my nose in a club that really looks French. I'm afraid everybody in the place will leap up and scream 'Paris by Night!' and sling their pâté at me."

"You know, they've got a right to be nervous. We don't leave 'em much space. If you're French and you're nice to tourists, next thing you know they're in your icebox, takin' pictures of the butter."

"Oh, I know, I don't blame them. But I still feel like I'm trying to pledge a sorority, and they keep moving the house. Sometimes I march Grace all over the city, looking for a place that isn't already overrun with hippies and gym teachers. We finally find some dump that even flies avoid. I drag Grace in and order something safe—like bread—but it's hopeless. The minute I open my mouth, every native bolts."

"Survival instincts of the decimated herd," said Dan.

"No, they can feel it in the tremor of the earth—the impending stampede! The natives bolt through one door, and thirty members of the Knoxville Auxiliary Vagabondettes stampede through the other. They push the tables together—"

"They order Bloody Marys and BLTs—"

"They want to know why there's no mirror in the ladies' room—"

"They ask for coq au vin without the sauce—"

"They ask us to join them!"

"Do you?"

"Grace does. I sulk."

"That's sorta how I ended up in Paris. Didn't matter what homey little village I'd find to spend some peaceful time—the bus was right behind me. Figgered if I joined a monastery, they'd turn it into a Hilton hotel. So I came to where the natives hate tourists even more than I do. Keep 'em off guard—that's the Parisian defense."

"That's fine for you—you live here. But me . . . I was so

mad to travel. But I guess I'm not the type. I get lonely. Everywhere I go, I want to belong."

"Now passin' through just suits me," said Dan. "Most places, a month is too long. Everywhere I go, I want to keep goin'."

Papers sailed across an empty street and a wedge of park. I brushed a pillar, patterned with one poster, beneath a conical roof. An old man in a blanket crouched on the dark side of the pillar. He wore a beret pulled low on his forehead. Motionless in his minimal shelter, he noted our passing. Cafés were shabby, with yellowing walls and chairs with plastic backs. Buildings were dark brick, the windows swollen with boards.

"Where are we?" I said.

"Near where I live. Want to show you one of my special places."

At the end of the street, we came into a small square park. The trees were squat, the grace of leaves and branches chopped away. Their thick trunks were bound off in stubby little knots. Trees stood around the pounded dirt courtyard like fat children raising their fists. I knew them, but they needed harsh outlines, and thick, caked color. Then I remembered where I'd seen the trees—in Van Gogh's paintings. "What kind of trees are they?"

"Plantain trees. They line the roads in the south of France. This is the Place des Vosges."

We walked among the trees. The sky was opaque, the stars widely spaced. White, pure, a slice off full, the moon sailed cleanly down the path of night. The trees breathed the quiet of the stars. We went into a courtyard of black, broken stone. The building surrounding us was stone, its corners smoothed to gentle curves by time. The ivory shutters might have been ochre under the sun. There were wrought-iron balconies and gabled roofs. Some of the windows where shutters gaped had cheap cotton curtains.

I whispered, "People live here?"

"Sure. And there's shops—grocer, baker . . . dentist . . ."

"Oh no!"

"Book and print shop's nice. Lots of Victor Hugo's books—his house is here." He pointed. We stood in the deep quiet, gazing at the dark, gabled house. The dank cold cut through my jacket and settled on my chest. But I rested at the center of a tranquil symmetry, suspended like an ornament in time. Dan's palm stroked my hair. " 'Be like the bird who halts in flight on wing too slight, yet sings, knowing that he hath wings,' " he said. I looked at him. He said, "Victor Hugo said that." His hair and beard were shining in the moonlight.

"Yes," I said, "this is what I wanted."

He kissed me. His lips were stiff and cold, like mine, but his tongue was warm as toast and honey. He was taller than I'd thought. I had to stand on tiptoe to hug him. His arms and his chest against me shut out the wind. "Don't move," I said to his neck. "This is the first time in Paris I've been warm."

He laughed, and said, "Let's go get warm."

The gables marched, antique, composed, above the rhythmic windows. The cold beat at my eyes, and I laughed. "Yes!" I exulted in my heart. "This is Paris! Night, the moon, a lover . . ." Dan didn't fit the picture. I'd envisioned Truffaut. But Dan was gorgeous, in a King of the Cookout way, and nice, and funny, and there. He might not be a native, but he was a citizen of Paris!

Would this story go over in Cleveland! I wouldn't have to buy my own beer for a year.

Dan opened the splintered door of a chipped plaster building with bolted shutters. He lit the light, a bare bulb suspended from a twenty-foot ceiling. The wallpaper in the lobby had faded to the color of ladies' room face powder, open to the public for forty years. The floor was discernibly marble, under layers of committed grime. It looked like they'd been using chewing gum for rosin. Brass cupids smirked from sconces dribbled with purple wax from depleted funerary candles. Cupids wallowed along the frame of a mirror with glass as scummy as a broken window in an abandoned garage.

"Who's the concierge," I said, "the Phantom of the Opera?"

"Six francs a day, with breakfast," said Dan. "Can't complain. Well, hell, I complain, I just don't leave." He was hustling me up the stairs. The staircase was hatched as if with an ax, and tilted to the open side. We were halfway up when the lights went out.

"What happened?" I said, as Dan said, "Shit." He groped for my outside hand and placed it on the balcony. "Economy," he said. "Light switches off automatically. They figure it allows you just enough time to sprint up the stairs."

"If you're a greyhound?" We moved down the black hole of the hall. I couldn't even sense the doors of the rooms, or the space where the corridor angled away. He turned me left.

"Stop here a minute," he said. I heard metal clinking. "Have to get my key. She hangs 'em on hooks in a hall with no lights—have to find it by touch. Mine's the third from the left in the second row."

Hands on my shoulders, he steered me through another tunnel. "Here's the toilet. You best do it now."

I stepped up onto a tile floor and felt for a light switch. The wall was clammy. The air in the hall had been frigid. But the tiles in the bathroom preserved a deep, mean cold. I groped along the wall, crinkling my face at the smell. "Where's the light?" I called softly.

"Sorry, forgot," said Dan, as I found a cord dangling, and pulled.

My left foot slipped into a hole. There was a subterranean explosion. A geyser erupted through the hole around my foot. I yanked, but the boot was caught. Water spewed over my boots, my jeans, my jacket, my face.

The light sprang on.

The toilet was a hole in the floor and two foot rests. I had stood in it, and flushed it.

"Jesus Q. Christ," said Dan. He started to laugh.

"Where was the light switch?"

"Here in the hall. Goddamn, I'm sorry. Let me assist you."

"Do."

I was soaked. He extricated my boot. I marched out to the hall.

"Don't you want to go?" he said.

"Thanks, I'm quite comfortable just as I am."

"Hey. Now, come on. I shouldn't have laughed. I just . . . you looked so funny. Like a pissed-off chipmunk."

His eyebrows were anxious, but over in the corner, his mouth was having hysterics. I had to laugh. "Paris pounces again!" I said.

We padded down another icy hall. "Here," he said. The key rattled. He opened the door and hit the switch.

His room was painted the same corpse pink, around the

faults in the plaster. The bed had a gulf in the middle, and the thin spread reeked of mildew. The room was even colder than the hall.

"Is this where we came to get warm?" I said.

"You better shake off those wet duds," said Dan.

"I'll die of exposure."

"Get set for luxury." The bureau was closer to kindling than furniture. Yanking out the bottom drawer, he dragged a blanket from under a tangle of sweaters and jeans. "If I left it out, the maid would steal it."

"This hotel has a maid?"

"Why, hey, little lady! This here's France! Every pension has a maid. This place is a pigsty, so the maid's a pig. All part of the plan. Shuck off, and put that around you." He tossed me the fleece yellow blanket. "Can't go back to Cleveland with a runny nose."

He took off his hat and his top two sweaters. I fumbled with my soggy jeans. A blotch of black and purple was spreading up my calf. Dan came to look.

"Ain't that a beauty? The little bastard creamed you good. Well, it's a cheap souvenir. Here, hold it. I'll get you somethin' to rub on that." He draped the blanket over my shoulders and went out. Alone in the cold on the cheap bed, I couldn't stop trembling. The walk, the night, the cold, the pain, the strange adventure—who was this hill-billy? What was I doing? I couldn't leave. I wouldn't be able to find my way home, or even down the hall. I had to catch a train in the morning. Did Dan have a clock? No. Hippies didn't believe in clocks. Clocks were tools of the Industrial Revolution. The blanket was downy. It must have been expensive. Probably the gift of another grateful American tourist. Probably Dan paid his rent by gratifying American ladies the nights before they sailed. He'd picked a steerage passenger this time out. I'd be lucky to pay for a Métro home . . . if he ever came back. Maybe he was a decoy for Grace's white slavers. He and a gang of Turks herded stupid, succulent females into trucks with airholes in the roofs. A brothel full of American lady tourists . . . what would we do on Stunt Night? Demonstrate baseball plays in the nude?

Dan came back with a tube of cream. "Woke up the landlady—told her I needed some salve for 'an injured friend.' She suspects me of lewd intent—sent my stock up. Most likely she'll reduce my rent."

"More likely she'll wait a day and tap on your door."

"I'll bet she could think of uses for this cream that you and me would think was downright outlandish. Let's see the injured party."

I stuck my leg out of the blanket.

"Lie on your stomach. I'll put some goo on it."

I lay in the gorge at the center of the mattress, my face in a moldy pillow. Dan hiked his blanket up to bare my calf and thigh.

"Can't get over this color," he said. "Wish I had my paint box."

"Grace should be here with her camera," I said.

The salve was cold. A shiver skittered up my scalp. "Ahhh . . ." I said.

"Feels good?" His fingers were callused at the tips. I wondered if he worked, or if he just played guitar. The cold salve, the warm fingers worked up my calf, easing the aching flesh.

"Dan . . . what do you do here? Do you just hang around? How do you live?"

"Oh . . . I get by. Play guitar and harmonica in the Métro—thirty francs on a good day. Do little jobs for folks I meet—carpentry, cleanin', workin' on boats. Once a week I tutor—I'm teachin' a French lady grammar." I could hear the amusement in his voice.

"Did she give you the blanket?"

"Reckon she did, now I'm reminded." He was smoothing salve into the soft, full flesh behind my knee.

After a silence, I said, "That's just lovely."

"Nice stuff, it'll help it heal."

"But what I want to know is . . . what do you *do?* Do you paint, or write, or . . . why are you here? You aren't the same as Dwight."

He laughed. "Hope not, ma'am, I thank you . . . I'm not that different. I'm aimless, mostly . . . been on the bum since I got drafted in sixty-nine and took the back door out. I like it. I like to see how people live, get to know 'em. . . . I like it in Paris, so here I am. Usually, I woulda wandered off by now."

His hand was so warm, so smooth with cream . . . the thumb and the palm caressing . . . the fingers kneading, stroking . . . I didn't ask any more questions. He didn't speak. When his hand moved under my hip and coaxed me to turn, I rolled over, moving the blanket aside. He lay with me, pulling the blanket over us, stroking the hair from my face with the sweet-smelling fingers of his kind right hand.

All I'm going to tell you is that making love with Dan was a far cry from the gunshot acrobatics on the college golf course. He took his time, and mine. In an hour, I almost got my money's worth of Paris.

We clung together beneath the blanket, his arm and leg hooked across my breasts and thighs, keeping me safe. "I have to get up early to catch the train," I murmured.

"What time?"

"About seven."

"Okay."

"Do you have a clock?"

"I'll wake up. It's a talent I have. Sleep."

But I couldn't sleep. I was too excited. My head was swarming with images: the minibike marauder in the phosphorescent darkness, looming over the bars of his vengeance machine; the wharf rats in the café, surrounded by natives holding their noses; the squatting ghosts of trees in the Place des Vosges, and Dan saying, "It takes a while to find your special places in a city"; and Grace on the plane, chattering to Turkle about Mom and Dad and Richie and Timmy and Sparky; my desk at Occidental, and my very own red leather manual . . .

What would it be like to be at home in Paris—dashing from clubs to cafés to rendezvous in swanky flats, wearing extravagant underwear monogrammed by swish designers, racketing around the Place de la Concorde in one of those corrugated metal cars that seemed to be made out of warped aluminum siding, smoking cigars, reading Malraux, going to Cannes for the weekend with a weary older man. How would I live when I wasn't skiing in Biarritz with Nureyev's double? I must be kept . . . or else I'd mooch on my rich, corrupt, and acquiescent (or dim and religious, rich) parents. From time to time I would go to a museum to refresh my recollections of Picasso and Rodin, or take a course at the Sorbonne: "Vin Ordinaire I and II"; "Dressing by Rote: A Mandate." My men would be charming and drained, their temples hollow, their droopy eyelids nicotine-stained by nights of exquisite debauchery. Perfume would emanate from my pores. My pants would be so tight across the crotch, I couldn't pee for an hour after undressing. Nothing would recall the freckled delinquent coding clerk, popping the tops off Ohio nights with boys who've known me since I'd wet my pants on the bus to the zoo.

What a grievous screw! I was just learning how to look for my own special places in Paris, and I had to go home.

I felt for Paris what I felt for Dan: a reluctance to leave him while he had the upper hand.

Night in the windows had a pearly cast when Dan awoke. "Rise up, little lady. We've got a goodly hike."

My right leg wouldn't straighten, as if the joint had rusted. I collapsed on every right footstep. "Poor little dude," said Dan. "Shame you don't live here. You could make a packet in Paris as a panhandling gimp."

Clouds of the Seine blotted the edges of buildings. Here and there a narrow tree etched its branches on the mist. The bakeries were open, sleepy people lining up to buy long loaves of bread. "Breakfast," said Dan. The woman at the counter handed him his half-loaf with a smile and a flourish of greeting. I caught the words "amie Américaine" in their exchange. The shiny glass counter was piled with flaky ridges of croissants, like sea shells, knobby brioches and folded sugar-glittered apple tarts and raisin buns and flat, sticky pinwheel cookies. Never again, o Paris pâtisserie! Home to the heartland, citadel of the stamping plant brownie! Dan bought me a pinwheel cookie. I pulled apart a spiral, delicately, melting each separate morsel with my tongue. Dan broke off hunks of the skinny, rich loaf. "It's warm," he said. "Bite." O fragile golden crust! O cloudy substance!

"You speak French," I said accusingly.

"Sure. I've been here a year. Couldn't say 'please' when I got here. Didn't have two nickels. If they'd had pay toilets, I woulda had to go on to Spain. I hear they pee in the streets."

Women and men in aprons bustled in cafés, setting out Cinzano ashtrays on tables, placing chairs; in stalls under green and yellow striped awnings, they unpacked fat-bottomed, wet, brown pears, dull yellow apples, plump bananas, frilly sheaths of vegetables and lettuce. A short grey-haired man in a blue apron bit into a brilliant red tomato, grinning at me as he caught the juice in the palm of his hand. I grinned back, brushing flakes of breakfast from my jacket. We drank café au lait standing up at a bar where workmen in eternal blue smocks were already knocking back cognac. I scooped all the foam from my coffee before I drank it, and licked the spoon. "I'll bet you eat the frosting before the cake, and then you want more," said Dan.

"It's true," I said. "I want it all."

What if I didn't go home?

I finally let the bubble of the idea surface. What if I stayed in Paris? I couldn't bear to go back to Cleveland. I'd airbrush my adventures for my family, and tell the truth to Randy. She'd buy me a pizza to console me. We'd go to the Churchkey my first night home. For one night, I'd bask in the glamour of Ulysses, just off the boat. The boys who'd refused to share my whirlwind tour would kick themselves and buy me a beer. They'd all try to take me home. The next day, we'd all realize that I was just another local girl, on tap, like the watered beer, and the twice-boiled water of the stagnant lake. My memories of escape would fade, like the bruise on my injured leg. In a month or a year, I'd marry some nice, dull boy who wouldn't mind my sporadic attacks of acidic ennui. In fifteen years I'd be sitting with Randy in the bleachers, watching my husband slide home for the P.D. All-Stars. I'd go home to make tuna casserole—and grilled cheese for the kid who hated tuna. Not even I would remember that once my spirit had been loosed from the bonds of morning-canned-orange-juice existence.

I didn't have to live that life. Dan had been adrift in the world for seven years! When he'd come to Paris, he hadn't even been able to say, "Because the record player doesn't work." ("Parskala-*peek*up-na-*mar*sha-*pah*.") Yet here he was living in a real, or surreal, French pension, getting through the day, getting by. If he could do it . . . and he hadn't had a friend to help him. I had him.

I also had a paper loophole: my plane ticket home. I was booked on tomorrow's plane. But if Grace told them I wasn't coming, the ticket would still be good. If I didn't make the expatriate grade, I could hitchhike to Luxembourg and take the next plane home. I'd never hitched in my life. But I'd never run away from home, either.

My father always says, "You can't leave home."

My mother always says, "You can damn well try."

What I didn't have was money. I had twenty-two francs —about five dollars. Could I wire my father for money? . . . no. All my life, I'd been coddled like an egg. This time I was going to depend on myself alone. Unless I ended up in jail and needed a bond, I wouldn't ask my father for a dime.

What about Grace? Could I con her out of her duty-free souvenir fund? . . . no. If I told Grace I was staying in Paris, she'd barrel, bellowing, across the square to the police station, and have me deported.

I couldn't borrow money from Dan. He didn't have any. Besides, I wasn't ready to tell him I was staying. He would be around when I needed him. But I'd better not need him till the plane had left. He might forcibly assist me on board. Greater fear hath no man than to apprehend the lingering of a one-night stand.

I said—in tones of idle speculation—"There must be other ways to make money in Paris . . . you know, besides panhandling. That circus girl, for instance—"

"Lisa?"

"*Lisa?*"

"Yeah, that's her real name. She's kinda weird."

I laughed. "What makes you say that?"

"I mean . . . she can get by on less than a regular girl. Like she doesn't remember to eat, unless you put somethin' in her hand. The Captain lets her live on the barge for free . . . she's no trouble. She's only maybe eight percent there, most of the time. Sorta like the place is haunted. They send her out for wood—course half the time they have to go fetch her, she's out there on the bank just wanderin' with her kneesocks fallin' down. When we were playin' on the street, we made her tambourine. But she didn't take to rhythm. She'd just gradually quit . . . and then she'd throw in a *clang!* Sorta grated on our nerves. Wrecked the ensemble."

"Right. But there must be American girls who *function* in Paris."

"It's tricky. Can't get a work permit unless you got a job, and vice versa. Best way for females to live here is au pair."

"What's that? Does it call for net stockings?"

"No, you take care of kids. Live with a family. That way you don't have to sweat out payin' the rent."

"You mean babysitting?"

"Sort of. You get your own room and all. I think. And eatin' French for free is a hell of a bargain."

I used to babysit in high school. I never went to the same house more than twice. The first time, I'd tell the kids stories; I'd let them stay up late; I'd pick up the litter and wash the glasses in the sink; I'd eat exactly half of the snacks assigned to me by the mother: corn chips, Pepsi. Home early, the mother would extol my qualities; the father would overtip me. The second time, the kids wouldn't go to bed till I was dropping from exhaustion after hours of elaborate tales and strenuous games. The sinks and counters would be stacked with encrusted dishes and pots. The living room would be heaped with debris, and the vacuum cleaner rampant. At 2 a.m., when the chores were done and the parents who'd promised to be home at midnight hadn't staggered in, I'd seek revenge on the hidden treasures of the pantry: chocolate-covered almonds, homemade Key Lime pie. I'd be finishing the ice cream as the car crossed the tree lawn. I'd keep my eyes shut on the way home, as the father drove through stop signs. At my door, he'd make a pass at me. Then he'd tell me all he had was a ten, and he'd catch me next time. Next time, I wouldn't go.

A resident Yankee nursemaid among the vengeful French . . . it would be a last-ditch, last-battalion effort. But better the final cartridge than the white flag: going home.

At the hotel, Dan kissed me goodbye. He had coffee foam in his moustache. "Look me up when you make your whirlwind tour of the Balkans," he said, grinning. "I might turn up anywhere."

Ho ho. And so might I. I'd made up my mind. Now all I had to do was get away from Grace.

I sneaked past the raccoon man, dozing at his desk. He started, twitching, and gaped at me. Then he gave me a smarmy smile of lewd collaboration. Shortly, he would slip a note, in perfect, filthy English, under the door of our room. Grace would read it. I hoped she'd get a thrill.

Grace was snuffling under the covers. By now, she should have been schussing around in her fluffy pink slip-

pers, quaffing Lavoris and aiming it with ineffective lady-
like spurts at the basin. She'd better get up soon. She had
an hour and a half to make the Luxembourg train. She had
to hoist her caravan out of the hotel, through hurtling
crowds, down the Métro entrance, in and out of the sub-
way car, across the populous vault of the railroad station,
and into a first-class compartment of the train. If she
missed this train, she wouldn't make Luxembourg tonight.
The plane for home left Luxembourg tomorrow. Once
embarked, Grace would numbly oil the gears of her return
to the Buckeye State, extending to pear-faced officials in
blue the ticket, the passport, the ticket, the passport . . .
But first she had to deposit herself on the Métro, with her
chattels: two suitcases, one weighing thirty-six pounds; a
train case; two plastic bags of presents; and a two-foot
stuffed turtle.

All my clothes were crushed in one canvas bag—sweaters, T-shirts, underwear—except the dress. As *The Book*
advised, I'd left home every garment that wasn't essential
for sanitation or warmth. But the day before we'd left for
Europe, I'd bought one gorgeous, slinky dress, and shoes
to match. I'd folded the dress with the delicate precision of
a head nurse making a hospital corner, and laid it on top
of the scrunched-up sweaters. In every hotel room, I'd
snatched the one hanger for the dress. But I'd never worn
it. No place we'd ventured in three weeks had matched
the romantic possibilities embroidered on that dress. If
I hadn't already thrown in my lot with gypsies, the sight
of the dress, hapless on its wire wings, would have cast the
die.

Light-fingered, tiptoe, I snitched the toothpaste and brush
from the basin. Grace had laid my flannel nightgown out.
I took it. After a hand-to-throat assault on the effete snob
within me by the pragmatist, I also lifted *The Book*. It's
fine to quit smoking, but you like to know you've got a
pack in the house. And I could use it for toilet paper. I
raided Grace's stationery (pink, with trellises and kittens
in the corners). Sitting in the hall on the canvas lump of
my bag, I wrote:

> Grace, don't worry! I met some Americans who live
> in Paris, and they asked me to stay. They can't ask
> you too because there isn't room. So I'm not going

home. Just take the Métro to the station and take the
Luxembourg train, like we talked about last night.
Give my regards to Richie and Timmy, etc. Good luck
finding a job—with all your stainless steel cookware,
I think you should open a luncheonette. Give this
letter to my parents, okay? Love, Kerry

The letter to my parents was harder to write. I couldn't lie.

Hi you guys! Don't worry, I'm fine! I know what I'm
doing! I still have money and my ticket home, as long
as I don't cash it in, which I won't. I'm going to try
to find a job and stay through the winter. If I can't,
you'll see me soon! But why not enjoy it when I've
got the chance, right, Mom? Write me c/o American
Express, Paris. Don't send money. Don't *worry!* I'll
write as soon as I've got more news, Love, Kerry
P.S. Mom, if I make it to Italy I'll send you a San
Marco pigeon!
P.P.S. Listen, Dad, will you call Occidental Insurance and tell my supervisor that I just met
Jesus Christ walking down the street and he
told me to get out of the insurance game.

I sealed the notes, addressed them, and took them downstairs to the desk. "S'il vous plaît, monsieur, donnez les
lettres à mon amie," I said, with care. "Et . . ." I knocked
on the desk, and pointed up.

"Mais bien sûr, mademoiselle," said the raccoon man
with a salacious smile. "Et bon chance." Bon chance: good
luck.

I didn't like his tone.

I trotted down the Rue St. Jacques, the canvas bag barely tugging my wrist. I took an observer's post in a glass-
enclosed café on the Boulevard St. Michel, near the Métro
entrance. Grace would not be able to see me, huddled in
the second row of tables. I could watch her go . . . and
Dan might stroll across the bridge and up the boulevard,
looking for a way to pass the morning. . . .

The café was jammed with teenaged dilettantes, fouling
the air with brown cigarette smoke. They babbled, conducting their cello and piccolo voices with twig white
hands. They wore jeans and furs. I wore a sweater I'd had

since seventh grade. I would have liked a grande-crème, a tumbler of whipped milk and coffee. But I propped my translucent wool elbows around a cheapo espresso. My left ear was barraged by the clamor of the pinball machine. At least the yahoos yammering and banging at my elbow were French. Pinball was proof that not all yahoos were Americans, a small touché.

9:45. If Grace didn't gladden my sight in the next five minutes, it would mean she'd roosted, squashing my eggs before I'd even counted them.

I saw her. She was puffing and chuffing, jouncing on inadequate aching feet, exhorting the human pachyderm who labored in her wake. The whorey chambermaid had twined her claws in the handle of the biggest suitcase. Bending from the waist, she heaved and strained, like a hooker trekking with her souvenirs to the last gasp of the T.B. ward. The nasty-minded clerk was toting the other trunk and two shopping bags, containing fifty percent of the available dynel and polyester replicas of Notre Dame, Grace's gifts for the home folks. Grace hugged Turkle, and her train case, and a bundle in cellophane—probably a dozen eclairs, to tide her over till lunch.

Grace dropped Turkle at the mouth of the Métro. A brown man in a black cloth suit with a Nehru collar took possession of Turkle. He smiled with twenty-four teeth. As he stooped to retrieve the turtle, the raccoon man butted his poplin bottom with the trunk. Steely in their overladen haste, Grace and her lackeys swept the Indian into the vortex of their descent, and vanished.

In a minute, the clerk and the maid reappeared. Their faces were purple with outrage. The silent rockets of their arms exploded. Traffic in and out of the stairwell bottled around them as they screamed at each other with semaphores, as if from the decks of neighboring ships. Knowing Grace, I guessed that they were signing voodoo on her head. She'd made them porters, and she hadn't tipped. I was surprised they hadn't seized her by her bulky ankles and shaken her for francs. They stalked up the avenue. I could trace their route by their popping fingers. Behind them, the Indian stood smiling to no purpose, like a neon sign on a defunct highway.

I was alone in Paris—a young, broke American, in a city where Americans were so much merde.

I stifled a volcanic impulse to overthrow the table and gallop down the Métro to oblivion, to a Cleveland winter of paper clips and meat loaf. I was terrified. No one in the world who cared about me knew where I was.

Dan was my friend. Naturally, I would seek a friend's advice. He'd have ideas about these au pair jobs, and how I could get one. I didn't have money for a room, till I landed a pallet in the servants' quarters of some posh French maison. Dan would be pleased to have me a tenant . . . briefly. I wouldn't push my luck. If I had a free bed, I could live on a dollar a day—two yogurts, one coffee. If I couldn't find a job, maybe Dan and I could work up an act for the Métro. I'd have to wire my mother to send my tap shoes.

I went to find Dan.

I had to keep unfolding my map as I walked. The route wasn't complicated, but I was distracted, and jostled by crowds. I changed the canvas bag from hand to hand. The peace of the streets once desolate under the moon was shattered by trucks. The planked windows yielded to doors agape, where workers shuttled boxes down the tongues of ramps. Dan's hotel was a peeling wreck.

As I heaved the door open, grey day leaked through the lobby. A hideous woman, a frog in a mobcap, sat on a stuffed velvet pumpkin. The basin of cheap black cotton between her ravaged knees was filled with francs, as if she were a wishing well for hopeless souls. She sifted and counted the coins. Her fingers trembled. She squirmed as the light dribbled over her eyes.

"Pardon," I said.

She dropped a coin into the well of cloth. Noiseless, it fell to oblivion between her thighs.

"Pardon," I said unsteadily. "Je cherche . . . un garçon, Dan."

The froggy head swiveled. The tiny rocks of eyes were imbedded in flesh. She could have been forty or eighty; her decrepitude had not been bred by age. "Que voulez-vous?" she said: what do you want? Her voice had the serrated edge of abuse.

"Un garçon. Il est ici. Dan, il s'appelle Dan." Terror had uncorked my high school French. Il s'appele Dan. Voilà! la bibliothéque. Parce que le pick-up ne marche pas. Je veux d'être présenter . . . "Dan," I said to the ceiling. "Dan!"

echoed up the garish walls. Could I bound up the stairs and blunder to his door before her icy claw was on my neck?

"Il n'est pas là!" The gritty ruff of her ludicrous cap shaded her face. Her fingers let fall a silent coin.

"Est-ce que . . . um . . . you mean he's out? Can I . . . est-ce . . . une lettre, s'il vous plaît . . ." How would you say, can I leave him a note? Had I deluded myself that I could function in a country where I couldn't frame a sentence?

"Il n'est pas là, mademoiselle, il est parti."

"Party? He went to a party?"

"Parti! Il est parti ce matin à l'Espagne! *Il n'est pas là!* Comprenez?" Holding the skirt of coins in her fists, she waddled toward the stairs.

Espanya . . . I should know that word . . . "Spain? You mean *Spain* Spain? No, no—the boy—le garçon sont ici aujourd'hui. Was, I mean. I was with him. Je suis—I was—" I'd never paid much mind to tenses. In French class I'd inhabited a realm of continuous action, marching and fairing and diting straight to the debacle of the final exam. I'd been conceded a D for the pains I'd taken with my scrapbook, *Monuments of France*.

"Et puis venez!" the bag bleated over her shoulder. She scooped the coins from her skirt and bunched the fabric in one hand, flailing the other fist at me as she stomped up the stairs. "Venez, venez, vous allez voir!"

"I hope you're not trying to rent me a slab in this mausoleum," I said, but I followed her. She hadn't understood what I was asking. Maybe Dan didn't call himself Dan. Maybe at the pension he went by François, or Jean-Jacques or Robespierre de Tour Eiffel. Skirts waddling before me through the tunnel, the frog lady flung open a door.

It was Dan's room. The cotton spread was wrinkled where I'd sat to put my shoes on. A black sock, stripped from a foot and abandoned, like a snail's shell, had drifted under the heater. I went to the bureau and opened the bottom drawer. The clothes, and the blanket, were gone.

"Il n'est pas là," I said to the woman with the sour, triumphant smile.

"Voilà," she said. "Espagne, il a dit." Dan had succumbed to his resident bug. Everywhere he went, he wanted to keep going. The hag took something from the table by the bed. As she waved me out, I saw that she held the tube of salve.

"Not Wounded, Sire, But Mad"

As my high school English teacher once remarked, "My ace in the hole was shot down in flames."

Out in the street again, I walked south, back the way I had come. When had he hatched his escape plan? When he was salving my bruise? When he was sharing his breakfast with me? When we were enfolded, sleeping? And why? After a year of unaccustomed repose in the kingdom of "Yankee Die," why would he pack up his blanket and make tracks for Spain? Maybe, like the French, he knew when to flee before the advancing army. Once he'd let down the bars for one small freckled Yank, could the bus be far behind?

He was gone, and I'd be gone by nightfall. The three-week Eurail pass that had tootled us around in little Swiss trains would get me to Luxembourg on the overnight local. What a fool I'd look, sending a letter to my parents through Grace, as if she were the Red Cross, and then sitting beside her on the plane. My eyebrows ached at the thought of her spasms of welcome. But broke, I didn't have a single day to look for a job in Paris. And alone, I didn't have the nerve.

I sat on a bench in the pie-wedge park. I took out Grace's mutilated copy of *The Book*. The Author wasn't good for much. In his little maps of neighborhoods, he numbered the Sights, but he left out details, like streets. He referred to his traveling companion as Faith, as in, "I had a plate of wurst and the native beer. Faith had a Coke." After several weeks of trying to follow his maps, I'd realized that he was speaking metaphorically. The Author and Faith were intimate; it was Reality from which he was estranged. But he did list the times of departure of trains.

To cheer myself up, I glanced through the Paris section

of "Tips from Our Readers." One of Our Readers had recommended the sewer tour. I could see her in hip boots
and a two-piece Arnel knit, popping flash cubes at rafts of
exotic offal. Then a paragraph smote my eye:

> A super way to live in Paris without spending
> money is to be an au pair girl. You live with a real
> French family, and get room and board and pocket
> money in return for taking care of the children for a
> few hours a day. One agency which places au pair
> girls with families is Liaison Nordique . . .

"All right. All right, Author," I said. "I'll have one last
Coke with Faith. If I can find Liaison Nordique, and if they
can get me a job—today—I'll do it."

It took me an hour and two lines of the Métro—with
tunnels—to arrive at a street two blocks from my point of
departure. I admit that I have no sense of direction. When
in doubt, I let my instincts sniff out a route. I follow it for
fifty paces. Then I retrace my steps and walk the other
way. It almost always works. I compensate for rotten instincts with fierce determination. My father always says
that I remind him of the impassioned young man who
jumped on his horse and rode madly off in all directions.

When I'd found the street, and the building, and the
office, the woman at the desk of Liaison Nordique looked
like every woman's nightmare image of her rival: tall,
slender, with hair the color of comb honey, and cheekbones fanatically defined. Physically, she was infinitely
more organized than I was. She smiled, and said, "Bonjour."

"Bonjour," I said.

"Est-ce que je peux vous servir?"

I laid my cards on the table. "Look, I don't speak
French very well. I'm American. I wanted to ask if you
have au pair jobs where they'd take someone who doesn't
—you know—who can't—uh—talk. And I need it right
away, like now."

"Very good. Will you please fill out this form?"

While I was groping through the French and English
questions on the form, she made three phone calls and was
charming in three languages, one of which sounded as if
she were singing while swallowing noodles. Liaison Nor-

dique . . . she must be Norwegian. No wonder she was so intimidating, coming from the country where they'd fought the Nazis on skis.

Question: "What duties are you willing to perform as an au pair?"

Who knew? But from previous dealings with Ditsy Dixie at Elite Office Aides, I knew better than to leave it open. If I did, my French employers would ship me to the scullery and lower me into hundred-gallon vats with scrub brushes strapped to my feet. They'd let me have Bastille Day off, and an hour for church on Christmas, after which the master would press a small coin into my palm for the year's wages.

On the other hand, with twenty-two francs and eight hours and a French vocabulary mostly consisting of "s'il vous plaît" and "c'est trop cher," I wasn't in a position to haggle. I wrote, "No heavy housework."

The Viking Princess was babbling in French to the telephone. I comprehended "jeune fille" and "travail." "Girl. Work." I translated in pidgin, like Tarzan.

Question: "What salary do you expect?"

"Um . . . pardon," I said, venturing over enemy lines. "Je ne sais pas . . . uh . . . l'argent . . ."

The Viking beamed, as if I were a toddler whose first step had landed me flat on my ass. "Yes, of course. The usual minimum fee that we ask for our jeunes filles au pair is two tundred francs a month. Of course you will also have your own room, and your meals. Do you want to take classes in French?"

"Oh, oui, yes."

"Good. There is a school called l'Institut Catholique where many of our jeune filles study. It is reasonable, and there are classes at many different times, so you can arrange with your family to have your hours off when a class is scheduled."

Two hundred francs a month sounded like a lot of money. She was talking so fast that I didn't have time to translate it into dollars. She should have been selling used cars on late night TV.

Question: "Character References—give three, one a former employer."

Randy and I had traded fathers for this purpose. Her father had testified to my moral fiber, and my father to

Randy's, since we were twelve. I also listed my college biology professor, who was senile and didn't answer his mail, and my supervisor at Occidental. The supervisor wouldn't give me a glowing report. But I couldn't see the Viking placing a transatlantic call to the Coding Department. She made another tinkly French phone call. Hanging up, she wrote down an address.

"This lady is very, very nice," she said. "She speaks some English herself, and she does not mind that you are not fluent. She has two little girls. She is looking for someone immediately because her jeune fille has gone back to Switzerland." (In a huff?) "I think she will like you very much. She expects you at one o'clock."

Madame Faurer continued to expect me till two. Her street was secreted near a park. The trees had slender, earth-colored trunks, and the ground was beaten brown, with no patch of green. I made a circuit of the park, looking for signs. Children swooped and dipped on the sepia horses of an antique carousel. Girls and women stood by the gate, jiggling navy baby buggies, weighted with chrome. Didn't kids go out to play on a carousel alone? Did they always have keepers? I stepped off the curb as an old man led a pair of pudgy ponies down the lawn of mud. The sky and the ground were filmed with grey, like the roofs and houses dimly walling the park. The children mounted on the ponies wore navy stocking hats that covered their necks and heads, with circles cutting their faces into moons. They sat erect and stern with cold, each child holding a little stick in one hand.

I rounded the corner into the avenue. Thin shrubs straggled up from the mud. More women in tailored coats were pushing more navy buggies. Dark-clad children with spindly dark legs trailed the buggies along the gravel paths. A troop of white-limbed boys in shorts scattered pell mell across the field, bashing a ball with their feet.

I stopped a woman leading two fat children, each one gnawing a fat croissant. "Pardon," I said, handing her a piece of paper. I attempted to say the name of the street. The woman was suspicious. But she gave me the correct pronunciation, and walked away.

Only the French would think you'd stop a stranger to ask a pronunciation.

The street, when I found it, was diagonal cutting away

from the park. I was disappointed by the fancy new buildings. I'd hoped for gables and chimney pots. The Faurers'
building looked like a Hyatt House, even to the glass elevator. I got off at the wrong floor and went to the wrong
apartment. I was always doing that in France, till someone
explained to me that in Europe, the street floor is the
"ground floor" and the second floor is the "first floor."
When I attained the Faurers' apartment, I was an hour
late. But I was well ahead of Madame, who was still in
her bathrobe.

I worshipped her at once.

Elegant wrists emerged pale and graceful from the purple
silk cuffs of her dressing gown. The dressing gown alone
would have won me over. She looked like Jean Arthur,
befuddled at finding herself in Cary Grant's bathrobe. Her
hair looked like a shiny brown cauliflower. Her voice was
tinkly. No wonder the Viking had tinkled on the phone. I
wanted to tinkle too, but I couldn't speak French.

"Bon*jour*, Ker-ray! Entrez, entrez, et donnez-moi votre
manteau!" That was all I got as she tinkled me down a
plushly carpeted hall and into a living room full of windows with white gauze drapes, velour sofas, glass tables.
She snatched off my coat and stuck me in an armchair.
She offered me a cigarette, sitting on a hassock, smiling
with her pretty mouth, tinkling in French. Hadn't they told
her I was illiterate?

"Madame, pardon," I said, "s'il vous plaît . . . un peu
lentement?" Lentement: slowly. I'd looked it up in my
dictionary on the Métro ride. Thank God in my obsessive
purge of luggage, I hadn't pitched the paperback French-
English dictionary. It was a high school remnant.

"Bien sûr, bien sûr, Ker-ray," she trilled, patting my
knee. The weight of her diamond must have cramped her
knuckle. She sang out, "Leah! Vien cherie!" A little girl
ran into the room. She hurled herself on her mother's knee.
The hassock nearly capsized. "C'est Leah, qui a trois ans,"
knuckle. She sang out, "Leah! Vien, cherie!" A little girl
dressed like a Ginny doll in a flowered frock with a full
skirt and puffy sleeves, white ribbed kneesocks, white stiff
shoes, and plastic bow-shaped clasps in her fine pale hair.
She had a round, pasty face, like a gingerbread doll made
of white flour, and huge raisin eyes which were turned like
beacons on her mother's face. Madame tinkled, "Dites

bonjour." Leah muttered something into her mother's arm-
pit. The kid was shy. At least she wouldn't give me any
hassle.

"Madame," I said, "est-ce que Leah comprends anglais?"

"Non, Ker-ray," said Madame sadly, "et c'est de ma
faute. Mais j'espère que vous allez faire professeur! Je
voudrais que vous parlez anglais avec les enfantes, tou-
jours!"

She wanted me to teach the kids English—I got that.
But she'd babbled on. A time lapse of two sentences fell
between her speaking and my getting her drift, if I did.
She kept asking me questions based on phrases I hadn't
tackled yet. I said, "Je ne sais pas . . ."

"Vous n'avez pas compris?"

"Non, Madame."

A look came over her animated face which I was to
recognize often, and come to dread—defeat, and a cheery,
strained patience. She forged into English. "You will 'ave
a room for yourself alone. Do you go to school?"

The relief of speaking English was exquisite.

"Yes, but I have to go there tomorrow and find out
when the classes are."

"Good. I 'ave arrange zat you 'ave sree hours each day
to go to school. I will pay you . . . two hundred fifty francs
each months . . . and if I am please' of you . . . I will pay
you more."

When would she know if she were pleased? But I'd start
at fifty more than minimum. What a nice lady! On the
Métro, I'd figured out that two hundred francs a month
was only forty dollars. Two hundred fifty francs was fifty
dollars—not much spending money for a month in Paris.
But then I wouldn't spend anything. I'd eat with the
family. I wouldn't go to cafés. Of course there was school
. . . Madame was tinkling in French again. She leaped up
and raced into another room across the hall, and came
back lugging a very fat baby in a potty chair. 'C'est ma
petite Anouk," she said, dropping the chair with a thud.

The baby gave me the same deep-eyed stare as her sister.
I hoped they'd liven up. I was beginning to feel like the
governess in *The Turn of the Screw*. I said, "Est-ce que
c'est tout, Madame?" Is that all there is?

She laughed. "Oui, oui, c'est tout! Toutes mes enfantes! Avez vous des questions, Ker-ray?"

"Non, Madame." If I did, I couldn't phrase them.

"Bon!" She leaned in with a conspiratorial smile. "I am very please' of you. You 'ave what we call 'dents de lapin,' do you know what zat says? 'Bunny teeth!' Très sympathique!" She tapped her photogenic teeth.

Trust the French to look a gift horse in the mouth. After a thousand dollars worth of wiring, it was ironic to be hired for my overbite. But what the hell. I might as well get started. "Je commence maintenant, Madame?"

"Oh non non!" She trilled a lot of stuff which seemed to imply that next week would be time enough. Hadn't the Viking explained at all?

"Madame, pardon . . . but, mais . . . il faut commence maintenant. Je n'ai pas l'argent pour le . . . hotel . . ." Now or never, lady. How do you say "destitute" in French?

That gave her pause. She looked at the khaki sack I'd dropped by the door. Her tinkle was a trifle muffled as she asked an incomprehensible but weighty question.

I gave her the usual sheepish, "Je n'ai pas compris."

"You 'ave ozer sings?"

"Sings? Oh—no. No, that's it. C'est tout. C'est moi."

She studied me, smiling, puzzled. I might have bunny teeth, but I wasn't the American debutante she'd figured on. She seemed to be wondering if I were just eccentric, or the product of a disadvantaged home.

"I travel light," I reassured her. I had to speak English as lentement for her as she had to speak French for me. "But I'll write my mother to send my clothes." Shipping wouldn't cost much. My mother could mail me "Tricia" and "Julie" in one manila envelope.

Poor Madame. I'd arrived on her doorstep like a baby in a basket. At least she knew she could trust me not to depart in a huff, like the erstwhile Swiss. I had no money; I didn't speak French. I was better than bonded, I was practically indentured.

The apartment had five rooms: the vast salon, the roomy kitchen across the hall, the master bedroom, the nursery and the maid's room. My room, "all to myself," contained a huge double bed, a dresser full of blankets and wedding pictures, a bassinet, and a white wicker basket, stuffed with cotton balls and diaper rash ointments, and crowned with a white satin bow. The walls were pink. The quilt on the bed was blue, with pink flowers. Who would have felt at home in that room—Mary Pickford's mother? In the basket, I saw a tube of the salve that Dan had brought me.

Listen, in a month I'd have so many Frenchmen mad for me, I wouldn't remember that hillbilly's name.

In the enfantes' room, Madame showed me a closet full of diapers, little undies, piles of white tights, and racks of Shirley Temple dresses. The bed for Leah and the crib for Anouk were white, with white canopies, the sheets edged with lace. The white pillow cases were framed in lace. The bed quilts were white, embroidered with flowers. The kids would be snowblind by the age of five. Madame was tinkling around in a cupboard, emptying a shelf for me to store my things. She watched me unpack: one thin sweater, one thick sweater, one flannel nightgown, two pairs of socks . . . I felt like the Little Match Girl. She was pleased with my French-English dictionary, and puzzled by *The Book*. She seized upon my only dress and made me hang it up in another closet, next to more of Leah's flouncy frocks. Leah observed this activity with olive-dull eyes. She kept clutching her mother's robe and tucking her head down to bump her mother's elegant bottom.

"Leah! Laisse-moi, cherie!" said her mother at last, the sharp honk of the first word not quite dissipated by the subsequent tinkle.

"Non, non," Leah wheedled.

Sounds of protest echoed from the living room, where we had abandoned the stolid Anouk, strapped to her throne, a baby Mikado. Madame sent Leah to see to the baby. "Allez, allez, vite!"

"Non, non, Mama," Leah whined, backing into the crib, round white face contorted with a kid's imitation of anguish.

"Allez!" Madame shrieked, the tinkle ascending to a dog whistle blast. Leah staggered out, bawling. Madame gave me a smile a little tattered by crow's feet. I smiled, somewhere ruefully. If Leah wanted to make my life a hell, she had all the tools.

"Maman! Maman! Maman! Maman! Anouk a fait po-po, Maman, Anouk a fait po-po!" sang Leah, dancing back from the living room with a bogus display of glee.

"Formidable!" Madame beamed at me. She raced off after the clapping, frolicking Leah. I lagged behind.

In the living room, Leah squatted by the blinking baby, peering between the baby's bulgy thighs. "Regarde, Maman! Anouk a fait po-po! Bravo, Anouk!" she hollered. Madame peered in too. Then she clapped her hands and kissed the baby. "Bravo, Anouk!" she trilled, jumping up and down. Leah frolicked around the couch, announcing the triumph of Anouk to greater Paris. All we needed was confetti and a band to play the "Marseillaise." I wondered how many times a day we'd have to reinforce Anouk. What did we do when she wet her pants? Beat ourselves with birches?

Madame and Leah retired from the arena when the cotton balls were called for. Anouk didn't cry as I leaned above her, swabbing. Austere, removed, she stared at my face. I tickled her. She didn't even blink. What fun! A catatonic baby, and a schizophrenic toddler. No wonder Madame stayed in her bathrobe. She wanted to pretend she was dreaming.

I stuffed the baby into the snowy jumpsuit provided by her mother. The jumpsuit was split at the seams. A baby in a white jumpsuit—maybe she wasn't allowed to crawl. Maybe she was toted till she was three. That policy would explain some of Leah's problems. Lugging the bulk—I'd have the arms of King Kong if I kept this up—I went to find Madame.

She was feeding cookies to Leah in the kitchen. She gave a cookie to Anouk, who slobbered it down the pristine bib of her jumpsuit. The kitchen was a large oblong room, with the door and casement windows facing off at the narrow ends. Along one wall stood a washing machine, a drier, a stove, a counter and sink; on the opposite wall loomed a monstrous refrigerator and rows of wooden cupboards. A square table made of some steely plastic obstructed the middle of the room. The table was flanked by two chairs, and a small square sittable stool. In the corner by the back door leading to the service elevator was a baby's bouncy canvas chair. In front of the window, the ceiling was hung with racks for drying clothes, and an ironing board, with iron at the ready, jutted out like the prow of a ship.

"Voulez-vous du café, Ker-ray?" said Madame.

"Oh oui, merci, Madame," I said. I hadn't eaten since breakfast with Dan. It was almost 5:30. How soon was dinner? In restaurants, no one ate till eight o'clock, but surely families choffed a little something at six to tide them over? Grace and I had spent most of our money on snacks to get us over the hump. The cookie in Madame's hand traveled past me to Leah, who was chewing on the one in her other hand, fat chins bobbling. "Deux galettes," Leah sang: I've got two cookies! Madame shut the cookie box away in the cupboard. She put a saucepan of water to boil. She got two flowered cups, each one big enough to put my fist in, out of the cupboard. At least I could quaff a big foamy cup of café au lait. Funny how espresso, which tasted like dirt, was so good when you mixed it with milk.

Madame handed me a jar of instant Nescafé. "Mais servez-vous, Ker-ray," she said. Help yourself.

We sat at the table drinking Nescafé. Madame took hers black. It tasted a lot like the fuel oil in the Occidental Coding coffee machine. Anouk in the bouncy chair was perfectly inert, regarding me and her dog-eared galette with the same suspicious gaze. Leah hung on her mother's knee, babbling. Madame fed the monologue with "Comment, cherie?" Was this the Children's Hour? Suddenly Madame leaped up—she had a tendency to spring from repose like a deer scenting hunters—and dashed for the bedroom, tinkling something about Liaison Nordique. In a minute, I heard her on the phone. She must be telling the Viking that I'd passed the audition. On the telephone, Madame's tinkle soared into a sing-song that reminded me of Glinda the Good in *The Wizard of Oz:* "Are you a good-a witch or a bad-a witch?" Leah had clambered after her mother, yelling, "Maman! Maman! Maman! Maman!"

I looked at Anouk. She looked at me. I extricated the nubby cookie from her limp, fat fingers, rinsed it under the tap, wiped it on a towel, dunked it in my coffee, and ate it. She watched me, not surprised. In seven months of life with Leah, she must have gotten cynical about the human race. She'd be raccoon-eyed and smoking opium by grade school. The soggy cookie stirred up the juices in my shriveled stomach. Snitching was chancy for the indentured; Madame might have an accounting eye. But I pulled very gently at the icebox door, listening for the thumping and scampering of Leah and Madame.

The shelves glistened, desolate and arctic in their isolated whiteness. Even the boys I'd known at college always had a bottle of catsup and a six-pack of beer. Madame Faurer's provisions consisted of a bottle of milk, a stick of butter, a rectangular plastic carton which I didn't take time to pry open, and a pear gone bad. A bottle of salad dressing and a jar of olives rattled in the rack on the door. There were two olives in the bottle.

Out of morbid curiosity, I opened all the cupboards. The bottom cupboards were chockablock with pots and cooking equipment. I caught two pans in my hands as they slid from a pile. There were three different grinders, each with an elaborate crank and interlocking pieces that mashed and sheared with bladed élan. There were skillets and saucepans, a double-boiler, a deep-fat fryer—french fried pear? french fried olives?—and five or six pie pans with fluted edges, ranging in size from tart to giant pizza. The lids outnumbered the pans. One cupboard slithered with half-shells—Olives St. Jacques?

The upper cupboards held six tomes of cookery and a bag of flour. Hunting, I found sugar, baking powder, salt and whole pepper, and some powdered stuff, like Pablum, for the baby.

The French are famous for whipping up feasts out of nothing. But even Jesus started with loaves and fishes. The Faurers didn't even keep a jar of peanut butter. Having eaten a peanut butter sandwich for lunch at least four days a week since infancy, I couldn't imagine life without a large jar of Crunchy, not Smooth, in the cupboard. My best friend Randy used to say that when she first knew me, she'd pictured our family at dinner, passing around a punch bowl of peanut butter, dipping in our fingers, like Hawaiians with poi. At that moment in the Faurers' kitchen, I would have run over my grandmother for a peanut butter sandwich.

Then I came upon a treasure trove: two cases of canned pudding. At least "La Crème," the brand name, might signify pudding, and the stuff in the crystal bowl pictured on the label looked like pudding. The flavors included "chocolat," "caramel," "vanille," "banane," and "fraise," which was pink. Why would Madame, who owned four ounces of butter, keep enough pudding to last a semester at a boarding school? Were the family all suffering from gum disease? Pudding wasn't my idea of dessert—I was a chocolate chip cookie person—but I would have wolfed down a whole tin of pink tapioca if I could have found a can opener. A frenzied silent search of drawers and cupboards yielded every utensil from an apple corer to a garlic press, but no sharp object capable of rending the lid of a can.

I stole two more cookies and gobbled them. Unless Monsieur arrived with a carton of take-out, we were in for a lean evening.

"Ker-ray!" sang Madame. Swallowing, I went to the door. She was dressed to face the faded day in slacks and a turtleneck sweater. Leah was stuffed into a white fur coat and hat, and white vinyl boots. She looked like an Eskimo go-go girl. Were they going out to eat? Madame rushed me backward into the kitchen. She raced to the ironing board and plugged in the iron, which stood upright on the board, cord dangling. She opened the door of the drier and hauled out armloads of diapers and lace-edged sheets and infant pajamas which by no stretch of the fabric could fit the baby Buddha. She babbled some words including "repasser," and made ironing motions. "Ces ne sont pas de vous," she said kindly, bundling two holey dishtowels and a huge sheet back into the drier. Only the ironing which pertained to the kids pertained to the kids' au pair.

The fly was taking shape in the ointment.

Half the load was diapers, which was a mercy. I started to fold them. She stopped me. "Ker-ray, regardez." She put a diaper on the ironing board, ironed it, folded it, ironed it, folded it. When it looked like a cotton omelet, she put it on the table. She invited me to imitate her.

She wanted me to iron the diapers. What about spray starch? Why not diapers embroidered to match the sheets? Where had Madame been raised—the Palace of Versailles?

I ironed a diaper. "Bravo, Ker-ray," said Madame, patting my rigid shoulder. She cleared out of the kitchen. Reappearing in a camel's hair coat, she tinkled something that ended "à tout à l'heure" and hustled the polar dwarf out.

I looked at Anouk. She looked at me. I knew why she'd adopted a poker face. I ate some more cookies, mindful of the level in the box, Anouk was one baby who could have gone hungry, or at least unstuffed, from time to time. But she was so resigned to abandonment that I felt sorry for her. "Here, sport. Worry this one for a while," I said, giving her a cookie. I did a desultory repasse on a frayed diaper. The doorbell rang.

I hated to open the door. I'd have to be lucid in French. But Madame bustled in, laughing, and scooped up a big straw handbag from a corner of the kitchen. She bustled out again. On her second exit, we gave each other edgy smiles, like distant cousins at a family reunion who keep meeting at the bar. If she had a habit of remembering on the sidewalk what she'd left upstairs, I'd have to keep my cookies under wraps.

I was done with repasser when they returned. In her straw bag, Madame carried milk, a block of Swiss cheese, a wet lump of lettuce, some carrots, two tomatoes, bananas, apples, oranges, three yogurts, and a small flat packet of butcher paper, which was later revealed to contain four scrimlike pieces of ham. Leah was smacking the head of Anouk with a half-loaf of new-smelling bread.

Madame's family provisions wouldn't have lasted me a two-day train ride.

"Hold it!" I wanted to holler. "Meals are part of my stipend, right? Where's the coq au vin? I'm not ironing diapers till seven p.m. for a yogurt and a banana!"

But duty called. Madame dumped Anouk in her playpen in the nursery. The white plastic cage was so packed with toys that the baby was lost in the crowd. Madame escorted me into the bathroom, a carpeted hall with a tub. They'd secreted the toilet next door.

She wanted me to bathe Leah.

The prospect horrified both parties. Leah screamed, "Non, non, Maman!" clutching herself in terror: the convent novice abducted by the neanderthal. "Leah! Ça suffit!" said Mademe almost sharply, retreating to the kitchen. Leah roared after her, tooting like a derailed locomotive. I sat on the edge of the tub, regarding the gleaming monolithic basin and the velvety carpet, and mulling over tortures which could be applied to a strong fat three-year-old in a large locked bathroom. I could hear Madame yelling, and Leah whining, pounding the floor, rattling a chair against the table. Madame dragged her, shrieking, back to my cell. Leah's face was patched with red. Her spine was rigid, and her feet in white laced shoes plowed twin tracks in the carpet. "Doucement, doucement," Madame said. "Sois gentille avec Ker-ray." Noblesse oblige, little princess, make nice with the nanny, or she'll split and I'll have to do this myself.

Madame closed the door. I locked it.

While the water was running, I got Leah down on the floor and tried to unlace her shoes. Even the laces were stiff with polish. She kicked and flailed. How could a kid who lived on galettes have so much energy? Her mother must feed her raw meat for a week before a new au pair arrived. Finally I sat on her stomach and held her left leg down with one hand. With my right hand, I unlaced the left shoe and yanked it off. She kicked my arm with her right foot. I slapped her chubby leg, hard. A red splotch appeared in the white flesh. She wailed horribly, her limbs falling limp in despair. During the lull, I got her other shoe and her stockings off. She began to recover as I flipped her on her stomach and unbuttoned her Rebecca of Sunnybrook frock. If Leah were my kid—God forbid—I'd dress her in combat khaki and a sign that said BEWARE OF DOG.

Hauling the dress over Leah's squirming arms, I tried to think of Helen Keller and her keeper. After months of struggle, even a deaf, blind child had yielded to discipline. Learning had followed, and finally love. Leah might as well be deaf for all the communication between us, till I learned her language or she learned mine. If I were gentle but firm, if I set up rules and enforced them . . . if I didn't yield to the impulse to hold her head under water till she stopped struggling . . . maybe in time she would come to respect me. Maybe we'd even be friends.

The title Beloved Teacher was much more appealing than Animal Trainer.

I hauled Leah over the side of the tub and dumped her in the water.

"Trop chaud!" she yelled: too hot.

"Non," I said.

"Oui, oui, c'est chaud! Ah-oo! Ai-ee!" She danced in the water. Waves belched up over the sides.

"Stop that! Knock it off!" I said.

She stopped. She opened her squinched-up eyes and stared at me. Ah ha! The power of cryptic incantation— the Voodoo curse! "Quoi?" she said.

"J'ai dit, 'Stop that!' You turd," I said. "Asseyez-vous."
I knew how to say "Sit down" because my mother used to
say it to me when I was little. Cosmopolitanism at our
house consisted of "Gesundheit" and "Asseyez-vous."

She sat. I handed her the soap and washcloth. "Soapez-
vous."

"Quoi?"

I made washing motions. "Comme ça." What was wash?
"Laver!" It was all coming back to me, my high school
vocabulary. Soon I would be able to say, "Hot dogs for
sure," and, "Where is the library?" just like I'd learned in
French lab, when we weren't having fire drills, singing "La
Vie en Rose," and pulling out the plugs of everybody's ear-
phones to see how long it would take them to notice.
"Lavez-vous," I said smugly.

Only an hour later, I hauled Anouk, in pink Dr. Dentons, into the kitchen. Leah, in blue, was already there,
sitting at the table, a dishtowel tied around her neck. A
man stood by the cupboards. He wore a black suit, a narrow tie, and a brushcut, like Ozzie Nelson's. He had a
homely, houndish face, and sharp black eyes. He looked
like a science whiz having his picture taken for the high
school yearbook.

"Ker-ray, c'est mon mari," said Madame, all aflutter. She
was courting steam burns, dumping boiling water from a
pot of potatoes and carrots into the sink. Vegetables tumbled into a colander. Where had she been storing potatoes
and onions—under her bed? Rushing to the cupboard, she
extricated—with much clashing and banging—one of the
mincing machines.

"Bonsoir," the husband said over the clash of metal.

"Bonsoir," I said.

He chucked Anouk under the chin. She maintained her
frosty gaze, like a socialite goosed by a gardener. Evidently
she wasn't Daddy's girl. Leah wasn't either. He stroked
the top of her head, and she reared away, yelling, "Ooch!
Ai-ee!"

"Leah," said her parents, gently. Monsieur retreated to
the bedroom with his briefcase. Didn't the poor guy need a
drink? My father went straight to the ice cube trays when
he came home from work. When I was little, I was so used
to seeing him back out of the icebox with a tray and his
briefcase, I thought he worked in there. This poor man

worked till 7 p.m. and came home to Goneril and Regan.
I heard the bathroom door close. There was a lengthy
pause—I hadn't swabbed the place après le déluge—and
then the sound of water rushing from the spigot.

The next half hour was a contest between Madame,
frantic to get the kids fed before her husband wanted his
dinner, and Leah, the human hurdle. Madame hurled potatoes into the mincer, wrenching the crank in jerking circles;
Leah stroked the back of her mother's knees, whining,
"Je voudrais du chocolat, Maman," monotonous as the left-
hand piano part of "Heart and Soul." Chopping the heads
off boiled onions, Madame burned her fingers in her haste,
and rushed to the sink to run water on her blisters, trampling Leah, who'd been hovering at her mother's butt like
a fly at a horse's tail. Leah lay in a heap by the ironing
board, bawling. "Ai-ee! Ooch! Oo-là-là!" Her mother
scooped her up, gave her a rapid brush-off, and rushed
back to sink, pot, and grinder, bumping her hip on the
table, and catching her ankle in the bent leg of the baby
chair. From hunger or from boredom, Anouk decided to
provide a soundtrack. She wailed great gusts of anguish,
her head lolling over the side of the baby chair, which
listed to port. This was the hour for which she'd been
hoarding emotional response. "Ah-nouk! Noo-noose!" Madame sang sweetly and hopelessly into the Banshee din.
Leah, as the Angel of Mercy, patted the baby's arm, mur-
muring soothing sounds which must have tempted the baby
to get her by the neck. I hauled the baby up from the chair,
her body a lump of moist despair. She screamed into my
sweater. I jiggled her. She screamed like a Paris police
siren: "Ah-ah-ah-ah-ah-ah-ah-ah-ah . . ." Madame was stirring the molten vegetation into soup. She dropped big pats
of butter into two flat pottery bowls. Tossing two spoons
on the table, she told Leah to sit.

"Non non non," Leah moaned, her blue pajama feet pat-
tering a dance.

Madame unleashed a stream of bel canto fury. She seized
Leah's resistant bulk, planted her in the straight chair with
a bulgy-bottomed whomp! and slammed a soup plate in
front of her. She dumped soup over the butter and stirred
with the spoon. Leah wailed, with less conviction and
volume than Anouk. Madame, with a haggard smile, waved
the baby over. I put Anouk back in the canvas chair. She

dangled, howling. Madame poured and stirred the second plate of soup, testing its heat with her tongue. She blew on it to cool it. Leah got the hint.

"C'est trop chaud!": too hot.

"Non, pas pour toi, c'est bien," said Madame, smiling at Anouk, who was listing in her chair and keening, oblivious.

"Non, c'est trop chaud pour moi aussi!" Leah threw back her head and let it loll on the back of her chair. She kicked the table with both feet, forgetting that she wasn't wearing shoes. It did my heart good to see her wince with real pain. Madame tied another towel with another hole in it around Anouk's neck. She spooned some soup into the baby's open, drooling mouth. "Hoopla!" Madame said gaily. Anouk sputtered, winced, shook her head, dribbled the soup out, and roared. "Trop chaud," Madame muttered, flapping one hand above the plate of soup. She ran water from the tap into the bowl, tested the soup, and spooned it into the wailing gulf. The soup dribbled into the towel. Madame kept spooning; the soup kept running out. Finally a spoonful slid down the baby's gullet. She turned purple and choked. Madame yanked her up from the chair and turned her upside down, pounding on her back. The dishtowel around the baby's neck fell over her face, muffling her breathing. I disconnected the towel.

The baby gasped. Her mother pounded. Even Leah was silenced by the drama, probably requesting that le bon Dieu grant Anouk a happy death.

The baby screamed. Her screams were awesome, tragically inspired. Her life was torture at the hands of an evil genius sister and a dingbat mother. The days when Leah didn't stick a fork in her, Madame dropped her on her head.

Madame abandoned dinner. She stroked the baby, who was belly-flopped across her mother's gorgeous knees, hollering as if she could keep it up till midnight. Leah attempted to recoup lost favor by stroking her mother's hair and cooing, "C'est jolie, les cheveux de ma maman . . ."— "My mother has such pretty hair . . ." Leah was the French Bad Seed. I hoped to hell Anouk would never win a spelling medal.

I took Anouk to my room and plugged her mouth with a bottle. I could have rolled her for it. I was so hungry my vision was fogged. If Madame dared to sling me the same hash rejected by the enfantes . . . if she never fed me at all . . .

When did I get to put my feet up and have a glass of wine? Even slaves repaired to the cabins at eventide, to sing sad songs and do imitations of the master. I was more like the body servants who waved palmetto fans above the ladies as they napped, and slept all night in the hall in case something was wanting.

Madame invaded my quarters. She shepherded me and the guzzling baby into the kitchen. Monsieur sat at the table, in the silk print dressing gown that had won my heart a few short hours before. Leah was enthroned on the other chair, smacking her lips as she spooned up the raspberry dregs of a yogurt. Her soup was untouched. Madame took Anouk from me, saying, "Asseyez-vous, Ker-ray." One more place was laid at the table, but both the chairs were taken. Monsieur got up and gave me his chair.

"Non non," I said.

"Mais oui, asseyez-vous," said Monsieur, taking the stool.

Horrified, Madame dislodged the squirming Leah, and made her husband take Leah's chair. Shifting Anouk to her shoulder, Madame took away Leah's bowl. I could tell by her hesitant wrist and shifty eye that she would have dumped the bowl back in the pot if I hadn't been watching. But she took it to the sink and rinsed it out. She dried it with a ragged towel, filled it with soup, and gave it to me. Leah's bowl. I regarded it with loathing. The Faurers, as the Viking had informed me, had beaucoup de bucks. But they only had two chairs and two soup plates, and their towels were full of holes. When I was a kid, I used to complain that the people who lived in the biggest houses gave out the two-cent lollipops on Halloween. "They're rich!" I'd say, and my father would answer, "That's *why* they're rich." If they had Halloween in France, Madame Faurer would ladle soup into every bag.

Soup was followed by a limp, oily salad. Salad at home was iceberg lettuce (guaranteed Chavez-approved by the hippie grocer), tomatoes, green pepper, onion, mushrooms, cheese cubes, croutons, and Russian dressing. Salad at Madame Faurer's was dark green stuff that looked like dandelion leaves, skimmed with oil and doused with gravel. Monsieur contentedly nibbled away, slopping breadcrusts around his plate. He offered me more salad. All this was less sustaining than the peanuts in a cocktail lounge. Where was dinner?

Madame opened the oven door. My heart leaped. Maybe she'd hidden a roast in there.

She set the entree before us. I looked, and broke off half the loaf of bread. The main course consisted of three small squares of real American bread, the kind that tastes like cotton batting, each slice coated with a film of ham and a scrap of Swiss cheese. How could the woman cut slices that thin without a laser beam? Monsieur took a sandwich. I looked at Madame. She was perched on the stool, still holding up the bottle for the stupefied baby, while Leah worried her mother's hair. Madame had eaten nothing. After a somersault of brain cells, I said, "Madame . . . vous ne mangez pas?"

"Non non, Ker-ray, je n'ai pas faim," she assured me, trying not to look at the two little sandwiches. She added something tinkly and deprecating about "diner." Dinner wasn't her favorite meal, which accounted for its disreputable state this evening. I took a sandwich and ate it. My stomach awakened from its torpor, and seethed. Monsieur was chewing faster than I was, and casting covetous glances at the puny third sandwich. I speeded up. We finished in a dead heat.

Madame picked up the platter and handed it to Monsieur. He deferred to me. Both of them looked at me: we know how you Americans feed your faces! "Non, merci," I said. If I hadn't been the envoy of American good will, I would have seized that sandwich and raced away with it into the night.

The diabolical design of slow starvation was accompanied by the water torture of questions, in French, from Monsieur. He spoke so softly that I didn't hear the questions. After he repeated them, I heard them, but I didn't understand them.

"Where are you from in the States?" he said at last, in the unmistakable nasal accents of the Great Lakes region.

"You speak English!" I cried with joy: thank God, reinforcements!

"Sure," said Monsieur. "I was a foreign exchange student. I went to high school in Ypsilanti, Michigan."

"Est-ce que vous connaissez Eep-see-lot-ee, Ker-ray?" said Madame.

"Oui," I said. My high school had bused our choir to Ypsilanti for something called a "sing-off." Madame and Monsieur awaited my comments. "It's in Michigan," I said.

Monsieur nodded brusquely: yes, yes, he knew that. "The administrators of the program tried to send me to a larger city—Cleveland."

"Est-ce que vous connaissez Cleve-lan', Ker-ray?" said Madame.

"Oui," I said, grinning, "in fact—"

"But my father refused to allow it," Monsieur continued. "He felt that a smaller town would be safer and much more typical of the American culture—the charming naïveté, the frontier rawness—"

"Yeah, right," I said, exuding a charming naïveté. My rawness spoke for itself.

"Also my father had been to Cleveland on business—he was appalled by the size and squalidness of the slums, the dirtiness of the whole city, the decay and the industrial atmosphere of the center, what you call 'downtown.'"

Trying to follow his rapid English, Madame was frowning in concentration and smiling in encouragement. Eager to please, I was nodding so hard my neck cracked. "Right, absolutely," I said.

"Where are you from?" said Monsieur.

"Cleveland," I said.

There was a pause. Madame got it. She bit her thumb.

"So that you will learn French more quickly, we will speak only in French," said Monsieur.

I said sadly, "Okay—I mean, oui."

As if to further demonstrate the downfall of communication, Madame had to tell me three times, lentement, to put Anouk to bed. Leah decided to befriend me by telling me stories and quizzing me on them. I kept saying, "Je n'ai pas compris": I don't get it. I could hear Monsieur Faurer at a later hour, saying to Madame, "But yes, the American has teeth of the bunny, but she is also a dumbbell, is it not?"

On the gastronomic front, I hadn't lost hope. I was praying, and fasting, for dessert. I expected pudding. We had what amounted to a pudding cellar. What we needed was a pudding rack. Sure enough, when the plates were cleared, Madame with frabjous tinkles threw open the door to the pudding lode and produced two cans—"banane" and "chocolat." She pranced to the table, flourishing the cans as if she were doing a hard-sell commercial in between Saturday morning cartoons. Leah and Monsieur regarded the cans with resignation bordering on sleep. Clattering around in a drawer, Madame emerged with an object which looked like a cross between an icepick and a scythe. She stabbed the pudding can. She dumped the contents of "banane" and "chocolat" in the erstwhile soup plates and set them before me, as if I were supposed to use my fingers, dipping from the left and the right.

"Voulez-vous de LaCrème, chéri?" she asked her husband. As one, Monsieur and Leah turned to the icebox and claimed the two remaining yogurts. Madame stuck a spoon in each bowl of pudding. She went to the sink and ran the water, dumping in dishwashing liquid. She was going to do her chores before she ate her pudding.

What was I to think? There were the bowls. There were the spoons. Madame hadn't stated a preference. Throwing good breeding to the dogs, I took the banana bowl and polished it off before Madame had turned around from the sink.

I was scraping up the last of the custardy stuff, only beginning to glean that a little banana pudding was more than enough, when I noticed the deepening silence. I looked up.

Monsieur and Leah were staring at me over their little cardboard cups of yogurt, each one-quarter the size of a pudding can. At the sink, Madame was wiping dry a tiny crystal dish and a teaspoon, which she was about to set before me. I was supposed to have served myself a few tablespoons of chocolat or banane and left the bulk of the pudding for display. Instead, I had eaten enough banana pudding for a French family of four.

My humiliation was complete. All I wanted was to collapse in the pink and blue Disney suite. But the au pair's labor ends only when the little charges are comatose. There followed two hours of putting Anouk to bed, letting her scream, hearing her mother go in and get her up, having her mother bring her to me, putting her back to bed . . . Leah, meanwhile, was playing the empress on a restless night: demanding that dolls be brought, and other dolls removed; requesting glasses of water, from which she took sips while her mother propped up her head . . .

At eleven, Monsieur dragged the blushing Madame to the master bedroom. I hoped they were taking drastic precautions. I thought of Dan, who had lured me and left me. Here I was, sleeping with a diaper basket, if I ever got to sleep at all. Was I supposed to sit up all night? What was I, a croup kettle?

Some romance! Some adventure! I wished to hell I'd gone home.

La Vie en Rose

I switched off the vacuum cleaner.

All was silent in the apartment. Leah was at nursery school. Madame had gone to fetch her. Emparo, the Spanish maid, had vanished down the freight elevator to have a word with her mother, who was a maid on the floor below. Anouk was in the nursery, stiffly propped in the plastic playpen among her stuffed companions.

I dropped the vacuum cleaner hose and went to the kitchen. I grabbed a spoon, opened the icebox, and scooped up mouthfuls of congealed cauliflower au gratin. No doubt Madame intended to heat it up for lunch. I couldn't wait. I'd be the only one to eat it anyway. Madame never ate, and Leah never ate what her mother prepared. Anouk and I were the only ones who opened our mouths for whatever was on the fork.

I noted previous spoon-troughs and fork-tracks in the lumpy surface of the casserole. Some were mine from a midnight foray, but some were undoubtedly Madame's, and I'd recently discovered that Emparo, the Spanish maid, also struck a finger in the meager pie. One of us was always turning her back and swallowing as another would-be poacher pussyfooted into the kitchen. The place was like a diet workshop in a week of low morale.

Emparo and I had good reason to be sneaky, and hungry. She was performing drudgeries à la maison Faurer from 8 a.m. to 1. Earning $1.60 an hour, she couldn't pack a box lunch of artichokes and pâté. I lived at the mercy of Madame Faurer's grocery list, which could have been sent by Western Union under the ten-word limit.

But the motives behind Madame's starvation were convoluted. She'd told me that she had "fear of getting fat"— which in her case was like my having "fear of being too fluent in French." Her breakfast was Nescafé, and she never

79

ate dinner, except for glasses of wine and charming little snatches from her husband's plate. Lunch was the culinary high point of the day. There wasn't a lot of it, but what there was, was tasty—vegetable casseroles, or small tender cuts of meat or fish, with salad—the sort of light repast that tides one over and makes one feel virtuous till around ten, when one orders a pizza. Madame didn't sit down and eat lunch, either. Instead, she snitched from pots and plates, even to the carrots and fish she pureed for Anouk, and she ate whatever Leah left, which was most of whatever had been set before her. (Leah only liked to eat what Madame had been saving for the dinner of Monsieur.) Often in the afternoon, I would come upon Madame, gnawing Leah's abandoned apple or scraping up the last jam in the baby's yogurt.

Twice in the month I'd been with the Faurers, Madame had taken to her bed with "mal au coeur"—heart trouble, as she told me. Monsieur and I would tiptoe around, while Leah attempted to burst into the darkened bedroom and hurl herself on her mother's bed like a Hindu widow leaping on her husband's funeral pyre. Monsieur hauled Leah off to school, Leah shrieking, "Ooch! Eech! Ai-ee!" At lunch the place was gloriously silent, and I scrounged for tidbits in the icebox with the maid, who kept raising her eyebrows and grinning in the direction of the bedroom. Leah lunched with the mother of Monsieur when her mother was stricken, a policy which may have brought on the attacks. I would ask Madame, when we bumped in the hall outside the john, if she'd like some tea or pudding. We always had pudding; pudding was the peanut butter of Paris. Madame would lay a hand on her troubled heart and tinkle wearily, "No, she had a pain, she couldn't eat." When I'd come in from taking Anouk to the park, I'd find the poor starved woman in the kitchen, breaking off hunks of bread and cheese.

More and more I had the feeling that I was the soubrette and Madame was the ingenue. She was afraid of her husband, her kids, her mother-in-law, the man who came to fix the washing machine, the concierge, the maid, the maid's mother, and me. After a week, she'd ceded me Anouk, like a rambunctious protectorate. I was Baby Boss. When Madame encountered Anouk and me, she snooked the baby under the chin and left the room. She would have liked to cede Leah too, but Leah was fanatically devoted to the empire. She trailed her mother from room to room like a clackety duck on a string, clacking, "Maman, maman, maman, maman . . ." When Madame wrote letters in the salon, Leah sat across the table, scrabbling with colored pencils on sheets of satiny writing paper. When Madame took a bath, Leah sat in a chair by the tub, eating cookies. Madame couldn't pee without Leah pounding on the door.

Madame should have made it her mission in life to get Leah to school, for her own peace of mind. But she was terrified of Leah's teacher, a master sergeant with a hairnet, whose contempt for the parents of tardy children was legend. If Leah weren't ready for Madame to drive her to school on time, she got to stay home. Mornings from 8:00 to 8:45, Leah and I were engaged in a tightly clocked sumo wrestling match. I had to get any clothes at all on that kid's body and dump her by the door by 8:45.

Her shoes were Leah's secret weapon. They were so small that the kid had corns on her toes. They were stiff from my nightly whitewash. Getting them on Leah's kicking, wriggling feet reduced me to trembling and tears. Finally I announced, with pidgin dignity, that I would not put on again the shoes of Leah. (I'd looked it up.) Madame was gaily apologetic: Leah was always a pig in the mornings, just like her father! After that, Madame forced the camel through the needle's eye, with much smacking of soles with the palm of the hand, and much squealing of the demon child. I asked Madame why she didn't buy Leah new shoes that were "plus grands." Wide-eyed, Madame said that children's feet grew so fast! Shoes were so expensive! Paris was the final stronghold of the Chinese art of binding.

Sometimes I won and Leah went to school. Sometimes I lost and Leah stayed home. Leah's cause was abetted by her mother, when Madame couldn't pull her act together by zero hour. Nothing gnawed like the sight of the Bad Seed in coat and boots and knitted hat, gamboling down the hall at 9:05, as her mother tore apart the kitchen in search of her car keys.

Who was Madame Faurer? She seemed to operate by rote, grinding out her day the way she mashed up vegetables for soup. She had no life outside her house. She took Leah to school at nine; she fetched her at noon. She returned her at two and cherched her at five. On the way home from these sorties, she bought the fruit and vegetables and cheese and fish. The rest of the time, she was in the apartment, fussing in the kitchen, watching TV, reading in her room. She took a lot of naps.

My mother ran a three-story, twelve-room house, with the dubious assistance of a cleaning woman one day every other week. On her Tuesdays, Orla spent the mornings clearing Coke bottles out of my brothers' rooms, and the afternoons at the kitchen table with my mother, drinking Tang and discussing the sorry state of the Cleveland schools. My mother didn't clean. She'd rather take us to the zoo, or read. We lived in a pleasant disorder, with dust and crumbs, and stacks of books on chairs. Twice a year, if my mother remembered to ask me, I washed the windows.

With two kids and a five-room apartment to manage, Madame Faurer had a full-time nursemaid and a cleaning woman five days a week. No wonder we kept meeting in the icebox—there was nothing to do. I cleaned the kids' room and my room and did the kids' laundry. Madame invented busywork for me: bleaching Leah's white tights, white caps, white gloves; polishing her white shoes; ironing diapers. Emparo cleaned everything else. Madame got so desperate for tasks for Emparo, she had her take down the white gauze curtains in the salon and wash them in the bathtub. Emparo had to lean over the side of the tub and scrub, like an Indian beating clothes on the rocks of a creek.

The Faurers saved money on servants, dishtowels, dinnerware, menus, shoes for the kids, and entertainment. They didn't go out. They didn't have guests, except for the mother and sister of Monsieur. They lived in Paris as if they were living in Nutley, New Jersey. When Monsieur went to Lyon on business for a weekend, Madame stayed in his dressing gown all Saturday—I thought she'd married him for it. Sunday, she stayed in bed.

Monsieur was an enigma too, a brushcut with a briefcase. At dinner, he conversed with Madame sub rosa; I couldn't hear it, let alone understand it. At breakfast, he didn't speak. He read the paper. Madame served him, straining scalded milk to pour in the Nescafé, slicing stale rounds of yesterday's bread, which she carefully charred to dry black husks on a grill that rested on a burner of the stove. Monsieur was so picky at dinner that he couldn't bear to eat a wilted lettuce leaf or a pear that wasn't brown. How could he stomach burned bread and boiled milk for breakfast? I'd never have the nerve to ask him. After the first night of Twenty Questions, answered by me with "Pardon?" he only spoke to me in English, and only when forced by Madame. When I spoke French in front of him, he corrected my grammar and pronunciation. He had the national accent fetish, whereas I was happy that I knew the French for "sit." My vocabulary was expanding. I was almost fluent on the topics of laundry and bowel movements. Certain phrases rippled off my Yankee tongue, for instance, "Stop that noise or I'll give you a spanking." Somehow the linguistic leaps never came into play at dinner between Monsieur and me. I took to eating cheese and fruit in my room, instead of dining en famille. The meager fare wasn't worth the strain of our silence.

Even if we'd talked, Monsieur and I wouldn't have understood each other. One morning I was sitting in the kitchen, wearing my Wendy nightgown, feeding Anouk. Monsieur hurried in, set down his briefcase, and started rifling through the laundry basket. "I'm looking for a handkerchief," he said in his Michigan-flavored English.

"I ironed some yesterday," I said. "They're on the counter."

"Oh, I have a fresh one," he said. With that, he found a dirty handkerchief, blew his nose in it, put it back in the laundry basket, and went to work.

What could I say to someone who would do that?

The front door opened. I swallowed. It was a reflex now: when a door opened, I swallowed. I closed the door to the icebox and opened the door to the washing machine. When Madame and Leah swooped in for the noontime contretemps, I was shoveling diapers into the washing machine. Tote dat barge, lif' dat bale . . .

Lunch was the usual free-for-all. After the production number, which featured Anouk, for once, and was based on the motif of expectorated fish, I roped the baby in her crib. If we didn't tie her down, she stuck her head through the bars and mooed, like a cow in a stockyard pen. I changed my fishy jeans and put on my coat. I took my notebook and pen and grammar book and good ole high school dictionnaire, and made my escape. Madame tinkled, "Bien etudier!": study well!

I didn't go to school.

Twelve hours a day with Anouk and Leah, I learned French from the bottom up, like the lab technician who only knows the patients by the contents of their stools. But Monday through Thursday, three hours a day, I took an excursion into one of a hundred worlds of Paris. I took the Métro to a new stop, and walked. I poked and marched and loitered till I was cold. Then I picked out a café. I sat for an hour, drinking nasty espresso, doing the exercises in the grammar book, and futilely searching for phrases I'd heard in my dictionary.

I felt a little guilty about lying to Madame. I'd discovered that I couldn't pay for French classes on the fifty dollars a month the Faurers were paying me. Being the Faurers' nanny was like being on welfare; I could survive, but I couldn't make progress. I debated whether to throw myself at Madame's knees and plead for a raise. But I knew that in a struggle between Madame's generous and stingy natures, there was no contest. If she knew I didn't have to punch in at school, she'd never let me leave the house. As management policy, this would be equivalent to cutting out the lunch break because the workers didn't earn enough to buy food. But I was learning how management thinks. And if I never got out of the house, I would feed Leah into the grinder and serve her to Anouk.

So I lied. Monday through Thursday, 12:30 to 3:30, I was like a prisoner on part-time parole. At first I only carried my books to back up the lie. Studying was something I could do at night, while Anouk the Human Siren was winding down. I wanted to use my free hours for exploration. Wandering in Paris, I expected to find . . . what? Some revelation. I examined the streets and chose the cafés as if I were scouting locations for a tryst. What Paris delivered didn't have to be a lover. In fact, between the ephemeral Dan and the enfantes-ridden Faurers, I'd cast my vote for chastity.

I found places where I loved to walk. Boulevards of trees, whose slender trunks almost ached as they curved into branches, and white stone houses glowing through veils of ivy and black-iron lace . . . streets cliffed with buildings of molting salmon-colored stone, blackened as if

with chalk . . . cafés with yellow awnings, propping up
the rotting timbers of houses that trembled in the raw
wind . . . alleys gay with blue berets and brassy pouffed
hair . . . the Place de Trocadéro, an enormous open air
ballroom overlooking the Eiffel Tower, where I expected
the burly man selling postcards to the little nun to whirl
her into a wild blue waltz . . .

"Paris must be the most beautiful place in the world," I
told myself, as the dull cold settled in the folds beneath my
eyes. "I'm so lucky to be seeing Paris." But when I was
depressed, homesick, and nursing the despot of a cold, I
told myself that all I was doing was looking. My expecta-
tions dwindled with the days. Now when I entered a café,
I only hoped the waiter wouldn't ask me to leave. In the
street, I only hoped some lovelorn Algerian wouldn't follow me home. How could I explain him to Madame?

If I'd ever hoped to have an encounter with a citizen of
Paris on the street, I couldn't have picked a worse hour to
venture out than midday. From twelve to two, any French
person who had a home was in it, taking the main meal
with dignity and grace. Exceptions were people like Monsieur Faurer, who suffered breakfast and dinner at the
hands of his wife, but needed one decent meal; and people
forced by distance of rootlessness to eat in cafés. The same
people lunched in the same café daily, for years. At lunch-
time, in Paris, one lunched. Only a fugitive from a barbarian country would enter a strange café at 1 p.m. and
order café. The waiter would look at me without expression. Then he'd take away the napkin. If I went back to
the same café twice, the waiters would treat me as if I'd
come to clean the septic tank. At least in cafés in the
student quarter, I wasn't expected to eat. But those were
the conclaves hardest to penetrate. Always, my entrance
would transfix the crowd. Bony youths in synthetically
faded blue jeans gazed at my mittens. They sneered at my
notebook, perceiving that it was a ruse to admit me to the
company of literates. Standing in a doorway in a glacial
hush, I wanted to whip out a concertina and launch into
"Lady of Spain." "*Da* da da *da* da da *da* da . . . and now
I'd like to introduce my monkey, Jean-Phillipe . . ."

I'd slink to the corner by the TOILETTES sign, bumping
the backs of chairs.

Three hours a day was exactly the dose of freedom I

could handle. Friday was my day off. I dreaded it. I slept as late as possible, given the racket and the sorties-on-pointe of Leah into my room to fetch the diapers and ointment. I made my usual Faurer breakfast, Nescafé with milk and two shards of flat, stale Zwieback-like biscuit with butter and jelly. It was a measure of the pitiful state of cuisine à la maison Faurer that I sometimes lay awake at night, praying for morning, so I could eat a biscuit. I ate breakfast in bed on Fridays, to avoid Madame, who had a tendency to think of little tasks I could complete before I made my escape. If Madame wasn't hanging around the icebox, or hadn't stationed Leah as guard dog, I stole some cheese and fruit to put in my purse and munch on later. Away from Deprivation Hall, I tried to make friends with my stomach again. Fifteen francs a day was my holiday limit: two for the Métro, five for a museum, eight for eats. Eight francs, $1.60. If I drank a grande-crème for once, instead of a lousy espresso, it might cost me two and a half francs. But if I went to a cheap café, I could get a Croque Monsieur for three, or maybe four. A Croque Monsieur was the hot dog of France, the all-purpose snack, a skinny open-face ham and Swiss sandwich, the morsel with which the Madame had dismayed me on my first night as a serf. Croques Monsieurs worthy of the name were more sustaining than the appetite depressants that Madame had tried to pass off as a meal. But Croques Monsieurs that filled me up cost more than three francs. If I had a grande-crème *and* a Croque Monsieur, I couldn't buy a pastry, not the sinful and sumptuous pastry that would momentarily put shine on my day. I was bound to be hungry again in an hour, whichever morsel I plunked for. My teeth ached for a good ole greasy bulky dribbly overladen cheese-oozing gristle-gnawing starch-enveloped hamburger with Big Boy special sauce. Haute cuisine in Paris might make steak look sick, but if all you've got to eat with is $1.60, you're better off in Parris Island, South Carolina.

Technically, the night of my day off was also mine to kill. Paris by Night, on forty centimes. By six o'clock, the city was dark, steeped in insidious cold as dankly pervasive as a fever. I was starving. My feet hurt. My eyes were crossed from hours of squinting at shadowy paintings through screens of heads. (I was still working on the

Louvre, which I had vowed to devour, as if it were a plate of something nasty but chockfull of iron.) All I wanted was a bath and bed.

Even at the top of physical and financial form—even in my one dress, poor bloomless bud of a garment—I would have been aimless and spooked on a Friday night in Paris. I lived in Paris now. But I didn't know—any more than some suspender salesman from Sandusky, asking an incredulous cabbie—where to go in Paris to have a good time. Wherever it was, I couldn't go broke and scented with diaper rash ointment. And I couldn't go alone.

I'd slink back into the apartment as Madame was force-feeding les enfantes a twilight dinner. When I wasn't on call, she plowed through the day like an Olympic heat. She thought the kids wouldn't realize that she'd tucked them in bed before the street lamps went on. Bedded sooner, they screamed with more gusto, and longer. I lay on the blue spread and looked at the diaper basket. Another frenzied, dissipated Paris night beckoned. As soon as le père and la mère were sacked out, I would be abroad, stealing cookies and cheese. Then I'd cuddle up with one of the two books in English in Monsieur's library: *Franny and Zooey,* and *Fanny Hill.*

Dear Mom and Dad. La Vie en Rose.

Saturday was awful, with no "French class" to escape to. Madame asked me cheery questions about my big day on the town. Leah only had school in the mornings on Saturdays and Wednesdays, which warped the afternoons. The maid didn't come—there was no one to make faces at when Leah was performing.

But the nadir of the week, in Paris as in Cleveland, Ohio, was the Sabbath. The Faurers were Catholic, but they didn't go to church. Monsieur was home, without an American ten-pound Sunday newspaper to give him activity and a sense of purpose. All day, all four Faurers were ensconced on puffy loveseats in the salon, dulling the pain of proximity with television and trying to act like the Waltons. I hid in my room: the cousin who's queer in the head. Around five, I heard Leah pounding on her parents' door and wailing, "Non, non, Maman!" Tableau: The Spirit of Fornication Past. Monsieur and Madame had locked themselves in the bedroom and into a fast embrace, abandoning Leah to rage in the hall, and Anouk to eat cigarettes off the coffee table. I rescued Anouk. I dragged Leah into my room and berated her in English. Sometimes she subsided into whining and snuffling. Sometimes she distracted herself by torturing Anouk. The least her parents deserved was a chance to console each other for their cross. But I hated Leah so much, I didn't want her sitting on my bed.

I couldn't believe that a three-year-old child was so fully formed a malevolent being. She didn't have a spontaneous moment. Everything she did or said was planned to get her mother's attention, or to get my goat. In peak form, she could ring both bells. She'd demand a cookie of her mother, "tout de suite"; her mother would refer her to me. Leah would choose her galette with care and make me butter it. Then she'd nibble it, play with it, drop it, make me wipe it off and rebutter it, rub it all over the carpet and the upholstery in the salon, and leave it, grubby and mealy, on the table, saying she didn't like it. She'd ask Maman for hot chocolate, "tout de suite." When I served it, she would complain that it was too hot, trickle it in and out of her spoon, spill it into the saucer and onto the table, splash it around with her hands, staining her pristine dress, and then cry, because it was cold. When her mother fed Anouk, Leah cried for baby food and made her mother feed her. She made a point of asking for whatever I was eating, especially if there wasn't any more. Always, she wanted something "tout de suite": right now! Always, her mother gave in. Madame Faurer was, how you say, a pushover.

Since I was the new au pair—the fourth in her three years of life—Leah was taking a survey of the boundaries of my patience. She didn't know that she was doing the splits atop the Berlin Wall, in sight of the guns. Standing right next to me, Leah would bang a fork on a chair. "Stop it," I'd say, several times: "Arrete-toi! Laisse-le!" Staring at me with dull brown eyes, Leah would maintain her catatonic rhythm. Finally I'd have to take away the fork and move her stiff little body away from the chair. Leah would take up a crayon and begin to draw on a linen napkin, never moving out of range of my spastically twitching hand. She knew that when Maman was in the house, I couldn't haul off and fetch her the clout she was begging for.

Apart from the preschool grappling in the morning,

Leah's favorite torture time was bedtime. She slept in the nursery with Anouk, but Anouk went to bed at eight, and screamed till eight-thirty. I rocked, or shoved, the crib; I whistled "Toora Loora Loora" into the tumult. Finally I lulled the screaming baby into sleep. Shortly after she'd collapsed, sodden and exhausted, and I'd crept away, Madame ushered Leah in. I hid in my room, feigning deafness or sleep. I couldn't bear to watch Leah, tiptoeing grotesquely in a pantomime of caution, whispering her last requests to Maman: a cookie, a doll, some water . . .

As soon as her mother closed the door, tinkling, "Bon nuit, cherie!" the Bad Seed would set up a clamor to rouse the guillotined saints. I'd rush in, hissing, "Qu'est-ce que tu as?": what's the matter? I was too late. Anouk was winding up and would be roaring for another hour.

Leah had worked up myriad variations on this theme. I could see disaster approaching every time, like a truck across a prairie. Madame walked into the wheels of the truck, eyes wide, smiling, the perfect dupe. While Leah was shrieking, I'd grip the bars of her crib, growling in halting, murderous French, "Shut up, the baby's sleeping!" "Go away!" Leah would holler, beating my hands with her fists, "I don't want you, I want my mother!" Anouk would roar. Madame would enter, hollow-eyed and white-limbed in her nightie, tinkling sweetly, as if she hadn't heard us yapping and snarling. Madame's word for Leah was "Insupportable!": "Little dickens, ain't she the limit?" My word for Leah was "turd."

"You are a turd," I told her when her mother wasn't listening. I looked up vicious phrases in my dictionnaire. How do you say, "You're a rotten kid, you stink"? I couldn't control her because I couldn't argue with her. I couldn't explain when she asked, and she always asked, why: pourquoi? It was the magic word with which my adversary made me helpless.

I could vent my pent-up wrath upon her when I dressed her. She must have had bruises. I was afraid to look. After I'd given her a few rousing wrenches, she was wary. I might be a functional mute, but I was bigger than she was, and mean. At night, in her bedroom, my apparition threw her into paroxysms of dread, as if I were the Angel of Death and my scythe had her name on it. It made me feel horribly guilty, inspiring gut fear in a child of three. But she was a wretched excuse for a human being.

Hating Leah was like shooting morphine. It drained me, but it gave a purpose to the day.

My only consolation was Anouk, the Baby Buddha. At first, she'd cried at the sight of my face. Then there was a period of mutual granite-eyeball. Like me, Anouk had ironic genes. But she got used to me. She even got to like me. Now we were in cahoots.

Every day when I got back from "class," I took Anouk for a stroll in the park. Together we descended in the elevator to the basement of the building, to retrieve the baby buggy. Bundled in knitted bonnet and mittens, which she enjoyed removing with her teeth, and a ziplock snowsuit, Anouk was solemn, like an astronaut ascending to the launching pad. The buggy was a Cadillac of bourgeois babydom: vast, dark, deeply cushioned, grilled, and copiously trimmed with chrome, one of a hundred thousand navy canvas limousines darkly dotting the dun earth and grey trees of parks throughout the wealthy pockets of Paris. If someone had conducted a Baby Scramble, it would have taken months for the nannies to identify their own machines and padded anonymous charges. Anouk's buggy was stuffed with cushions, lacy pillows, fuzzy quilts. When the hood was up, she was only two spooky eyes in a cavern. I squashed the hood flat, except when it rained. She preferred to ride sitting upright, facing me, watching the monochromatic scenes of people and trees reel backward on either side. As we rolled along the gravel paths, her mushroom nose grew rosy. We paused at the gate of the faded carousel, to watch the somberly clad children floating up and down to wheezy accordion music. The little clouds of their breath seemed to issue from the pallid mouths of the specter horses.

Once, a mother in a sleek furred coat stooped to wiggle fingers at Anouk, who sat rigid in her bank of pillows. "Coo-coo!" said the mother, "coo-coo!" Anouk's grave regard never wavered. She responded with a magisterial silence. I saw her as Queen Victoria, viewing from her carriage the carpeting of Cockneys on Guy Fawkes Day. "Comme elle est serieuse," the mother said, drawing back her fingers from the baby's teeth: She's so solemn!

"Oui," I said, wheeling away the queen.

The mid-December air was cruelly damp. My mittens were soaked and my fingers were numb after one circuit of the park. Some days Anouk was so banked in wool that only her eyes emerged to stream in the wind. But our misery was companionable. A trek in the dismal park, past the freezing, lonesome ponies and the frost-slick swings, was the baby's only escape from the hothouse with its manic attendant and her demon helper.

In Paris, my only friend was eight months old.

Once, I was invited to a party at Liaison Nordique. The Viking had called Madame—the old "if your mother calls my mother" routine—and informed her that the agency was tossing a little "do" for toutes les au pairs, with door prizes: BOYS. Madame was ecstatic. You would have thought I was the last maiden daughter, instead of the weak link in the chain gang. My elopement would have sent Madame—in desperation, and maybe in her bathrobe —into the highways and byways in search of another vagrant with bunny teeth. But romance, in France, was the Great Emancipator. Madame took charge of the dinner melee so that I could spend a whole hour in the bathroom, decking myself for a tryst. It was a novelty to take a real bath. Using the tub seemed too much like encroachment when Monsieur might want the bathroom. I'd gotten my nightly splash in the bidet down to a breakneck seven minutes. After the bath, I had half an hour to kill. Fairing my toilet took five minutes, since all it entailed was changing my pants and brushing my teeth. I sat on the hamper and made faces at Leah through the door.

Monsieur arrived, with briefcase, as I was about to sortir. Madame announced the felicitous tidings that I was to parry and feint with BOYS. They bade me godspeed— he gravely, she joyfully. All I needed were patent-leather pumps and a wrist corsage.

The party was a bust. It was held at the office, with the Viking presiding. She was svelte in gaucho pants and chandelier earrings, and taller than any BOY in the room. She greeted me graciously, as if to say, "Oh yes, just put the carton on the back porch, will you?" I was a member of the crudest class of imported domestic, since the Viking had sold me for peanuts to people who were in trade. The offices, the waiting room and the hall were stuffed with bodies, interspersed with coats, as if the guests had been packed for shipping. The air was torpid with heat and winey breath and the curling acrid vines of smoke. There was "sangria" to drink. I drank it, sitting in a corner. "Sangria" seemed to be equal parts red-pop and gin, with a twistful orange rind beached on the rocks in the plastic cup.

Most of the jeunes filles seemed to know each other. They yodeled back and forth across the chaos, in singing-noodle language. Like the Viking, they were chicly garbed. Either they were the daughters of kings in their homelands, disguised as maids for a glimpse of French life in the raw, or they were earning more than diaper-ironing fees. The BOYS, on the other hand, could only be described as dogs. As a fraternity, they would have had to shanghai pledges. Half of them were pimply and stringy, with slide-whistle tenors and bangs in their eyes. Addressed by jeunes filles, they were sullen, like my brothers stonewalling little girl cousins at family picnics. The Viking must have had to pry their fingers from soccer balls, and carry them, one by one, kicking and hollerng, up the stairs. The rest of the gigolos were stork-legged men with lumpy foreheads and noses like beaks. They wore suits with rusty lapels, and cameras on straps that bent their necks. They kept taking pictures, no doubt for the brochure.

If I thought they were a freakish lot, they weren't duel-ing over me either. I was the wooden stranger. The fumy room could have been a high school gym, clouded with balloons and streamers. I was fourteen again, clamped to a folding chair, my feet tucked under it to hide my anklets. In junior high, Randy and I had founded a club called the Wall Blenders. We'd held meetings in the john at mixers. I'd spent so many evenings sitting on cold porcelain basins, I'd been lucky not to have piles. Now, in Gay Paree, a sophisticate of twenty-one, I drank sangria, and blended into the wall.

The Wall Blender beside me on the horsehair loveseat had waxy white, bulbous cheeks and flaxen spoolie curls. She was holding her coat, and watching the revelers with an expression of willed but inarticulate frolic. Since we were members of the same lodge, I made overtures. "C'est bon," I said, dangling the plastic cup. I thought I'd start off on a positive note. If she thought I was crazy for praising the eighty-proof red pop, I could pretend I was drunk. But my amenity died unshriven. She didn't speak French, or English. She was a Finn; she showed me her passport. Consulting her Finnish-French pocket dictionnaire she managed to explain that she was employed by a Finnish diplomat's family. I asked if this were her first au pair soiree. No; it was her fourth. Was she a masochist? Was she a management spy? Or was she so lonely that even a backstairs wassail at the Tower of Babel was better than another night alone? I felt sorrier for her than I did for me. I held my cup, and chewed the ice. She held her coat.

Then a surrealistic touch was added. The Viking instigated dancing. She brushed three birdmen off the desk and uncapped a record player. Noodling in tongues, with embellishments of tinkles français and American slang—like "swell"—she accomplished the supernatural feat of clearing a space the size of a shower stall. She threw a stack of 45s on the spindle, appointed a stunted twelve-year-old as her consort, and led off the jitterbug to "Reelin' and a-Rockin'." A few other weirdly grafted couples joined the sock hop—a boy in Eton collar and a girl in leather pants; a pair of bosomy Swedes—pressing spectators into the ranks of the masses in the hall.

One of the cameramen asked me to dance. Rock-and-roll was as natural to me as the Carioca. I'd never jitterbugged in my life. I shook my head, but he dragged me into the pinwheel of flying bodies. "Voilà!" he kept yelling to pump up morale, but I couldn't get the hang of it. We took turns flinging each other into the furniture and our fellow boppers, testing the stress on our shoulder sockets. Ours was a minuet with overtones of martial arts. At least in the crush, no one could see to rate us on technique. After two disc-slipping numbers, I palmed off my partner on the silent Finn, hacked my way through the jungle of elbows, and limped for the Métro and home.

In the morning, Madame was crushed when I admitted that I hadn't met my knight. I was changing the sheets on the enfantes beds. I had to change them twice a week. White embroidery didn't stand up to a three-year-old cookie mauler and a Buddha who leaked. Madame was rummaging in the cupboard, sorting piles of underwear into smaller piles. She felt impelled to look busy in front of me. Suddenly she gave me a little smile, and asked if I were sad.

Apart from inquiring the profession of my father, she'd

never asked me a personal question. I said I had a cold.
I'd looked it up: "Je suis enrhuméd."

At once, Madame hustled me into the cavernous bathroom. She rattle through a medicine chest that was almost
as big as the icebox, and as crammed as the icebox was
bare. It was a warming moment. We both felt lousy, and
Madame wanted to share her solution with me. Abruptly,
I said, "Aussi je manque ma famille." I said it wrong, but
she knew what I meant: I miss my family.

Her eyes filled with understanding, and relief. "Moi
aussi, Ker-ray," she said. A stream of babble followed.
Sorting through the syllables, I gleaned that Madame was
from Lyon. She missed her family too. She missed her
town. The only people she knew in Paris were her husband,
her in-laws, and her kids.

Quelle horreur!

I needed a friend. Madame needed a friend. Maybe we
could work something out. All morning, I kept going into
my room and looking up phrases I could drop over café
au lait in the afternoon. Madame and I would develop rapport, like my mother and Orla in Cleveland. There was a
lot of ground to cover. "When I was ten, I broke my leg."
"In America, we don't iron diapers." "What's with all the
pudding?" I sat on the bed with my dictionnaire, piecing together confidences. I could hardly wait for four o'clock.

We sat facing off with our Nescafé, mine in a boat with
milk, Madame's in a demitasse of double-strength ink.
Anouk stood under the table, gripping my knee with both
hands. She butted my thigh with her head and peered up
at me, sharing her appreciation of her wit. Leah was off at
fascist nursery school. The silence was taut with expectancy. We were griding our loins to o'erleap the language
barrier. For me, asking a question in French of a French
person was like stepping off a platform onto a tightrope,
two hundred feet above the floor of the tent. Madame was
already wearing her look of effortful nurture, the same one
she used to encourage Anouk on the potty chair.

Rather than tearing into gut issues—"Why don't you
spend the money you save on food on a psychiatrist for
Leah?"—I started on something safe. I said, en français,
"You are from Lyon?"

We were off to the races. I could have spared myself
stage fright. Except for "oui" and "non," I didn't set foot

on the tightrope. Madame Faurer had not a soul to talk to. I wasn't much at girlish chatter, I of the bunny teeth and thirty-word vocabulary; but I was a wonderful listener. I nodded compulsively, sometimes in the wrong places. In the shadows beneath the table, the baby was glaring up at me, aping my expression. To pick out even key words like subjects, I had to concentrate so hard I bit my tongue.

The interview ended at 4:45 when Madame had to fetch Leah. She was quite jolly, patting my arm, giving me a grateful smile as she went. I put Anouk in her playpen and collapsed on my bed. Making friends with Madame was going to be a one-way proposition. She hadn't given me a breach to leap into, even if I'd had the ammunition. Since I couldn't comprehend any given sentence, let alone follow her pattern of thought, I didn't know her any better after our heart-to-heart chat than I had when I'd found her in her husband's dressing gown, the day I'd arrived. One riddle was solved: the pudding. Monsieur was the brains behind LaCrème, the largest pudding company in Western Europe, with plants in Paris and Lyon. I was au pair to Pierre Faurer, the Pudding King. Madame was the Pudding Queen.

But at least our relationship was elevated from the plane of mistress and servant. If Madame began to think of me as a person, I could lobby. She'd already promised me a raise, if I were "please' of me." Once I was her confidante, she'd have to come across.

Monsieur read *Time* in English every week, and gave it to me when he was through. That night, I was sitting on my bed, reading "Leisure," and eating slices of apple and gruyère, when Madame tapped on my door. She was holding a pale pink cashmere sweater. She apologized for interrupting my dinner, but she wondered if I'd like to have the sweater. Lentement, she explained that the cleaner had shrunk it and it didn't fit her. She'd be glad for me to have it.

"Merci," I said. Madame gave me a kindly smile and went out, softly closing the door.

What a sweet thing to do, I thought. Madame had asked me several times if my mother were sending the rest of my clothes. She seemed to expect the arrival of two bearers with a steamer trunk. I said I hadn't asked my mother yet, which was true. I shivered in the park; I dreamed about the bulky sweaters and corduroy jeans I'd left at home. But I didn't know how long I could stick it out, au pair. If my clothes were in transit, I'd be trapped. If they arrived, and then I took flight, I'd have to buy another khaki case and tote two cases on the road. Madame had begun to suspect that I had no other clothes, and possibly no mother. She wanted to share her bounty with me.

On the other hand . . . if she'd paid me a decent wage, I could have bought my own sweater. Was she regretting our chummy afternoon? Was this a donation, to put me in my place? I'd feel conspicuously dependent, wearing Madame's sweater, like a Zulu in a mission rummage suit. I'd have to demonstrate my gratitude by being cheerful at my tasks, a wee willing worker. My mother used to give my outgrown clothes to Orla, our cleaning woman, who had a daughter two years younger than I was. Had the daughter ever worn the cast-offs? I'd be embarrassed to wear the sweater in front of Emparo, who would have received it if I hadn't intercepted it by playing earphone for Madame.

Then again . . . I didn't have any clothes. Madame had clothes. Why throw away an expensive sweater when she knew I needed it? I decided to believe in the generous impulse of Madame. She liked me. I felt good. Maybe we'd find as I learned her language that we were more alike than different. Sisters under the skin . . .

The door banged open. Madame dragged in Leah, who was roaring "Non, non, Maman!" as if her mother, in the flush of newfound communalism, had ordered Leah to kiss me good night. With a gay laugh of apology for one more interruption, Madame tackled Leah, heaved her on my bed, yanked down the flap of her Dr. Dentons, and shoved a four-inch ice-blue suppository where, as we say in Ohio, the moon don't shine.

"Ai-ee!" shrieked Leah, her nose in my plate.

Madame snapped the flap, said, "Excusez-moi, Ker-ray," and took the little sufferer off to bed. I had to get up to close the door.

It was several weeks before I broke down and wore the sweater.

The Bissiclette of Père Noël

In the middle of December, I reached a low point, where I scraped along. I kept thinking of Christmas at home. My family was very cool till Yuletide, when we ran amuck. We decked the halls, and even the bathroom, with anything green that came to hand. Even my father decorated cookies and cut out loops for paper chains. All my mother's gifts as a social director came into play. Our house became the Christmas depot; branches of both sides of the family shuttled in and out by chartered bus. My parents, my brothers, Aunt Martha, my grandmother, Great-Uncle Al and his girlfriend and I chose the Christmas tree, assembling in a prickly committee the night before Christmas Eve. In the parking lot of the Baptist church, the only evergreen mart where the stock wasn't stripped to stumps by December 10, we resorted to compromise and fistfights. Finally we voted and hauled home a tree. My father played carols on the saxophone: "Bring your torches, Jeanette, Isabella . . ." My mother accompanied the sax on piano, plying the ensemble with bourbon laced with eggnog, "to warm the vocal chords." Everybody sang. Aunt Martha made fudge. My brothers ate the candy canes. We lassoed on the lights and draped the paper chains. My father made more eggnog. The decking of the tree took on glitter and dash. By the time we slung the tinsel on, the tree looked like it had been trimmed by a basketball team in the last three minutes of play.

Tree Night was the kick-off of a two-week binge which sated even my mother's lust for boogieing. The ringing of the doorbell counterpointed the popping of corn, the crackling of the fire, the squalling of little cousins, the pounding of feet on the stairs, the blooming of rich cinnamon and turkey smells and the odor of roasting mittens from the

97

radiators, the wassaily quavering of Bing Crosby, and the profligate scattering of tissue paper.

Christmas at home was an unholy mess. I couldn't bear to miss it. Every night, I took out my airplane ticket and stroked the greying edges of its fold.

Christmas as it galloped upon us also trampled the feelings of Madame. I got more mail than she did. In bed at night, I'd been writing lonesome letters to my best friend Randy, to my family, to close and distant friends. All my money that didn't go to the Métro went for stamps. Girls I hadn't seen since high school were suddenly receiving four-page tracts from the servants' quarters. Almost everyone wrote back. My mother forwarded everything sent to me at home, even the hopeless yearly appeal from the high school alumni fund. She sent me newspaper clippings from the suburban rag we called the "Scandal Sheet," of brides I'd been to milk plants with in scouts, and kids from the block who'd been busted for dope or trespassing, and uncles who'd been nabbed in the speed trap on Cedar Road. She sent me bulletins in what my father called the "Cousin Update": "Your cousin Joey won the Standing Broad Jump in the district playground olympics." She sent me outstanding columns by Bombeck and Buchwald. Mom was afraid I'd lose touch. With the onslaught of Christmas cards, some days I got five envelopes and poor Madame got none. Maybe Christmas cards weren't hip in Paris. Maybe the Faurers were overlooked, like the gawky on Valentine's Day. The mail came three times a day, at eight, twelve, and four. The afternoon coffee ceremony took a rancid turn when for the third time in a day, Madame took the mail from Leah and handed the envelopes, one by one, to me.

"C'est très bien, Ker-ray, vous avez bien des amis," she said, her eyes puzzled and pained: how nice that I had so many friends! I put away the letters. She urged me to open and read them, but I said I'd save them till after dinner, like dessert. I couldn't read them in front of her. Her family in Lyon, like Randy, wasn't much for correspondence.

Randy had always hated to write. We'd been best friends since we'd teamed together in the apocalyptic Girl Scout Cookie Campaign of 1960. Cookie week in Cleveland had coincided with a six-day blizzard. But Randy and I had

slogged through sleet as if frostbite were required for the
Peddlar's Badge. Together we'd set an Ohio record, two
hundred seventeen boxes. (Part of the credit must go to
our troop leader, otherwise known as my mother, the
Vince Lombardi of sandwich cremes and mints.) Maso-
chism crowned with glory had bound us forever, like Everest climbers. For the next six years, we were never apart
for more than a week. When we split up to go to separate
colleges, I found out that Randy couldn't write. Even from
Rome her year abroad, she only sent me two postcards,
both of the Spanish Steps, both with the same message,
printed in caps: "KER—YOU WON'T BELIEVE! ! !"
Now at my lone outpost, ringed by hostile natives, all I
got from Randy in response to my demands for *any* piece
of mail were interoffice memos from Kraft, receipts for
payments on Randy's National Defense loan, cocktail napkins from the Churchkey scribbled with "Hi!" in various
hands, and parking tickets.

My parents had sent my Christmas present early, and I'd
opened it. It was a beautiful leather-bound journal, which
I was too depressed to use. Why describe the wildlife in a
psychic swamp? Not one of the cards from relations was
gladsome with a check. It was my own fault. At the com-
mencement of travail, I'd written, "I'm all right, don't send
money! I want to do this all by myself!" My relatives were
sticking to the bond. Not even my father had cheated. I
wished he'd send me just enough money to buy a decent
pair of pants. The three-week minimum wardrobe I'd
brought had been ravaged by seven weeks' wear. The
elbows had gone from the sweaters. I'd lost weight at the
Faurer spa; my jeans were so baggy I looked like Harpo
Marx.

Then a carton arrived in the mail. It was addressed to
me. I found Madame examining the box, probably looking
for the CARE stamp. DO NOT OPEN UNTIL XMAS! ! !
was printed in thick letters of peacock blue beneath the return address: "G. Pitasky" and a street in Middleburg
Heights, Ohio. The carton was labeled REVEREWARE.
My address at the Faurer house was also written in peacock blue, and ended, PARIS! ! ! ! FRANCE! ! ! ! !

Who bought Revereware in cartons the size of a TV
console, and scattered exclamation points like feed to
starving chickens?

Grace—G. Pitasky—whom I'd abandoned, had sent me a Christmas present.

My mother had written that Grace had called her, to see if they'd netted my corpse in the Seine. Mother had given her the Faurers' address. When I hadn't had a letter or a card from Grace, I'd felt ashamed, but I hadn't been surprised. But the spirit of Christmas must have oiled the springs of Grace's charity. Maybe she'd mailed me Turkle for company. Turkle, or Sparky, or Richie and Timmy . . .

Leah wanted me to open the box, no loubt hoping that there was something she could break inside. Madame was in transports, thinking that my phantom wardrobe had appeared. When I explained that the package was a present for Noël, Madame was overjoyed. I mustn't open it, I must wait. I was willing. For my birthday, Grace had given me a purse made of red plastic beads, with earrings to match. She'd said happily, "Don't you just love coordinating your accessories?" From the size and heft of the package, I suspected that she'd sent me a vacuum cleaner, or the contents of her fantasy file. In any case, I wasn't eager to reveal to Madame the glories of my only present from America. I took the carton to my room and made it a nightstand.

On December 23, in the four o'clock mail, I got a Christmas card from Randy. The envelope was typed. Randy didn't write and she didn't type. In college, she'd printed out her papers in caps on yellow legal. She must have coerced some dingbat in the Fudgie typing pool into sending it for her. I looked at the picture on the card. An albino Jesus was exchanging gassy smiles with Mary and Joseph, as played by Barbie and Ken. They were observed by the token chorus of Third World kings, holding mosquito lamps, a crippled shepherd boy, an ox, two donkeys, an Irish setter, a flock of doves, and a crowd of gawkers such as gather beneath the window of a jumper. There was a backdrop of quonset huts. One gross, isolated star hung like a hundred-watt bulb in the turquoise sky. A blizzard ceased at the fringes of the golden aureole above the stable roof, as if the divinity of Baby Jésu functioned like solar heat. Huge in the foreground, like a stunted elephant, hulked a mouse in a Santa Claus hat. Under the whole obscene composite, a yellow scroll proclaimed in spidery scarlet script, *The Legend of the Christmas*

Mouse. No doubt inside the card I could read the history of the costumed rodent whose manger had been commandeered for Christ.

Okay. The card was funny. Okay, it even beat the three-dimensional postcard of the Last Supper I'd once sent Randy from Raleigh, N.C., where I'd spent a wretched week with wretched adolescent cousins one summer. But on Christmas, she could have sent me at least a box of chocolate chip cookies, or a fruitcake, or a letter—something real! I was hurt. To get even, I didn't read the card. I taped it on the wall above the diaper basket. Next time she blundered into my room, the sight of my five by seven mural stopped Madame in her tracks. Anxious not to hurt my feelings, she didn't know whether to applaud my taste or my sense of humor. After a pause, she pronounced the Christmas Mouse, "interesting."

"Oui," I said.

I was in a subterranean state. At home, it was Tree Night. My family was having a collective hissy in the Baptist parking lot. I wanted Bing piped over the speakers of a shopping mall, and sparkly garish cookies burned on the bottom; I wanted *Holiday Inn* at 2 a.m. as my brothers and I sat transfixed and stupefied with Hershey kisses in the luminescent orbit of the television, and *Miracle on 34th Street,* and Scrooge, any Scrooge. If Tiny Tim had appeared in my bedroom with his inane benediction, I would have turned him over to Leah. It was almost time for her bath. Perhaps tonight I'd hold her under. What was the policy in France on mercy killing?

Madame and Leah burst upon me, bright-cheeked from the evening sortie. They still had their coats on. Leah bent over Anouk and nattered in a soupy imitation of her mother's tinkle. Madame, manically atinkle, steered me into the nursery, stuffed Anouk's snowsuit into my hands, and yanked my coat from the closet. I couldn't even pick out the subject in her stream of Lyonnaise. At this hour, I should be scrubbing Leah's absurd white tights and polishing her silly white shoes. It seemed that the four of us were going out together. Was this a suicide pact?

Outside, where the low double lamps of cars cut arcs in the wooded night, Madame led the troops to her little red Citroën. I'd never been in the Faurers' car before, and I never was again. Except for Madame's sorties to Leah's school, the car was only used on infrequent Sunday excursions to the home of Monsieur's mother, Madame Faurer-père. Madame Faurer-fils never ventured out of her own arrondissement. She didn't need to drive. And given her compulsion to collide with every object within ten feet of her path, Paris did not need her certain contribution to automotive mayhem.

Leah insisted on sitting in the death seat. I said I didn't mind. I would have sat in the trunk to get away from her. Anouk and I gazed out the window at the muzzy moons of street lamps and the hustling crowds. We bowled down crescent avenues to the close-ranked lanes of the business district of Passy. Madame, as I might have guessed, was a nervy and tentative driver, hesitating one beat too long before darting the Citroën into a gap, lightly tapping the horn in response to a bellow of hoggish invective. Leah bounced and chattered. "Doucement," Madame kept saying, "softly, my little one," which was like raising a finger to chastise a flood. Eyes on the rear-view mirror, slender fingers poised above the horn, Madame was frantic but cheery, contained but all abubble. Wherever we were going, she was having a wonderful time. She asked me something, and didn't even take a pained pause before she repeated it. "Pantalons" was part of the question. Slowly I grasped that we were going to buy some pants, for Christmas. Christmas pants—a custom in Paris, like new shoes for Easter? I said, "Pantalons pour Leah, Madame?"

"Non, non, pour vous, Ker-ray!"

Madame was going to buy me a Christmas present. She wondered if I'd like some new pants.

A used, shrunk sweater was one thing, but brand-new pants were something else. Good ole Christmas! Madame might stint on linens and eats, but in the season of giving, she gave. I got excited. Even Anouk took an interest. When we went into the store, she regarded the shelves piled with rich velours and corduroys and wools with an alert, judicious air, exactly like her mother's. Madame, for once, was not intimidated by the salesgirl, who had the artificial brows of a female bee in a cartoon. I had to try on several pairs of pants, guessing sizes. The numbers in the waistbands must have been kilometers or square roots of hips. The pair that Madame and the bee lady liked were so tight in the crotch, I felt like I'd just gone over a bump on my bicycle. They were cut like jeans, made of deep green velour with a soft flared leg. They were gorgeous. I had no use for them. My sweaters, even the castoff cashmere, weren't worthy of the pants. But Madame had the bee lady wrap them. She took Anouk around the store, showing her the piles and racks of jewel-toned fabrics, making little cluckings and cooings, as if to say, "Some day, chérie, all this will be yours!" Leah was nonplussed by the attention Anouk and I were getting. She had made it so clear to all of us that I didn't suit. Her day was blighted every morning when she rose to discover that I had not been dispatched during the night.

Back à la maison, Monsieur, en dressing gown, was waiting for his dinner. Madame made me show him the pants he'd paid for. "I'm going to save them for a special occasion," I said, despicably obsequious. It was a knee-jerk response to a gift from an unexpected quarter. Already, doubt had roosted in an unlovely corner of my mind. Was I supposed to reciprocate? I could hardly pay for my daily espresso. By Thursday, I had to chance being seen in a neighborhood café because I didn't have Métro fare. I couldn't buy presents.

Perhaps in the tradition of impoverished family retainers, I could render with my own hands some feeble loyal tokens: for Madame, crocheted covers for the vegetable grinders. For Leah, I could whittle a shoe horn.

Madame had told me that the mother and sister of Monsieur were coming to dinner Christmas Eve. Dinner would be very festive (would it be catered?) and very typique of France. Would I like to join them? "Merci," I said. And Christmas Day, they would visit the father of Monsieur, who was no longer avec la mère. I would have the whole day free. "Merci," I said. I had exactly three francs—sixty cents—to paint the town purple on Christmas. I'd better pray there'd be leftovers from the festive, typique dinner. If I had to get through Christmas Day on breakfast biscuits and Leah's galettes, I'd hang myself from the kitchen linen rack.

Leah had been home all week for Noël vacance. By six o'clock, maddened by inactivity and Christmas, she jittered like a hyped-up chimpanzee. Her incessant babble fea-

tured a phrase combining "Père Noël!" and a word that
sounded like "bissiclette." "Bissiclette . . ." Some kind of
pastry? Probably Leah had asked Father Christmas to
bring her a French fruitcake. That was appropriate. Madame had me dress her in one of her Norman Rockwell
frocks, a red checked number that was too big for her.
Madame explained that the dress had been a gift from her
husband's mother—"ma belle-mère." When Madame
Faurer-père arrived, Leah must remember to thank her
for it. Leah must remember not to call Madame Faurer-
père "grandmother" because it made her feel old. Leah
must call her "Dodo."

Leah was tranquil compared to her mother. Early in the
day, Madame had broken down and bought real food. The
packages took up two whole shelves in the icebox. All
afternoon, Madame had been fiddling with pie crust, in a
a huge tin fluted-edged pan. The first attempt had cracked
in baking. Madame had put the fragments in a bowl in the
icebox and tried again. In the course of a few hours of
softly padding feet, the broken crust had vanished. I
hadn't eaten as much as Madame, who'd been slicing
apples in dangerous proximity to the icebox door. To save
both our faces, she fed the remains to the kids, pretending
they'd eaten it all. As I was giving Anouk her bottle at
seven, Madame was frantically stirring a mixture of milk,
flour and mushrooms in the top of a double-boiler, her
nose in a fat, faded cookbook. In the oven, little fowls
squatted in roasting pans. Anouk wore a two-piece jersey
ensemble, not intended for a baby whose yogurt consump-
tion was conspicuous. Her mother—in the midst of stirring the sauce, setting out the silver tray of cocktail glasses
and the crystal bowl of pretzel sticks, unearthing the chest
of silverware from the linen cupboard, shrieking at Leah
for picking at the second, successful pie shell, soothing
Leah's hysterical tears lest the guests arrive and find her
weeping—kept plucking at the baby's jersey top, yanking it
over the bulging stomach.

Madame had set the table in the salon with delicate
china patterned in blue. I'd never seen it before. Four
chairs with grey velvet seats were set around the candlelit
table. I thought of offering to eat in my room, for the
sake of symmetry. But Leah was an extra wheel too; we'd
have to wreck the picture with two kitchen chairs. I

hoped Madame had hidden linens too. If she didn't have extra napkins, Leah and I would have to dine with bibs on.

I left Anouk in the baby seat, watching her mother run into the table and drop the plates. I went to clean up. I scrubbed the white shoe polish out of my nails and gave myself a sponge bath in the bidet, with a fleeting and affectionate thought for Grace. I put on the dress. Wearing the pantalons of Madame would have re-established my subservient position. As the delegate from the penal colony, I owed it to my true identity as college grad and former coding whiz to stun the French with home-style chic. I brushed my hair and teeth, and put on the only pair of panty hose I'd bought since 1971. Slipping into my fancy shoes, I felt a minor pang for my languished fancies of Paris frolics. "Listen," I told myself, "if I were in Cleveland, in two days I'd have to go back to Occidental, and code."

I joined the family.

The belle-mère and the sister of Monsieur had arrived. I could hear them in the kitchen, tinkling with Madame. Faurer women spoke to each other like pediatric nurses coaxing their patients. *"Why* don't we want to take our lovely *massage* today, *hmmm?"* Their trio aria could have been dubbed by Jeanette MacDonald. But the visitors had sharp black eyes, like Monsieur's. They wore black dresses and carried black coats. The belle-mère was decked in bracelets of florentine gold, and lobe-stretching earrings. The sister wore pearls at her skinny neck and ears. The mother was thin but tough, as if she stretched her skin tighter and coarser across her bones every day, by an act of will. Claude, the daughter, who was thirty like Madame, was frail, breastless, and hipless in her narrow black dress. Her arms and legs were white and brittle, like twigs in sheaths of ice. She wore her black hair long and teased, the rich lady version of car hop bouffant. Claude smiled and said "Bonsoir" as I came in. Madame exclaimed over my transformation. The belle-mère swooped upon me like a velvet vulture.

"Bonsoir et bon Noël!" she trilled, sharp eyes scanning me for evidence of gaucherie or cellulite deposits. She opened the ice box—Madame looked relieved that there was something in it—and put in the cake box she'd brought. She surveyed the goods and asked their prices.

When Madame answered, the belle-mère shook her head. Her hair-do didn't move. Madame gave a sad little glance at the cake box. The apple tart she'd labored over rested beneath wax paper on the bottom icebox shelf. The belle-mère lifted the paper shroud and made a cooing noise, which sounded patronizing, as if Madame had burned the brownies. She said, in such distinct explanatory tones that even I understood it, that she knew she wasn't supposed to bring anything, but she'd seen a little cake in the window of a shop, and she'd brought it along for fun. We all knew that the apple tart would lose the beauty contest.

Claude lifted the spoon from the pot of mushroom sauce and tasted, no doubt exhausting her caloric allowance for the day. She complimented Madame. Both of the ladies called Madame "Sooree," which, she explained in an aside, was her nickname—"Souris": Mouse. She wasn't mousy, but somehow it suited her; it sounded sweet and inept. Madame Mouse chattered, smiling. She was wearing a black crepe tunic and pants, and rhinestone clips in her ears. On Christmas Eve, everyone was dressed for a wake. My dress was bright orange knit. I felt like the setting sun.

Leah was oddly subdued. She kissed Claude as if she meant it, Dodo as if she were making an effort not to shut her eyes. Prompted, she thanked Dodo for the pretty dress. The ladies made her stand on a chair while they retied the sash her mother had tied four times. Unsatisfied, Dodo sent Claude for pins. She tugged and tucked the dress in bunches, close to Leah's ribs. Leah's expression was a mixture: excitement, pleasure at getting attention, apprehension, and a kind of strained charm that was like her mother's. She seemed unsure of what was expected of her, of what was coming to her. When they finished and Leah got down, Dodo took Leah's hand and led her from the kitchen. Leah accepted the dry fingers gingerly, smiling as if she were braving the first day of school. I almost felt sorry for her.

After she'd been kitchy-cooed, and her mother had been told to put her on a diet, I took Anouk to her room and put her to bed. Since it was an hour before her bedtime, she was taken aback. She roared. Dodo and Claude barged in, a pair of strange dark birds, scaring hell out of the baby. They soothed her and cuddled her, briefly. When she was ready to boogie all night, they threw her back and closed the door. I looked at Anouk. She looked at me. It was another half hour before she wore herself out, and nodded off.

In the salon, the Faurers were assembled on the plushy chairs, holding glasses. People sitting in the salon never seemed convinced, especially Madame. The room looked like a lounge in an expensive sanitorium. Everyone perched, and watched the door. They looked up at my entrance, ready for any news. After an awkward gap in the chat Monsieur asked me in French if I'd like a drink. Liquor in the house was news to me; I'd figured it was over the budget. Maybe they'd kept it from me in case I had the servant's tendency to tipple. He turned the key of a cabinet beneath the bookcase and opened the door, revealing a shelf full of bottles. Most of them were sealed. Taking the advice of Madame and Claude, I asked for port. It was ruby dark and rich. On an empty stomach, I got fuzzy-minded quickly, a tactical error. I needed all my faculties to answer questions. Claude tried to put me at ease by asking me about myself, which had the opposite effect. After a series of thudding pauses, she launched into ecstasies about New York. She'd spent two weeks there with friends. She listed her favorite sights: "Bonweet Tellair . . . Socks a Feef Ahvenoo . . ." I kept nodding, as if I followed and heartily concurred. Suddenly Dodo asked if I'd ever been to New York.

"Non," I said.

That knocked out that conversational gambit. It was hard to identify with Claude. Some vacation—two weeks in Ladies' Lingerie. But who was I to sneer? Claude saw New York as a sales slip. I saw Paris as a diaper pail.

The family resumed its self-contained babble. I tried not to grimace as I listened. What with the hectic pace and the descants, I could hardly pick out nouns. The droning of Monsieur was a relief. Leah was scrunched between Dodo and Claude. She fidgeted. Finally she whispered to Claude, who laughed and trilled something about Père Noël. Everybody laughed, including me. I hoped no one would ask me to explain the joke. Madame kept jumping up, nearly overturning the drinks, and scampering into the kitchen. I didn't know whether to offer aid and succor or to keep out of her way. Dressed up and twiddling a goblet of port, I'd lost my serf identity. I didn't know if I were Exhibit A in a cultural exchange, or a scullery maid who'd won a dinner above the salt playing bingo in the servants' hall. Monsieur and the ladies carried on, taking no overt notice of the crashes and little mews of "Hoopla!" that issued from the kitchen. I went to Mouse's rescue.

She was attempting to remove the top of the double-boiler. The hot pads she was using as she wrenched at the pot were worn through. She kept dropping the holders and sucking her fingers. She grabbed a grimy towel and wrapped one end around a handle of the bottom pot. The other end of the towel dangled in the flame.

"Ah! Ah!" I said. What's the French for "burning"?

The fringe of the towel was on fire. The kitchen filled with thin black smoke. Madame plunged the end of the towel under the faucet. She cursed, and then laughed lightly, to reassure me that she had the conflagration and the dinner under control. She rushed at the stove and pried at the clasps of the two parts of the pot with a wooden spoon. She was pirouetting on the brink of a breakdown over this meal. No wonder Monsieur was willing on most nights to take pot luck. I got some diapers. We used them to hold the pots and pull them apart. As she poured the mushroom sauce into a serving bowl, Madame confided that the belle-mère was a gourmet cook, and very choosy about her food. Was that why she and Claude looked so unhealthy? Didn't any victuals come up to their standards? She put the lid on the bowl and set it on the second shelf of a tea cart. The top shelf of the cart was stacked with plates that matched the ones on the table in the salon. She'd been hoarding a service for twenty, while Leah and I were passing one pottery soup plate back and forth. I hoped all the crockery didn't mean more guests were coming. We were out of chairs. One more guest meant someone had to perch on the kitchen stool. I was going to nominate Dodo.

Tossing the salade, Madame ejected croutons and lettuce from the bowl. The vegetation shot up and out in parabolic arcs, settling on the counters and the floor. I picked a crouton out of her bangs. "Merci, Ker-ray," she said, setting the salad bowl on the cart. The cart held, in addition to the plates, two bottles of wine, a platter of lox, a butter dish, and an empty silver tray. Madame opened the oven door and cautiously plucked out a dozen slices of good ole American toast. I was possessed by an almost visceral longing for peanut butter. I stifled it. Madame buttered the toast—she had a future as a short order cook—and stacked it on the tray, and covered it with a napkin.

"Voilà!" she said.

"Voilà quoi?" I almost answered. Toast and lox? I helped her wheel the cart across the carpet to the table. I was so hungry and so dizzy from the port, I didn't employ much force. But Mouse had enough crazed energy for both of us. Everyone gathered around the table, exclaiming about God knows what. Even in Cleveland, lox is no big thing. Leah made a fuss about sitting next to her mother, who was so exhausted she could barely cut her toast. I watched the belle-mère for a model of etiquette. So did everybody else. She had the female contingent tightly reined. They were supposed to grow up to be her. Claude and Leah would make it or die trying. I wouldn't be around long enough to save Anouk. The thought depressed me.

We ate the cold lox and buttered Yankee toast. It was delicious. The ladies nibbled. Leah crumbled up her crusts and picked from her mother's plate. Monsieur and I had seconds. In response to "Would you like some more?" I'd learned to say, "Volontiers," which meant, "Just pass the platter."

After we'd demolished the first course, Madame and Claude collected the plates and stacked them on the cart. They passed out fresh ones. Madame raced into the kitchen, tinkling, "Excusez-moi!" We waited, drawing on the tablecloth with our forks. The belle-mère lit a cigarette. Claude followed suit.

There was a hideous crash, and silence.

Monsieur, with a look of grim patience, marched to the kitchen. Mouse blocked his entrance, dismissing him with a little laugh. He marched back, avoiding his mother's eye. We waited. At last, Mouse bore in a vast china platter, on which the crispy little fowls were arranged in rows. It looked like a parking lot of Volkswagens. She circled the table, playing the butler, and we helped ourselves. The smell of the crackled skin was so rich, I felt faint. Madame put the platter on the cart and lifted the serving dish of sauce. She ladled mushrooms au crème on the slices of meat on my plate.

We ate.

Mouse had outdone herself, which was no challenge: she would have surpassed her previous efforts by making a tuna loaf. But laboring under the shadow of the belle-mère bomb, she had produced a masterwork. The first bite of little-bird-with-mushroom-sauce was paradise on the palate.

A long-drawn wail emanated from the nursery.

I stared at my frantic knife and fork. I chewed. Madame Mouse, on my right, was chewing too, and in public. Even Claude, the princess of malnutrition, was chewing behind her attenuated fingers. In the hush of reverent munching, the wailing intensified. The plea became a summons.

Madame inverted a bowl over my plate.

Anouk was delighted to see me. She chose to overlook my clear and present intention to off her with a pillow. Rocking her crib, I could almost hear my dinner cooling. I got her up and brought her to the table.

Oohing and cooing, the ladies passed her around. I hadn't taken the time to change her diapers. She didn't sit well on black velvet. The belle-mère put her down to crawl and went to wash her hands.

Claude and Monsieur had finished, and were smoking. Madame was picking at the bones on Leah's plate. Monsieur watched, bemused. He had never seen her eat before. Watching me ravage the fowl, Claude asked sympathetically if we had this dish in America.

Monsieur, with his usual brusque assurance, said that of course we did. His tone implied that he'd frequently been served the dish in Ypsilanti, the hot-roast-beef-and-mashed-potato-sandwich capital of the world. "What are these birds called in America?" he asked me.

"Cornish hens?" I guessed. "Pheasants?" Somehow my mother had never slipped them in between the Sunday roast and the Friday chicken.

Monsieur said, "Non, non," and sent me for the French-English dictionary. Madame inverted the bowl over my plate. I had to identify my dinner before I could eat it.

Name That Bird. Monsieur leafed through the dictionary, muttering, "Pointard . . ." I chewed. Beaming, he announced, "Guinea hen!"

Beaming, everybody looked at me.

"Ah," I said, nodding. But of course, guinea hen. In Cleveland, we eat them at baseball games, with mustard. I scraped the plate.

Lines were drawn over dessert. Madame presented the tart and the cake with seemingly neutral grace. The tart was flat, covered with papery apple slices, slightly charred at the edges, like the crust. Dodo's gâteau was a downy pile of pound cake, topped with pale, glazed friuts: strawberries, blueberries, pineapple slices. Dodo was deprecating, like a winner who'd cheated at the Pillsbury Bakeoff. She had only bought the gâteau! It was Mouse who had made her own tart—and such a large one!

Madame served me first.

I was on Mouse's payroll, not Dodo's, thank God. Besides, I could eat leftover cake all day tomorrow, if Leah didn't eat it all tonight. I had the tart. Claude took the coward's way out and skipped dessert. Monsieur from diplomacy and Leah from greed ate both. Mouse had the cake; Dodo had the tart. Both pronounced the opposition "delicieuse."

I helped Mouse clear the table. We rinsed and stacked the dishes as she babbled. Having qualified as cook to son of Dodo, she was giddy with relief. I had established my loyalty by opting for the tart, and my savoir-faire by not putting my elbows in it. Mouse was proud of me, and I was fond of her. Next to her in-laws, she was homespun.

Mouse the Magician produced an espresso pot and coffee. She set me to boiling water and pouring it over grounds. Only forty minutes later, we took our coffee in demitasse cups. Then, at long last, after a month of build-up, it was the magic time, the hour of Père Noël. I sat back in one of the overupholstered chairs and watched the pageant unfold. Sucking a strawberry plucked from the cake, Anouk observed the grownups with her calm, ironic eye.

Everyone else was in a tremor of suspense. Mouse and Claude kept giggling and poking each other. Monsieur disappeared out the front door, proclaiming that he couldn't understand why Père Noël hadn't shown. Evidently Père Noël was driving around the Bois de Boulogne in a Citroën; Monsieur was going to flag him down. Dodo, efficient as ever, suggested that Leah call up Père Noël— who had a telephone in his Citroën?—and demand an explanation. The two of them went into the bedroom to ring up Père Noël. Mouse and Claude ran into the hall by the elevator and capered about, staring down the glass stall, hugging each other, watching for Leah. We could hear the belle-mère on the phone, tinkling basso, like a cracked bell. She was having trouble getting through to Père Noël. Leah was mum. She was so excited, and so confused, she was hardly breathing.

The elevator rose. Monsieur had arrived from the basement with Noël. Claude held the elevator open at our floor, while Mouse helped him haul in and set up a decorated Christmas tree: white nylon needles and turquoise dacron fiber balls, sewn to the detachable branches with white plastic thread. The stand was a pink plastic claw, like the foot of a flamingo on a low-brow's lawn. Running on tiptoe, Monsieur and Mouse toted load after load of loot, wildly waving at each other to hurry. The bonanza package was three feet high and four feet long, covered with silver foil and red and green bows. All three adults had to haul it into the room and prop it behind the Père Noël. "Bonne nuit! Bonne nuit!" Mouse and Claude fluffed up the bows.

"Attention!" hissed Monsieur. He ran to the kitchen for his camera. When he was poised on a chair to take the picture—having first removed his shoes and placed a diaper on the upholstery—the ladies raised a chorus of farewells to Père Noël. "Bon nuit! Bon nuit!" Mouse and Claude kept kept yelling, laughing and collapsing on each other.

Leah came roaring out of the bedroom. Dodo was squawking, "Vite! Vite!" Mouse and Claude moaned: what a shame, Leah had just missed Père Noël! Leah's face was a smorgasbord of hastily summoned reactions. She was eager to respond, but she wasn't sure what the grownups wanted. Was she supposed to be disappointed that Père Noël had gone? Or overjoyed that he'd left the inventory of a small boutique in her living room? She tried to play it both ways. When her father snapped a flashbulb in her face, she burst into tears.

Her grandmother threw up her hands. Impossible to comprehend the ways of les enfantes! Her mother soothed

her, wiping Leah's face with a cold cloth so that the
camera wouldn't capture the effects of her tears. She was
allowed to attack the presents, but it had to be choreo-
graphed. Leah knelt before the gay display. The grownups
called out instructions to improve the composition of the
picture her father was about to take. "Move a little right!
Turn your head! No no, turn it the other way! Pick up a
present—no, the blue one! The one with the silver bells
on the ribbon! Good, hold it up! Up, up, we can't see it!
Good, now smile!"

"Should I look surprised?" said Leah.

Impatient, Claude rushed forward and adjusted Leah's
taut limbs—spine turned, profile out, package up, right
knee on carpet, left leg bent and foot implanted—the posture of the crippled shepherd boy on Randy's Christmas
card. I burst out laughing. Everybody looked at me. I
stuck my nose in my port glass, as if I'd been overcome by
fumes.

All the while, Leah was struggling to maintain an expression of artificial joy, like a Delsarte actress miming
RAPTURE. Her father took pictures. Claude took pictures.
I would have had time to make a quick sketch if I'd
brought a pencil.

"Bon!" said Dodo, descending on the canyons and buttes
of boxes. Leah could open her presents now.

The first one they let Leah open was a present for
Anouk.

While we were admiring the undershirts that Père Noël
had woven for Anouk, Leah asked, in a timid voice I
hardly recognized, about the "bissiclette." Leering at each
other, the grownups bemoaned the oversight of Père Noël,
who hadn't come across with the mysterious but très im-
portante bissiclette. I wondered if Dodo would get him on
the phone again. Leah's glee mask gave way to disappoint-
ment, with a dash of suspicion. She didn't trust these god-
like grownups, arbitrarily dispensing strokes and buffets.
They made her open her presents in dribbles, in between
opening presents for Anouk and handing around the gifts
exchanged by the adults. Dodo kept taking away a package Leah was opening and doing it herself to preserve the
bow. After she opened every package, Leah had to say,
"Merci, Père Noël!"

But she made a good haul: a two-foot doll that looked

liked an embalmed midget, with a wardrobe of frou-frou
frocks that Leah could borrow, as if they were roommates
at school; new shoes, which pleased me, which were white
—which didn't; a sweater and some trousers from, of all
folks, Dodo; more outsized and sugarplummy dresses;
books, records, paints. Anouk got more stuffed animals to
add to the overpopulation in her playpen, and—in the
fraying nick of time—pajamas. The grownups "awwwed"
about the golden book of *Babar* and the rubber ducky
which guilt and pride had made me buy for Leah and
Anouk. My gift prompted Leah's first spontaneous reaction
of the evening; she was thunderstruck. The grownups gave
each other rich leather bags—a wallet for Monsieur—and
rhinestone jewelry, and cashmere sweaters. Mouse gave
the Pudding King a new bathrobe—just what he needed.
I had to get my new trousers and trot them around, so
everyone could admire them. I was also humiliated by
tokens from Dodo and Claude: three sets of plastic loop
earrings in primary colors, and a black velvet cigarette
case. I didn't wear jewelry, and I didn't smoke. "Merci," I
said.

Something was still afoot. The huge foil box had not
been opened or assigned. Leah eyed it. The grownups
nudged each other. Leah didn't have the guts to ask Dodo,
who was helping her garb the zombie doll, but she whispered to Claude. With hearty declarations of ignorance,
Claude approached the box and examined the tag.

"Mais c'est à Leah, de Père Noël!" she tinkled.

Quelle surprise!

Only fifteen minutes later, with the assistance of her
mother, Claude, Dodo, her father, a knife, a scissors, and
the claw end of a hammer, Leah unwrapped her "bicyclette"—a bicycle. It was red and shiny, with training
wheels. It was almost as big as Anouk's baby buggy. Leah
went into the requisite transports. After a night of climax
and anticlimax, of carefully orchestrated disappointments
and artificial thrills, she couldn't get it all the way up; but
she tried. They made her holler "Merci, Père Noël!" up the
chimney, though he'd supposedly arrived by elevator. Perhaps he had a switchboard on the roof. Everybody tinkled.
Monsieur took pictures. Anouk ate ribbon. I thought about
home.

"Mais Ker-ray!" cried Madame. "Votre boîte!"

I had not opened my present from America. I must cherche it, vite, vite, vite!

Too disheartened to be apprehensive, I cherched the box from Grace.

I borrowed the scissors and knife to cut the string and slit the tapes. Inside was another large box wrapped in Christmas paper that only Grace could have found: pinky cherubs soaring across a background of blue, holding aloft banners, as if they were standard bearers for the marching band, each banner inscribed, HE IS RISEN. Grace must have been seduced by a door-to-door salesman for the Seventh Day Adventists. There was a large pink envelope scotch-taped to the package, addressed, *To Kerry, Gay Paree!*

I opened it. On stationery with cocker spaniels frisking in its margins, Grace had written:

Merry Xmas! I bet you thought I'd just send a plain old card. SURPRISE! ! ! I was sure relieved when your mom told me you had a real home with a family, instead of just "bumming around" with "hippys" or something! At first I was real "pee-owed" at you! My gosh, I thought you were kidnapped or something! You always made jokes about white slavers, but some things aren't so funny! But your mom says your a real "jet setter" now! Guess what! ! ! ? I have a job! ! ! Remember Craig, that handsome boy I bought all my cookware from? He called me up to see if I wanted to buy a convertible sofa on time—it's half price if you bought the vacuum cleaner, and it's only $10 a month and it takes three years to pay it off so by the time it's delivered I'll be married to Richie or Timmy! But anyway I told Craig about losing my job at Occidental and he said anybody like me who believes in looking ahead and paying for quality would make a super super "sales rep" for his company! So now I go to all these neat-o parties! I take my sample case and a little box of personalized mints that Mom makes for me. She buys boxes of Merri-mints, the flat kind that are pastel colors, and she uses a cake decorator and writes on them GRACE and our phone number! Its so cute! Of course, the "prospects" eat the mints, but I guess the phone number sort of seeps into their brains because I sold more cookware my first two

weeks than any other "rep" they ever had! ! ! The
company sent a photographer to take my picture for
the "Rep Rap" in the magazine they send to all their
offices!

And since I'm mentioning pictures, aren't these just
the neatest pictures you ever saw in your whole life?
I'm only sending you the Switzerland ones cause your
not in the Paris ones, poor you! Some of the Paris
ones had people in them I didn't even know! I think
there was something funny going on! Richie thinks
maybe there's some way they could sort of fog up the
air in France with some chemical that would make
your camera take pictures of the wrong people? Anyway I've got all mine in this neat-o scrapbook with the
plastic envelopes of pictures in a long row so I can
flip through them real fast and pretend I'm in a movie
of Europe, especially since there are so many shots of
the same thing! Well, I guess I better "sign off," Richie
is taking me to see Jerry Vale tonight! Timmy was
supposed to take me, but then he found out it was the
same day as the Firearms Show so he finked out, the
rat! Write real soon! But don't write in French, ha ha!
Merry Xmas, and God bless!

Sincerely,
Grace (Pitasky)

The Faurers were watching me.
"She says, 'Bon Noël,'" I said.
A Kodak envelope was enclosed. I tried to hide it, but
Madame spotted it. The whole family passed around
Grace's shots of Kerry in Yurrup. Comment was minimal.
What could they say about a dozen overcast, tilted views
of a small, grim figure backed by anonymous mountains? I
opened the box.
Grace had filled it with smaller packages, each wrapped
in a different paper. If the belle-mère saved all of them,
she could make a paper quilt. I said to Monsieur in rapid
English, "You don't want to sit here while I open—"
"No, no, go ahead," he said. The ladies chimed, "Allez,
Ker-ray! Ouvrez les petites boîtes!"
In a silence filled with my confirmed misgivings and the
growing confusion of the audience français, I revealed the
articles that Grace thought essential to an American im-

prisoned in Gay Paree: the super box of 64 Crayolas and a Sesame Street coloring book; clamps which would hold my mittens to my coat sleeves, the kind that are known in Ohio as "idiot clips"; Chapstick; Howard Johnson brownies, probably lifted from Gloria, who would never recover; a box of a chewable caramel-coated product called "Poppycock"; red plastic bracelets, completing the set of accessories Grace had given me for my birthday; a deck of cards for Animal Rummy; a bottle of bubble-blowing liquid and a blower; a Cleveland Indians pennant; a purple sleeveless turtleneck sweater; mohair wool knee-socks, striped fluorescent green, orange, yellow, and brown; three knit headbands, blue, pink, and white; a pair of Dr. Dentons, exactly like Leah's, complete with feet and flap; and a roll of toilet paper.

By the time I'd opened the pajamas, there wasn't a sound. Grace's package had eclipsed the bicyclette of Père Noël.

How do you explain Grace in French? I thought of passing it off as a joke. But in my dictionary—I'd looked it up—there was no French equivalent of "joke," which should have told me all I needed to know about the French. All I'd been able to find was "s'amuser"—"to amuse oneself." I waved the Dr. Dentons and said in a small voice, "C'est pour s'amuser." Only Mouse nodded, with a puzzled smile; how would the au pair amuse herself with pajamas with a flap in the seat? I should ask to borrow a suppository.

Thoroughly routed, I said "Bon nuit" and trundled the cursed thing to my room. I put it in the corner and kicked it a few times. Then I sat on the bed.

I pictured myself entering a café on St. Michel, wearing a headband and jeans rolled up to show my mohair knee-socks; out on the town in my new velour pants and purple sleeveless sweater and plastic earrings; sitting in the kitchen in the long, bitter January evenings, playing Animal Rummy with Monsieur, me in my Dr. Dentons; celebrating New Year's Eve by throwing wide the casements and festooning the Paris night with bubbles and toilet paper. The brownies and the Poppycock wouldn't be wasted. If Mouse lost her head and ate the rest of the cake during the night, I could feast on Grace's provisions Christmas Day.

I had to laugh. Good ole Grace. Dear Mom and Dad.

But in the morning, after the Faurers had eaten their

burned bread and left to visit Monsieur's father, I moped. I was broke. I'd hoped for a little cash surprise from Madame, but she'd fluttered out with only "Bon Noël!" Even if I'd had money, there was nowhere to go. The museums were closed. Everything was closed. It was a family day in a city where the family was the only thing that came before the franc. I'd already read *Time,* even the sections on "Science" and "The Philippines." I could color in my coloring book. I could get a scissors and cut holes in Leah's clothes. But Christmas Eve had mitigated my loathing for Leah. If she were a monster, she'd done the research for it.

I opened the icebox. The cake was gone. But half the tart remained, congealed in a gum of burned mushy apples. I made myself a gravy boat of café au lait and got back in bed with the cup and the entire remaining tart. Screw the Faurers. Screw everybody. At home, they'd be eating tangerines out of stockings with inadequate tabs of scotch tape on the tops. We didn't have a fireplace, so my mother always taped the stockings to the top of the stereo. They always fell down. She never seemed to realize that scotch tape wouldn't hold a full stocking.

I started to cry.

"Oh, knock it off!" I told myself. What could be more self-indulgent than crying with a mouthful of cold apple tart? There were flakes all down my Wendy nightgown, all over the pink and blue bed. I gave the sheet a mighty snap! The reverberant ripple propelled a host of crumbs upward and onto the carpet. I'd have to vacuum. Nothing like servile work to top off Christmas Day.

I looked at the pink wall across from my bed. The diaper basket was displayed on the bureau, like a door prize. Across the wall, I had taped my Christmas cards and Randy's postcards of the Terminal Tower, Cleveland's fatalistically christened landmark. From the bed the effect was of a rainbow of little colored squares, ending in a wicker pot of diaper rash ointment. The artsy arc of paper harked back to open house displays in student teaching. Once I'd thought myself too good for Split Rail Middle School. I should notify the college placement office of my present position. I'd like to see them work it into their statistics: "Of last year's graduating class, the Education Department has helped to place 2,056 secondary teachers,

4,531 elementary teachers, 315 guidance and counseling advisors, 12 librarians, and 1 bonded servant."

I considered calling my family. By the time Monsieur got the phone bill for five hundred francs, I'd be back in "The Best Location in the Nation," gluing Roman collars. But I had enough trouble grappling with the guilt of stealing cookies. I could call collect. My father would accept the charges. But he'd laugh. I was supposed to be independent of family and country, sinking my American teeth with voracious abandon into the meat of an alien culture. Did Henry Miller and Anaïs Nin call home collect? Did Dan? How was Dan spending Christmas in Spain—playing "Jingle Bells" on flamenco harmonica?

That train of thought was chuffing straight for the washed-out bridge. I got out of bed. If I couldn't call home, at least I could read my cards and letters. Like the Swiss Family Robinson, I had to use what I could salvage. Later in the afternoon, I would rifle Grace's package. I would eat the Poppycock and blow the bubbles. I would frolic if it killed me.

Standing on the crumb-speckled carpet in my bare feet, I read from left to right. I felt better already. When I got to "The Legend of The Christmas Mouse," I laughed out loud. Good ole Randy. She was illiterate and lazy, but she had an impeccable sense of the tawdry. I opened the card for the first time.

Over the printed message, Randy had stapled a twenty dollar bill. Under it, she'd printed, in what looked like crayon:

> MERRY CHRISTMAS, KER!
> Love ya, Ran
> P.S.: Courtesy of Kraft, I got a bonus
> from moving marshmallows!
> P.S. Again: As your father would say,
> SPEND IT FOOLISHLY!

I cried again.

Then I got dressed in my Christmas fancypants, and went out to show Paris.

PART THREE

Teamwork

Plum Pudding and Aylesbury Duck

First I went to the nearest railroad station, to change my money into francs. Only the desperate traveled on Christmas. The wispy men and blowsy women framed in the streaked glass panels of the Café de la Gare seemed to be lingering under false pretenses. They crumbled rolls and toyed with sugar. As I clacked across the echoing hole of the station, a French girl accosted me. She could read the legend emblazoned in Esperanto on my forehead: BLEEDING HEART.

"I am very hungry," she said en français, winning me to her at once, since I'd been hungry since November 23. Most Parisians who were forced to speak to me spoke English, couched like a squint-eyed query to an ear trumpet. She was complimenting me by pretending she thought I was French. She wanted to dun me out of a franc. Knowing the big house was scattering lollipops, she was trick-or-treating in the quarters. "Pourquoi pas travailler?" I said: why not work?

She fluttered her fingers along her flat belly and murmured, "Je suis enceinte."

A little bun in the oven! If she were pregnant, it was a very shy fetus. I said, "You could be that pregnant and shovel snow in Duluth."

"Comment?" she said, smiling wanly.

"Come-on is right," I said.

But it was Christmas, and the Lord, via Randy, had blessed me. In the spirit of "The Legend of the Christmas Mouse," I gave her a franc. After all, chucking a franc to Dwight D. E. Clanski, the hippie from Dayton, had bought me the best time I'd had in France. I had no regrets about my night with Dan. As we say in Ohio, "Sorry don't bring the hay in."

I traded Randy's twenty dollar bill for less than its equivalent in francs to a hamster of a man behind bars in a booth. France had a whole breed of clerks with the beady protuberant eyes of rodents, who scrunched inscrutably in booths and cubbyholes, changing money, selling cigarettes, taking Métro tickets. I took a Métro, deserted except for one lone, lorn Algerian. His hair lay in tightly kinked furrows along his turnip head. He wore a tweed sport coat and an open shirt, with a purple and green striped muffler that was more for flamboyance than warmth. He took the seat across the aisle and concentrated fiercely on my face, alternately leering and glaring, as if he were sending me greetings in Morse with his gold bicuspid. When I got up at the St. Michel stop, he sidled behind me and hissed in bad French, "You have never known love."

It was a poetic kick-off.

I made a flying visit to Notre Dame. I had been there before with Grace, who had taken pictures with her camera ensconced in the armhole of her bunny-fur coat. She had snapped the Rose Window, and the meek monk who rattled his coin box at the door. I had been impressed by the phalanx of hamster clerks in cassocks who pittered around replacing swampy candles with fresh ones under the noses of supplicants poised with lit matches. There had been so many gapers that people praying were an embarrassment, like grandmothers crying at high school graduation. I'd stumbled on a chapel in a backwater behind the main altar and found a real Mass going on. The priest had had his back turned, but the eight who worshipped had looked a little sheepish.

But for Noël, the long, soaring hall was banked with greens and lilies, and swirling with the red snow of the robes of clerical bigwigs. Ten confessionals cranked out lines of the hastily humble. I wondered if the Faurer family had buzzed church en route to the house of Faurer-père. I could see them in a front pew, Mouse and Leah locked in a tinkling struggle for decorum; Anouk, on the arm of Monsieur, grandly flinging the fifty-franc note into the basket. I pictured Leah mincing up the aisle to the crèche to ogle Baby Jesus.

At home, the crèche spread itself over the top of the upright piano, cotton batting drooping over the corners of "Minuet in G." My mother always hid the Baby Jesus under a wad of cotton, a little snowdrift of expectation, till Christmas morning. One year, simultaneously making Russian teacakes and answering the door, she misplaced him. We looked, but we never found Jesus. My father wanted to write up this incident and send it to Hallmark, but my mother talked him out of it. Right about now, I thought, they're opening the presents . . .

"Never mind!" I told myself, "this is Paris! Noël, already!"

The day was white and opaque as I walked across the Pont and into the Cathedral. When I came out, dizzy with incense, pressed in a throng of dark-furred women, hooded children, and somber men, grey-white flakes were thickly rushing out of the pallid crater of the sky. I burrowed into the stiff, upthrust collar of my coat. If this cold and wind kept up, I'd be round-shouldered in another month. I pulled my knit hat down to my eyes. Only my iced, lonesome nose confronted the wind.

The church crowd had gone home to pointard and excessive gâteaux of their own. A café was the bleak alternative to the blasting holiday silence of the street. I sneaked a peek from my cave at the buildings on my right. They were little houses, with gables and soap-smooth stoops and tattered shutters. A piece of cardboard was taped to the door of the end house. In pencil, the lettering said:

OPEN HOUSE
CHRISTMAS DAY
HOT BUTTERED RUM AND
PLUM PUDDING FOR ALL

I must be hallucinating. But over the shop was another sign, beaten by wind and eaten by mist to an ivory smoothness:

SHAKESPEARE & COMPANY

Next to the name was a pastel cartoon of the dome and goatee of the master himself.

Shakespeare and Company! I knew all about it—I was an English major. It was the twenties' hangout, the corner candy store for Joyce and Pound and Gertrude Stein. The lady who ran it, Sylvia Beach, had discovered *Ulysses*. She used to buy Hemingway shoes. I'd never known that the place still stood, glowing through the polyester artifacts of Paris like a good book in a neon world. Sylvia Beach must be ninety-six by now.

I went in.

Mold partout. The interior looked like a canyon in the final stages of erosion. Crumbling books were stacked, propped, leaned, perched, tossed, inserted, scattered on shelves, tables, chairs, and the floor. The books had the look and smell of having been stored in a cavern, exposed to the droppings of bats and the dripping of rivers through seams in the rocks. Their covers were split and mossy, their pages tea-stained, parchment stiff, their spines thready, their backs sprained, their edges nibbled and raw. A book freak could cry for such lichenous neglect. The air of the place was fetid with river rot, a weedy wet stench that pervaded the books, the sprung seats and leprous upholstery of the mildewed armchairs, the sour-smelling mattress and blanket on the floor of the upstairs loft. I could see my breath. Insidious damp dug into the pores of the backs of my hands as I edged, crabwise, among the toppling shelves.

Several chilblained American hippies huddled by a space heater, drinking cold cider out of broken teacups and eating supermarkets cookies off a paper plate. Here we come a-wassailing among the leaves so green—ho!

"Well, it's not as billed in the advert, is it?"

The girl who had spoken stood behind me. She was stocky, with cheeks like peaches. Her white-smeared eyelids seemed to have been foisted on her steady blue eyes. Her plum-colored coat was made of thin wool, and she wore sheer stockings and three-toned platform shoes, instead of boots. But she was the only person in the place who didn't look cold. Her peachy cheeks were glowing, while the rest of us were dribbling into wads of sozzled Kleenex. "Bit cheesy, isn't it?" she sniffed.

"We had some other stuff before, but we ran out," said a boy in a worried-looking sweater. That seemed unlikely, since it wasn't noon yet. The boy was reluctantly in charge: minding the lemonade stand.

"Had to keep eating to get warm, I should think," said the girl. She eyed the encrusted spidery burners of a gas stove in the boxlike kitchen tucked between two shelves of books. "D'you cook on that? Don't the French fuss about wiring? They fuss about everything else," she said.

Encouraged by a fellow cynic, I said, "This isn't the real Shakespeare and Company, is it?" Whoever ran this dump couldn't have loaned a writer a pair of dry socks.

The boy in the aggravated sweater said, "No. This owner bought the name and some of the books when the real place closed."

Pinball took the old cafés and mold got the books. The Paris of the twenties was gone. With my luck, the seventies renaissance would blossom in Middleburg Heights.

Grace Pitasky would be smack in the heart of it, dispensing mints, while I was washing diapers in Passy.

"Thanks for the Christmas cheer," said the girl with the startling eyelids. "But call that pudding . . . they wouldn't stand for it in England, I can tell you."

I followed her out. She was too good to lose. Someone who spoke English, who was rude in the teeth of retracted promise—a comrade! I'd never in my life approached a stranger. Even in kindergarten, I was the one who stood by the paste pot, waiting for someone to ask me to pass it. But here in Paris, I would either learn to make friends, or resign myself to silent nights and days of pidgin po-po talk. I said, "Excuse me. Uh . . . are you going anywhere special? I mean . . . would you like to have coffee or something?"

"Don't mind if I do," she said. "My name's Doris, actually, but I loathe it—can't think where me mum rooted that up—I'd thank you if you'd call me Dee." After we found a café she warmed the frosted cockles of my heart by ordering a grande-crème and a raisin bun. "I don't eat cakes in cafés, as a rule, they're a bit pricy," she explained. "But I'm bound to feel abused if I don't tuck in enough to be sick on, seeing it's Christmas."

Sensing that I'd found the British counterpart to Randy, I joined her. She almost came to blows with the waiter over the ordering of the cakes. In French, she trampled over vowels and shored up consonants, dragging the battered body of the language over English ramparts. She was from Aylesbury in Buckinghamshire. "Two hours from London by train. Ever heard of Aylesbury duck?" she said.

"Oh, I know a joke about Aylesbury duck," I said, to break the ice.

"Let's have it," said Dee, grinning. She had glorious teeth—like Chiclets.

"This is my uncle's joke. Let's see. I think this old lady

goes into a butcher shop and says to the guy at the counter, 'Have you got an Aylesbury duck?' And the guys says—"

"Is that how you'd do an English accent in America? All that gnashing of teeth?" said Dee, amused already.

"That's how Great-Uncle Al would do it," I said. "It's his joke. Or else his dentures. Where was I? Okay. So this guy brings out a duck—"

"Can you describe it? An Aylesbury duck?"

"No, no, that's not the point. See, this lady sticks her hand up the duck's rear end—"

"She does what? . . . Is this supposed to take place in England?"

"Maybe I'm not telling it right."

"No, no, keep on, I'm intrigued."

"Well, uh . . . so then . . . she says, 'Young man, this is not an Aylesbury duck. I want an Aylesbury—' "

"How did she reckon that, I wonder?"

"I don't know. They don't say. I mean, she doesn't . . . *anyway,* that all happens a couple more times—"

"With the one duck?"

"No. Different ducks. Finally she sticks her hand up the third duck's ass and she says, 'Yes, this is an Aylesbury duck,' and—"

"Duck must've said, 'Leave off, it's too flippin' cold,' " Dee chortled. "That'd be an Aylesbury resident, I'd figger." She beamed at me. "Press on, Kerry."

"Then. The guy wraps up the duck. The Aylesbury duck. Right? And the lady says to him, trying to be friendly—"

"Bit late to chat him up, I should think."

"—'I haven't seen you in here before, young man—' "

"I believe I can guess the end of this," said Dee. "Does she put her hand up his bum?"

"No," I said. "No." I inhaled a lot of coffee. "She says to him, 'Tell me, are you from the town here?' And the guy says, 'Why don't you stick your hand—' "

"Waiter," called Dee, "garçon encore une grande-crème, s'il vous plaît!"

" '—up my arse and find out?' "

Dee turned her chalk-awninged eyes on mine. She nodded. She said, "Is that considered hilarious in America, Kerry? I shouldn't think it would raise great howls of mirth in England."

"What's it like in Aylesbury?" I said.

"Well, for a start, I'm not even from Aylesbury, which is a quite large town. I'm from outside Aylesbury, two and a half miles, to be precise. Our lot are stuck in a council house right out in the country, farms, you know, cows, all that rubbish. Well, I mean, there's nothing there. I mean it's all very well for children and old people but not if you want any sort of life. I can't bear it any longer than three days, then I get cheesed off and go to London. I love London. Mind you I'm one of the few girls from the district to leave it. All my friends fell pregnant and got married at fifteen and that's it for life! I said I'd get off on my own and I have. But Paris isn't what I'd been led to believe, I don't mind telling you that."

"You're not kidding," I said.

"Well, there's the bloody French for a start. They don't think like the English. Always shoving you about in the shops. I don't call that manners."

Dee was an au pair too. "You know why we're called 'jeunes filles au pair'?" she said. "It used to be they'd ship you over in twos. Makes a great deal more sense, that. You'd split the work, and you'd have someone to talk to. But then there'd be two eating, as well—the French put a stop to that." She worked for a family in the Faurers' neighborhood, the Seizième Arrondissement or 16th District. Good ole 16e. "You can come round to the flat and have a meal tonight if you like," she said. "Danièlle and Marc are going to a party, after Elise toddles off. Are your people anything? My people are Comtes. He is, I mean, Marc's a Comte. Of course I don't suppose that means much to an American, does it?"

"My family's just rich. Monsieur is the Pudding King."

"Poor old Marc hasn't got sixpence to himself," said Dee. "Comtes, you know, they're common as pigs over here."

We were sitting at a table in a corner of the Café de Notre Dame, gazing through fogged glass across the Seine to the shrouded spikes and square peaked turrets, steeping in the mist. It wasn't four o'clock yet, but the day was in retreat.

"Right about now . . ." I said, "What are they doing at your house?"

Dee said, "Right about now at home? . . . just getting up from the table. Me dad's saying how's about we have the pudding later. Soon they'll be settling down to have the Queen's speech on the telly. She'll wish us all a happy Christmas, thank us for the rise—she gets more than a million a year now, that's in pounds, a pound's two and a half of your dollars. Well, she needs it to keep up all those castles and footmen. And it's the Jubilee, you know."

"Seems like an awful waste," I said, social conscience saluting.

"Oh, the tourists eat it up—you wouldn't believe all the masses and masses of people who go to Buckingham Palace for the changing of the guard and all that rot," said Dee. "Well, that's why people come to dear old England, isn't it, to get what they can't get at home. Then we'd have *Disney on Parade*. But you must have that in America too. Disney's yours, after all."

"*Disney on Parade*? No, I don't think so," I said.

"That's peculiar, for a start. What's on the telly on Christmas Day, then?"

"I don't know . . . *Amahl and the Night Visitors* . . . *Celebrity Bowling* . . ." I didn't want to state baldly that in our house, TV was considered a necessary evil. "Then what? Do you have turkey? My mother makes the best dressing in the world. She even cans her own cranberry sauce."

"Oh, me mum usually manages to truss up a turkey. It's quite grotesque how much we eat at Christmas at home. About six, we'd force down a bit of Christmas pudding— been eating nuts and chocolates all day, feeling a bit stodgy by now. I'd have packed away about a box of sweets my-self by now—mind you, I put on about a stone over the Christmas holidays. I quite enjoy it."

"I love to eat," I said fervently.

"We know how to eat in England," Dee said. "I've heard enough about the French and their food. All they do is pick! Let's see, where were we? Right. Then we have the pantomimes on the telly. Then we stagger off to bed. Never move all day except to get up and get more sweets. Next day being Boxing Day, the whole rubbish starts all over."

"What's Boxing Day?" I said.

"You don't have Boxing Day in America? Well, it's the day after Christmas," said Dee, as if that explained it.

"What're they doing right now at your house, d'you reckon?" said Dee, playing fair.

"Right about now . . . my mother is trying to make my brothers eat the grapefruit that she sections every Christmas and no one ever eats. My mother thinks that eating grapefruit is a family Christmas tradition. But really the tradition is *not* eating grapefruit, because we've already eaten the tangerines and Hershey's kisses and walnuts in our stockings, and the cookies that were too burned to pass out to guests. After we don't eat the grapefruit, my father makes us all go out and play Fox-and-Geese on the baseball diamond."

"You have your own baseball diamond?" said Dee, eyebrows catapulting into the baby-mild skies of her forehead. "Is that popular in America—like English toffs having tennis courts?"

"No, no," I said, "our whole yard's a baseball diamond. My father can't grow grass." Thinking of the Fox-and-Geese game and the snowball free-for-all that followed, I grew morose. "While we're doing that, a lot of surprising people show up to visit. People like . . . my father's old Latin teacher . . . and my mother's college roommate and her husband . . . girls I used to make bottle resealers with in Junior Achievement . . . kids in my brothers' basketball league. . . . One of my great-uncle's girlfriends brings us a candy wreath, which my brothers destroy by eating all the toffees." I mooned at the dusky fairy tale towers in the glass. "You never know who'll turn up, it's like the last scene in Shakespeare. Even cousins we have no use for, who like to embroider hunting scenes on toilet covers."

The café was empty. Small bright lamps bored holes in the fog along the deserted quai. "Right, Kerry, shall we go back to the flat and cherche the Christmas pudding?" said Dee. "Danièlle bought me some at the Monoprix, she reckoned I'd miss it. It's in a tin, but we mustn't be choosy. Marc and Danièlle are simply terrific. And Elise is a good sort, but she's badly spoiled. Well, they coddle them, don't they?"

Some treat: pudding. But sharing it with Dee would give even tapioca a novel appeal. Trudging to the Métro past shop doors sealed against the cold was hardly dispiriting. Dee was impervious to the malignant snatchings and bruisings of the wind. After a fierce blast sent me reeling into a kiosk, she said cheerily, "That was a nasty one, wasn't it?"

Wiping my nose on my sleeve as we waited for the Métro, I said, "You don't seem to feel this weather."

"Well, it's very similar to London, Kerry, Paris is. It's right across the Channel, you know."

"I've had a cold since I got here."

"I put it all down to the central heating. Though I suppose you've got that in America too, haven't you?"

"I guess so," I said, with the Yankee air of apology: if it makes life easy, we have it. "Uh . . . what is it?"

"A furnace, you know, and all the rooms warm? . . . We don't have that at home. I'm quite accustomed to a room with a bit of a chill on it. It's healthier, full stop. The British don't get colds, as a rule."

The Métro was half full of holiday outcasts like us: American hippies, straining under Everest peaks of packs, maps clutched in raw red hands; a dirty old lady wearing two coats, neither of which had buttons; Algerians. A tiny black man stood at Dee's elbow, his nose on the level of her chest. His long black coat was twice too big. He looked sinister but shrunk. He kept rolling his eyes at Dee's sumptuous purple breasts and grinning. She gazed down upon him.

"Look at this one," she said in a clear voice. "Looks goofy, doesn't he?"

Several passengers looked at us with the emotionless, measuring glance of one Métro rider to another.

"But then the only blokes in Paris who come round foreign girls are the bloody Algerians in the Métro, aren't they?"

Now the whole population of the car was leveling its marbleized—in some cases, Algerian—eyeballs on us.

"Keep your voice down, okay?" I whispered. "He might speak English."

Dee broke into a chuckle, the first truly appreciative recognition of absurdity I'd heard her utter. "English! Him! I doubt it!" She beamed on the Hottentot, who was transfixed by the effects of the jiggling of the train on Dee's breasts. Dee let out another hoot. "Oh, come on, Kerry!"

Dee's Comte lived in a flat in one of the glowing white stone buildings that shone through the twilight like enormous sugar cubes filigreed with black iron gates. When we arrived, Danièlle and Marc were dressing to go out to dinner. Marc crouched, resting his hands on his knees and arching his back, while Danièlle, hidden in the mantle of his flipped-up jacket, was fiddling with the back of his shirt. "It doesn't meet," she announced to us in English, emerging from beneath the black cloth like a photographer using a powder flash. "He is too fat. C'est à toi, tu es gros!"

Marc laughed, with the merry assurance of the beautiful that no one will care if they get fat or their underwear has limp elastic. Danièlle fetched some diaper pins from Elise's room, and used them like frogs, fastening the flaps of the shirt into two-inch proximity. "C'est ça. Personne n'en devine," said Marc, winking at us: who'll know?

I was in love with both of them. They were gorgeous, with sculptured bones and graceful, wry smiles. They looked like their wedding had been photographed by *Vogue,* which it had. Danièlle had a floppy bang of pale brown hair that all but hid her pointy fox's face. She wore a white crepe shirt with billowy sleeves, and black velvet knickers embroidered down the sides with flowers, and the most beautiful russet leather boots I ever saw. She looked like a frail but highly successful female buccaneer. Marc was tall, with black hair and turquoise eyes. He looked like a model in a Windsong ad. He was so handsome in his tuxedo that he seemed to be a mirage. If I'd been twelve years old, I would have made a scrapbook of them, and hung around outside to carry their groceries.

Elise was a bright-faced, elfin thing with cherub ringlets. She was dressed in a sweater and trousers. Not all French mamas got their kiddies up to look like Patty Playpal. She was two and a half and didn't talk much, except to roar "Maman!" and gallop down the long hall from her bedroom to hurl herself at her mother's wispy pelvis. She called Doris "Doughy." Doris seemed to regard her charge and her employers with the same serene indulgence. While Marc was adjusting his monkey suit, Danièlle joined us on the sunken couch that cut a square horseshoe in front of the fireplace.

The salon had been designed and structured in platforms, carpeted in dull red with a pattern of blue fleurs-de-lis. The raised levels were splattered with pillows, the sunken levels inset with rectangular cushioned "conversation pits." The white walls were lined with glass shelves of paperback books, records, a stereo, three rows of liquor bottles, and a rack of wine. It was so much like a two-page layout that I felt like a decanter.

But the ashtrays were chockablock with butts. Elise's toys were stuck in the crevasses of couches and strewn across ramps. There were crystal globes half dark with wine on the glass-topped table. Dee's people lived in their living room.

And they spoke English!

Marc dashed in, a vision of pulchritude in his frontally flawless tux. He plumped a bottle of champagne in Dee's lap. "Merry Christmas," he said with his *Vogue*-spread smile. The Comte and Comtesse shrugged on furs—what else?—and swept off into the suddenly festive Paris night. Kid, pass the popcorn.

"That's who I wanted to be in Paris!" I said. "I got the wrong job. Where's the Comtesse bureau?"

When Elise had recovered from a cloudburst at the door, we whizzed her into her carved oak bed, pummeled her with kisses, weighted her down with foam-filled critters, and said, "Bon nuit."

We attacked the kitchen.

Concentrating on the salon, the Comte had blithely skipped o'er the cuisine. The cupboards weren't painted and the pipes were coated with slime. But compared to the Faurers' icebox, Danièlle and Marc's was a lumberjack's dream. There was food in it—at least when we descended on it.

"When all's said, it's Christmas," said Dee as she placed a buckling tray on the coffee table. We drank champagne, listened to Dylan records—Marc's collection was heavy on sixties folk—and gorged ourselves. We commenced with a small Camembert, some grapes, and a whole loaf of bread. Demolishing a dainty, dull salad, we stormed the entrée— Christmas pudding out of a can, like Howard Johnson's canned brown bread, a congealed, spheroid fruitcake redolent of its aluminum casing. Dee had heated up the pudding in a saucepan—"In Britain, of course, we'd steam this"—and drenched it with cream. It was a Christmas confection fit for the second winter in the fallout shelter.

"This is a big deal in England, huh?" I said, prying with my spoon at something that might have been a marshmallow.

"Well, this isn't the real thing, Kerry, this is no example," Dee said, scraping her bowl. "You might like a bit of brandy on that, it can make you quite tight when it's properly laced." We plundered Marc's liquor supply and poured cognac on top of the cream. I tasted the results.

"Foul, eh?" said Dee. "Here, that's a trifle, chuck it in the waste, I've got masses of treats."

She went off to the cruddy kitchen with the tray, and bore in Round Two. "Regarde!" she said: more bowls, an ice cream cake roll the size of a cannon, and a Sara Lee fudge cake, intact in authentic foil pan. I fell on the fudge cake, wetting it with Midwestern tears. How many nights of Finals Week had Sara Lee rewarded my toil . . . how many times had I hidden the last precious hunk in the lettuce drawer . . .

"Where did you find it?" I shrieked.

"Oh, the French will ship in anything that sells. Mind you, they'll tell you that nothing's worth eating unless it's made in France. But they'll sell you anything you like, and make rude remarks while they take your money!"

We mowed down most of the chocolate cake and all the ice cream roll, swilling down glutinous mouthfuls with champagne. In lieu of *Disney on Parade,* Dee gave me a tour through the glossy wonderland of Danièlle and Marc's wedding album. Her pride was affecting. She could have been the upstairs maid exhibiting the mistress's monogrammed undies to the slattern who swept out the hearth. Having been a wildly popular bridesmaid, I'd slogged through whole encyclopedias of "Bride's Hand and Groom's Hand on Wedding Cake Knife," "Bride Makes Bouquet Foul Shot," "Groom's Mother Dances with Father of Bride," "Bride's Great-Grandmother Dances with Former Violin Teacher of Groom," etcetera. But Danièlle's wedding portrait had been taken by Richard Avedon. Her veil had been embroidered in petit-point by nuns who must have had to go to Lourdes to get their eyesight back. The svelte and cap-toothed guests at the reception had the mirror-eyed smirk of folks bred to the flashbulb.

"They had Radziwills at the reception," said Dee.

"What's that, like Swedish meatballs?" I said.

"No, they're related to your Kennedys, you know."

"This is one class act," I said, stirring cake and ice cream into a cold, crumbly porridge. "You're so lucky!

Danièlle and Marc are so nice! They give you presents . . . they let you eat . . . they're gorgeous . . . their place is so neat . . ."

"Like the platforms, do you? I don't. But then it's I who has to Hoover them."

"Danièlle talks to you like a person! My Madame talks to me like I'm a dog act. Tinkle tinkle. And I hate the kid! Anouk's okay, she's the baby, we get along—but Leah's the worst turd I've ever met, she's like something out of *Village of the Damned!* . . . Elise is *cute!*"

"Cuteness isn't the whole story, Kerry. When I first came to Paris, her bawling was bloody continuous. Every time she saw me she started in. I thought I'd go mad—"

"Ha! Crying is nothing! You should try putting on Leah's shoes! You'd pay Danièlle and Marc to let you work for them!"

"Not much chance of that," said Dee, chortling. "Though I would have taken this job for four hundred francs, I was quite pleased whey they offered five hundred."

"How much?"

"Five hundred francs a month. It's quite decent, really."

My innards were churning: fudge cake brandy ice cream champagne fruitcake salad cheese bread grapes . . . "I think I'm about to throw up," I said.

"Yes, I know it's Christmas now, I feel quite sick," said Dee.

I had to lie down on a platform and breathe very deeply. After an interval murmurous with the rapids of stomach acid, I said, "You know what I get? Two-fifty."

"Two hundred fifty francs a month? That's rather shabby, isn't it? It's not as if they can't spare it, really, living in this neighborhood. But then, that's the French for you, penny wise and pound foolish. Packing off their kids with any needy case who'll work cheaply. I don't mean you, of course, Kerry."

"Of course," I muttered to the carpet.

"But then I'm not really a jeune fille au pair at all, am I, I'm a nanny. Legally in Paris you have to pay a nanny more."

"Maybe I'm a nanny. What's the difference?"

"Bugger all, as far as I can make out. It's all in what you call it, really. You should talk to your Madame about it."

"I would if I could talk to her at all." How would I

phrase it? "Je suis nanny . . . est-ce que je suis nanny? . . . je me s'appelle nanny . . . Alors! Je demande . . ."

"Well, come. They understand what they want to understand, don't they?" said Dee, picking frosting off a fork. "I met an Irish girl in the park, who's au pair for a baroness. Another useless title. This baroness told this Irish girl that French law says you only have to spend seven francs a day on a servant's food, and the baroness preferred to spend her money on clothes. She was quite frank about it, give her marks for cheek. She said she didn't intend to go over the minimum, so when the little girl and the au pair were eating, the baroness stood and watched to make sure the au pair didn't eat more than seven francs worth."

"Seven francs . . . I bet I don't even eat *that* much," I said. "You know what she gave me for lunch one day last week? You have to realize I don't eat dinner, hardly, and all I have for breakfast is two crumbly crusts and coffee—by noon I'm so hungry I could eat a raw dog backward. So Tuesday she gives me, for my whole lunch, half a cauliflower and a whole artichoke—raw. Both of them raw. And she stood there and watched me eat the whole cold, prickly mess! I had to take off every artichoke leaf and bite off the end, but the leaves were cold and stiff and I had to sort of worry them . . . not only was I filled up like the Hindenburg with gas all day, but my gums hurt! It was like chewing a rose bush!"

"Sounds a bit barmy, your Madame. Well, it's in the nature of the job, Kerry. They'll all take advantage of you."

Foment in the servants' hall. Mutinous rumblings below the salt. Did au pairs who sat in the park, with their bloated blue buggies, knit? Did they all call each other a code name? "How goes it, Jacques? . . . How are they treating you, Jacques? . . . Making you iron the diapers again, Jacques?" It was only a matter of time till we converted the buggies to tumbrils.

"You must be working for the only human beings in France," I said. Suffering from the glorious excess of the Christmas stuffing she'd given me, I grudged poor Dee her job. Maybe the Comte would let me understudy.

"When all's said, Danièlle and Marc are still French. Now take the salon. It cost—stop, I'll reckon this into your money—right, seven thousand dollars. Marc's uncle lent them the money. Seven thousand dollars for boards and a bit of rug, don't see the sense in that, but here's the point . . . they've no hot water. Haven't had for six weeks. We have to heat water on the stove to wash up. What's worse, when I wash Elise's nappies, I have to heat water for that—gallons and gallons of it. Now, I ask you! In England, we can make do with absolutely bloody rien, but we wouldn't borrow to landscape the parlor, if we didn't have a shilling in our kip for coal!"

"How come they don't have hot water?" I said.

"Oh, it's the landlord who's the villain, according to Danièlle. She rings him up and screams at him. But she and Marc aren't frantic about it because it's I who gets lumbered with heating the water. There you have it."

We brooded.

"More champagne?" said Dee.

"I can't swallow. I think I have glottal arrest," I said. "This is the most fun I've had since I became a serf. But I have to go home now. I want to die in bed."

"It was luck running into you, Kerry," said Dee, pumping my hand at the door. "I've been quite lonely since I've been in Paris. I've only met that one Irish girl, the one who's au pair for the baroness, and she's useless, won't go about at night, just mopes by the fridge and writes letters to nuns."

"Thank you for everything," I said, but more was called for. I tugged at the unraveling edge of my mitten. "This was a neat Christmas present—making friends with you."

Dee grinned. "Always happy to be of service. I've never had much use for Americans, after what I've seen in London—they run in packs, you know, mucking up the streets with Polaroid negatives, trying to truck their Wimpies into the House of Commons—but you seem fairly sane." She gave me one of her John Wayne nudges. "Look here, let's go and cherche some blokes this weekend, shall we?"

Glints of good times coming broke across the murk of au pair travail.

"You're on," I said.

Chercher les Blokes

What with the vivid social profile of the Comte, it was two weeks before we got out à la nuit. New Year's Eve, for a wonder, even the Faurers had a party to go to. I celebrated their absence by taking an hour-long bath in the tub. When I was puffy from steaming, I took my Dr. Dentons out of tissue paper and put them on. Pajamas with feet . . . I'd forgotten the sensation of sweat and lint between the toes, and the smell of heating rubber in the sheets. I wished Grace could see me. The caramel corn had lost any semblance of freshness in translation; it tasted like my duck feet smelled. To wash it down, I stole a glass of port from the locked cupboard. I had discovered the key on a bookshelf, while cherching a French "góod read," something between a Gothic and *Dick et Jane*. Abandoning the quest for culture, I saw the old year out in my pink and blue padded cell, propped up in bed, chewing plastic popcorn, swilling pilfered port, and rendering a 64-Crayola portrait of the diaper basket. I sent it to Grace as a thank-you for her Christmas package. Randy's thank-you for her life-saving twenty-dollar bill was the set of head bands Grace had given me, and the Indian pennant. "No doubt you'll have more use for these than I will, come spring," I wrote with hollow gloating. In the morning, roused by the wolfish howls of Anouk, I woke in a flannel sauna, every pore open and yielding. Sleeping in Dr. Dentons in a steam-heated room was better than jogging. The highlight of the New Year was Monsieur's expression when we met in the kitchen—he in his valedictorian suit, I in my snap-flap sweat pants.

By January 7, I was mad with cabin fever. In a burst of of post-Noël malevolence, Leah had bedeviled her mother into collapse. Madame lay in a state of Victorian prostration in the double bed, with the drapes drawn. The table

beside her was an altar to anesthesia, banked with so
many bottles of pills and jars of syrups, I had to set her
tea on the floor.

After a week of playing doctor, Monsieur made tracks
for Lyon, probably fleeing the prospect of teaching Leah
to ride the *bicyclette*. In addition to my *typique travail*, I
had to haul Leah to school, leaving Anouk with the
Spanish maid. Emparo was killing the time of Madame's
vapors swabbing out the pristine ashtrays in the salon.

A permanent twilight had descended, of charcoal skies,
gloom grey drops, scurrying black rubber boots and umbrellas, and a truckle of grainy mud. Leah fell down twice
in mudholes as we slogged across the boggy park, between
the gutted torches of birch trees. The intensity of her
shrieking drew horrified glances from the faces shielded
by westbound umbrellas. I expected to be nabbed for child
abuse—or worse—for disturbing the peace. There must be
harsh laws against that in France, I thought: making a
public display of oneself. INTERDIT DE FAIRE LE SPECTACLE.

Once I'd delivered the demon child, snowy boots and
tights and gloves desecrated with mud, I took a prescrip-
tion to the pharmacist. He received me with suspicion and
dispatched me with cautionary farewells. What was Madame taking—arsenic? "Ça n'est pas pour moi," I assured
him: not me, buddy, I'm an aspirin person. But I could tell
he thought I wouldn't even get around the corner before
I'd have the lid off the vial.

Since the telephone was in the sickroom, I hadn't been
able to call Dee since Christmas. At last, on the Friday
after New Year's, the phone sent up its crass alarm. Madame groped her way to the kitchen. Leaning on the door-
post, she tinkled on a dying fall of notes, "Ker-ray! C'est
pour vous!"

I apologized profusely, but she smiled bravely, waiting
in the hall to give me privacy. I wondered why she didn't
stay in the kitchen to introduce herself to Anouk, who had
regarded her with vague welcome, as if memories of her
mother were pleasant but dim. I stood by the bed, holding
the receiver, observing the chaos of pills and tinctures, the
paperback book on the floor, the bottle of wine behind the
dresser, the bread fragments scattered over the sheets,
the broken bar of Lindt chocolate peeping from under the
pillow.

"I'm so depressed," I said into the phone.

"Gooo-d! I'm fairly well round the bend myself, after a fortnight cooped up in the flat with Elise on account of this bloody rain!" Dee's voice strode briskly into my ear, marshaling forces of humor and sense. "Can you get your Madame to let you out tonight? Danièlle and Marc have been gadding about since Christmas, but they've thrown up the sponge, so I'm off. What would you say to a trot round the Latin Quarter?"

"It would save my life," I said in low, rapid English. "If I don't blow this popstand, I'm going to snap. They'll find me hanging from the drying rack. I'm sure I can go when the kids are in bed. That's eight-thirty, more or less—if they aren't raving."

"Get her to couche them for you, can't you? Then we can set off at seven. I'm after making the most of this, Kerry, Christ knows when they'll let us off the leash again."

Madame was willing to pick up the maternal torch for a few hours. To show her good faith, she put on Monsieur's dressing gown and had a cup of tea. Then she foraged around in the ghost town of the icebox for a rubbery onion, some languid carrots and a flowering potato, and set them to boil. When I left the apartment, wearing my Christmas fancypants and carrying Monsieur's vast bat of an umbrella, she was mustering the bowls and the mincing machines. Dinner equals soup: the same old grind.

Hunched beneath the black tent, I slopped across the park, deserted in the weeping blackness. The farflung globes of street lamps dangled on their drooping iron stems. I watched the sidewalk rivulets running under my suede boots, now matted with accumulated rain and mud and sand from the park.

"Bonsoir . . ."

The voice was less a whisper than a gasp, as if the impulse to speak had been strangled by the fearful withholding of breath. The hissing cry came again: "Mademoiselle, bonsoir . . ."

Off in the dingy recess of the sparsely wooded crescent to my right, thicketed by a sodden hedge from the damp streaks of lamplight, stood a figure in a raincoat and soft-brimmed hat. I doubled my pace, umbrella bobbing. From the corner of my eye, I could see that he didn't move except for the sad, bouncing motion of his hand at his crotch.

"How do they find me?" I said to Dee as we waited for the Métro.

"It's Paris, isn't it? You don't find that in London. All this talk of amour is just talk. If you ask me, the French are repressed." As Dee talked, I gazed at her eyelids, which were taupe and turquoise marvels. "I don't know about you, Kerry, but I haven't been besieged in the streets by amorous Frenchmen. Except loonies like your bloke in the raincoat."

"Two blokes. One just now and one at the Louvre."

"The Louvre! Well, precisely. Fancy a Briton making a scene like that at the National Gallery!" she chortled.

The steep cobbled paths of the Quartier Latin were streaming with black umbrellas. I wondered what Paris was like when it wasn't cold and wet. My fingers glistened with droplets that had slithered down the stem of the umbrella as Dee and I bumped beneath its shelter. In an attempt to avoid the gauche, I had left my mittens at home.

"I've got Christmas money left," I said. "We can even see a movie if you want." We were passing the glittering entrance to a cinema which charged more for admission than I spent on my whole day off. What the hell! Unearned money was meant to be squandered. Umbrellas mounted on the stumps of boots sprouted like mushrooms in a line to the entrance. I looked at the posters. The movie was *King Kong,* the remake, in English subtitled in French. I could wrestle down the environment and pretend I was home at the drive-in.

But Dee said, "We'll never meet a bloody soul sitting in a film, unless it's one of the knee-nudging sort. Had enough of that for one evening, I'd say. What say we cherche a club or a disco?"

"Lead on," I said.

We marched, unsynchronized, beneath the umbrella, up and down the rues. At last we found a place that looked promising, a club called the Lilli Balloon. "Now for a start, we shan't come up with a couvert unless they've got live music," said Dee. We folded our tent and stole behind enemy lines.

Inside, the club was dark and jammed with blokes. No one seized us to extort an entrance fee. No one demanded that we ante up for drinks. After the initial barrage of eye-balls as we entered, no one looked at us. Dee and I stood in a corner by the bar, imitating stools.

After a decent interval of mourning, we petitioned the bartender, evidently another slumming Comte, who consented to trade us two shots of sour wine in exchange for four dollars. "Charming!" said Dee.

The juke box was clotting the smoky air of the room into grey cotton candy—festoons of it clung to the rafters, like the extraterrestrial webs in the movie *The Great Spider Invasion*—with the syrup of "Love Is Keen" by Donny and Marie. In the next stultifiying hour, our ears were clogged with treacly tunes: Neal Sedaka, the Carpenters, Lesley Gore, even the Cowsills. I hadn't heard "I Love the Flowergirl" sung since sock hops in seventh grade.

There were three other females in the place, each draped like a furpiece over a sullen youth. The rest of the mob were sleek, raccoon-eyed café habitués, pinball majors of the Sorbonne. They lounged at spindly tables with their legs in the aisle, assessing the cost of each other's boots, or splayed themselves over the bar, testing the seams in their undersized pants. They didn't talk much. Mostly they smoked. From time to time, a lout with an air of precocious decadence would drop a phrase. The lout beside him might or might not nod. The bon mots I could translate were at least as profound as commentary in a checkout line: "Chicken's up two cents."

Dee and I conferred in a humble undertone. Then I was stunned to find one of the loungers eyeing me. I smiled, suppressing terror. What if he wanted to talk in French?

He approached, with a graceful, ambling gait, like a cat grazing a food dish. He had ringlets and tight pants and a short, tight jacket. He looked like a cross between a juvenile delinquent and a bell boy.

The Wastrel's Apprentice.

"Don't look now, I think we've struck a bloke," I said.

"You are Amurrican?" said the bloke.

"Yes," I said. Huzzah! A bloke who spoke English!

He smoked five of Dee's cigarettes and allowed us to buy him a beer. He was Hungarian, presently based in Paris. His invisible means of support was his mother in Bucharest. (I asked.) He made sculptures out of wire and plaster stolen for him by female dental technicians. Paris was all right, because people there knew how to live. But he hated the rest of France. He also hated England. "It is all dead, the people are dead, the time of England is over," he said.

"All said, we're paying our way as we go," said Dee, watching him take her last cigarette.

"Money, this means nothing." He turned his droopy gaze on me. "You are an Amurrican. Amurrica is dead too, but too stupid to know it. Amurricans think they can buy culture. An Amurrican tried to buy London Bridge."

I said, "Yeah, and they sold it to him."

"Have you been to America?" said Dee.

He shook his ringlets up and down, waving an exhausted hand, as if he'd toured with de Tocqueville.

"Where?"

"New York . . . Buffalo . . . Vail, Colorado."

"I guess you've experienced the spectrum," I said.

"What do you call those stores? Some numbers. Seven . . . eleven, yes? That is Amurrica. All one seven-eleven."

I said, "Aren't you needed to spread world peace to the rest of the patrons? Or whatever else you're spreading?"

He sneered, detaching himself from the wall. "You will not make many friends in Paris," he said. Several of the neighboring wastrels stared at us.

"No loss, if you're any example," said Dee.

"Amurricans will find out they cannot buy friends," he declaimed for the boys in the backroom.

"They can if they smoke cigarettes, can't they?" Dee called after him. "Look here, Kerry, these are a useless lot. I don't even fancy them, they're all so sort of weedy-looking. Have you heard about this American Center?"

"Oh, I went there one day when I was supposed to be at class." I tossed down my wine. I was disgusted. One bloke all night, a bigot from Bucharest.

"What's it like then?"

"It's dumb. There's a snack bar all made of formica, and a mural on the wall of all these wholesome hippies' faces, you know, 'Youth, Our Envoys to the World'—it looks like a billboard for 'Up with People.' And they sell coffee that makes me homesick, it's so awful—they must have it shipped direct from the vending machine at Occidental Insurance. They sell hot dogs too, in genuine U.S. cotton buns, and they have all the American magazines and newspapers. The last outpost of *Redbook*. There are posters advertising their little theater group doing something like . . . *America Hurrah,* or *The Sandbox* . . . something that was a crushing indictment of the American way of life in 1962."

"What sort of Americans go round there?"

"Oh . . . former Vista workers. You'd hate it."

"Doesn't sound right. Where is it?"

"In the Rue du Dragon. I found it by accident, like I find everything."

"This place I heard about is in the Boulevard Raspail. They have music at night, groups and all that, and it's three francs or something, quite cheap for Paris. Shall we toddle round? If it's a bore, we can chalk it off to experience and press on."

The alternative American Center, when we found it, was a cavernous house of blackened turrets and pock-marked verandas. The rooms were filled with tight groups of overdressed French hippies, with a sprinkling of Eurasian girls and chummy Arabs in cartridge belts. The only Americans were blacks in outgrown Afros macraméd into braids that fairly squeaked. The blacks were addressing hushed claques of Parisians in Chicago-tinted French. The French kids could have been rushed by truck from the Lilli Balloon. The tile floors were littered with instruments and cases. Any guitar in the place would have covered my bond for a year. Poles in the central hallway were papered with French and English schedules for classes, and prices. "This is bloody cher!" said Dee. "I don't think I'll be signing on, thank you!" We could have taken psychodrama, electric flute, mask-making, contrapuntal theory, kiln technique, Haitian cookery, tribal dancing.

"I'd swear we were in Shaker Heights," I said.

A pretty French girl in stolen Levis was taking francs at the door of the auditorium. "Are you paying or performing?" she said.

Three francs might mean a Croque Monsieur on a cold, bored Friday. I said, "What would I have to do?"

"Sing or play an instrument . . . It isn't necessary to audition." It was clear that she considered that fortunate for me.

"I'm performing," I said.

The girl took my name—as it were, between finger and thumb.

"Well done, Kerry, keep up our side," said Dee, as we settled on folding chairs, facing a small stage. "But can you actually do this sort of thing?"

"Heck yes, I grew up in the sixties, I can play 'Blowin in the Wind' in G–C–D."

"But you haven't got a guitar."

"I'll borrow one. I'm the only American in the room. They'll have to lend me one to save face."

"Perhaps you should set your sights lower. You could recite, for example. 'My Last Duchess.' Or as it's the American Center, the Gettysburg Address. Especially as no one in the audience speaks English."

"The only poem I know by heart is 'Breathes there a man with soul so dead,' which would not be a crowd pleaser."

"Don't think I'm familiar with that one."

"I'm not about to recite it for you, after that business with the Aylesbury duck."

"Mustn't be touchy, Kerry. You may need a friend at court."

When the chairs were filled with bony louts in battle jackets, and the walls reverberated with machine gun babble, the stage lights came up and the house lights came down. A pudgy man danced out, to somewhat derisive applause. He wore a mustache and a beret and a sweater whose warp and woof were distinct. He made us a speech of welcome to the American Center, in French. Now and again he tossed in an American idiom, for color, like "off the wall" or "down home." His speech was punctured by shouted insults from the teenyboppers, and his rattling responses. Trying to be pals, he couldn't keep the little beasts at bay. Finally he called the first performer to the stage.

Tight pants; fat boots; droopy eyelids: same ole same ole. The guitar was a hefty instrument choked with strings and bejeweled with knobs. He played the Beatles' song "Blackbird" proficiently. But he didn't sing. I missed the soothing wobble of the countertenor and the simple, moving words. His number was received with a brusque slap of palms that didn't even see him offstage.

The next five guitarists wore the same boots and the same expression of exhausted lust. They played, on grandiose guitars, the Beatles, Jimi Hendrix, Eric Clapton, Dylan. They didn't sing. Was singing illegal? Pronunciation might have been a stumbling block. Having been a frequent butt of accent jokes, I'd have relished a Parisian rendition of "Up on Ze Rrroof."

During the fifth number, I began to sense unrest in my intestines. My hands were cold. My neck and ears were tingling. I had to go to the bathroom, but I was too weak to get up. By the time they called my name, I'd be foaming at the mouth, and my hair would have turned completely white.

Once in my life, I'd performed in public. My mother had insisted that every child should learn to play some instrument. One of my brothers played drums, which barely qualified, and one played clarinet. My father was a sax man. My mother played piano. I knew that she envisioned little galas, with the family group essaying, if not Mozart, at least "In the Mood." I said I'd take harp. I figured in Cleveland she'd never be able to rent one.

But she found one and acquired it just for hauling it away. For two years I fluttered my grubby fingers over the cursed strings. Finally my teacher, Mr. Passelaqua, drafted me into the Christmas concert. I did everything but slit my wrists to get out of it, to no avail. Ten years old, the harp, the freckles, the number I was playing, "Silent Night" . . . I was the crippled shepherd incarnate. I closed the bill.

By the time my number was up, I was suffused with fatalistic calm. I had given all I had in the ladies' room. My father and my uncle had been at the bourbon in a heroic effort to withstand six variations on "The Spinning Song." When they trundled my harp onstage, they bumped a pedal out of position, flatting the E. As soon as I played the first two bars, I knew. "Silent . . . night . . ." The "night" sank into sour, sulphurous depths. I didn't know how to fix the pedal. If I ran screaming into the ladies' room, my mother would never forgive me. So I played it all the way through—two verses. "Silent . . . night . . . holy . . . night . . ."

After the concert, my father took me, all by myself, to Howard Johnson's, and bought me a tin roof sundae with peppermint stick ice cream. The next day he called Goodwill and told them to come get the harp.

After that, I'd refused to participate in school plays, varsity volleyball, Stunt Night, pom-pom squad, public jump rope. I never went out to dinner on my birthday, for fear that a flock of waitresses in Croatian dirndls would bring me a crepe with a candle in it and lead a hundred strangers in "Happy birthday, Kerry." I didn't even like to be waited on in department stores. I liked to be ignored.

Here I was on hostile turf, about to make an ass of myself and a laughingstock of my country, just to save three francs. I should have known I couldn't pull it off. Apart from stark fright at the image of all those eyeballs, steely with the "hanging judge" regard of a Frenchman for an outlander, I was unworthy of any guitar on view. And I sang. I'd be driven from the temple of Franco-American harmony, and cast back into an outer darkness I hadn't known since Harp Night.

There followed a ten-minute interlude in which a shy, dark-skinned boy played some twangy object laying in his lap, looking and sounding like a harp that had died. The louts in the house gave him brief attention. Then, as the twanging extended, incessant, without the respite of a bridge as we know it, the natives grew restless. They sniggered. They shouted, "C'est fini!" They broke into applause three times before the shamefaced boy dragged his act to the wings.

"Rudest bloody people in the world," said Dee, as we quarantined ourselves by giving the boy sincere applause. He never emerged, no doubt having ended his Parisian torment by taking lye. "I thought he did quite well. Mind you I wouldn't seek out that sort of music, but it's what he learned at home, isn't it?" She patted my knee. "I'll cheer you on, Kerry. You don't reckon they'll storm the stage, do you?"

"No, they're too lazy. I'm not worried. What can I lose, my au pair franchise?"

"That's the spirit."

The beret man bounced onstage and into English. "Next we have, for your amusement and edifica-see-one, a genuine American art form!" He rubbed his palms and all but licked his chops. The audience muttered "américain" in verying tones of discord. My stomach said, "Hi there, aren't you sorry you did this?" My brain had mounted an armed assault on memory to retrieve the lyrics of the second verse of "Blowin' in the Wind," and was now in full rout. The beret man crowed, "It is an art form born dans les rues, in the streets, which has now moved into the cafés and concert halls—"

"Art form, my word," said Dee.

"I only know three chords," I said.

"—and which has now achieved worldwide renown and respect, changing the course of political events and helping to end the war in Viet Nam!"

The audence booed. "Oh, fine," I said. "What am I doing, leading the Yankee Die songfest?"

"Well, after all, Kerry, your government—"

"I don't want to hear it. I was stuffing envelopes for McCarthy when I was twelve years old. But I don't want to hear it from the French, especially—they started that mess in the first place."

"It has come to be called 'guerrilla theatre'!" boomed the beret.

"Huh?" I said.

"S'il vous plaît, dites 'Bienvenue' à 'Les Trois Guerrillas d'Amérique'!"

They came from the wings as if from under a rock: Dwight D. E. Clanski, the Captain, and Duse. Three American Gorillas. Dan's amigos, who had emptied a café with their folksy aura, had honed offensiveness into an art.

"It's not you after all," said Dee.

"You said a mouthful."

They must have discarded their layers of wool in the rank and sweat of a cloakroom, and costumed themselves for the . . . what can I call it? It wasn't a performance. It was a cross between a ritual and a riot. It took them ten minutes to drag out their equipment and arrange it tastefully in heaps: harmonica, bongo drums, dulcimer, tambourine, and guitar; three small American flags on sticks; two wooden spoons; a lot of raw hamburger; a plastic gun; an egg beater; a copy of the *National Enquirer;* two pomegranates; two empty beer cans; Wonder Bread; candles that looked remarkably like the votive candles at Notre Dame; a faceless dummy dressed in a black suit—for which they must have rolled a seminarian—

and a tie, but no shirt; a baseball bat; two green plastic G.I. Joe helmets; glitter, in an envelope; a twenty-five-pound bag of peanuts; rope; a butcher knife; a poster of Farrah Fawcett-Majors; and a wooden crate with airholes, which proved to contain a chicken whose cries of "Cheap" were self-descriptive.

The gorillas were swatched in sheets which dragged around their shoes and made trundling the properties tedious. Glimpses of Duse's green-and-orange striped shirt and checkered kneesocks signaled through the gaps in her toga. Her greasy hair was bound down with an Ace bandage. Dwight D. E. Clanski wore a cowboy hat, which rode above his mashed-potato countenance and reheated-lima-bean eyes like John Wayne on a spaniel. The Captain retained his nautical headgear, lest he forget who he was.

During the gorilla act, we witnessed: the inauguration sequence, in which Duse waltzed with the dummy in the black suit, as Dwight played the bongos and the Captain threw peanuts at the audience; the redneck sequence, in which Dwight and the Captain swilled from beer cans, played baseball with a pomegranate, made obscene gestures to the poster of Farrah Fawcett-Majors, cut a pomegranate in half and glued the halves to her larger than life-size chest, beat up the poster with the baseball bat, cut holes in the poster with the butcher knife, and set fire to the poster with the votive candles, while Duse all the while was attacking the mound of hamburger with an egg beater, and making whimpering noises; the wish fulfillment sequence, in which Dwight and the Captain tied up Duse, beat her with wooden spoons, and force-fed her Wonder Bread, after which Dwight hit her over the head twenty times, counting, with the tambourine, while the Captain ate the remaining pomegranate in front of her, making appreciative moans, and spitting the seeds in her face; the low-budget nuclear holocaust sequence, in which the Captain, as the power plant, exploded, by shouting, "KA-BOOM!" and flinging glitter all over the stage, and Duse and Dwight fell dead; the art-and-the-media sequence, in which Dwight sang "Blood on the Saddle" to his own guitar accompaniment as Duse did an interpretive dance, seemingly based on a lemming stampede, and the Captain read aloud from the *National Enquirer* headlines such as, "Two-headed Baby Found in Vacuum Cleaner Bag, Twelve-Year-Old Mother Sobs, 'I'm Innocent.'"

In the finale, Dwight and the Captain, in army helmets, armed with the dimestore gun and the butcher knife, discovered Duse making love to the dummy, hurled her aside and, as she groveled at their feet—walking on her knees, she kept crawling up her own sheet and strangling herself—they shot and stabbed the dummy. The massacre's effect was muffled by the gun's sound, a humiliating click! which Duse supplemented by interspersing her wails and shrieks with cries of "BANG!" Next they kicked the dummy, and stomped on the dummy, as Duse fired off blasts on the harmonica, probably orchestrating the gradual collapse of the victim's lungs. Dwight planted lighted candles around the dummy, the Captain sprinkled the dummy with the shredded raw meat, and the two of them knelt and pretended to nibble on the meat as Duse played "Rock of Ages" on the dulcimer. (Several fainthearts departed at this point, and Dee whispered, "Seems a bit gamy even for Paris.") Throughout the debacle, any of the apes who had a free hand was waving an American flag.

At the curtain call, I was first on my feet, but the French sheep leaped up all around me, bellowing "Bravo!" drowning out my cries of "Get bent!" In the midst of this storm of sophomoric acclaim, the three gorillas began to sing, "My Country 'Tis of Thee." "Horsefeathers! Garbage!" I hollered, jumping up and down. "Steady on, Kerry," said Dee. Still singing, Dwight and Duse opened the wooden crate and took out a terrified, starving chicken. The Captain brandished the butcher knife.

"Bloody hell!" Dee grabbed my arm. "You don't suppose—"

"They will in a pig's eye," I said, struggling out to the aisle and through the throng of hysterically yelping yahoos to the stage.

Stage fright was vanquished by the pure flame of my rage. I came down on the trio like a wolf on the fold. I belted the Captain with a backflung elbow that sent him caroming into Dwight. "Give me that bird," I demanded, snatching the apoplectic chicken from Duse. The chicken squirmed like a gerbil doing a rhumba. It tore with its beak at my thumbs. But I pressed it to my breast, where it showered my hand-me-down cashmere with feathers and poop.

Flicking hamburger out of his beard, the Captain gaped at me. Then a sickly illumination, like TV backwash, slid over his face. "Cleveland!" he said.

"You're damn right!" I cried. "You thought you could pass off this . . . pageant of twaddle . . . as Life in These United States because nobody here would know any better, didn't you? You lose, Sinbad!"

Dwight tried to palm off the no-offense-taken grin of the full-time jellyfish. "Hey, what's happenin'?" he asked me.

"How could you malign your own country just so these Golden Book Marxists could get their rocks off?" I said.

The audience was in a lather, a sprinkling of voices cheering me on but the chorus roaring dissent at interference in the sacrifice. Now that my Joan of Arc charge was over, I was aware of the eyeballs, the lights, the booing, the faces in the front row, ghoulish in the spill of light. Clutching the antic chicken, I felt like an animal trainer whose act had bombed.

The beret man had vanished. He must be summoning the crew with the hook. I was losing my affection for the chicken, who was attacking my chest like a homesick woodpecker. But if I tried to leave the stage, I'd be torn to bits—or at least severely goosed—by the disappointed groundlings in the pit.

I turned to the audience and pitched my plea into the din. "C'est fait à Dieu"—and I waved the blinking chicken—"Laisse-le! Le poulet va libre!" It wasn't a deathless slogan for a banner: "This is God's chicken, leave it go free!" The crowd roared "thumbs down" on the chicken and my grammar.

"We weren't going to kill him, honey," said the Captain with a condescending smile. "It was all part of the act."

"Ha!"

"He's Duse's. He lives on the barge with us. We wouldn't hurt him. Duse!" Duse was fairing the janitor, bundling up the props. She gazed aloft at hearing her name, thinking the roll was being called up yonder. "Duse! Come here and get D'Annunzio."

Duse received the chicken, which immediately sank into a trance. She sat on the crate, cradling the zonked-out fowl and swaying. All four of their glassy eyes were fastened on my ear. They were soulmates.

Now that peace had been perpetrated, the cannibals thought I was part of the act, a deus ex monkeywrench in the works. A cry went up of "Rrrreep-off!" "Rip-off" was an expression Parisians were familiar with, since it was always on the lips of Americans in Paris.

"This looks bad," said the Captain.

"Maybe we should sing," said Dwight.

"I don't think that's a good idea," I said. Eight bars of "Blood on the Saddle" could precipitate mass executions.

"Duse can sing the Marshallaze," said Dwight. "That always gets French people on your side."

"Only in the movies," said the Captain.

But Dwight was hauling on Duse's toga. Her sheet was twisted, coiled, and matted, smeared with hamburger and chicken shit, dusted with glitter and feathers and pomegranate seeds. She looked like a leading chracter in *Night of the Living Dead.* Dwight led Duse and D'Annunzio to center stage. Duse was still in Disneyland. Her eyes were metallically reflective, like hubcaps. But prompted by Dwight, she started to sing.

She must have learned the French words phonetically, since she had only a layman's grasp of English. What was more astounding was her voice. She could sing the cigarettes out of a dilettante's pocket. She had a haunting, wrenching alto that soared up and swelled on the high notes, gaining strength and timbre and the power to move her listeners. In a room full of musicians who couldn't sing, Duse had a great, pure voice.

The venal Parisians had to capitulate. Educated from birth to be picky, they had to bow to Duse's talent just to prove that they recognized true art wherever it appeared. She was a zombie. Worse, she was American. But she had the gift. The rabble quieted. Halfway through the song, where the cymbals should have crashed with the cry to march, a few of the listeners tried to join in. They were quelled by their neighbors. A Frenchman would rather hear his anthem sung by a barbarian on pitch than by a tone-deaf français. But at the triumphal final chorus, a dull, pleasant humming, like an air conditioner, could be heard throughout the hall.

Duse got an ovation. The rest of us got out alive.

To celebrate their underserved deliverance from the mob, the gorillas invited us back to the barge for tea.

"Tea?" said Dee. "At this hour?"

"That's all we have," said Dwight.

"In that case, it's quite decent of you to offer." Dee turned to me and said in the same clear voice, "What do you say, Kerry? It couldn't be worse than what we've already put up with this evening."

"Bet me." My contempt for these specimens of Yanks was almost palpable, a mudball in my fist. Besides, I had a vivid, crawly recollection of the noxious hour I'd once murdered with the Captain and crew, au café. All night I'd been reviled by European youth. I'd made a crusader's charge to rescue a chicken which had only been masquerading as a martyr. I felt like a fool. All I wanted was the Métro home. Dee and I crouched, debating, beneath the umbrella of Monsieur, in the dense rain outside the black iron gates to the Anti-American Center. The Captain, Dwight, and Duse, encumbered with instruments and burlap bags of props, loomed uncovered and dripping, a tactless gap away. I whispered, good manners being my downfall. Dee didn't lower her voice.

"I grant you, I don't much fancy this lot. But all said, it's better than sitting on our bums in the salon, packing away the fromage."

"Listen, the Bowling Banquet at Occidental Insurance would be scintillating, compared to tea with these turkeys! In the first place, they don't even wash."

"I had noticed a bit of a ripeness, I don't mind admitting that. Still, we'd be out on the water, wouldn't we. Ought to be a breeze."

"Who knows *where* we'd be? Somewhere on the Seine!

If we had to spring for the exit to save our sanity, how would we find our way home?"

"Stop a minute." She raised her voice, needlessly, addressing our proposed hosts. "How far is this barge, then?"

"Just down by the quai," said the Captain, all sunny reassurance: the slave trader to the tribal chief. Why was he so eager to escort us to his home, unless he hadn't ensnared a subject for insult lately, and planned to whet his blunted ax on us? And of course he needed extra hands to lug the props.

"There, you see," said Dee. "If it's nasty, we can easily make our way back to civilization."

"What if civilization won't take us back?"

But Dee hauled me over to the leper colony. She said, "Lead on, Captain Bligh."

I went along quietly, declaring my resistance by making faces. I would have struggled to the death to avoid the Captain, except for an ulterior motive which slunk, rubbing its hands and chuckling, in the alley of my mind. The Captain might have news of Dan. Having been left at the church, even by a groom who hadn't heard about the wedding, I demanded at least the satisfaction of knowing the present location of the culprit, with his blanket and his harmonica. Was he in Spain, or had he just moved down the rue? Even now, was he back at the barge, masterminding an encore?

This last consideration went to my knees and quivered. We were plunging in and out of puddles, up and down curbs. Under our batwing roof, Dee and I tracked the burlap bags jogging ahead. As the bags halted, allowing a vicious beetle of an auto to cut across their owners' path, I called out, "Hey . . . does anyone live on this boat besides you guys?"

The Captain turned and leered at me from under the eaves of his yachtsman's chapeau. "Sorry, little lady," he drawled, in a lame imitation of Dan's Tuba City twang. "Ole Dan Spencer done gone to Madrid."

Dan was worse than flighty. He was a blabbermouth.

"Who's this bloke in Madrid?" said Dee.

"Isn't there a Métro around here?" I said, prepared to get a hammerlock on Dee and yank her down a stairwell. But we had arrived at the quai.

"We're moored just down that bank," said the Captain,

pointing into the fathomless deeps of darkness beneath the bridge. The cold breath of a river in winter crept along my shrinking flesh, insinuated its clammy nose beneath the cuffs of my trousers, shinnied up my legs. Below, in the lapping blackness, here and there a fuzzy white or yellow globe outlined the prow of a boat.

"Where's your boat?" I said. "Don't you have a light on it?"

"A sailor doesn't need a light. He can smell out his own ship," the Captain said.

Any group of sailors with a less distinctive collective scent than the three gorillas would have needed bloodhounds to sniff out their craft in that blind cold stench of decaying fish, oil, tar, mildewed wood, moldly rope, river slime, and mud. I watched the burlap mound of the Captain's back jounce down the darkness. His legs disappeared, chopped away by night as he slipped down the mud bank. The rain had screened the moon, and the pale drowned images of lights on the quai behind us shivered in the inky flowing ridges bordering the stream.

"See, we don't really have a permit to put our barge here," said Dwight, a wispy albino spook at my elbow. "We couldn't front the bread for it. So we can't let anybody find out we're here. We hid it under the bridge."

"You mean you're illegally parked?" I said. "With no lights? What if another boat hits you?"

"Allez, Kerry, onward to the barge," said Dee, brisk and dauntless, the intrepid Britisher, bearing the Union Jack and a tin of pudding into the trackless wilds. She set her platform shoes firmly into the thick, resilient goo, and vanished downward, accompanied by a rhythmic sucking and releasing thwomp! at every step, as if she were being gummed to death by an octogenarian whale. Dwight guided me, never shifting his vapid gaze from my face.

"I wish you'd look where you're going," I said. "And where's Duse? She's likely to fall in the water and sink without a murmur."

"No, she went first. The Captain has to follow her. She's sort of like his divining rod, you know—she's the only one who can find the boat in the dark."

Dwight was listing to the left, downhill, beneath the weight of his lumpy bag, and the guitar tucked under his left arm kept slipping past his shelfless hip. He had to keep trying to stop in the middle of a mudslide, to realign. Since his right hand seemed to be welded to my arm, I had to stop when he did. When his own brakes failed, Dwight made me his emergency, casting the combined weights of his gangly, odoriferous body, his Santa Claus bag and his dangling guitar on my meager arm. Each time, I almost pitched over into the mud. The whole grotesque, precipitous struggle reminded me of a spring rite at college known as the Sigma Chi Mud Tug, in which teams of brawny or dainty Greeks played tug-of-war in a swine wallow. "Leggo," I kept telling Dwight. But he needed me for ballast.

Each slithering spurt of descent brought us further under the enamel-black shadow of the bridge. As the slope eased into a horizontal flat, and the sound of the water, glancing on the banks and dancing under the boats, drew near, Dwight ceased his ball-and-chain drag on my arm. "Now we go single file," he said, "there are planks. Somewhere. This is where I always get lost. Grrrooo!" He sent out a call, half growl, half coo. The call was returned from a spot vaguely left. He wandered toward it, cooing and growling. The river resounded with the mating calls of sado-masochistic doves. I clung to Dwight's jacket, fearing in the blackness on all sides the aching of a ravenous abyss. There were no shapes that I could discern, no sense of space as distinguished from mass. I could see Dwight, not even as a denser, darker form. We were under the bridge, where night gathered, hooded from any light.

"Oh, here's the plank. Okay, follow me," said Dwight—as if I were about to strike out on my own. I found the board and placed one foot toe-to-heal with the other, like a child walking a crack in the sidewalk. If I'd let go of Dwight's jacket, I would have been utterly lost in the dark. I could tell the direction of the water by the spray. But I didn't know how close the river was till I stumbled and stepped off the board into ankle-deep water. I gasped. The shocking cold shot up my spine. My foot went numb. I groped for the board and found it. I swayed. The board swayed, and Dwight swayed.

"Gee, watch out," said Dwight. "This board turns into the gangplank, but it doesn't get much wider. If you step off then, the water's pretty deep. It'd be hard to find you."

If Dee hadn't gone before, I would have taken my

chances backing up, without the dubious support of dippy Dwight. But Dee's voice, quite close, belled out, "Steady ahoy, Kerry! Welcome aboard!"

"Aboard where?" I said.

"Sshhh! Keep your voices down," the Captain hissed.

The jacket I was clutching was wrenched away. I grabbed at dank, wide air. For an instant I was propped, rocking, on one board in the cold yawn of a void. Then hands seized my arms and pulled me forward. My boot brushed the rough wood ridge that bordered the barge and found footing. I was on board.

"Why in hell are you parked halfway out on the river?" I said to the Captain, whose face, a triangle of fragments not blackened by beard, hovered by my cheek like a wind-ripped cloud about to cross the moon. To my right, Dee's splendid teeth gleamed in a disembodied Chiclet grin. I said, "I thought the whole point of a barge was that it was flat, so you could park it on shore!"

Arms tugged me across the boards. We halted every other step to dodge some trap: a coil of rope; a raised square hatch; a pail of tools; the drifting form of the wraithlike Duse, the phantom of the barge.

"Cops patrol the shore, looking for illegal boats," said the Captain. "We have to stay out in the mainstream and run out a plank for access. They'll never find us."

"As long as our karma is good," said Dwight.

My ears pricked up: karma! I thought karma had gone the way of contact-paper daisies. I hoped we weren't in for ginseng tea and I Ching casting. I muttered to Dee, "If they ask us what our mantras are, let's swim for it."

The Captain thrust aside a burlap bag nailed above the entrance to an unlit cabin. Striking a match and plunging ahead, Dwight was transformed to a hunchback as he entered. Filing in, we attempted to stand without pressing into each other. When Duse had entered, cradling D'Annunzio, the feeble-minded chicken, there wasn't enough residual space for a turtle to pass among us, or enough good air to make the turtle's journey healthy. Dwight's second match went out, probably for lack of oxygen. The atmosphere was suffocating. We might have been trapped for the fortieth day in the cat house at the zoo.

"Can you open a window?" I said. "Quick?"

"Here, let's sit out on the deck, shall we?" said Dee.

"Too noisy," said the Captain, "might attract attention. If we don't put the lamp on, we can uncover the windows."

"How will we make the tea without a lamp?" said Dwight.

"I'd quite enjoy a cup of tea," said Dee, nudging me. Sportsmanship was on the ebb. Already we were eager for the slaughter. If Dwight tried to make tea in the dark, either he'd set fire to the curtains, or we'd be here till Tuesday while he scrambled in the muck. But sabotage would be suicide; we were captive hostiles. And we'd never make it up the slope in the dark without Duse and her seeing-eye chicken.

"We can't make tea with no light," said Dwight, adhering to the bit between his teeth. He had assumed the role of solicitous host, as if he had a tray of hors d'oeuvres in the oven, if there'd been an oven. Duse was sending and receiving with her chicken. She wasn't likely to take our coats or run to fetch ashtrays, if there'd been ashtrays. Dwight lit another match.

"Duse doesn't need light to make tea," said the Captain, pulling up the burlap rags masking three hewn-out windows, and tucking the tail of each curtain into the gap between nails at the top. Household arrangements were rustic. Burlap was the motif. At last the Captain allowed us a plumber's candle stuck in an anchovy tin. The Captain set the tin on the floor of the cabin. The four of us sat around the flame like a family in a storm cellar sitting out a cyclone.

Duse was busy with the tea preparations in a mercifully murky corner. Her hair was still bound in the splattered bandage, and she wore her basic conglomerate costume, topped by layers of lumpy sweaters. She looked like a wounded goalie. The chicken was perched on her padded shoulder. He hunched like a vulture, with cold. In the weak light, they cast a doomful shadow on the cabin wall as Duse fed tinder and paper into the jaws of the stove.

It was hard to believe that anyone could live in that floating lean-to. The cabin was smaller than the Faurers' kitchen, and as bare as the Faurers' icebox. There were no built-in bunks or shelves, no breakfast nook, no nailed-down crates, not even a ratty mattress. In one corner were heaped some sour-smelling blankets; in another, the prop bags and instruments with which the gorillas earned their marginal keep. The stove was crippled in one leg, the stump supported by an overturned No. 10 can. The iron of its porky body had rusted away to holes which were patched with punched and twisted tin foil plates. The stove's corner was banked with tinder, newspapers, greasy rags. The place was a fire marshal's nightmare. Only the dampness prevented the craft from exploding in flames.

It was so cold that I was plastered against Dwight, clinging to his bony and comfortless arm. The head cold which I'd been doctoring with Mouse's pills and suppositories ever since the first week of au pairdom had blossomed. I had to keep wiping my nose on my shoulder, which was beginning to look like D'Annunzio's perch. And I was hungry. I would have killed for a box of those tough little caramels in the Métro's vending machines. There wouldn't be eats at this bash, picking out the hamburger and making patties, assuming the abused meat was still good for packing. The tea, at least, I hoped, would be boiled. I needed a heat transfusion.

Dee, as usual, didn't mind the cryptlike chill. She was engaged in a verbal joust with the Captain, who was expatiating on the subject of England for a change. He had just mentioned, in one sentence, croquet, pukka sahib, Suez, and boiled spuds.

"You're living in the past, aren't you?" said Dee. "As to India, I don't see we did them harm in the long run. We did get them reading and writing, didn't we? Before the British gave them a hand, they were squatting in the gutters and eating out of leaves."

"England thinks like Amerika," said the Captain, with the contemptuous intonation that imports Amerika spelled with a "k". "The same capitalist-imperialist-bossist mentality. India was your Viet Nam. You tried to impose a corrupt, dying system on a pure peasant culture, a genetically, culturally, religiously, politically heterogeneous population. You forced them to set up a phony Parliament to worship the white bitch goddess—"

"Here, keep a civil tongue about the Queen," said Dee. "She's not much use in the practical sense, but she does represent the British people. She has more admirers in India than that woman who's running the show right now! Calls herself Ghandi, my Christ! but she's chaining her relations up all the same."

"That's a typical imperialist ploy, blaming the natives for the evils they acquired from your invaders. The American Indians didn't know what syphilis was till the British colonists arrived on Plymouth Rock with their flies unzipped."

"What rot! Perhaps that's the custom on American ships —we shall have to watch out for ourselves, Kerry—but the British fleet would hardly have become the greatest navy in the history of western civilization if the British seaman went about—"

"England hasn't had a decent navy since the thirteen colonies told the mother country where to shove it," the Captain said.

"No taxation without representation," I said.

"No kiddin'," said Dwight.

Dee glared at us. I grinned.

"Look here, Kerry, you can't go along with this blather. I mean say what you will, there are some standards of decency in Britain. Not to put too fine a point on it, we haven't had to throw out all our government and start over, like America did not long ago. You wouldn't find Britons content to let a blighter like Nixon go scot free on a lifetime dole! Churchill's widow only gets eight pound a week as pension and wouldn't take more! A British citizen pays his own way!"

The Captain's face was empurpled with wrath. In a political boxing match, Nixon was a rabbit punch.

"Score one, up the British," I said.

"Far out," said Dwight. His eyeballs rested wetly on my face. It was like being passionately besought by a large, smelly dog, whose cold nose and sloppy tongue hovered within contact range of my nose. I was afraid to look to the right. Despite the cold, I detached myself from Dwight's arm. I didn't want to encourage the fantasies ambling in the wide open spaces of his brain.

Since he was losing the argument, the Captain changed the subject. He noted the romantic overtones of Dwight's concentration on my nose. Subtlety was not Dwight's weapon in pursuit; at any moment, he'd be humping my ankle.

"Another conquest, eh?" the Captain leered at me. "How was Victor Hugo's house?"

The nausea that rose in my throat was partly caused by cold, fatigue, fetid air, and swallowed mucus. But it was also a manifestation of certainty: Dan was a rat. With one phrase, the Captain had stripped me of my warmest memory of Paris.

"I wouldn't have figured Dan was a men's room confidant," I said.

"Oh, no fear. He didn't *tell* me anything. I haven't seen him since he gave you the three steps of decency. I just know Spencer's pattern. Step 2 is generally Victor Hugo's house. Why vary a sure-fire technique?"

I was so relieved I almost hugged Dwight, which would have been a grievous error. I didn't even mind being Notch 306 on the folksy Casanova's sword, as long as he hadn't told the other fellas the details of Step 3. I'd hate to have the Captain know the color of my underwear, or what I muttered in unguarded moments. I said, "You mean you didn't even know he went to Spain?"

"Here, who's this chap you keep rattling on about?" said Dee.

"Just some bloke I met when I first came to Paris. No big deal," I said.

As if on cue, Dwight stuck his finger in my ear.

No one had ever played with my inner ear before. Maybe a master of the art of foreplay could have made me like it. But Dwight was such a wet smack in every way that his finger just made me cranky. I was also afraid of infection, having seen his fingers in strong light. But then my ear wasn't clean. I hadn't puzzled out where Mouse hid the Q-tips.

"Quit that," I said.

Dwight retreated to spaniel distance.

The Captain said, "Hell no, we didn't know Dan was in Spain—"

"Duse knew," said Dwight.

"We just found out when he wrote for money. Claimed he'd lent me some absurd sum—"

"Yeah, but you really borrowed more than that. Really," Dwight said mildly.

"He wanted me to send it to him care of American Express, Madrid! American Express! 'Madrid by Night'!"

Duse was distributing tea. She wafted around our tribal circle, handing out tin cans of a tepid liquid that smelled like the dishwater left in the sink after cleaning pots for a Thanksgiving dinner. Dee demonstrated the courtesy and courage that had been the foundation of the British Empire ascendant, by tasting hers first.

"Tastes a bit like beans," she said. "What sort of tea is this?"

"Duse makes it special," said Dwight, nurturing his can of tea, as if it were warm, against his concave chest.

"That's all we need to know," I said. I held my can, averting my eyes from the scum around the rim.

"Herbs," Duse barked into my neck. She was sitting behind me, having lit without my notice. She sat in the lotus position. The chicken roosted on his mistress's checkered wool ankles. Duse held her can of tea—still blotched with a partly peeled label, a picture of an animated pear—in a ceremonial attitude, elbows akimbo.

Dee leaned over and whispered, "What are these little floating specks, d'you reckon?"

"Fleas," I whispered. " 'Ours not to reason why.' "

"That's all very well, but do you know the rest of that quotation?" 'Ours not to reason why! Ours but to do and die! Into the Valley of Death rode the six hundred!' . . . *The Charge of the Light Brigade.*"

"Cheers," I said.

My tea tasted a little like aspirin and a lot like Franco-American spaghetti. I got half of it down. Luckily, my sense of smell had faded, thanks to the accumulating blockage in my nasal passages. Dee won the White Man's Burden Award by polishing off a whole mug.

"Hate to drink and run," I said, "but since we have to grope our way out, we better get started."

The Captain assured us that we were welcome to sleep on the barge and go home in daylight. But we said that our French families would be in a formidable swivet if we didn't get back tonight. Our hosts were broken-hearted. Wouldn't we like to hear Duse sing another song? "Does she take requests?" I said. We looked at Duse. She had trailed her muse into the transcendental wilderness behind her jungle eyes. She wasn't even capable of speaking, unless in tongues. She looked so Delphic, I was tempted to ask her my future: "How long will I be stuck in Paris?" But I didn't want to know.

"Don't think she's in the mood," said Dee.

"I could do some magic tricks," said Dwight, perking up. "I used to do 'em at parties. . . ." His voice tottered off down Memory Lane. Parties were jewels of the dear dead past. The barge was not awash with invitations.

"It's sort of dark for magic tricks," I said. "We wouldn't really get the effect."

"Oh, they work better that way. You can't see my mistakes," said Dwight. ". . . Sometimes I get confused. . . ."

"Next time, perhaps," said Dee. I squeezed her foot. She said, "Right, sorry."

In a last gasp of hospitality, the Captain offered to demonstrate the intricate knots he'd learned to tie in his two years before the mast in the Merchant Marine.

"What sort of ship did you sail?" said Dee.

"A tanker," said Dwight. The Captain harpooned him with his eyes. "But there was nothin' else to do," Dwight continued blithely, "so the Captain got into rope."

"Rope and dope," the Captain smirked.

If we were into marijuana jokes, it was time to go home. The next phase would be Spin the Bottle. "I think we'll pass up the rope tricks," I said. I didn't care for the notion of knots when the menfolks were so desperate for the company of ladies. Duse, the female head-of-household, was as sexually effervescent as a masthead. Dee and I weren't spurning Hollywood offers, but at least we smelled like soap, and talked.

"Thanks for everything," I said, "but we have to go. Madame'll call the cops if I'm not in by midnight."

"What're you on about?" said Dee. "You've told me she hardly knows what day it is— Sorry."

Dwight turned his doggy eyes upon me and almost whimpered. I wanted to tell him, "Stay!" Duse and the Captain prepared to lead the return expedition. As a pledge of our good faith, we had to write down the telephone numbers at the Faurers' and the Comte's. There was some consolation in knowing that the three gorillas, far from having a ship-to-shore hookup, didn't even have the coins to use a pay phone.

We lined up to walk the plank. "If I don't make it out," I said to Dee, "you can have my mohair kneesocks."

As Dwight attempted to tip me into the Seine, I could hear Dee politely saying, "You must come round to the flat some time." If I could have found her in the dark, I would have strangled her.

The route back to the world was easier to cherche than

the route to the floating hovel. As soon as we emerged from the blind hole of the bridge, we could see the lights of the quai. But our hosts insisted on walking us to the Métro entrance. I had to peel Dwight from my arm.

"Maybe you and me could go out some time," he offered doubtfully.

"Stranger things have happened since I've been in Paris," I said.

Then we ran for it.

"Well? Was that better than sitting around the salon, eating cheese?" I said as the desolate tunnel of the station received us.

Dee considered. "What sort of cheese?"

"I'd rather eat warm Velveeta."

"D'you know, I believe they hadn't any plates."

"Probably eat from leaves, like they do in India."

"Oh, you may laugh. But I'll tell you frankly, we wouldn't stand for that in England."

Shoveling against the Tide

The sky was disgorging its customary dribble as I bundled Anouk and Leah in their sortie regalia—it was Wednesday, one of Leah's half days off from school—and trucked them to the park. In the absence of a monsoon, Madame believed that les enfantes would benefit, as she would, by their being aired. Dee's Madame Danièlle had the same fixation. We'd agreed to rendezvous at the "sable," a circular pit of sand.

On most afternoons, the sand pit was overrun with enfantes in overalls, butting scooters into castles, shoveling sand into little tin buckets and dumping it in each other's hair, filing primly up the ladder of a slide and chuting gaily down. The benches were lined with au pairs, jiggling the sweeping chrome handles of the navy vessels of their youngest charges; knitting; reading; chattering in French, Spanish, German, Swedish, English; and pausing de temps à temps to cry, "Alexandre! Non non non! Ça suffit!"—Knock it off!—"Viens ici, maintenant!" One by one, nannies languidly ushered the toddlers to the cottage where a fig-faced woman in gardening gloves sold boxes of caramels, and hot waffles, gummy with powdered sugar.

But today, the sand was a moldy, deep brown, like leaves on a forest floor. Nannies, preceded by buggies and trailed by stiff woolen dolls of children, moved in lazy eight-shaped paths among the barren hedges.

"Is this your lot?" said Dee, gazing with interest at Leah and Anouk. Leah stood like a cardboard cut-out, watching the boys on the soccer field beyond the bars of trees as they flailed with their raw knees at the white ball. Dee said, "Does your Madame always get her up in frills like that?"

"Always. And always white. Every day's a nuptial day at our house."

Dee's charge, Elise, was dressed for the sand pit in over-alls, a shabby jacket, and a hat with earflaps. Her button nose and nubby cheeks were red. She toddled over to Leah, pushing her bright little face up to Leah's statuary mask. " 'jour!" said Elise.

Leah backed off a step, almost losing her balance. Her huge chocolate-centered eyes were apprehensive. "Dites 'Bonjour,' " I said. But she didn't speak. She stared at Elise.

"She's a spooky one, isn't she?" said Dee. "What say we give them a go on the carousel? That'll bring her round." She chortled. "Gooo-d, I'm a flippin' comic!"

We crossed the paved avenue, bound off from traffic, where children on roller skates were hurtling, ankles sling-ing, wheels ringing rhythms on the damp cement. Anouk sat erect among the pillows, assessing the leafless branches passing over her head.

"Hallo there," said Dee, giving the baby a tickle. Anouk dropped her gaze to Dee's face, and allowed it to remain there. "My Christ, she's spooky too," said Dee.

I felt like my dog had bitten my date. "No, she's great, once you get to know her," I said. To show Anouk's fun-loving side, I sang, "Anouky, my coo-kie!" which always made her laugh. She gave me a gaze so austere that it singed my eyelashes.

"Well, you have my sympathy, Kerry," said Dee.

We arrived at the fenced-in patch where the carousel churned up mud. An old woman in a stocking hat took our money. In the shadow of the roof, Dee hoisted Elise to the once-red saddle of a once-black steed, I heaved the dead weight of Leah onto a peeling blue-white pony. The old woman strapped them on. She placed a wooden stick in Leah's stiff, gloved fingers, and another in Elise's mitten. "Tiens!" said the old woman: hold this.

"What's the stick for?" I said.

"Don't you have the brass ring in America?" said Dee.

"Only as a metaphor," I said.

There were two other children on the carousel, both insulated in layers and scarves till they were almost inert. One, like Elise and Leah, was strapped on a pony. The other was a solitary egg in the basket of a coach resplen-dent with blistered carvings, with rococo decay. The child in the coach wasn't wielding a stick: no dreams for the carriage trade.

The old woman grasped a post of the carousel and leaned her weight on it. The wooden tent shuddered, and slipped to the right. The gears of the music box in the center began to wheeze, as if speaking for the faded horses. As the old woman pushed and walked, the creaky little carousel picked up speed. She gave it a final heave and let it go. The platform circled freely, sailing of its own accord. It tilted and tootled and moaned. The music was a hurdy-gurdy tune, as familiar and anonymous as cotton candy. Elise and the two enwrapped strangers creaked upward and downward, around and around, soaring toward the brass rings shining in the eaves, plummeting just as their batons tipped the bright perimeters in the gusty air. A mink-encased maman clung to the gate behind us, shouting "Allez, Christian!" at the little mummy on the pony, who was assailing the bras rings so vigorously that he would have landed on his noggin if he hadn't been battened down. Not to be outdone on the field, Dee yelled, "Allez, Elise! Prenez le . . . how d'you say 'brass ring' d'you reckon?"

I shook my head. I was watching Leah. She held the baton out gingerly, uncertain of its purpose.

"Ça!" hooted Elise, stabbing her stick at the air two feet from the brass ring. "Ça! Ça! Regarde," she commanded Leah, demonstrating her fruitless thrusts with bold élan, as if she were shadow-boxing. She turned her merry face to us and cried, "Doughy! Regarde! Ça!" She made a curlicue in the empty air with her ambitious stick.

"Bon, Elise! Bravo! Allez! Give her credit for spirit," said Dee. "Yours hasn't got the hang of it, has she?"

But Leah was watching Elise, and holding her awkward baton out toward the rings. I found myself calling, "Allez, Leah!" Leah turned her solemn little face toward me and gave me a stilted smile. She sat straighter on her shadow mount, like a princess riding side-saddle. She speared with her stick at the air. With each ascending curve of the wooden horse, Leah's baton dived closer to the brass ring. On the last groaning circle of the carousel's journey, she snared it.

"Bravo!" I yelled. "Bravo, Leah!"

Leah smiled with all her teeth, in a paler rendition of her Père Noël smile. The grownups were pleased. She'd done right.

Christian, the rich mummy's mummy, also speared a circlet.

"Make it easy for them, don't they? That's the French for you," said Dee.

"What happens now?" I said. "What's the prize?"

"Damn-all, that's what. Rien du tout."

"Then what's the point?"

"Precisely. Now in England, it's quite tricky to catch the brass ring, but if you manage, they let you go around for free. However, small chance of getting anything gratis in Paris."

We paid for another round. Anouk complained. I turned her coach around so she could watch the ponies, racing in circles to a rickety-tickety tune. On the second voyage, Leah speared another ring. "Bravo," I called, and she waved it. But the thrill of the conquest had dimmed.

"Maybe that's why they're all crazy," I said.

"Don't follow you, Kerry," said Dee.

"What they do to them when they're kids! Get them excited about the brass ring, make sure they get one without a struggle—and then tell them it's worthless!"

To recompense Anouk for her stint in the bleachers, we strolled down to the muddy path that ran along the closed road for skaters. We had to tread lightly in the muck, which was landscaped with the tracks of ponies and their redolent deposits. Leah and Elise held hands and trotted, leading our small parade. They were an unlikely pair: Leah in her fake fur coat and phosphorescent boots; Elise in her cords and earflaps. As we rolled along the brown track, Leah turned her head and smiled at me, as if to say, "Look, I have a friend."

"You know, I could like her if she'd let me," I said.

"She's a queer, stiff little thing," said Dee.

"Only in public. At home, she's a madwoman. 'Je voudrais this, je voudrais that—' "

"Oh, well, in the ordinary way, Elise would be belting off all over the park. She's like a puppy, I don't know where she's got to half the time. Miles ahead of me, miles behind—then someone reckons she's lost and makes off with her, and I've got to chase them—"

"Leah's going to need about ten years of therapy before she'll be a decent human being," I said. "And Anouk'll be nuts too, in a couple of years. That's what kills me. Yesterday, Madame and I were playing peek-a-boo with Anouk, and she'd come to me before she'd come to her mother. Madame made little jokes about it, trying to pretend she didn't care. But Anouk must think *I'm* her mother by now. How will she feel when *I* desert her? and she gets a new mother? and another one six months after that? Madame told me Leah's had five au pairs in less than four years! No wonder she acts like a skin graft when her mother's around. She's afraid to let her mother leave the room, for fear she'll never come back!"

"You mustn't get emotional about it, you see. Otherwise you'll end up promising to stay for a year. They suck you in, don't they? After all they're not our children."

"I get so depressed."

"Well, it's a wonder we're not certifiable, shut up all day with these buggers."

We moved our troops into the hedges to allow the pony man and his shambling pair to pass. The ponies humped and bumped along, their bellies drooping from their ribs like depleted concertinas. The mounted children shrouded in hoods were pinchfaced and dejected. They lurched, passive, wretched. Seeing us, they assumed expressions of diehard pleasure: they were having a real live pony ride! The guide was an old man in a worn coat, the collar pulled up around his grey-tufted ears, and a hat with a limp brim. His face was chalky with stubble, except for the pink, flaccid sockets of his angry eyes.

"Doesn't care much for his work, does he?" said Dee.

Back à la ranch, Leah burbled through her bath and dinner, which she ate with minimal complaint, about the petit baton and the petit truc she'd captured, and her petite amie. Madame was stunned at this transformation, and further impressed by the news that my amie anglaise worked for the Comte. Marc and Danièlle were unimpeachably "in" among the cliques of the Seizième. Leah's little playmate was a find. Perhaps, suggested Mouse, I might invite the petite amie and her keeper to tea? "Très bien," I said.

Mouse went all out for the tea party, setting the kitchen table with unstained napkins and uncracked plates. Leah and Elise got the only chairs; Dee took the stool, and I stood. We had croissants and Coca-Cola. After twenty minutes, the floor beneath the chairs was a sea of pastry flakes. The sight of a quart of Coke nearly doubled me up with nostalgia. "Drink a lot of this stuff in America, I should imagine," said Dee. "Shocking what it does to your teeth."

Mouse adored Elise. "Comme elle est mignonne!" she kept exclaiming: isn't she cute! Too bad kids weren't baseball cards; she could have made a trade. She marveled at how tranquilly Elise and Leah played together. Dee was also impressed with Leah's company manners. In a voice which undoubtedly carried to Madame, who had retired to her room, she said, "Don't know what you're on about, calling that sweet child a turd. I should think you ought to have a medal struck—'Leah, For Good Conduct.'"

"You've just seen her Dr. Jekyll side," I whispered. "Two seconds after you guys are gone, she'll turn into Mr. Hyde."

But Leah was so winning, so gentle, when she played with Elise. I almost could believe there was hope for her to develop into a person. When Dee had hauled Elise and her earflaps off to the elevator, Leah stood at the window in the salon, waiting to wave as Elise emerged below. Seeing her, pale and small in the twilight, still with expectation, I felt a surge of affection for Leah, or for the child I would have liked Leah to be. I stood behind her, and rested my hand on her downy hair.

"Ai-ee! Non!" she cried, jerking her head away and slapping at my hand. "Pas vous!": not you.

She ran to her mother. I took Anouk into my room and played with her till dinner. Anouk's fingers clung to mine as I bounced her fat bottom on my knees. I sang softly: "Trot trot to London, trot trot to Lynn; careful when you get there you don't fall in. . . ."

If I quit, it would be because of Leah. She was a child, so I kept trying to love her. She wouldn't allow it.

La vie au pair was bearable with Dee to share the angst. We faired an excursion whenever we got the chance. We'd discovered a pub called the Red Boar, which had been reconstructed in the Champs Élysées, like London Bridge in the American desert. From the outside, the Red Boar looked like the pubs in movies: a wooden signboard; a heavy door with frosted windows; the name WHITEBREAD'S printed on a band of black wood that hemmed the gabled roof. But inside, the glossy, walnut-colored paneling was plastic, and the milk glass globes of the lamps had gilt tin bases. The tables and red-plush-cushioned chairs were made of simulated wood, wrought in molds to look carved.

"Still, it's a taste of home," said Dee, as we tried to lean our elbows on a table without tipping it over. But she was disgusted when the French bartender said he couldn't make a shandy. "Call this a pub! Next you'll be saying you can't make gin-and-orange!"

The patrons were mostly disenchanted nannies and Irish rugby players, which gave the pub an atmosphere half of a scrimmage and half of a tea party. The rugby team had crossed the channel—probably in an open boat—in response to a challenge from a Parisian team. The French had been deservedly creamed, and the Irish were celebrating by "drinking their eyes out" and demonstrating for the nannies how they had "murthered the frogs." They kept asking the nannies to dance, and failing that, assaulting their teammates. Conversation was slight, partly because of the volume of the immutable stream of disco music. Even the rugby players had to bawl to be heard.

The nannies were all in a funk, as if they were out in the park on a wet day. They drank gallons of watery beer, without ever leaving to pee. From time to time, one would inquire, "Gotten a packet from your mum yet, Bess?" Bess would answer, "Sent me some cigs. Me brother's lost 'is kip." The nannies around the table—they cruised in teams as large and tightly knit as the rugby brotherhood—would cluck, and hoist another jar.

I had an unmagical encounter with a Cockney who wanted to know my views on the American ban of the British-made Concorde. I said I didn't have any views. "They claim it's noise pollution, but your government's afraid of British competition," he said, leaning over the table with the air of a jouster whose lance has struck home. Once I'd failed to parry, he offered to take me to the cinema. Nodding at Dee, who was arguing with the bartender, he said, "Ask your chum how she likes the smell o' me mate—the ginger-haired fella."

I related this to Dee. "I don't fancy *him*," she said. "I mean, frankly, Kerry, that's what I came over here to get away from."

The evening ended abruptly, when a bloke with a face like a brick and the athletic grace of a dump truck sat on Dee's lap and tried to thrust his hand up her skirt. "Sod off!" Dee shouted, belting the bloke on the side of the head with her purse. In the ensuing unpleasantness, the management was summoned, the nannies took Dee's part, the rugby team played a match with the effete French bouncer, and we made our exit just as the cops arrived in a Keystone clamor, with a wagon to cart off the feisty Celts to the lock-up.

Poor Dee had terrible luck. On the way home, in one of the connecting tunnels of the Métro, an Algerian tried to steal her purse. He yanked it. She yanked it back, and thumped him on the chest. He slapped her across the face and fled. "Bloody cheek!" she said.

Most of the time, Dee was "stuck in the flat with bloody Elise." Four nights out of seven, I slumped on my spine in the Comte's conversation pit, imbibing the Comte's vin ordinaire, harking to the plaint of the Comte's au pair. Dee and I were perfecting the technique of mutual condolence.

Paris in winter was overrun with people to feel sorry for. Apart from the Faurers, whom I pitied collectively and separately, and the Spanish maid and her family, and Dee, and me, the parks in the Seizième were hopping with children who didn't know their mothers or like their attendants. The streets and shops of Passy tapped and twittered with mothers who'd given their children away. Outside of the rich, condensed little neighborhood, men with bruised faces and chapped hands slept in doorways, and skinny whores in miniskirts stood on the boulevard at noon, staring with eyes like jagged tin.

Train tracks bound off the park and the graceful wooded streets where the Faurers and Dee's Comte lived, secluded from commerce: a land of tranquil trees and extraneous servants and sated infants in ponderous carriages. A tunnel stretched beneath the tracks to streets of shops and cafés and the Ranelagh Métro line, chuffing toward the outside world, the world not shined and buffed with money. If I were walking to visit Dee, or to have an overpriced espresso in a chic café, I cut across the park, drilling my eyes down into the sidewalk for fear of lonely figures in the shadows. But if I wanted to explore another of the multitudinous versions of Paris, I entered the tunnel and crossed beneath the tracks. I emerged in a street. Already gabled houses and boxed cafés seemed more clearly drawn on the screen of mist.

As if to signify that raw life would pounce as I escaped the passageway, a beggar had taken up residence in the tunnel. The creature was female. She was a remnant, a harridan out of Lautrec. Her hair, which announced itself in torturous wisps, was the dimestore gold of paper stars. Her skin was colorless, as if the effort of maintaining life had drained her body of any semblance of it. Inside the sack of flesh, her organs must be dried, like fruits, withered, light and hard.

The sight of her—a woman reduced to a passive, whining thing, scratching a dreadful existence from the barren soil of French compassion—filled me with horror which increased each time I had to pass her. She wasn't always there. Often after I'd braced myself to block her out, her spot by the freezing, damp-patched, concrete wall was empty. But her presence pervaded the tunnel even when she was gone. She was the reminder of the terror of want that gnawed at the underbelly of comfort, of security, of money and form. Madame, shopping for fruit and cheese in Ranelagh instead of in Passy, would have had to pass the beggar. Were those the days she came back with such niggling parcels in her basket that the Spanish maid, observing, poked me with the vacuum cleaner hose?

Madame and I could talk a little now. In the tedious twilight that held the city in its February thrall, we sat in the kitchen discussing les enfantes. At our feet, Anouk played with the half shells for Coquilles St. Jacques. Mouse was worried about sibling rivalry. She'd noticed that Leah yearned to flush Anouk down the toilet like a Tinker Toy. She was lenient with Leah, Mouse explained, to show her that Maman loved her just as much as the baby.

What's the French for, "Don't throw Anouk out with the bath water?" I said, lentement, "But if you make life too easy for Leah now . . . it will be difficult for her . . . in the real world." The Old Philosopher, stitching the phrases together . . .

Mouse smiled and nodded. She'd missed the point. She took my simple sentences and hung them with the complexities of her own ideas, not mine. I could talk. But I couldn't make myself heard.

It was easier to talk to Emparo, the Spanish maid. Like me, she was only semiverbal in French. Our subject never varied. We plodded along in the present tense of grievance, peasants paired behind a plow, never casting an eye toward the farther furrows. Emparo was married and had an infant son. Her husband was a construction worker. They lived with Emparo's mother, a maid, and her father, a construction worker, and a shifting mélange of relations, in a housing project outside of Paris. The tenement was teeming with Spanish domestics and laborers. Emparo called it "une petite Espagne": Little Spain. I got the impression that on Sundays there were bullfights in the courtyard. Even on the cheesy wages that the French squeezed out for foreigners, Spaniards earned double what they could in Spain. But Emparo and her countrymen could hardly wait to go home. They socked away every centime that they didn't send back to the branches of the family who weren't already sleeping on their Paris bathroom floors. They went home for feastdays and holidays, jamming the third-class compartments of trains.

Emparo hated Paris. The French, she gave me to understand, were the stingiest people on earth. Worse, with all their money, they didn't know how to have a good time! They went to bed at ten o'clock! They never ate! (She grappled with a narrow half-loaf of bread, wrenched off a hunk and gnawed it, tossing the remnant on the counter.) Call that bread! In Spain, when you made bread (spraddling her fingers as if about to pass a basketball) you made a loaf! And when you ate (somersaulting arms) you ate! In Spain, families helped each other. Here— (She aimed a backhand swat at the door, with a contempt which I took to include Monsieur's omnipresent, piss-elegant mother and sister, and Madame's almost mythical family in Lyon.) In Spain (she shrugged) nobody had a peseta. But they sure as hell (arms outflung) had fun! And as for the way the French brought up their children—! (She blew out her cheeks; her eyebrows leaped; her head waggled; she groaned.)

We grinned in complete accord, and had a glass of wine on it.

Dear Mom and Dad,
I'm fed up with this sodding cold! In France they say
every cold lasts eight days, but I've been enrhumé
tous le temps since I got here! Of course it's always
bloody "pig time" lately—that's lousy weather, "temps
de cochons!" Aussi, the lift is kaput. Il faut haul the
little buggers up four flights of stairs. The only bonne
chose is I get to use one of the only phrases I kept
from high school français—"L'ascenseur ne marche
pas." "The elevator doesn't work." Quel thrill!

I was smoking along through the French grammar book.
I was up to Leçon 24, "La Salle de Bain." I could name
the features of my face, and the items on the breakfast
table pictured in the book—items which did not include
burned bread and scalded milk. I could tell time. I could
spell "pyjama" like they did in Paree. I could say "bird-
cage" and "dog." I was learning the future tense, which
had implications, in view of my present prospects, that I
didn't care to ponder.

Each day I mounted the ladder of decreed routine, and
slid down the greased chute of a stupefying evening into
the brick wall of dawn. Anouk's wail fueled my choo-choo
shuffle to the kitchen to plop her breakfast bottle in the
pan. After the antipasto of lunch, I toddled off with my
dictionnaire and half a pound of Kleenex to a local café. A
franc in the bank was a step toward the exit. Spurning the
Métro, I studied in cafés I could walk to. When I felt devil-
may-care, or my nose was running too briskly for hiking, I
hung out on a café smack in the middle of Passy four
blocks from home. I almost hoped that Mouse, on one of
her rare promenades to the vegetable stalls, would drop in
for café au lait and find me playing le hookey. As at Occidental Insurance, I was scraping together an escape fund.
But on the pittance Madame begrudged me—the raise she'd
promised "if I am please' of you" had never appeared—I'd
be putting money in a stocking till I wore support hose. As
at Occidental, I prayed to be fired.

Then, like a note from the governor on execution morning, an envelope came from my father containing my income tax return. Computing my coder's wages versus the
weekly extractions made by Uncle Sam, my father alleged
that the government owed me $231.21! ! ! I seized Anouk

and taught her to polka. The date was February 28. If the
IRS didn't diddle with my file, I could shake the mush of
Paris from my boots by May, with enough swag to launch
Son of Whirlwind Tour. I was a certified miser; I could
last months on $231.21. And this time I would do it right
—alone!

I signed my name and sent the paper off in the afternoon
post.

Then I went into a walking decline. The barrier of two
more months—sixty-one days of digging my fingernails into
my thighs to keep from shoving Leah down the ascenseur
shaft—was more than faith could overcome.

On one of my lowest days, I wrote to Dan.

Ever since the night we'd had tea on the barge, I'd been
running the newsreel of Dan, stepping up to the counter
at American Express, Madrid, to claim his mail. On one of
my free days, I'd made a sentimental journey to the Place
des Vosges. The shutters of the houses were chipped ochre
in the daylight, and the bunched arms of the trees were
mottled grey. Inside Victor Hugo's house, the French had
carefully preserved a plaster cast of Victor's arm and hand;
death masks and deathbed photos; two pictures of his
eldest daughter on the occasion of her First Communion;
and an entire room transported from the country home
which Victor had built for his mistress, who must have
been a mandarin—the room was red lacquer, with dragons.
It looked like a restaurant in Cleveland called the Yangtze
Palace. The weirdest decorations were sketches and paintings done by Victor: manor houses, ships in tossing seas,
and wind-torn landscapes all overcast with VICTOR
HUGO in letters of fire. There must have been forty of
these monomaniacal renderings. Was "hugo" French for
"ego"?

I bought a postcard of the plaster cast of Victor's arm.
After keeping it on my dresser for a month, I wrote on it:

Guess who's still in Paris! How's Spain? Has the tour
bus found you yet? This is a picture of Victor Hugo's
cast. An art lover saw Victor's sketches and broke
Victor's hand. If you look closely you can see an
autograph on the cast—"Better luck next time, ha ha!
Flaubert." Bon chance! Kerry.

P.S.: Look me up when you take your next tour. I might turn up anywhere!

I addressed the card to "Dan Spencer, American Express, Madrid, Espagne."

I carried the card for another week before I put a stamp on it and chucked it in the mail. What could I lose? Maybe he'd have an attack of nostalgia and send me a souvenir of Spain: the ear of a bull.

A Hamster in Winter

In March, a month of unalleviated dankness and domestic animosity, I became wary of two phrases français which recurred in the torrent of yattering issuing from Madame and the Bad Sister. One phrase was long and one was short. The long phrase always preceded a charming request from Madame for some little service in addition to my slavey routine—like shining the shoes of Monsieur, a task she generally took upon herself; or overseeing a tea party for Leah and the frou-frou enfantes of friends of Dodo, three petite princesses whose simpering and tantrums made Leah look like a noble savage by comparison. In twelve weeks, I had proven that I had qualities—a not subnormal I.Q. and an element of doormat in my nature—which suited me for extra duty. Every time I heard the phrase—it sounded like "Celeryville de Rendezvous," which makes sense if you know Ohio—its syllables filled me with foreboding which was immediately fulfilled.

The long phrase had the same disquieting effect on Emparo. When it was directed at her, she assumed the posture and expression of a basilisk. She waited for Madame to feel silly for talking to a monument, and go away. After Madame had slunk from the kitchen, Emparo would erupt into Spanish, rolling her eyes, slapping her palm on her forehead, punctuating her aria with "Aye yi yis" and (in asides to me) "français! incroyable!"

Sometimes Madame would solicit me in English, saying, "It don't mind you?" I looked up variations of this question in the dictionnaire, and found the heinous phrase: "If you don't mind: si cela vous ne dérangez pas." It seemed appropriate to speak of au pair favors in terms of derangement. Madame didn't know how close the nanny was to going bonkers.

The shorter phrase had variations, but it always included

the word "omstare." I had no luck with "omstare" in the dictionnaire. Printed phonetically in English, it looked like a description of the gaze of Krishna freaks. "Omstare" was batted back and forth between Mouse and Leah like "bicyclette" the week before Noël. The much-vaunted bicyclette reposed in the closet, awaiting the arrival of fair weather or a private coach. What were they buying the kid this month? "Omstare" . . . French for "tractor"? I pictured Leah in overalls by St. Laurent, digging up rich kids and sand in the park.

Leah had hardly been in school since Christmas, between vacations, which seemed to occur bimonthly, and ear aches and chicken pox and vaccinations and her mother's malfeasance and mal au coeur. But after the "omstare" talk commenced, she attended faithfully for almost two weeks. At the end of this peaceful term, Mouse went to pick her up one night and returned with not one rat but two. Leah burst into the kitchen, where Anouk and I were sneaking cookies, and displayed a wire cage containing some matted hay, a wheel, a diseased-looking carrot, and a small, brown, terrified critter. I gazed at it in horror. Madame entered, wearing the same expression, which she tried to disguise with a valorous smile.

"C'est Omstare," Mouse said. She added something genteelly introductory about the "jardin des enfantes," Leah's school, the home of the nasty little beast in Leah's nasty little clutches. The ratlike beastie was a lump in the corner of his prison as Leah bore him to the counter where we kept the bread. As she set down the cage, the beast began to skitter around, uttering piteous shrieks.

"Regarde! Omstare!" Leah cried, clapping her hands.

"Yick," said Madame and I in unison.

It was days before I figured out that "omstare" was "hamster." Omstare was an odd name for a rat, I thought, but perhaps it was French for "Frisky" or "Spot." Anyway, Omstare was an odd rat. He displayed unusual insight by refusing to come out of his hayrick when Leah cooed at him, her nose inserted between tthe bars, or to eat any of the carrots with which she barricaded his corner. Anouk, when Mouse held her up to look at him, responded with her George Sanders eyebrow raise, and never looked at him again. Emparo had the same reaction as Madame and I. When Leah was away at school, Omstare would sometimes scuttle out of his hiding place and take a furtive fling at his wheel. At the sound of the metallic clatter, Emparo and I would turn, watch the critter in the wheel, look at each other, roll our eyes, and say, "Yick!" Disgust, like love, was a universal language.

Omstare was our suffered guest for a week. Mouse explained that every enfant in the jardin got to take him home for a visit. The philosophy behind this program might have been to teach the kiddies animal husbandry. But a caged rat in the kitchen was a symbol not lost on the Mouse. She shuddered and retreated to her bedroom when Omstare came out to turn the wheel. I didn't much care for his scuttles and snuffles, but I felt reluctant kinship for him. What a life! Transported from the kitchen of one rich, willful little turd to another . . . they should have named him "Au Pair."

The most peaceable part of my day was the hour when I walked Anouk in her sumptuous baby-voiture around the park. We trundled along the looping paths, through brown light and dead trees, the carriage wheels sinking into sodden mud whenever they left the gravel trail. We passed the soccer field, where bare-limbed boys danced madly in the frigid gloom, and the creaky carousel. The islet of the park was the eye of a storm, the infield of the Indy 500. The streets that swept around it, pouring their jumbled rush of traffic into Passy, were dragways for the frenzied French. Crossing the street with a baby buggy was an act of ruthless courage. Oncoming cars continued coming on. Anouk was nearly sideswiped several times, once by the smug red voiture of a woman who had bundled her petite darling's trike into the trunk five minutes before. Most of the contestants in the Passy Petit Prix seemed to have a code d'honneur against mashing bébés français. If pressed, they would have swerved to avoid Anouk. The season on au pairs was always open. French drivers would have loved to leave Anouk intact and flatten me like a Yankee crepe. I was very cautious on two-lane streets.

On Tuesday of the week of Omstare's visitation, the sun came out. It hung reluctant and pallid in the muzzy sky. For weeks, the park had been a sink of sludge, oppressed by portentous yellow clouds. The shy emergence of the sun was an event. I enmeshed the baby in mohair and lace in the carriage, and marched her into light. After our circuit of the park, I settled on a bench which was actually dry. I turned Anouk's carriage so that she could watch a gaggle of little girls jumping rope.

But Anouk was frisky. She had acquired the trick of standing up. She performed it whenever she was bored. To amuse us both, she took hold of the edge of the carriage and pulled herself up. She stood far forward, the skipper in the prow, and the craft slowly tilted under her weight. I grabbed the handle before she capsized.

"You're going to land on your head," I told her, "tu vas tomber, numbskull!" I sat her down. "Reste-toi, get me? Stay there." But she was delighted with the new game. She pulled herself up; the carriage rocked; I sat her down. "Quit it!" I said, slapping her chubby fingers. She laughed, or fronced her sourcils—a terrific French description of an eyebrow squinch—but she wouldn't stop. I whacked her on her bonneted head with the palm of my hand. "Non!" I hollered. She laughed.

"You are abusing that baby!"

I was shocked to be overheard by another American. The man who had spoken sat on a bench a few feet away. He had the hoary cheeks and leaky eyes and torn, anonymous coat of any wino. He glared at me, his body wavering on its perch. "I saw you! You were hitting that baby!"

Two mothers of the Seizième, fox-faced and furred, regarded me. The white-legged little girls, jumping to the beating of the rope on the wet-stained pavement, turned their cloud breath toward me. Anouk fronced her sourcils at the drunk. Who was this rowdy interfering with her game?

"You're crazy," I said.

"That poor child ought to be taken away from you!"

"Listen," I said, growing hot, "this baby loves me—"

"You ought to be locked up! Hitting a little child! Parents who let someone like you take care of their children ought to be thrown in jail!"

"Shut up! You don't know what you're talking about!" I got up and wheeled Anouk's carriage around toward the nearest path. As if I'd signaled that play had resumed, she gripped the carriage side and staggered upright. The carriage rumbled and swung. Anouk toppled forward. I grabbed her by the shoulder of her snowsuit. "See, I told you! Asseyez-vous, you jerk!" I shoved her down. The mothers watched, clucking, with the virtuous maternity accrued on the one day a week that they passed with their own kids, when the au pairs were sprung. I was already a scandal to the Seizième, what with my mittens and jeans. Even the Spanish maids dressed better than I did. If I were arrested for child abuse, it would justify the Parisian conviction that what shows, tells.

"I'm going to report you to the police!" yelled the drunk as I wrenched the carriage around in a slough of mud. "I'm going to follow you and tell that baby's parents how you abuse her!"

I could hear him yelling as we rounded the curve of the path by the carousel. We went straight home. I kept glancing back, into the watery sunlight setting the trees afloat, for the weaving specter of vengeance, witness to tortures suffered by Anouk at my hands. "He was crazy, wasn't he? Anouky, my coo-kie," I sang. She giggled. But she was puzzled by the termination of our ramble in the sun.

I was shaking. Along with fury at the drunk's accusations—I loved Anouk and she loved me!—there was the recognition that what he'd said was true. I hadn't hit her hard, but I'd hit her with impatience, almost with anger. I'd hit her on the top of the head, where a baby's skull is fragile. And other times, when I'd been enraged by her temperamental squalls, her refusal to eat what I'd prepared, to sleep when I wanted to sleep, I'd handled her roughly. I'd abused her.

I played with Anouk for hours that night, with a solicitude born of love and guilt. Sticking it out à la maison Faurer might prove that I had fiscal fortitude—or at least that in a cow barn, I could hold my nose with one hand and shovel with the other. But I'd also demonstrated to myself that machines were my meat. I was lousy with people.

In the next few days, I approached the park with trepidation. The wino could spring from behind any tree, trumpeting my villainy to all of Paris. But no one sprinkled ground glass in my path as I rolled Anouk's carriage through the arch of birches. The blackness of my nature was a secret I shared with a wino and les enfantes. To everyone else, I looked too insipid to be evil. The Freckled Sepulcher.

Friday dawned: my day to frolic. Monotonous damp

had closed over the city again. The morning was steeped in insistent fog. I had scheduled visits to Napoleon's Tomb and the Arc de Triomphe, interspersed with a masochist's hike that would spare me the price of a Métro. Madame was waging the battle of the decibels with Leah in the nursery. I nipped into the kitchen and swiped a lunch. There was so little food that whatever I took would be missed. But time had made me careless. I wrapped a block of cheese in a ragged diaper and shoved it into my purse. I packed a banana, like a six-gun, in either pocket. There was a loaf of new-made bread, which I'd gone out to cherche for Madame that morning, "if it didn't derange me." I broke off a reckless third of the loaf. Cradling the bread in my elbow, I shoved my sketch pad into my purse and ran for the elevator.

Inspired by the success of my earlier work, "Diaper Basket: Crayon and Manila Paper," I'd bought a sketch pad. It had cost as much as a four-star pastry. It would be worth the money, I thought, to fill the droning hours between errands and ironing. Soon I was bored with "Still Life of Playpen." I carried the pad and a pencil in my purse when I set off to explore the city. At first, I tried drawing people in cafés. But the subjects, once aware of my furtive scratching, kept coming over to look at their portraits. Sometimes they snickered. Sometimes they took offense. Then the waiters and pinball fans and cognac drinkers sent delegates to view my efforts. Their reports were given to hearty guffaws. I hated being critiqued. I knew my style was primitive. I was drawing for something to do, not to be judged on points.

I took to the parks. Hunched on a bench, I sheltered my smeary scribbles with my elbows. But in the Parc de Trocadéro, as I cartooned the Eiffel Tower into a wire giraffe, policemen and nannies and lean, mean old ladies whose lapdogs were snapping at pigeons drifted behind me and breathed condemnation all over my neck.

I had taken up art in a nation of critics. What I needed was a tent and a periscope.

Sketching, or even walking, in the park was further complicated by the conviction shared by all mankind that no female liked being alone. Every man who saw me lolling on a bench in the Bois de Boulogne—not lolling in the grass, since that was a felony in Paris—or leaning on the wall overlooking the Place de la Concorde, the Versailles of cloverleafs; or perched on the concrete rim of a center-piece of flowers in the gravel path of the Luxembourg Gardens, felt honor bound to lighten the burden of my solitude. Most of these philanthropists were odd ducks of one kind or another: foreigners, like me, or Parisians who were outcasts because they were funny-looking . . . or fourteen, or seventy-nine, years old . . . or rheumy-eyed . . . or open-flied. By the third month in Paris, I'd been confronted so many times by gaping zippers, I was afraid to drop my eyes below the belt of any man I passed. On the Métro, I gazed at the ceiling, springing for the door if a man in the same car reached in his pocket for change. When I crossed the children's park at evening, every birch tree seemed to shield a man who was making his private public.

I asked myself: was Paris the capital of exhibitionism? Did Frenchwomen accept the flapping raincoat and the frantic leer as unfortunate offshoots of the urban scene, like litter? If not, why was I the recipient of every pervert's favors? How did they find me?

The penis vendors were the most depressing of these sad-ass Casanovas. But it hardly mattered whether the male who shattered my peace was a sixteen-year-old Dutch boy or a forty-year-old Frenchman or an ageless, toothless, friendless Pakistani who could only bob and grin. Each of them thought he was an unmixed blessing. Each of them punctured my little sphere of privacy on the only day in the week when I had one. Saturday through Thursday, I could only be certain of being alone in the toilet. Friday, I had a chance to draw a breath . . . to gaze at something beautiful . . . to linger over café au lait without the con-stant proding of the hands on the clock. But even on a Friday, I had to keep moving. A stationary female—even a female in ratty jeans, whose nose was running—was a public resource, like a water fountain.

"Mademoiselle, pardon . . ." Did I want a cigarette, wasn't whatever I was looking at "jolie," wasn't I "jolie aussi," would I like to go drink something, what was my name? They always wanted to know my name, as if it would give them a grip on me. I wouldn't tell them, or I said, "Leah." The pursuer would not go away until I'd said, "Leave me alone!"—"Laissez-moi tranquille!"— and he'd rendered a judgment on my cold and selfish nature. When I wouldn't neck with the Dutch boy in the Tuileries, he passed the verdict, "It is the world's great tragedy that people will not communicate."

I could only respond, "Oh, raspberries."

I have to admit that if someone who looked and talked like Truffaut had approached me, I wouldn't have hollered, "Sod off!" I still would have thought he had some nerve, but I would have made allowances. Somehow men like Truffaut didn't pick up grubby American servants in parks. I attracted the homeless, tempest-tossed. Feeling sorry for my persecutors was just more aggravation. What was I, a social worker? I had enough troubles of my own.

Now, as I hurried across the bleak, stripped arbor of the park, the raw air scorched my lungs and flickered up my sleeves. The new-made smell of the bread I was hugging was rich in my nostrils. Dizzy with hunger, I tore off the soft golden cone of the loaf and stuffed it into my mouth. Chewing, I descended the cement ramp to the tunnel beneath the railroad overpass, hoping that the Ranelagh beggar would be lighting some other nook with stale despair.

But she was there in my granite-bound path. I swallowed the morsel of bread. My mouth had gone dry.

Her face was hidden. She had burrowed into her nest of blankets against the right wall, where the granite was beaded with cold. The heap of cotton was too thin and saturated with damp to give the illusion of warmth. As I passed her, the bulky apex of the mass shifted, and a head emerged. My foot brushed hers. I stumbled. She muttered, and a lizard's hand groped at the air from a hole in the rags of her nest.

I dropped the torn loaf. It bumped the scaly palm of her hand and fell to the blanket as I ran up the ramp toward the wet black sky.

I was the only mourner paying respects at Napoleon's Tomb. A bridal party rushed from the building into the courtyard, clucking like chickens, as I entered. The little leader's mausoleum seemed like an odd place to get married, but the French were crazy for military trappings. The bride's bouquet of irises graced Napoleon's coffin. A monstrous dark marble object on a dais, installed in a rotunda of white marble, the coffin looked like a whale in a hospital bed, holding his get-well bouquet. Statues of Justice, Truth, and War were standing around in helpless attitudes. I could hear them offering lamely: "So, you look good. . . . How are they treating you? . . . How 'bout those nurses, huh?"

As a salute to Napoleon, I ate my two bananas.

The walk up the Champs Élysées to the Arc de Triomphe was more than bracing. The wind cut straight down the boulevard, ripping at the gaucho pants of paired, sleek ladies. The windows of boutiques thrust out their artificial cargoes: bamboo mannequins, chrome mobiles, garments of stripped elegance, fluorescent prisms. The verandas of plushy cafés had been abandoned. Portly, greying Frenchmen in camel's hair coats and their red-lipped, leopard-swathed doxies sneered from interior windows, framed in white wicker and potted palms. A waiter in emerald livery stared severely down upon me from the second-floor window of a restaurant. Even an espresso in this chi-chi joint was out of my league. I'd have to eat my cheese in a doorway.

"Shut up," I told myself. "Who are you—the Orphan of the Storm?"

The Arc de Triomphe was set on an island in the center of the Étoile, a zooming unlaned racetrack fed by the ingress of traffic from twelve broad avenues. The speed and viciousness of competition in the Étoile made the traffic assassins in Passy look like kids on the Dodgem ride at Euclid Beach Park. The Étoile was appropriately placed at the mouth of the Champs Élysées, where it was fed by tributaries piled by the very rich. When life at the periphery of real life made them crazy with boredom, idlers and cruisers from the Avenue Kléber, the Avenue D'Iéna or the Avenue Foch could sail numbly into the automotive maelstrom of the Étoile and end the voyage.

There was an underground passageway from the curb to the island. But only cripples and tourists took the low road. Parisians sallied out among the whizzing Fiats, Volvos, Peugeots, and Bentleys, nimble and bold, outfacing their fellow citizens in games of lethal chicken. Not to let the side down, as Dee would say, I stepped off the curb.

A Rolls-Royce ran over my foot.

Luckily, my Swiss boots were too long in the toe. The would-be murderer didn't even mash a metatarsal. He only left a tire mark on the suede. But the shock of the impact, averted only by an accident of pace—I hadn't even seen the car till he'd run over me—overwhelmed me. I stood in the street, speechless. A man hauled me back on the curb. "Ça va?" he said. I nodded, trembling.

I had to stand in the wind for a while to get my courage back. Then I plunged into a gap in the onslaught. Brakes keened as motors died in anguish. Balked contestants in the "Brush with Death" event berated me in French, Italian, and German as I scampered into the safety zone of the island. Breathing hard, I turned around and grinned at the livid faces of the losers. The Arch of Triumph could have been named for the victorious visitors who'd made it there alive.

Near the entrance door in one thick leg of the base of the arch, a man was performing a private ceremony. He had laid his long cloak and beaver hat on the cement, near the tomb of France's unknown soldier. The man had a dark, thick mustache. His shirtsleeves, in the sharp wind, were rolled above his elbows. The grave was set into the ground, flush with the surface of the pavement. There was no whalelike sarcophagus, only a small torch, a plaque and a bunch of red roses. As I watched, the man performed a series of maneuvers in front of the grave: wheeling, clicking his boots, shooting out his right arm in a spasmodic salute, pivoting and rapidly bowing, jerking upright, and marching two steps. A family of Japanese were staring at him, the oldest son fiddling with the camera around his neck. The boy was dying to take a picture, but hesitant to violate the privacy of even public mourning.

I paid the entrance fee and began to climb the twisting stairs to the museum and the observation platform at the top of the Arc. The walls of the tubelike stairwell were unmarred ivory. The steps, like the sidewalks, the trees, the rooftops, the sky—like winter, like Paris—were gray. The steps rose, upward and right, curving, climbing. The muscles in the backs of my calves and thighs began to ache. I had to open my mouth to breathe. I unbuttoned my coat, and then I took it off, though the ivory walls were frosted with cold, like the walls of the Métro tunnel where I'd tossed the beggar my bread. I forced myself to breathe evenly, shorter inhales, longer exhales. My heart protested dully. I slowed my pace. My thighs ached and burned, but I pushed them up and down, up and down. I might not be good for much . . . I told myself . . . and breathed in . . . but at least I could climb the same stairs . . . a Frenchman could climb. . . .

On the top step I halted, my jaw clamped, sucking in air through my nostrils. My legs sank into the floor with the dead weight of wooden pilings under a pier. I stood, and breathed, and watched the elevator deposit a load of babbling French children and the family of Japanese. The oldest Japanese son took my picture.

In glass cases, toy soldiers in the uniforms of all the armies of France's history marched in an unbroken double line to battle. The walls were hung with photographs and paintings of the Arc at moments of historical importance—for instance, the Arc draped in purple and black, crowded close by carriages and men with torches, as Paris mourned the death of good ole Victor Hugo. Artists had competed to design the Arc. My favorite of the entries was the sketch of a monument shaped like an elephant, with its interior cut into four extravagant salons. It was a shame that Richard Nixon hadn't seen it; in his heyday, he would have had it built at San Clemente.

I went out onto the observation platform and leaned against the wall.

The mist rose, and the city shifted and rose beneath it. I looked down at the foot of the Champs Élysées, at the little beetling cars, the people reduced to flocks of specks moving in patterns, like birds in flight. Removed from the difficult city by height and mist, I could see the precise, articulate beauty of its design: the long pale ribbon of the Champs Élysées, bordered by little brown buttons of gardens, dividing the fabric of grey, neatly bunched rooftops, and leading to the sepia patch of the Tuileries and the pinkish medallions of the Grand Palais, and the Louvre, laid out like medals on a general's suit. To the left rose the bone-colored dome of Sacré Coeur, an image of mythical purity; to the right, the rickety derrick of the Eiffel Tower, and the undulant mist-sheened crescent of the Seine.

I made the circuit of the platform. The Étoile was the waistband of Paris, and the city a flaring circle skirt of geometric patterns, bedecked with the bright knobs of monuments, embossed with the triangles and rectangles of dark parks that would be, in a month, soft green.

I looked at Paris and nursed the pain in my throat, the ache of unrequited love. So cold, so fair! I could have lived in Paris for the rest of my life; the city would never have taken me into its heart. Paris and I both knew that I had no place in a city lush with parks, where no one could sit on the grass.

I left the roof, passing the cases of metal soldiers, the mounted swords. I began the descent.

The endless stairs: down, down, deeper into the tight spiral, into the slick stone walls; the gray steps rising, unchanging, marching between the drapes of my hair; rising with the immutable rhythm of my falling feet, step, step, step . . . I seemed to be going down and around inside myself, like a corkscrew. Step, step, down, down, smooth well of ivory, burnished, cold, devoid of variation, smooth succession of piled firey blocks, curving downward, sinking into a chamber leading only into itself. I started to panic.

I stopped. I planted both feet on one step, arresting the almost effortless motion of turning, turning, turning—with a sick fear that stopping was useless, that my spirit, my self, had not ceased its singular plummet, its colorless fall. In the cold that moistened the ivory walls, I was sweating. I leaned my forehead against the stone, the cold, wet stone, and breathed.

Voices from the chamber below issued up the tunnel. I was not isolated in this grayest, coldest cell in a gray, cold, unchanging city. People were below, moving upward to meet me. I began to move again, step, step, step, step, faster and faster, descending toward the saving voices. But the voices came no nearer, and their rise and fall became the voice of the sameness, the score of the dream. I changed the rhythm of my steps, one-two, one-two-three; I touched the walls for the sensation of their icy roughness, minute variations in their texture. Twice more I had to stop and seize hold of my panic, the panic of monotony, before I reached the bottom and a wide room and a door, and air, and the sky.

I sat for a long time in the window of a snooty café, looking down the double lines of trees and lights to the Place de la Concorde. I drank a grande-crème, slowly.

When the bottom half-inch was as cold as my hands, I ordered another. The waiter banged the saucer on the table to express his French opinion of my American skin-flint ways. I didn't even flinch. My impervious profile said, "Screw you, Pierre, this is a café, and that's what I'm drinking—café." I watched night settle wetly over the poppy field of lamps. When it was full dark, I picked up my bag—I hadn't had the heart to eat the cheese or use the sketch pad—and went out. I walked down the boulevard, past the parading faces. On the Métro, I stared at the ceiling.

I plunged into the shaft of the railroad underpass, sealing off my senses from the clamorous presence of the beggar. But I knew she was there. Propped against the dank wall, bedded in tatters and filth, she clutched in her lizard hands a pencil and a sketch pad exactly like my own.

I ran. I ran up the ramp and across the park, the brown trees jouncing across my vision, the light rain flying into my face. I kept running till I touched our door.

It was only eight o'clock. But the house was dark, the rooms thick with steam heat and silence. Monsieur was in Lyon, and Madame had forced the enfantes into sleep—perhaps with the same drugs she used to soothe herself? In my bedroom, standing up, I ate the piece of cheese, picking off lint from the diaper. Then I put on my nightgown and got into bed. I wrote Randy a seven-page letter, which I knew by page two I wouldn't mail.

The door popped open. In rushed Madame Mouse in her little white nightie, her nose bright pink with cream. Hopping and gibbering, she swiped at the air with a bread knife.

At long last, Leah had prodded her mother over the brink.

Giggling, Madame squealed, "Ker-day, venez, venez à la cuisine! Omstare va sortir!"

Omstare was up to no good in the kitchen. Maybe he'd eaten Leah. I put down my letter and followed the madly giggling, lethally gesticulating Mouse. If she turned around to explain, she'd lop my ear off. I put a car-length distance between us.

Omstare was making a bid for liberty. Maybe he knew that Monday he was due at the jardin des enfantes. Life with Leah was Shangri-la compared to the circumference of monstrous eyes and gross fingers that represented nursery school to a hamster. Omstare's refusal to eat his carrots was now revealed as part of a plan. The carrots were stacked like logs along one wall of his cage. Omstare was perched on his hind legs on top of a mound of carrots, smashing with his nose at the lid of the cage. The lid wasn't firmly latched. Leah must have left the hook dangling when she'd dumped in the last load of carrots. The hook was caught in one of the bars, instead of in the eye of the latch. With each blow from the nose of Omstare the Valiant, the hook shuddered, the lid bounced, the carrots shifted, the tinny bars rattled, and Madame Mouse screamed. The cage danced along the counter with the force of Omstare's assault. Burbling to me of the consequences horrible if Omstare gained his freedom, Madame crept forward, her bare toes curled with repugnance, the knife a sword in her upraised fist. She snatched at the hook to push it into the eye. Swiftly the mighty Ostare nibbled at her fingers. "Ooch! Eech! Ai-ee!" she squealed, leaping backward.

Omstare squeaked a war cry. Breathing deeply, Mouse ventured forward again, tinkling fiercely, "Allez! Sortez en bas!": Get back, Simba! But Omstare had the determination of a man at the foot of a gallows. He knew that Mouse's sword was useless. Mouse couldn't stick it through the narrow gap between the bars. To skewer him, she would have had to raise the lid.

Mouse turned to me. Her face was flushed with suppressed revulsion and hilarity. "Ker-ray!" she beseeched me. Her plea was clear: if it don't mind you, save me from this hamster!

Approaching Omstare, my nose wrinkling, the very pores of my skin closing in retreat from his bulgy warm body and slimy teeth, I also felt a traitor's empathetic guilt. I could identify more with Omstare, hurling his body against the bars of his cage, than I could with Mouse, wielding the sword of the master race against the uprising enchained.

Saying "Yick" at intervals, I shoved Omstare gently back with the bowl of a wooden spoon, and hooked the lock.

Omstare, a sore loser, yelped a few times and slunk off

into his mound of disgusting hay. Madame pressed a hand
to her heaving breast and laughed, ashamed of her terror.
In a burst of camaraderie, she offered me a glass of wine.
"Merci," I said. We sat at the kitchen table on the two
chairs, drinking wine from the enfantes' plastic glasses.

We sat in silence. From time to time we smiled and cast
humorous glances at the cage, now hushed as a tomb. I
thought of all the things I'd wanted to say to Madame,
about Leah, about myself. I looked at the plastic glass.
I said, lentement, en français, "Madame, I would like to
leave at the end of the month, if it doesn't derange you."
When she looked at me, startled, I added quickly, "I
want to travel more before I have to go home."

She nodded brightly—"Bien sûr, naturellement," she
said—but our eyes met and locked for an instant of com-
prehension, an honest, wry exchange. We finished our wine
and went to bed. An hour later, when I couldn't sleep,
I heard her in the bathroom—running water into a glass,
shaking pills from a bottle.

The next evening, as I was changing Anouk in the
nursery, Mouse was giving Leah her bath. Leah was being
"rambunctious," as my mother would say, or, as I would
say, "fairing the Turd." Suddenly I heard her mother
shrieking at her, "You are insupportable! That's why
Kerry is leaving you, because you are a brat! She loves
Anouk, but she doesn't love you!"

"Goodbye, Leah," I told her, speaking to the wall.
"Goodbye, Anouk," I said to the baby's laughing face.

"God help you both."

Better Late Than Never

"Well, I must say, I shall be sorry to see you go," said Dee, when I told her. "I shall likely go right round the bend in a fortnight and take up with an Algerian. Let it be on your conscience."

I did feel guilty, leaving the other half of the pair on her own. When Dee got "cheesed off," all she could do was stick her head out in the alley and yell at the sky. "I've a feeling I shan't be here much longer either," she said. "It's not as if you can have any friends in Paris. The only people I've met in six months are bleedin' foreigners. No offense."

"None taken," I said.

Danièlle and Marc had decided to go to their ski lodge in Switzerland for the last week in March. The lodge had been in the Comte's family since the days of boar hunts. Danièlle had thought of taking Dee and Elise, but she'd concluded that Elise was too little to ski.

"Tell you what, Kerry—as I'll have the flat to myself that week, I'll have a bit of a farewell party for you. Granted, I don't know who we'll invite. Might have to drag in some of those loonies who take off their trousers in parks."

I planned to leave Paris on April 1. I didn't know where I was going. Since it would only be a loan till my income tax refund came through, I'd written to ask my father if he'd wire me $231.21. If I kept to the same parsimonious habits I'd refined in Paris . . . if I headed for a poorer country with a warmer climate, where I could sit in the sun insead of sitting in cafés . . . reckoning on the magic figure of five dollars a day, I'd be able to stay in Europe for forty-six days. In France, five dollars wouldn't last for twenty minutes. But in Greece, five dollars was a lot of olives. I could stay in student hostels if pressed, though the thought of all those hearty hikers and wispy hippies gave me hives.

I had to go to the Paris office of American Express to collect the money wired by my father. The office was on the Rue Scribe, in the fearfully suave and moneyed district of the Opéra. The ground floor boutique sold expensive, hideous costume jewelry, and perfume which cost, per ounce, as much as a cheap week in Morocco. Dusty American youths lounged around the glass cases, reading their mail, or slumped on backpacks, devouring chocolate chip cookies packed in shoeboxes by loving hands in Wisconsin. A number of hopeless souls sat on the floor near the cashier's desk, waiting for wires to transmit their allowances. Spraddled on a blanket, two males and two females ignored the admonitions of the guard to clean up their act. Intertwined, they were eating eclairs and reading different volumes of the Don Juan series by Carlos Castaneda.

I thought about that: were all of them reading the books in order? Was the girl who was now reading Volume IV the most spiritually advanced? Or did all of them finish their volumes at the same time and pass to the left, the left end handing off to the right? They didn't look that organized. Maybe each one swapped with whoever had finished, reading the volumes separately for form, but in toto for content, like the Betsy-Tacy series: *Betsy's Wedding . . . Betsy Was a Junior . . . Winona's Pony Cart . . .* The readers had the unkempt look of seekers after inner peace. But who could read a paperback and eat an eclair without getting chocolate on the pages?

The man at the counter, whose suit and expression had a cellophane surface distinctly French, called out a name. One of the seekers leaped up, dislodging his female alter ego, squashing eclairs and his buddy's fingers in his haste to claim his cash.

"Hot shit!" he bayed. "Five hundred dollars! The cheap old bastard came through!"

"Yeah? Oh, I'm gonna tell *my* old man I'm stranded!" said the other boy, running to the counter to send a wire. "Here, c'mere, tell me what to say," he called to his ecstatic friend, who was all but humping his girlfriend in his glee. As the boys were composing a piteous plea, one iron-deficient girl said to the other, "I already told my parents

I was stranded. Next time I guess I'll have to say I'm in jail."

"We should get an answer tomorrow if my mom gets this," said the second boy, "she's a soft touch." They gathered up their spiritual reading and their consorts. "We can split for Istanbul Thursday."

The girl groaned.

"Fuck Istanbul," said the first boy. "Linda can't handle the flies. You know what five hundred bucks means, man? That means *Amsterdam!*"

They whooped, and split. The guard had to scoop up mashed cream and pastry with a handkerchief.

The Frenchman at the counter gave me a look of contempt for which I wanted to congratulate him. In an attempt to redeem myself, I used an Irish accent. "Could y' tell me, is there money for me from Ohio, for I've relatives there, though I meself am a native of County Meath."

He wasn't fooled. He knew what godforsaken moral abyss I hailed from.

The American youths who had gone before me on the low-budget route had swept across the fringes of the Mediterranean coast like the plagues of Egypt. I could expect to be greeted with bolted shutters and vicious dogs. (Or perhaps, in Sicily, vicious goats?) I almost wished I had a plaid cloth suitcase, as a badge of prosaic decency. Like Grace, travelers wtih plaid cloth suitcases didn't comprehend the concept of the Reel Yurrup Tourists Never Dig. But what they found in Yurrup, they photographed and left intact. And most of them kept their mouths shut. Discretion, I'd decided, was the better part of travel.

Dee's fête was taking shape. Danièlle and Marc would be gone from Sunday to Sunday. "We'll have our do on the Friday," said Dee. "That'll give us two days' time to Hoover the flat and pitch out the bottles. Not that I expect there'll be a great deal of drink consumed. Wine is all I'm willing to spring for."

We sat on a bench by the sand pit, making up the guest list. Elise and Leah were waiting in line for the slide, Leah with her usual public decorum, Elise hollering "Ça!" and butting the little boy ahead of her with her belly. In the carriage, Anouk was zapping noisome children and dizzy mamas with her sourcil fronces.

"Right then, so far we've got you and me, and that

dreary Irish girl, and that Cockney lout you met at the Red Boar—"

"He keeps calling me up," I apologized.

"Perfectly all right, Kerry, it's your party. But you'll be the one to entertain him, full stop. Probably have to listen to tales of him and his mates flinging crockery off the schoolhouse roof. That'd be his idea of a humorous anecdote, I know his sort. I suppose he'll want to bring his mate."

"I guess."

She sighed. "Well, they'll have to bring their own drink."

"I'll tell him. And I'm chipping in for food and stuff too."

"Pas nécessaire, Kerry, though it's quite handsome of you to offer. You'll need your money to travel. Who've we got, now? Oh, that Irish girl claims she knows a bloke she can bring. Can't imagine where she met him, unless he delivered a package. She never leaves the flat. She says he's quite a good dancer. Mind you, the Irish don't look at dancing the way we do in England. I hope she doesn't mean jigs." She shuddered.

"So that's three blokes."

"Well . . . if you call those blokes. I'm sure I shan't fancy any of them. I mean Irish blokes are goofy, judging from what I've seen in London. Dreadful socks."

"Those rugby players at the Red Boar were Irish too."

"My Christ! You don't suppose— If he's that sort, I shall simply tell Meiread not to bring him round. Picture a rugby player in the flat with all those glass shelves and bottles! And he can bloody well bring his own drink as well. You know the Irish!"

Since Friday was my journée libre, I offered to help her shop for refreshments and do any cooking and baking that was called for. "No fear," she said. "I'm not about to knock meself out for this lot. We'll have the usual bread and cheese and salad, and I'll get some fruit and some cakes. Perhaps we could open a few tins of pudding for auld lang syne." She nudged me.

I would miss Dee. I almost wished she were coming with me. Traveling alone had been a glorious prospect when I was lumbered with Grace. But a lonely winter had cooled my lust for solitude.

On the other hand, Grace had struck me as an interest-

ing study till I'd taken the intensive course. Maybe nobody wore well when you traveled together. It came as a
shock to realize that while I'd been putting up with
Grace, Grace had been putting up with me.

As if to woo me back from imminent escape, spring
had poked up its head and was feinting with winter. In
the park, dull branches were gauzily wreathed with round,
translucent buds. The sky was a fragile blue, and sun
suffused the trees' damp bark with lemon light. Anouk
and I spent all afternoon in the park, basking in the tentative warmth of the sun. "Regarde!" I said, pointing at the
satiny, fibrous shoots spiking the trodden earth. Anouk
leaned over the carriage side, directing her solemn gaze
at the shreds of green. Madame had presented Anouk with
a hat to shield her from the vaporous sun. It was a white
cotton pith helmet. Anouk threw it on the ground a couple
of times, to establish that she wore it by choice and not
by maternal fiat. Then she decided it suited her. Her eyes
merry, she peeked at me from beneath its scalloped brim.
She surveyed the ant farm of enfantes in the sand pit with
deanlike dignity, as if the hat conferred an honorary degree.

I couldn't bear to leave her. Her mother would shackle
her with useless trappings. Her grandmother Dodo would
turn her into a starving doll, like Claude. She'd have a
string of begrudging, nonverbal au pair mothers, till she
was so bewildered that she'd refuse to love.

Would it be easy or hard to thumb a ride with a year-
old baby? Her sunhat would be handy for the road. Where
would I change her—in a field? On the shoulder of a highway? How would I wash the diapers? Working out the
details of the kidnap fantasy gave me a little comfort. I
wanted to run away at once, so I couldn't see Anouk's
reserve melt, just for me, in a smile of delighted con-
spiracy.

Madame kept giving me wistful looks. If she wanted
me to change my mind and re-enlist, she didn't offer any
inducement. She'd already asked me, management-style,
"if it didn't mind me," to stay an extra week till the
seventh, a Thursday, when my replacement was due. We
might pass in the park, I and my doppelganger. I'd know
her by her bunny teeth. Mouse added that she hoped the
new model would sign on for a year. I didn't have the

nerve to say, "Trying paying more than fifty dollars a month. Try buying food."

The day of Dee's party was my last day off in Paris. I didn't want to spend much. I could get by on an apple at noon and a cake at four, since I'd get fed at Dee's. I decided to blow a few francs on a last museum, the Jeu de Paume. I'd been saving that museum because it housed the Impressionist collection. At the Art Museum in Cleveland, I used to visit the Impressionists the way I'd visited puppies in pet shop windows as a kid. Strolling through the hazy green of the Tuileries, I smiled at the birds, peckish in the seed beds, and thought about Italy. I was leaning toward Florence, and maybe Rome. To stretch funds, I'd hitchhike. Italian men were notorious lechers, which would make flagging down rides a breeze, but the rides themselves yawned. What's Italian for, "I am a virgin, I know not man"?

The air in the Jeu de Paume was moist with the tropical breath of hordes of appreciators. Corners of paintings were framed by shoulders and heads. Pairs of rich French females in embroidered blouses and kneeboots stomped from room to room. They looked like serfs on the Tsar's feastday. They stomped up to the single painting in each chamber which had been declared by some sage to be the masterpièce-de résistance. They stared at the painting, about-faced, and stomped away, scattering obsequious Japanese and abashed Americans. The Americans were rather sweet, gawking with uniform awe at Monet's cathedrals and the water fountain. I grew fond of two ladies who wore the same coat in different shades of blue. They were a team; one of them looked at the painting and the other read the title. I passed them as they were pondering Manet's *The Card Players.*

"What's this?" said the lady who looked at the painting.

"Gamblers," said the lady who looked at the title.

They moved on.

In the Gauguin room, I was wafted into bliss by the fleshy warmth of the painted women, the bursting blooms, the swollen streams. I could feel my face flushing, as if I were lying in the sun.

"Vous aimez Gauguin?"

I turned around.

The man who stood looking at me had large dark eyes.

"Comment?" I said: French for "Huh?"

"Je croix que vous aimez Gauguin, mademoiselle. Je vous regardais."

He thought I liked Gauguin. He'd been watching me. I couldn't believe it. After four months in France, was I about to have a conversation with a masculine native on the subject of art? Gimme a postcard! "Dear Randy . . ." I said, en français, "Yes, I think he is marvelous." My voice cracked. I wished he'd look away for a moment, so I could collect myself. No doubt beneath my freckles I was a sophisticated shade of hot pink.

"So do I," he said. His eyes were the color of Swiss milk chocolate. The soft-black pupils were enormous. I had an impulse to back away, as if I'd entered the mouth of a cave. Then he turned away, and looked at the painting before us. "Here, for instance, he has painted such women . . . there is a ripeness, a fullness, that is completely physical . . . so sensuous, don't you agree?" The rich brown of his eyes engulfed me. My knees buckled. When this man looked at me, he made contact.

I said weakly, "Oui."

He said that he was also a painter, that he had made a study of Gauguin. He took my elbow and guided me to the next painting. Now that he wasn't nailing me with his eyes, I could get an impression of his "presentation." In France, nobody just got up and got dressed in the morning. A man's haircut, or the color of his tie, was the summation of his life. This man, who looked about thirty, had thick dark hair, clipped off an inch above the collar of a shabby turtleneck sweater. His pants, for France, were baggy—I couldn't see the jut of his hipbone. He wore black wrinkled-leather boots. He was well-cast as an artist who'd made a study of Gauguin.

Thank God, I thought, that I'd worn The Dress and grownup-lady shoes, in anticipation of Dee's party. Dressing that morning, the sight of my bare legs had given me pause. I hadn't exposed them to the world since Christmas. They were so white, the right calf still faintly discolored from the minibike bruise. The yellowish bruise in the pale flesh had a lascivious, unhealthy look.

For the next hour, the gorgeous one guided me through the techniques, the flaws, and the personal quirks of Gauguin. By two o'clock, I knew more about Gauguin than

I knew about anyone outside of Cleveland. After I got used to his accent and his eyes, I was delighted to find that I could follow the sense of what he said. I missed the subtleties. Luckily, he wasn't interested in my opinions. He was an artist. His role was to illuminate, and mine was to perceive.

I perceived that he was an improvement on anyone I'd ever seen at close range.

He'd stopped talking. He was looking at me again. I'd missed something crucial. "Pardon?" I said, expecting the typical response: strained patience and slow, loud repetition into my almost visible hearing aid. But he smiled and asked again. Unless I was hallucinating from hunger, he was inviting me to lunch. Two free meals in one day!

I said "Merci" with such gratitude, he must have felt free to drag me into the mop room at once and take liberties. But he helped me on with my cruddy coat, which hadn't been cleaned since Cleveland, and averted his eyes while I hid my mittens, shoving them into my purse on top of the apple formerly known as "lunch." A real French dejeuner with a real French artist! "Please God," and I crossed my fingers, "don't let him take me to Wimpie's!"

He took me to a tiny room in a side street off the Rue de Rivoli. The room's six tables had linen cloths and napkins of the same blue as the smocks of Paris workmen. The young woman in black at the door said, smiling, "Bonjour, Jean-Paul, comment ça va?" She took my coat. The other diners looked up and nodded or smiled as we passed. The menu was handwritten on parchment, without prices, which was a mercy. I'd gotten so used to poverty, it pained me to cost another person a franc. Perusing the menu with mystical concentration, Jean-Paul rattled off a string of dishes and asked me what I liked. "You choose," I said. He beamed.

Ordering involved much consultation with the waiter, who had to make two trips to the kitchen to verify his facts. I smiled with what I hoped was adorable naïveté and hid my broken fingernails in my lap. I would absorb Jean-Paul's artistic judgments; I would defer to his gastronomic creed. I had no choice; I couldn't talk. Feeble French had turned me into the Total Woman. If I didn't understand a question, I said "Oui," and let it pass. Several times, catching a startled glint in Jean-Paul's eyes, or a word that took me aback by the time I'd translated it, I wanted to retract the "Oui." But by then we'd pressed on.

We commenced with a bottle of lovely, mellow red wine and some tiny lobsteresque things in a thin brown sauce. There didn't seem to be any meat inside of the brittle torsos and protuberances, but I sucked away, trying not to dribble, smiling agreement with the spare praise bestowed on the dish by Jean-Paul. He was devouring something or other with gusto, while I licked up sauce and listened to my stomach rumble. In this case, "appetizer" was the right word.

Jean-Paul had a cigarette and I had wine while we waited for the next plate of sauce. He didn't talk, preferring to focus on palatal sensations, which was just as well. Wine in the vacuum of my stomach was rendering translation impossible. Response had narrowed down to "Pardon?" and "Oui." Anything could happen.

Next we had either chicken or duck in a different brown sauce, accompanied by little cute potatoes and carrots. I could have eaten the contents of the casserole by myself. Jean-Paul dished us unassuming portions and poured us more wine. He tasted his sample of the entrée with critical reserve. Gradually, as he chewed, the stern cast of his features relaxed. He nodded, not necessarily wth approbation, just with recognition. The chef had attained an approximation of the perfect variation on this dish for which Jean-Paul had searched long years in vain. I had to grip the chair seat with my hands to keep from seizing the casserole and scooping out the rest of the stew with a hunk of bread. But my restraint was rewarded. During this course, Jean-Paul paid me the only compliment I ever got from a native of la belle France. After Jean-Paul cut his meat, he didn't change his fork to his right hand to eat it. In the Continental manner, he stabbed the meat and conveyed it to his mouth with his left. Watching me transfer the fork to the right, the knife to the left, again and again, he gave me an admiring smile. The only thing Americans did with class, he said, was cut their meat.

More wine. Another cigarette. I was wondering whether I'd be able to weave to the door without toppling over one of the little blue tables. I braved bad manners by eating a piece of bread for its absorbency. The waiter arrived with a modest salad which wasn't amusing. We nibbled a fragment of Brie. I was beginning to suspect that Madame Faurer's starvation policy was only the extreme of a trait endemic to the race of persnickety French. Eating was minor; the point of the meal was the critique. If having lunch with a Frenchman was hard on the nerves—what if I polished off my half with relish, only to find that he'd left his half untouched, because it didn't measure up?—what would sex be like? Probably a lot like a visit to my Aunt Martha, the scenario of which never deviated: I would say, "I got a ninety-five on my history final, Aunt Martha." She would say, "Who got a hundred?"

Still, he was gorgeous; every time he turned his rich, wicked eyes on me, I wanted to cover his hands with kisses to show my appreciation. After we'd had a taste of dessert—a slice of apple tart for him and two tablespoons of chocolate mousse for me—he escorted me to the door. We moved with an underwater languor which in his case was grace and in my case was drink. I hadn't drunk so much since my twenty-first birthday, when the crowd at the Churchkey had bought me eleven shots of Jack Daniels and I'd drunk them in an hour. I wanted at all costs to find a soft surface and lie on it. As we emerged in the dull gold light of late afternoon, he said something which sounded like, "Care to make a pilgrimage to my attic of the arts?"

"How far is it?" I said. I didn't want to pass out on the Métro. Someone might think he'd drugged me and offer to buy me. Artists are always in need of cash; he might sell. But his car was handy, parked a few blocks down the rue. We walked. My blood was buzzing with the blatting of taxi horns. Every curb was a chasm. He gave me his arm. I hoped he'd think my grip was tight from ardor, and not from fear of landing on my ass. His car was a grey Fiat, pockmarked with dents, as if he often had to drive past gangs of urchins armed with stones. As we drove, clearing corners and voitures with a slinging motion that made me feel like a raw egg in a blender, he pointed out the sights shooting past and "explained me" the history—none of which I comprehended—of the palatial structures littering the central city, unclaimed wedding cakes in a bakery catering to the brownie trade.

His studio was on the fifth floor of a rock-and-plaster tenement on an alley off the quai of the Ile St. Louis. I had to stop and sit on the steps of the third and fourth floor landings to rest. Jean-Paul dragged me up the final flight. I wanted to say, "Why didn't you rent the roof of the Arc de Triomphe?" But I couldn't breathe to speak. Besides, I didn't know the French for "rent."

The studio was one high-ceilinged room with cathedral windows on one side. The melting light of the sun glistened on the white plaster walls and the pale grey counterpane of the bed. Two pairs of trousers and some sweaters hung from hooks along one wall. The only other furnishings were a hotplate on a broken wooden folding chair and a sink shaped like a birdbath. The outside of the basin was the color of tartar-coated teeth; the inside had been slopped with red and purple and black and snake-green paint. No wonder Jean-Paul ate out. There wasn't even an icebox. The only door was the one we'd entered. The bathroom must be down the hall—or down four flights. Heat, like chairs, had been dispensed with. The fervor of inspiration sufficed to warm Jean-Paul. For a nanny, accustomed to the orchid-breeding atmosphere of Paris nurseries, it was bleedin' flippin' cold.

"Asseyez-vous," said Jean-Paul. He didn't have to ask again. I sat. At once, the muscles fighting the lassitude of wine abandoned the battle. I could barely prop the corners of my mouth into a smile. Lifting each eyelid to an open position was like heaving up a window painted shut. Jean-Paul seemed to be oblivious to my comatose state. He removed my coat—I could hardly feel the rough wool brush my neck and arms—and began to fetch his paintings and sketches for my review. I said, lentement, "Oh yes . . . how good . . . uh . . . how beautiful . . . formidable . . . I'm sorry, do you mind . . . ?"

"Non non non, pas du tout," he hastened to assure me, gently thrusting a pillow behind my head. As he sat beside me on the bed that was fading from my vision, floating off on a golden river of sun, borne away by the current of reverberations eddying up from the street, I had the dim impression that he was a little disappointed. I hadn't stayed awake for the etchings.

. . . I rose slowly toward the surface of sleep, pleasantly aware of a soft, comforting closeness, a feeling of warmth and enclosure. Eyes closed, I savored the reassuring presence, the slowly separating sensations of a dulcet stroking along my thigh and a wet, warm pressure on my neck. I didn't want to open my eyes. I wanted to reap these dark pleasures without the inconveniences of place and mechanics and timing.

". . . chérie . . ." The whisper curled inside my ear and settled. ". . . chérie . . ."

Resisting, I opened my eyes.

The room was dark. The whole field of my vision was spread with the devouring blackness of eyes. Jean-Paul was pressed against me, his left hand smoothing the skin of my thigh through the nylon stocking, his thighs insistently hard and warm against mine. His mouth had been nuzzling my neck. Now he nibbled at the corner of my mouth, his eyes pouring the limitless pools of their darkness into mine.

From the bottom of my heart, I wished I could brush my teeth.

I hardly had to do anything. Jean-Paul was as much the perfectionist, the singleminded, concentrated artist, when he made love as when he explained Gauguin or ordered lunch. I had the feeling that like a lackey turning pages for a concert pianist, all I had to do was pay attention and give intermittent, minimal responses. I couldn't complain about Jean-Paul's technique. He was formidable. He was so good I didn't even have to reinforce him with groans. Any noise I made was superfluous, as if the pianist's lackey had laid a rose on the piano bench when the stage was banked with bouquets. As when he'd told me how to interpret Gauguin, Jean-Paul wasn't interested in my opinion. His role was to illuminate; mine was to perceive. As when he'd orchestrated our lunch, I could appreciate the form, but the content didn't fill me up. When Jean-Paul sat up and lit a cigarette, I was still hungry.

"Oh, my gosh!" I said. "What time is it?" I was supposed to be at Dee's place at seven to help her set up for the party. "Uh, pardon, quelle heure est-il?"

"Comment?" Jean-Paul was affronted. I was supposed to be spent with appreciation, and here I was asking the time. Besides, French people never said, "Quelle heure est-il?—that was a high school holdover. French people always said, "Avez-vous l'heure?" I added, retrenching, "Avez-vous l'heure?" The way I pronounced it, "Avez-vous l'air?" it sounded like I was asking for oxygen. That should salve Jean-Paul's ego.

Pulling on my pantyhose with more haste than finesse, I made him understand that I was due at the house of my friend. "Il faut aller!" I said: time to split. Jean-Paul slinked elegantly into his jaded turtleneck and pants. He said, with dignity, "I will escort you to the house of your friend."

"Merci," I said, relieved. I was still half smashed, and confounded by the materializing of my Parisian fantasy lover, a week before I was set to leave Paris for good. What was this pattern I'd developed of taking lovers on the platform as my train was boarding? Not that Jean-Paul, any more than Dan, was the ultimate love I'd been saving my seventh grade sonnets for. But it would have been nice to get more mileage out of each of them than one underinsulated quickie.

Dee's Bash

Searching for Dee's place, Jean-Paul and I grew to loathe each other. I had no idea how to get there by car, from the Pont Neuf. I'd always walked there from Mouse's house, cutting across the park, taking short cuts through alleys. I didn't know the names of the boulevards crossing the route. From the car, I couldn't see the tree-obscured houses that were landmarks when I walked. Jean-Paul kept asking me with effortful politesse if I recognized anything. I kept saying, "No, I'm sorry." What was there to recognize when all the trees were birches and all the houses looked like sugar cubes with roofs? At last we found the Faurers' building. We set off for Dee's from there. I assumed that the car could circumnavigate the park and pick up streets that paralleled my walking route. I'd forgotten that most of the streets were one-way. We'd swoop down a thoroughfare and brake, the whole car shuddering, at yet another "exit only" entrance. Soon I was horribly nauseated, thanks to a hangover and tension and this journey in an unheated, sprung-seated car reeking of gasoline and Gauloise fumes. Between bad temper and tight brakes, the car leaped and halted in a violently spastic trajectory, like a tank in a conga line.

I sensed that Jean-Paul would have liked to put me out on a corner and let me wander. When I offered to sortir, he wouldn't hear of it. His fanatic nature had fixed its sights on the distant star of Dee's flat. After twenty minutes of swooping and shuddering, he parked the car and we walked. I staggered, and sucked in air. Jean-Paul gripped my arm. I seemed to be in custody. I noticed for the first time that his head was on a level with mine. He'd been so right all the time, I hadn't noticed he was small.

When I finally stumbled on Dee's front door, I expected him to drop me and run. But he pressed the bell. Duty on his part and humiliation on mine had made a bond between us that was stronger than love. I would never get rid of him.

"Bloody hell, where've you— Hallo, what's this?" said Dee, catching sight of the glowering Jean-Paul.

"C'est Jean-Paul. Il est artist," I said. "Sorry I'm late— we got lost."

"What's he, French? Won't speak any English, I suppose? Well, that should add zest to the evening. Bit of a shrimp, too, isn't he? Still, we mustn't complain. He couldn't be more of a dead loss than the silly sots I've been lumbered with for the last half-hour. Oh, and I've got some more disastrous news—you'll be simply raging when I've told you but they bloody well bludgeoned me into it—"

Dee had to amplify her naturally clarion tones to crest the swell of a nasal tremor and a vibrant plunking that shook the wiring in the walls.

"What's that wailing?" I shouted, as we followed her down the hall.

"Oh, it's a record—your American country-and-western drivel. One of those Cockney twits you insisted on having brought it round, in your honor—thought you'd be missing it, I gather. I think it's perfectly foul, myself, but what can you expect?"

"Why did you say I'd be mad at you? What's this disastrous—"

"Here we are!" Dee broke through the twanging and wailing chorus with a brisk soprano cheer: the nanny ushering in the vicar and the curate for tea. Dee had marshaled Jean-Paul with the rest of her charges. Obedient and spruce, he awaited orders.

The doleful caterwauling of "Yew lef' me in the mine shaft like a lump o' coal" was appropriate scoring for the atmosphere of bereavement in the salon. The Cockney from the Red Boar and his mate were sitting on one of the cushioned banquettes. They both wore three-piece suits with collars that stretched in folds from the buttons wrestled into strained slits at their necks. They were balancing brandy snifters of beer like teacups. On the cushions on their left sat a girl who appeared to be costumed for a three-day hike on the moor. She was wrapped in three or four tweedy sweaters and a hobble skirt. Her oxblood

lace-up shoes might have had hobnailed soles, and her
socks—I remembered Dee's remark about the socks of the
Irish—were kelly green. Despite the head mistress ensemble, she seemed to be in the last wasted stages of consump-
tion. She had eyes of heartbroken blue. Her skin had the
bluish transparency of skim milk, and her cheekbones and
collarbones protruded like the knobs on a dresser. She was
sitting primly on a cushion, clutching a wineglass, but I
had the impression that she was propped on a shawl-cov-
ered couch by a peat fire, while an accordion outside the
window sobbed through "Danny Boy."

"Well, now, Kerry, you remember Denny," Dee shouted
over the rodeo music, indicating the lad on the left, who
was frowning at his goblet of beer as if it had hairs in it.
He was the one who'd championed the Concorde at our
last encounter. "Cheerio!" he shouted. "This here's me
mate, Clive!"

"Cheerio!" Clive shouted.

"You too!" I shouted. "This here's Jean-Paul!"

"Bonsoir," said Jean-Paul severely.

The eyes of the Anglo-Saxons glassed over. They had
come British, been received as British; they expected to
conduct themselves as British. As an American, I was the
most exotic element they were prepared to contend with.
Besides, Denny already knew I was a pushover on international topics. Representing the publicly sullied honor of
America, I could be reduced to aspic by any of a host of
slogans: "Viet Nam . . . General Motors . . . C.I.A. . . ."
In the wrestling of political argument, I had a limp wrist.
Jean-Paul, on the other hand, was French, which meant
that he could be pinned to the mat in six places and still
look smug. And he cheated by not speaking English. It
was as if he'd demanded that they wrestle in high heels.

"Hallo," said Denny firmly, hoisting his Parisian version
of a pint.

"And this is Meiread. She's Irish," said Dee. "Kerry . . .
Jean-Pierre . . ."

"Jean-Paul," said my escort and I, but Dee had dashed
around the corner to the kitchen, calling, "Make yourselves comfy, I shan't be a mo, I'm just fetching some
treats."

Knowing Dee's notion of treats, I pictured Jean-Paul
confronted with a serving bowl containing half a sponge

cake, self-resurrecting from an ooze of chocolate sauce. We sat on a cushion facing the two boys, the languishing lass on our right. She was drinking something white, marbled with yellow, that looked like buttermilk. I asked her what it was. It was buttermilk.

"Had a bit of a tour of the city today, did you?" said Denny heartily.

"Yes, we went to the Jeu de Paume," I said, adding when it seemed necessary, "that's a museum."

"Oh, how lovely," said the Irish girl wistfully, as if museums were too taxing a pleasure for her. How had she arrived at Dee's flat—on a litter? Trying to extend the circle of our intercourse to the native, I said, "Jean-Paul is an artist."

Meiread, the Irish consumptive, turned to Jean-Paul and asked in French with a lilt more Gaelic than Gallic, "What sort of things do you paint?"

I expected him to say nastily, "Houses." But Meiread's blue eyes were fastened on his. His contemptuous glance was caught. He matched her, focusing his big brown beacons, trying to draw her in as he'd done with me. It was fascinating to watch the two-way beam of their powerful pupils. There was no fly in this string-winding contest; it was spider to spider. Meiread took out a cigarette—proving that she still had one good lung—without removing her delicate sea-colored gaze from Jean-Paul's. Both the slicked-up Cockneys spilled beer on the Comte's rug in their haste to provide her with flame. But Jean-Paul, master of the sexual overtone, slipped from his pocket a flat gold lighter, not so much engraved as chiseled all over, a Rosetta Stone of feminine congratulation. The boys were still grubbing around with matchbooks as Jean-Paul covered Meiread's hand with his left to hold her cigarette steady, and brushed the end of the cigarette with the lighter in his right.

By the end of the cigarette interlude, Jean-Paul had shifted to the cushion beside Meiread. He was launching his Gauguin routine. Meiread looked shocked. No doubt Gauguin was thought racy in Ireland, where a respectable painting had cows in it. With Jean-Paul and Meiread a French-speaking unit, the boys in banker suits were stuck with me. Denny had to store away the file cards he'd been organizing for a hot debate on the Irish question. I waited for news of America's latest salting of the world's old wounds. After four months in Paris, America seemed more like a concept than a country. "America": it floated in the outlying waters of my mind, an island swarming with over-achievers, every palm tree hollowed out and turned into a separately franchised MacDonald's. Bali Hai for the hyper-active.

"Look here," said Denny—I looked, sharply—"what about the plight of the old?"

"I haven't put everything out, as we've got more people coming," said Dee, setting a tray on the glass-topped table. She had arranged on the Comtesse's crystal plates a chunk of Swiss, a triangle of Brie, chocolate-covered cookies, foil-wrapped toffees, some greyish hard-boiled eggs, and, in a gilded basket, crackers à la Ritz.

"Good grief!" I said. "Ritz crackers! You haven't found peanut butter, have you?"

"Je regret, Kerry, je regret," Dee said, "but I have found an American specialité that's all the rage in Paris—potato crisps that come in a tennis ball can. I'm saving them up for later—'pour après,' as Elise says. Haven't you given Jean-Claud any wine?" Dee cut into Jean-Paul's epic monologue. "Voulez-vous quelque chose à boire?" she said carefully, holding the syllables up to the light like jewels sure to be flawed.

Jean-Paul took a swift gander at the Comte's liquor showroom and requested a tumbler of twelve-year-old Scotch, which cost twice as much in Paris as it did in America. "Trust the French," Dee muttered, pouring a scant shot. "What's he up to with Meiread? Well, don't give it a thought, Kerry. She's got her bloke on the way, he'll deal with Jean-Claud."

"Jean-Paul," I said. "Is that who else is coming?"

For the first time in the period of our acquaintance, Dee's eyes slipped away from mine in a manner so patently shifty that she could have been doing a music hall routine called "The Poor Liar." She said, "Yes, well, not exactly, that is to say, there's a bit of a chance, only the remotest possibility of course and I really, quite frankly, profoundly doubt that it'll come to a head—"

She rushed to answer the doorbell in a flurry of relief. Who had she invited? . . . Leah?

Jean-Paul had become impassioned on the subject of Art-Truth-and-Beauty. He was leaning in so far that

Meiread was semi-recumbent. She was the perfect foil for
Jean-Paul; she didn't talk and she didn't eat, though she
kept sneaking little melting looks at the crackers whenever
Jean-Paul took a drag on his cigarette. Dee had told me
that Meiread was au pair for a Baroness who wouldn't let
her eat. Now she was starving for appearances' sake while
captive in a cafeteria. Somewhat cruelly, I demolished half
the Swiss cheese and four cookies, washing them down
with Coke which Dee had bought me for "bon voyage" in
a magnum, like champagne.

When Jean-Paul got up to pour himself a half-liter refill,
the wispy Meiread darted out a blue-white hand, snatched
six crackers and a hard-boiled egg, shoved them into her
mouth and chewed violently, meanwhile slashing off a
hunk of Brie and tucking it into her lace-edged hanky. I
hoped she'd get a chance to eat the Brie before it ran.

Denny and Clive were guzzling beer, replenishing their
goblets from an inexhaustible supply of warm bottles, and
talking football. I was the only witness to Meiread's raid.
She might be a barracuda with men, but she was also a
fellow prisoner of Parisian icebox torture. I slipped her a
handful of toffees and muttered, "My lips are sealed."

The rodeo soundtrack died in a gallop and a moan, like
a small herd of depressed cattle stampeding over a cliff.
In the glorious silence, the boys looked up, startled. Jean-
Paul was still pouring Scotch as if it were draft. Meiread
was trying to swallow without making noise, the grotesque
mouthful bulging out her sunken cheeks and making her
eyes tear up. From the hall, we heard the front door open
and close, but no booming hallos from Dee. Maybe she
and the unknown guest had skipped. I was about to make
some merry jest that would have sandbagged an already
stupefied evening, when Dee toddled in, her mauve-aw-
ninged eyes apop. Behind her in the doorway floated the
sleek black skull and bone-white teeth of an Algerian.

Clive and Denny set down their beer. I gave Dee a look
of consternation, which she returned, Algerians had dogged
our steps, hissing, leering, grabbing, taking up the Métro
seats and tables in cafés that might have been occupied by
real French blokes. Algerians wandered woeful in Paris,
like spirits atoning for sins, scapegoats for the despised
colony of aliens of which we were a part. Now an Algerian,
symbol of our failure to be French, had invaded our final

fête. He was as welcome as the plague victim at the Masque of the Red Death.

Meiread swallowed. "Ali!" she said.

The Algerian grinned and edged past Dee. He wore a coat of buttery yellow-gold suede and carried a loaded pannier. He took Jean-Paul's seat beside Meiread. They kissed.

Jean-Paul nearly fainted. He actually staggered backward into the shelf of bottles. The English boys were so astounded that their mouths opened and closed, like the mouths of fish. Then, as one, they drained their goblets. The symmetry of movement would have appealed to Jean-Paul, if he hadn't been half-dead from social stroke. He waved me over and clutched my arm. But it was insupportable! He had never been in a home with an Algerian! Was this person of color a guest? It was not done to drink with Algerians—

Meanwhile the bubbling Ali was removing waxed paper parcels and plastic containers from his straw bag, and displaying their contents: stuffed black olives; flat soft discs of bread; mounds of something that looked like cream of wheat, on a bed of lettuce; another version of the same stuff in green; huge raw mushrooms; oranges; four kinds of straw-colored pastry, all squishy with honey; something slimy in a thin red sauce; something chunky in a thick brown sauce. Each time he revealed another treat, Meiread gave a happy little cry, and Ali tucked a sample in her mouth, as if she were a ravenous baby bird.

Ali had also brought a coffee maker and coffee, and two bottles of red wine. When the table was loaded with succulent novelties, Ali ceased his happy chatter—he spoke in a French so garbled that I could understand him perfectly —and beamed around at us. He was overjoyed, he said, to make this very small contribution of delicacies from his country. He was overjoyed to be among us.

"I shall just go and fetch some plates," said Dee faintly.

Meiread conducted introductions. Jean-Paul either couldn't or wouldn't move. He barely nodded. Ali leaped over the back of the banquette and ran around the platform to crank Jean-Paul's shrinking arm. The English boys regarded Ali and his delicatessen with bewildered hostility. They expected meals and people to be uniform. Life, to

Clive and Denny, was just a procession of overboiled brussels sprouts.

Dee returned with plates. She had assumed an air of missionary cheer: the air raid warden at the height of the blitz. "We shall have to make the best of it, full stop," she said to me, her voice restored to its painfully audible strength. With that, Meiread introduced Dee as the hostess. Ali threw his arms around Dee and kissed her on both cheeks.

I grabbed the plates.

Clive and Denny were scarlet. They were sweating like hogs from the combination of beer and central heating. I didn't like the grumbling way they conferred, shifting their disgruntled double gaze from Dee to Ali to Meiread to Ali. As I watched, they removed their jackets and laid them out carefully on the platform. Ali, merry as a grig at a maypole dance, had taken some records out of his magic bag. He put them on the stereo. He was babbling to Dee, who stood back, poised to bolt if he lunged.

Meiread was arranging the food, snitching and gobbling morsels of whatever came to hand—bread, olives, pastry, green stuff, white stuff—cramming down fragments and driblets, scraping packages, licking spoons. Jean-Paul watched her, appalled. He was clinging with both hands to his glass, in the paralyzed throes of indecision. The only thing he wanted more than escape was to polish off the top-shelf Scotch.

The music began.

How can I describe it? If you recorded and amplified and played—simultaneously—fourteen different pieces ranging from "Eight More Miles to Louisville" to "Questa o quella," rendered by eleven musical saws, a washboard band, a fog horn, a dozen kazoos, a bagpipe, twenty-three sets of spoons, a Moog synthesizer, and a milk bottle played by a seal . . . you would produce a more coordinated musical mutant than the one that writhed, gnashing its atonal teeth, from the gasping speakers of the stereo.

"Crikey!" said Dee.

Ali began to caper around the platform. He grabbed Dee's hand. He hauled her, as if she were a tree stump dragged from the unyielding earth by a team of mules. "Here, what are you on about?" Dee demanded, trying to extract her hand from his grip.

"He wants to dance, it's in his blood," I said. "Don't they have dancing in England?"

"Oh, you may laugh," panted Dee, determinedly lumpen in the zephyr of Ali's homage to the muse. "But dancing to this infernal racket—you might as well waltz to the sound of the Hoover picking up marbles—" Ali clutched her to his breast in a slow-drag mambo. Dee cried, "Whoa there . . . laissez-moi tranquille . . . bugger off!"

Clive and Denny thundered to her rescue.

Dee would have been the first to admit that she wasn't a cringing flower. I'd seen her take on a rugby team and a purse snatcher all in one night. But her countrymen were glad of an excuse to do a little good-natured Paki-bashing. As Dee yanked her hand away and scurried to ringside, they charged.

The doorbell rang.

"Bloody hell! The racket must have mustered up the police!" Dee shouted, making for the door.

Denny pounced, hooking Ali's left arm to pin it behind his back. Clive rared back, prepared to belt Ali once Denny had him placed. But Ali, misjudging their intent, crooked his own elbow, linking it with Denny's, and capered in a circle. The two of them did a figure combining a judo throw with a highland fling. Whirled off his stance and propelled in the opposite direction, Denny bashed head first into the wall. Meiread screamed. Jean-Paul retreated to the kitchen, rescuing the bottle of Scotch. No doubt he was afraid of damaging his artist's hands if he intervened. Clive, seeing his mate immediately scuttled, reassessed the enemy.

Ali was having a wonderful time. He executed a leap which incorporated splits and a backward spinal snap that would have severed less elastic vertebrae. Clive flinched and ducked, the masses of his ill-distributed muscles bearing him over sideways. He toppled off the edge of the platform and landed on a banquette in the conversation pit, with one gargantuan boot in the plate of . . . eels?

Meiread screamed. Standing on the flanking banquette, she was eating all the toffees, hardly troubling to unwrap them. Her gums were so impacted with toffee that she couldn't wrench her teeth asunder to scream. She screamed with her jaw locked, in a descant growl, like a nasty Yorkshire terrier.

The irredeemable racket of the record had soared to such a pitch—smashing crunching tinkling shrieking scraping—that we seemed to be in the midst of a two-hundred-vehicle chain collision. (I thought of the gang at Occidental Insurance. How they would have relished such a report!) Ali had crippled his dancing partners. He was momentarily stymied. In the cause of peace, I did a few hops. Dancing an Algerian tango couldn't be harder on ball-and-socket joints than jitterbugging at Liaison Nordique. Ali's delight was boundless. He swept me into a swiftly cantering two-man troika, embellished with dramatic slashes of the arms, little balletic rufflets of the toes, unheralded twirls, flamenco claps, and occasional cries of "Éhé!"

The belligerent Cockneys had rallied. Now their assault was checked by my role in the frolic. How could they defend the honor of the womenfolk, when the womenfolk kept throwing their skirts over their heads?

We had reached an artistic climax in our pas de deux—Ali was attempting a lift—when Dee slunk in. She was blushing. I couldn't believe it till the cause of her guilty look entered behind her: the Captain, who should have gone down with any ship going down; Dwight D. E. Clanski, the human embodiment of absolute zero; and Duse, Miss American Zombie, wearing D'Annunzio the chicken on her head like a crown.

Ali rushed forward to welcome them. He mistook the Three Gorillas for a small unsanitary carnival. Introductions were impossible. The soundtrack had shifted into the second movement, a symphony for screech owls and nutcrackers. Duse was too far gone for social graces. With the instinct for self-preservation of a child suckled by wolves, Duse drifted to the table spread with the eclectic disarray of the buffet. She took one of the wine bottles Ali had brought and uncorked it with her fingers. As Dwight might have put it, "Duse doesn't need a corkscrew." Meiread hovered over the eats, protecting her homestead from grazers. As soon as she tried to make eye contact with Duse, she realized that intimidation was useless. If Duse were mystically moved to munch, not even a footprint in the plate of eels would stop her. For now, she devoted herself to the wine. She poured a small amount in a crystal ashtray for D'Annunzio to peck at. Leaving the chicken to scratch up its Baccarat saucer, Duse wandered away to the kitchen.

I followed her as far as the hall, to watch her meet Jean-Paul.

In the kitchen, with its lichenous pipes and its ceiling flaking like a week-old sunburn, Jean-Paul was sitting on the counter—in the absence of chairs—hugging the bottle of Scotch. His pants were hiked up at the knees and his black silk socks had wilted around his ankles, exposing glimpses of worm-veined, hairy calves. His expression was morose. But his eyebrows shot up into the region of his previous hairline at the entrance of the Sweetheart of the Living Dead. Duse's transcendental eyeballs outspaced on any level the orbs of Jean-Paul. Jean-Paul didn't stoop to eat if the repast was flawed; Duse didn't need to eat at all. She was more than his metaphysical equal. She didn't acknowledge his presence. She sat on the floor and removed her socks: three pairs. Jean-Paul might be France's gift to femmes, but to Duse he was just another kitchen appliance.

Duse drifted out, dropping socks. Jean-Paul set down the Scotch with thud of renunciation. He followed her, probably to see if she were real or a sign.

The cacophony in the salon had redoubled. Dwight and the Captain had taken up their instruments and turned the musical traffic jam into a session. Dwight banged away on the exhausted strings of his guitar, which yielded a toneless metallic moan, like bedsprings creaking. The Captain plucked at a dulcimer, wincing, as if it might pluck back. Ali regarded the musicians with doubt. He applauded their zeal but had qualms about their technique. He kept trying to get them to dance instead. But Dwight had trouble putting one foot down before he picked up the other, and the Captain thought of dancing, like everything he couldn't do, as counterrevolutionary.

Then she appeared . . . the terpsichorean muse incarnate . . . Duse! Barefoot, waving the bottle of wine, she leaped to the platform. She struck a pose that would have been classic except for her MSU sweatshirt, red flannel long johns, and man's serge trousers. She passed off the wine to Ali and began to dance. Ali threw back his head and cocked his elbow, drinking from the bottle as if it were a wineskin. The wine ejected in a fat stream, most of which splattered into the carpet.

Dee uttered a strangled cry and bounded to mop up the wine with the nearest remnant to hand, one of Duse's socks. "Yick!" Dee said, dropping the sock and running to get the sponge. Ali and Duse paid no heed to this philistine preoccupation. Wine stains—pah! Who cared for carpeting when one must dance! Duse twined her red flannel arms and swiveled her floppy serge hips. Ali flung aside his suede coat, revealing a woven caftan in six colors, most of which seemed to be turquoise or pink. Crouching, he snaked around Duse in a semicircle, arms spread, like a basketball guard. Duse stomped her bare foot, flamenco-style. Ali began to chant, his eyes fastened on her blissed-out face. I couldn't hear the chant above the splintering discord of the music. Was voodoo big in Algeria? Dramatic tension built, despite the mundane note of Dee, center stage, mopping up wine.

Denny and Clive had been completely routed. The arrival of Ali's new troops had scrapped their plans to surround him and bounce him around. They'd been lubricating their pique. By now, they had consumed enough beer to float the Captain's barge. Propped, swaying, on their heavy boots, they hulked and glared at the revelers. Meiread had eaten everything she'd missed for the last six months. She was lying flat on her back on a banquette. She had lost Jean-Paul's respect, but there was something about her present posture that appealed to him. He pussyfooted over to her, edging around the platform with his arms up as a shield. Clive and Denny watched him, their eyes enflamed with pickled vengeance.

Ali got a hammerlock on Duse and dragged her around in an attempt at an apache dance which looked more like Saturday afternoon wrestling. Duse went limp. Ali flung her around with one arm, dousing the salon's white walls with wine from the bottle in his other hand. Dee had hysterics. She snatched up a carved gourd from a shelf and attacked Ali, pounding him over the head in an effort to permeate his transport before he wrecked the flat.

On the western front, fresh disasters bloomed. Jean-Paul sat beside Meiread. He took her hand and murmured low, "Chérie . . ." Clive and Denny saw Jean-Paul as the fleshy symbol of the forces in Paris that conspired to keep Cockneys horny, self-conscious, and sad. He was also weak. As one, they descended on Jean-Paul. With a philanderer's instinct for the husband's entrance, Jean-Paul saw them coming. He swiveled, blenched, and seized the only weapons available—Ali's deli.

The confluence of noise, brutality, and flying eels was too much for D'Annunzio. Loosing a countertenor aria of pain, he flapped three feet straight up and whizzed around the room, dropping turds like a balloon releasing air.

It would have taken radar to track the flight patterns in the cafeteria riot and dance marathon that ensued. The sounds of breakage, spillage, and wastage added a percussive effect to the music's crescendo.

The carnage called for a biblical blackout—a flood, without an ark. I couldn't flood the fools, so I pulled the plug. I took the needle off the record.

The relative silence of thumps, grunts, and splats! put a dent in the wholesale frenzy. D'Annunzio braked his erratic spiral, slamming sideways into the chandelier. Ali dropped his arms, which were supporting Duse in a fireman's carry. Duse slithered down his back and rolled off the platform, landing on Meiread with a spine-buckling thwomp! Meiread was huddled on her face on the cushions, protecting her neck with her arms. Trapped in the heart of the fracas, she was splotched with red stuff and green stuff, and finely dusted with cracker crumbs. She looked like a fricasseed duck. Similarly decked and basted, Clive and Denny were trying to kick Jean-Paul through the television. The apartment looked like Public Square in Cleveland after the four-day Ukrainian Festival. I had to force myself to look at Dee.

Dee's face was fixed in a waxen mask of horror. But she wasn't looking at the junkyard that had been the salon; she was facing the door to the hall.

Framed in the doorway were the perfect couple who had borrowed seven thousand dollars to construct a salon that was a perfect setting. The Comte and Comtesse had returned from Switzerland in time to see the fall of Paris.

I heard Monsieur's alarm go off—seven o'clock—before he tapped on my door. I'd been awake all night, rolling into various positions, ordering my muscles to relax, concentrating on a blue lake, a blue sky, courting sleep. But I might as well have been bolt upright with the light on, reading *Gone With the Wind*. My whole being was poised for departure. By eight o'clock, I would be making the first real gamble of my life, even gambling with life itself. Hitching a ride with a stranger in a strange country was trusting entirely to luck. When I walked to the border of the autoroute and stuck out my thumb, I would be betting that human beings were decent, friendly, sane. Every time I climbed in a car, I would be putting my chips on a number and chance would spin the wheel.

I took off my nightgown, rolled it up tight, and tucked it into a niche I'd made in the bulk of possessions in my canvas bag. The bag was crammed tighter than when I'd arrived, because of the cashmere sweater and the velour pants Madame had given me, and a fat paperback book. I'd gone back to the bookstore where I'd met Dee, old and moldy Shakespeare and Company, and bought a new copy of *My Life* by Isadora Duncan. She'd been a free spirit. Maybe she'd give me the courage to be really free myself.

As a sacrifice to the spirit of freedom, I'd thrown my watch into the Seine. The watch had been a high school graduation present from my Aunt Martha, a fan of promptitude. Aunt Martha wouldn't have understood the gesture of throwing a timepiece away—she hated waste. But I needed a symbol to give me nerve. If I wanted to know the hour, only to enjoy the lifting of the burden of some responsibility once yoked to that hour, I could ask a stranger. I had to learn to make strangers my friends.

I'd almost tossed *The Book* in after the watch, partly be-

cause I pictured Our Readers on the sewer tour, watching
the pulpy raft of *The Book* bob past their leased canoe.
Besides, the thing weighed as much as Turkle and was
equally humiliating to consult. After five months on the
Continent, I shouldn't need printed guidance. On the other
hand, as Aunt Martha was so fond of saying, "People who
think they know everything will find out different." I ripped
out the France and Italy sections—I didn't read them—
and jammed them in the canvas bag between my good
shoes and the toothpaste. I chucked the mangled corpse in
the incinerator.

I was traveling light. I didn't even have maps. Drivers I
flagged would know whether or not they were headed for
Italy. Once in Florence, I could get a map of Florence.
When in Rome, if I got to Rome, I'd get a map of Rome.
I was flying free.

I'd mailed home the letters I'd accumulated in Paris, all
except "The Legend of the Christmas Mouse," which I'd
kept for a bookmark. Grudgingly, loathing my hypocrisy,
I'd given the bubble-blowing mix and the crayons from
Grace's box to Leah. I'd wadded up the articles of clothing,
fluorescent kneesocks, Dr. Dentons and all, and shoved
them into a paper bag. I'd intended to put the bag in the
incinerator too. Then I'd found myself dragging it down
the street to the Métro tunnel. The spot where the beggar
made her nest had been vacant, blotched with a patch of
damp like a stain. I'd dropped the bag and fled.

I pulled on my stalwart jeans and family retainer sweater. The jeans were floppy in the hips and seat, and white
in the knees. The ribbing of the sweater was nubby and
the elbows were nearly bald. I didn't want to wear Mouse's
hand-me-down on the day I reclaimed my freedom. My
socks were worn through in three toes. I'd set out my
boots and coat in the kitchen the night before, as if this
were the first day of school.

I wanted to be off before Anouk awoke.

I'd said goodbye to Dee the week before. She was back
in England. The Comte had packed her off home the morning after the holocaust. We'd passed a hideous night that
Friday, crying, pleading with Marc and Danièlle not to call
our parents (collect), the British and American ambassa-
dors, my employers, the cops. Jean-Paul and Ali had taken
the back door out to the alley, escaping retribution. The

Cockneys had been stupefied with drink and unspent aggression; they didn't speak French, and their English might as well have been Urdu to the Comtesse. They were hulks, Exhibit A for our indictment. But they were English, which established them as civilized at heart. We'd dismissed the three gorillas as crashers—obviously no one would invite them anywhere—and the Comte had thrown them out. Duse had had to improvise a sling from her sweatshirt to carry D'Annunzio, who had fainted, exhausted from looping the loop. Glimpses of Ali that the Comte had garnered as Ali had taken the tradesmen's exit had almost sealed our deliverance to Devil's Island. What perverted pleasures might we have indulged in, right in the Comte's salon, with that swart exotic! I'd sworn that Ali was an old friend from Cleveland who'd dressed as a Turk for a joke. American blacks were hot properties in Paris; it was very "done" to drink with les noirs. When the Comte remained suspicious, we'd let Meiread take stage. She'd manned the pumps enough to empty Galway Bay. The Comte had promised not to press charges.

Clive and Denny had lumbered out, dragging a sack containing three dozen bottles of beer that they hadn't had time to drink. The Comte had assisted Meiread, who was spent with emotion, into a taxi. Dee and I, who were also spent with emotion, had passed the rest of the night scrubbing walls and shampooing the carpeted platforms. In the morning, I'd gone back to la maison Faurer, to start my nanny chores. Dee had packed. She'd been quite chipper as she took my hand.

"Enjoy your voyage, Kerry. Can't say I'd fancy a trip to Italy myself. My friend Cloris went to Rome on a package tour, and she stopped at one hotel where they used newspaper for toilet paper—ripped it into strips and stuck it on a wire ring twisted out of a coat hanger. Well I mean Italians aren't brought up like we are in England. Not to put too fine a point on it, they've got no moral sense. You'll have to mind your bag."

"Marc and Danièlle were pretty nice about all this," I'd said.

"Yes, it was quite decent of them not to fetch in the police. I can well imagine what prison's like in Paris." She'd nudged me. "Still and all, it was quite a good party, wasn't it? I mean it might have been a bleedin' bore."

Madame as Lady Bountiful had urged me to take along some cheese and fruit—"whatever I would like"—for the road. But I had heard her tiptoe down the hall to the kitchen during the night. When I opened the icebox to pack a lunch, I wasn't surprised to find that the cheese was gone. Apart from a few resentful-looking bananas, we were back to basics: butter and two olives.

Madame had come into the kitchen behind me. "Kerray," she said sweetly, "si cela vous ne dérangez pas . . ."

The fatal phrase. Celeryville de Rendezvous. If you don't mind . . .

My hackles leaped. What the hell was Mouse doing, asking me a favor? I had retired. "Je suis libre!" What's the French for "one foot out the door"? I put the weary banana I was holding back on the shelf and closed the icebox door before I turned around. My face, I hoped, expressed no emotion whatever. It was a monument face, adopted from Emparo. El Rocko.

Madame wore her frilly nightie and her most ingratiating smile. But the sockets of her eyes, like mine, were dark from lack of sleep. We faced off, two raccoons. I said, "Oui, Madame?"

She was desolated to have to ask me, but she had completely forgotten that this morning at the ninth hour—she gave a little giggle and tapped my arm: what an hour!—she had her first lesson in le golf. Her husband wished her to learn to play le golf for making foursomes with his pals de commerce. But Mouse had faired the idiot! She had just recalled herself that Emparo couldn't come till nine today! Mouse had to leave la maison at eight-thirty to make it to her lesson by nine. If it didn't mind me, if it didn't derange me, could I just stay with Anouk—Monsieur would take Leah to the jardin himself—just Anouk, just till Emparo arrived at nine?

"Madame," I said, lentement, en français, avec the face of rock, "you know that I am going to hitchhike and I have to start early. I don't want to be still on the autoroute at night. . . ."

She nodded steadily, compulsively, saying, "Oui, oui, oui, oui." But at the end of my careful explanation, she smiled with all the haggard charm she could muster. She was desolated, but if I wouldn't mind?

"Bien," I said, turning away. I took off my coat and

made myself a café au lait. Anouk was launching in-
quiries in the nursery. I got her up and changed her, hard-
ening my heart against her game of Queen Victoria Roused
by Incompetent Lackeys, which she interspersed with wry
looks from under her froncing sourcils, to gauge my appreciation of her style. What if the next nanny didn't have a
sense of humor? Enough of that! Remember Dee's advice.
"After all, they're not our children, are they?"

I gave Anouk her bottle. Cries of bedlam rang from the
rear of the flat. Leah, as usual, was fairing the turd. Mouse
was trying to dress herself and Leah toute de suite so that
Monsieur could take Leah to school and get to work on
time. Her panic was excessive, I thought. Monsieur owned
all the pudding. It wasn't like he had to punch in. Monsieur
arrived in the kitchen, looking hunted. He fiddled with the
pots for water and milk, the jar of instant coffee, the grid
for toast. He'd never had to make breakfast in his life. He
snatched a glance at me. Did he dare ask me to make him
coffee? or to sit on Leah while her mother shoed her, as if
the little turd were a calf that needed branding? "Bonjour,"
I said coolly, presenting the face of El Rocko.

"Bonjour," said Monsieur meekly. He took a dead banana from the icebox and sidled out.

Madame stumbled in, done up in slacks and layered
sweaters—her golf ensemble—that had cost more than I'd
budgeted to last a month. She dug her shoes out of the
laundry basket and flew out the doorway, tinkling, "Au
revoir, Ker-ray! Merci mille fois!"

"Don't mention it, Mouse," I said for Anouk's ears only.

The Pudding King dragged Leah in "to say goodbye."
She was partly buttoned into one of her "Sunday in Little
Rock" outfits. I could judge the fury of her mother's intent
to be gone by the smudges on Leah's shoes. I'd skipped the
whitewash the night before, and Mouse, the Bleach Freak
of Paris, hadn't noticed. Leah wasn't talking. She hid her
face in her father's trousers—I could see his fingers twitching to get her little mitts off the Prussian-style creases—
and said, "OOch! EEch!" when he tried to make her look
up.

"Ça va," I shrugged. What, me worry? *You've* got to
live with her.

"Bon chance," said Monsieur.

"Same to you," I said.

As he went into the hall, Monsieur said, "Oh, there is a letter for you." He brought it in and put it on the table. When the door to the outside hall had closed on Leah, the only enemy I'd ever had, I picked up the envelope. It was addressed in an unfamiliar hand, a forward-slanting print that reminded me of my youngest brother's writing, the one time I'd seen it, when he'd sent me a birthday card my last year in college. I set Anouk down on the floor to play and opened the letter. I read:

Hey there, little lady—
How'd you like Victor's house? The dining room appealed to me the most, looked like a Chinese powder room. Sure was a surprise to get your card, I figured your buddy would of dragged you back to Bismark. I recollect your home town was Bismark, N.D., wasn't it? You didn't say what you'd been doing in Paris and I take it you must have some type of job as you don't strike me as the type who'd keep writing home for bail-out money, a popular way of declaring independence amongst our compatriots. I hope you had better luck finding a job in Paris than I had in Spain. I started out in Barcelona but the place was crawling with hippies, you couldn't cross the plazas for the frisbees. I tried some of the smaller towns on the coast, but the hippies are all over the place looking for the real Spain. So I ended up in Madrid. There's a fair number of tourists here but they pretty much keep to the buses and are easy to avoid. I wash dishes in a bar to make enough pesetas to pay for a room and two meals a day in a pension. So far the only bullfight I've seen was on TV in a bar. They had instant replay too. I bought an old guitar from a guy so now I'm learning flamenco, not dancing, playing. I'm a slow student but then time is what I've got.
    Well, if you should hit Madrid in your wanderings look me up. I'm staying with Señora Murillo in the Avenidad Jose Antonio, the apartment is on the fifth floor so you might want to holler up and spare yourself the walk. I can't offer you a place to stay as the Señora is hardline Catholic and wouldn't go for a lady guest on the premises. But I sure would like to resume our

acquaintance. I figure to be in Madrid till June or so.
Give my regards to Victor!

Dan Spencer

P.S.: Did you take the tour of the Paris sewers yet?

"Well, well," I said. Anouk looked up and cocked an
eyebrow. "Well, well, well . . . what do you say, Anouky?
How about a side trip to Spain?"

I put the letter in my purse. Now I knew someone in
Spain. Hmmm . . .

Emparo showed up at 9:15. She was amazed to see me,
since we'd said goodbye the day before. When I explained
about le golf, she nodded, the corner of her mouth curling
sourly into the servants' smile. I put on my coat and got my
bag. We hugged.

"Bon voyage!" said Emparo. "Prenez garde en Italie—
prenez garde le sac!": Watch out in Italy—mind your bag!

"Oui, oui," I said. Italy seemed to be known among
Europeans as the Land of the Severed Strap.

"Venez à l'Espagne!": Come to Spain!

"C'est possible," I said, grinning.

I looked at Anouk. She looked at me.

"Allez!" said Emparo, laughing. She shoved me out the
door.

I only had to walk four blocks along the curbs of tree
lawns bordering the Bois de Boulogne to reach the auto-
route. I stood among the trees, looking down on the great
curved shaft of cement, wondering how many thousands
of cars, how many thousands of strangers swept along those
yellow lines every day. Hitchhiking—fairing the autostop
—was saying "Oui" before you understood the question.
Anything could happen.

I walked out onto the berm and stuck out my thumb.

PART FOUR

The Free Spirit

The Moving Target

It was midafternoon.

The pale grey blanket of the highway lay silent under the sun. The neat fields of bud-green grass and sun-rich soil were painted through an Impressionist haze of light. A small brown farmhouse and its hovering barn were drawn simply, cleanly against the sky. Looking out the windows of cars and trucks, I kept wondering how they did it, the French; how they made paintings everywhere. The whole country looked like the masterwork of an artist so sure and so mellow in technique that he could sketch in a tree with offhand affection and achieve an effortless clarity, a symmetry not only within the single painting but with every other painting of his life.

Smoke and a growling motor in the distance heralded another potential freebie. Shouldering the leather purse and taking up the canvas bag, I stuck out my thumb and smiled. Like anything for which I'd found I had a knack— hurdling in track and field class, selling Girl Scout cookies —hitching was fun. What power! Stopping a Frenchman's oblivious motorized passage with one upraised digit: revenge on France!

Hitching was a piece of cake in France. I was a young girl, alone. All I had to do was point my thumb and smile into the windshields of approaching voitures. When they saw my outstretched female arm, Frenchmen pulled over so fast that I never even had a chance to pee between rides. Before the car I'd alighted from was out of sight, another eager beaver was reining in to take me aboard. In fact, peeing, or not peeing, was the only problem. How could I ask a Frenchman to stop his car so I could pee? The first day, I rode in bloated agony for hours till I asked a trucker, Jean of Lyon, to pull off the road while I retired to the bushes. He was delighted; he had the same urge I had. He took the field to the left. I took the hedges to the right. When we rendezvoused, our relationship was chummy. The cab of the truck was a clubhouse. Mutual human frailty had made us pals.

Three rides, each with a lone male driver, took me as far as Lyon. The first man, Georges, was a paunchy salesman who had a daughter my age. He asked me if I preferred men of experience. I asked him if his daughter did. That put a snag in his line. Jean from Lyon drove a produce truck. He offered to take me fishing. Jean from Aix drove a fish truck and bought me lunch, a bowl of chowder, in a diner. He told me that Richard Nixon had ordered the murders of every political figure who'd died since 1952.

All my hosts were bearish on Nixon. It was useless to point out that Nixon wasn't President any more. "Ah, oui?" said Georges, Jean I, and Jean II, each with the same ironical smile. Retirement! Ha! They'd heard the same tale from De Gaulle.

Rides were so easy to come by that after Jean II dropped me off, I spurned the next two offers. One veto went to a withered old coot in a panel truck that chuffed along at twenty-five, as if it had a bellows for an engine. The underbelly of the truck was so eaten with rust that the muffler was tied to the bumper with twine. "Merci," I said politely, "but I'd like to get to Nice tonight." (Nice, Jean from Aix had advised me, was where I should couche for the night.) The ancient caboose chuffed away. The other reject was ripping up the road in a flame-orange shark-tailed chariot, when a bestial instinct told him that the blur he'd passed was female. He threw his weight on the brake at eighty. The tires bled rubber for a quarter of a mile. The orange fish backed up, snarling, and halted with a chrome tusk nudging my hip. The greaseball driver wore a T-shirt that fitted like a wax cast of ribs. His eyes rolled over my camouflaged chest. His tongue quivered as he asked where I was going: "Où vas-tu?"

"Tu," yet! Who was he calling "tu"?

He opened the door of the demon machine. I noted the trash heap of cognac bottles, the black lace peekaboo panties dangling from the mirror, the huge pair of pliers on the seat. "On va faire l'amour après," he said to put me at ease: we'll make love later.

What's the French for "That'll be a cold day in hell"?

"Kiss off," I said.

"Comment?" he said, slavering.

"Non!" I said. "Allez!"

The flame-toned jalopy blasted off.

I was gazing at the farmhouse, cut small and clean as a diamond on a cloth of blue, when a bright yellow sports-car pulled up. The driver was a woman. She didn't speak when I got into the car. "Merci bien," I said. I thought she was about thirty, which was the age of sophistication to me. But one of the first and last questions she asked me was, "How old are you?" "I'm twenty-one," I said, speaking French as she had. "Moi aussi," she said.

If we were the same age, we had nothing else in common. We looked like Before and After shots in an article called "Can the Feminine Gender Be Saved?" Split, grimy fingernails, frazzled hair, beat-up jeans, lint-ridden holey sweater: I looked like I'd been ginning cotton. My alter ego wore a white silky dress, slashed low between her heavy breasts and high up her smooth brown thigh. I could tell by the sheen of her stockings that they were silk. White plastic chandelier earrings tinkled dully in the glossy fall of her long black hair. Her lips, her cheeks and finger-nails, even her toenails, peeking out from the white straps of her high-heeled sandals, were dragon's-blood red. Her sunglasses had an opaque, metallic sheen that hid her eyes, giving her an air at once enticing and remote. She smoked the way I breathed, automatically, lighting a new cigarette from a dying nub. Her cigarette case was gold, inset with a lump of stone of a milky marbled blue.

"What are you doing in France?" she said.

"I was an au pair in Paris," I said. "I quit."

"Yes, I have done that," she said tonelessly. "I hated it."

She didn't speak again. The silence was restful after the political and sexual panel show conducted by the men. I watched the smoothly rolling grass of lemon-dusted green, the curved-roof houses, the wind-wrought trees.

The sun was melting across the grass as we left the auto-route. The green shoots in the neat brown fields were tipped with gold. The narrow road, white in the fading light, was flanked with the mottled trunks and fisted branches of plantain trees, the sentinels of the Place des Vosges. Plantains would always remind me of the night I'd met Dan, the night I'd decided to stay in Paris. I smiled at the trees in greeting and affection. Over the hum of the motor, the girl said, "You have courage, hitchhiking, a woman alone."

"No," I said, "I'm terrified. I do it because I have no money. If I want to travel, it is necessary to hitchhike."

"Yes," she said. "If it's necessary, one does it."

The sky darkened downward as night sank toward the earth. Trees and fields were glimpses of glaring color in the sweep of headlights. We moved through utter night, a country blackness not broken by stars. I had nodded into sleep, my neck bent crooked to rest my head on the seat, when the car stopped. "This is Nice," she said. "That is the railroad station. You should be able to find a pension that is cheap in this neighborhood."

I'd seen hotels near the Greyhound station, Cleveland's idea of a depot. I didn't want to sack out in "Flo's Rooms, By the Week, the Day or the Hour." But I got out. "Merci bien," I said.

She smiled, not turning her mirror-coated eyes from the road. Driving into the grassy blackness, she'd kept her sunglasses on. "Good luck," she said. The little yellow car nipped away.

I went to four full pensions before I found a fifth one with a vacancy. Each pension was a single floor, or a single large apartment, up at least three flights of nearly vertical stairs. Dragging my bag up the last groaning rung of each ladder, I was shunted aside by triumphant descending travelers who'd booked my room. I knew they all had *The Book* stashed in their purses and knapsacks. They were the Author's people: cheery ladies with stringy calves who carried flashlights and Tums; shopworn hippies, arisen from the ashes of the burnt-out sixties, and their teenaged clones. "How's America?" I wanted to ask them, inquiring for the health and state of mind of a old friend whom I wished well, but had no desire to see. But they wouldn't have understood the question.

At last a man consented to sell me a horizontal space. Like the raccoon-eyed concierge in Paris who'd snubbed Grace and me, he didn't speak English. But now I spoke French. I tried not to smirk as I bartered for use of the single shower stall, at an extra charge. He would have offered to rent me, at an extra charge, the single towel, but I had my own. The cubicle assigned to me was stark, with fissured walls of insurance beige. In the pasty sink, one lone faucet dribbled yellow water. Each plop on porcelain echoed in the rigorous silence. Either I had the whole floor to myself, or the rest of the tenants were monks. At least the lobby wasn't filled with Greyhound station remnants, peddling watches for $2.98, or flesh for the price of a meal.

I ate the hard-boiled eggs I'd swiped from Mouse, and an apple. I could hardly stay awake to chew. Being adorable in someone else's language was exhausting. Asking a stranger for the favor of a ride, I felt compelled to be perky and bright—for every question, a witty response. Hitching so far had been one continuous Q and A. Also, I had a secret conviction that I alone could dispel the French image of Americans. America was the in-joke of Europe, the lovable lame-brained jock in a family of esthetes. I could change all that!

It wasn't enough for the French to truck me around their country free of charge—they had to love me.

I cherched the shower. What I found resembled a shower, in that the water fell down. The spigot yielded a niggardly sprinkle that rolled off my scalp in a mist. Shampoo would have rubbed in like gum. Disgusted, I put on my nightgown and carried my purse back down the hall. The purse contained my passport and airline ticket and three hundred dollars, accrued from the kickback of Uncle Sam, the pittance I'd saved out of Mouse's stipend, and twenty-five bucks from my father, "an early birthday present." My birthday wasn't till August. (Leo or Virgo—you figure it out.) Like a seasoned traveler, I was minding my bag.

The lobby was hushed. Even the proprietor had vanished. I wrote him a note, asking him to call me at 9 a.m. I had the eerie feeling that I was the only guest he'd ever had—that the pension had appeared as I'd rounded the corner of the street, and would dissipate like smoke as soon as I'd departed. I could hear Rod Serling's ironic tones: "Some call it Nice, some call it . . . the Twilight Zone."

I pattered back to my drawer in the morgue. The bed had the springs of a concrete slab. I wound my arms around my purse and slept like the dead.

The rattle of the doorknob woke me. I sprang into an upright coil, my feet on my purse, as if it were a hot water bottle. "Mademoiselle, il est neuf heures," the doorknob growled.

"Merci," I said. The room was dark. There weren't any windows. I dressed and brushed my teeth again, speculating on the number of species in a drop of yellow water. I trundled my bag past the empty desk in the empty lobby. Halfway down the block, I looked over my shoulder. There was the sign: CHAMBRES.

A bag on each arm, I jounced downhill toward the sea.

Morning in Nice, a harbor town: even at the peak of the hill that propped the city out of the sea, the misted essence of aqua waves and creamy ivory foam from which the city had arisen clung fresh and damp to the sidewalks, the glass-fronted, cheap cafés, the shabby hotel doors. On the market street, its green central ribbon of lawn staked down against the breeze with palm trees, the sidewalks were an asphalt bargain basement of cheap cloth, glass made of plastic, garish souvenirs. Dark-skinned, dumpy women were already plowing through bins of parrot-colored garments. Dark men, skinny and intense, clustered in the doorways of tenements, arguing in violent spurts that climaxed in braying laughter. The Spanish workers of Nice were harder to quell than their Paris relations. Some of the granite doorstoops were strewn with bottles like the flowers on a grave. Men hissed as I passed them: ". . . sssssssss . . . Señorita, bella señorita . . ." The hissing and mumbling made me feel befouled. Why did they wait till I'd passed them to speak endearments? Were they afraid I might respond?

The main drag of Nice was the Boulevard des Anges— the Street of Angels. Beyond it swept the aqua sea, fenced by the boardwalk and the beach of white pebbles. On the town side of the boulevard stretched the line of palaces, grandiose, ornate, that housed the rich on holiday: the grand hotels of Nice. There were pink stucco piles ringed by palm trees, with doormen stationed beneath the tile-roofed porticoes to scoop old ladies out of the plushy pockets of limousines. There were white-pillared shrines, set behind gravel crescents lined with waxed fat cars, each limousine's front window starred with a silhouette head in a smart-brimmed cap. The grand hotels had hundreds of rooms. Each room looking out on the tranquil bay cost hundreds of dollars a day. The placid, surging waters were a deep greenish blue, a blue that seemed exaggerated, calculated to charm.

I threaded my way through cruising, purring limousines and custommade sportscars. Lanes of traffic moved slowly, luxuriantly, richly as beaten cream poured from a bowl. Gaining the curb, I crossed the grass to the boardwalk and leaned on the wooden rail.

The sky was a gentler blue than the sea. Gulls beat their antic wings above the skittering play of the tide. On the beach of white rocks, teenagers in modish robes sat cross-legged, smoking, in the cool glow of morning. Their brown skins were dusty, as if from the white drifts of stones mounded on the beach like hard round snow. I turned to watch the idlers on the boardwalk. A few fat children in spiffy suits or hampering petticoats were eating buns. The children looked cranky and hot. Here and there a buggy bounced, shoved by an au pair who was steaming with boredom. Some sturdy boys in T-shirts sat on the edge of the boardwalk facing the street, calling and whistling to every nubile female who passed. For the most part, they leaned on the rail, bereft.

Everyone else was old. The benches twittered and sighed with old ladies in lace-up shoes and dark dresses, and a few old men whose yellowed suits retained the creases of many mothballed winters. The only concessions they'd made to the sun were straw hats, and straw fans shaped like spades on a playing card. The rhythms of the gulls' wings were balletically echoed by the flutter of straw fans down the miles of benches, down the multitudes of the old. Nice was the Miami Beach of France.

In my boots, with my heavy coat over my arm, I looked like a visiting penguin. I forded the highway and found a café, set among low hedges. The waiter gazed at me, undiluted horror in his eyes, as I set my bag and purse on a white wicker chair and took a chair myself. My table could be seen from the street. He thought I'd be bad for business. No doubt he was right. Any qualms I'd had about invading such a high-falutin' saloon were squelched by the waiter's pained expression. "Un grande-crème s'il vous plaît," I said flatly. My tone implied that I had reserves of outrageous behavior to draw on, if thwarted. The waiter backed away, chewing his lip.

The place looked like the lounge of a retirement home

for the rich. Ladies with blue hair, sandbagged with diamonds, conversed in the lumpen dialects of New York, Kentucky, Los Angeles. Businessmen with sagging bellies and chins drank whiskey sans ice at three bucks a shot—it was just after 10 a.m.—discussing the state of corn shares in Chicago. Three old codgers, each at a separate table, were French—I knew them by their triple-ringed eyes and unsullied handkerchiefs, by the brusqueness with which they dismissed the fawning waiter. The three of them eyed me. I felt like a plate of veal. The waiter set my coffee cup down as if it were a dog's dish. But the café au lait was thick with milk and bounteous with foam. I ordered croissants for sustenance, and to make a point. The waiter was not impressed.

When the American businessmen had hauled their attachés to the Hilton, or somewhere like the Hilton, a young woman entered the café. She was dressed in silky white. She chose her table carefully—a table brushing the waist-high hedge at the sidewalk. But she sat with the chair set sideways, her full body displayed to the café's patrons, only glancing at the street, as if she were testing the swing of her white plastic chandelier earrings.

I thought it was odd that she wore the same ensemble as when she'd picked me up outside Lyon. I smiled and started to signal. She'd brought me all the way to Nice. At least I could buy her coffee. Sun glanced off the cold-chrome shields of her eyes as her glossy head turned. She didn't acknowledge my smile. I stilled the tentative movement of my hand.

After she'd ordered Perrier from the goggle-eyed waiter, she slid her glasses off and perched them atop her head. Her brows and lashes were thick and black, but the fleshy lids of her eyes were almost closed against the light. If she were twenty-one, she'd have worn out fast. After a moment, she plucked the glasses off her head and toyed with them—blowing on the lenses with pouty red lips, wiping them clean with the fabric of her dress where it fell in a loose fold, revealing her breast. Hers was a very smooth act.

The hurt that I'd felt when she'd snubbed me was gone. She had come to the café for a purpose which I would have hindered. But I was puzzled. Why was she wasting her floor demonstration on octogenarians? I cast a glance at the street. No one of virility was passing.

The blue-hairs collected their sparklers and their credit cards, shoulders rigid with distaste for persons of a certain stripe who tried to drink Perrier with high-class folks. When the delegates of decency had cleared the hedges, two of the three lone lizards beckoned the waiter. Terrified of losing either tip, the waiter hesitated. Then he padded to a midpoint between the two furiously scribbling old men, blocking their views of each other. "Oui, monsieur?" he said to his fingernails.

The old coot on the waiter's left finished first. He handed the waiter a folded note and pointed one horny finger toward the damsel, who was picking lint out of her little white purse with an air of unconcern. The waiter started toward her, edging past the table where the second old coot was winding up his pitch on the back of a card. The runner-up yanked on the waiter's arm, dragging the waiter's ear down to his own mouth and whispering instructions. The waiter took the card. As he moved away, his back to both ambitious swains, he tucked the card in the folded note. He laid them together on the lady's table, smiling, bowing, dancing backward, ensconcing himself in a gap in the hedge where he might be discreetly of service.

What a life! toadying to the desiccated rich! No wonder the waiter was such a snob. He had to worship money to keep his self-respect. If he judged his clientele by any standard but wealth, he'd set fire to the hedges.

The former au pair read her mail, turning over the card, unfolding the note with cruel red fingers. The old men waited. The waiter waited. I waited too; the suspense was terrific. Then the tie was broken. The third old coot, who'd been wistfully passive, probably forbidden by his doctor to write, got interminably to his feet. Shoving himself away from the wicker table with his cane, he hobbled to the fleshpot's table. He poked his quavering fingers inside his baggy lapel, drew them out, and dropped a ring with a red stone the size of an olive on the table.

She put the ring in her little white purse and assisted the invalid out. But I noticed that she also kept the note and the card. The thing to remember in sales, it's not your contact, it's your follow-up.

Maybe she thought whoring was a step up from taking abuse from a turd like Leah. I didn't know what she'd left at home when she'd come to Nice, dressed in white silk, driving her yellow sportscar. I didn't know what she'd escaped or how she'd come when she'd made her first trembling venture which had been more courageous than mine when I'd stood on the highway and stuck out my thumb. But the scene had depressed me. She was the same age I was. I paid the waiter—since neither of the old coots had tipped him, I made it unanimous—and cut through the purring parade of limousines on the Street of Angels. With my youth and my smile, I bought passage out of Nice.

Autostoppers note: It is harder to get out of Monaco than it is to get out of Cleveland.

The ride to Monaco in a yogurt truck was a dizzying dash along a cliff—a chunk of rosy dust tufted with pine trees, between the vivid blues of sky and sea. As the truck was twisting and swooping over the azure sea, like a butterfly carving a flight against the sky, I was explaining to my host, Pierre, why I wouldn't like to cop a quickie on the mattress nestled against the seat behind my head. Pierre was disillusioned by my refusal. He'd thought that all Americans in jeans were Hollywood hippies—politically rabid, dope-benighted, sexually insatiable. The fact that I looked like Huck Finn's stand-in didn't dent his dream. Pierre had very specific questions to ask a captive hippie. When I failed to grasp his import, he resorted to graphic gestures that nearly shot us into the bay. Reluctantly persuaded that I was not your typical American coke freak and nympho, packing flint and steel in hopes of an encounter with a dynamite fuse, Pierre still wanted to know what I, a female alone on the road, did for sex. I said I was engaged to a narrow-minded man in Ohio.

"Eh bien alors!" said Pierre, shrugging and shifting gears: so what?

But Pierre was a gent. He dropped me off at an intersection where, he declared, I would snag another ride tout de suite! It was eleven o'clock on a sunwashed morning. Pierre predicted that I would be in Italy by noon.

At noon, I was standing in the same spot, shifting my feet to prove I hadn't taken root. I felt terribly aggrieved. After a flying start, here I was, stuck in the hard heart of Monaco!

Faces frozen in smooth chunks of windshields, as if suspended in ice . . . slippery, darkly burnished fenders, swelling out of shining grills, like wet seals lolling on floes of ice . . . Monaco was arctic, its rivers of traffic choked with the glacial metallic transit of the fearfully rich. I tried to single out a face behind each chunk of glass, eyes that might respond to the appeal in my eyes. But I kept finding the long, anonymous faces of chauffeurs, suspended like icicles from dark-brimmed rocks in the caverns of limousines. The smaller, dimmer globes receding in the depths of back seats were haloed in the hoarfrost of sparse white hair, or stamped on the starkly pink, fleshy knobs of hairless skulls. Even in Nice, there'd been a few youngsters, a baby or two for ballast. Had I stumbled on the elephants' graveyard of the jet set? Or was Monaco a Shangri-la in reverse, where anyone who crossed its border was instantly shriveled to a husk of hard arteries, tough sensibilities, and heavy pockets? I checked the wrist below my hopeless thumb for liver spots. I shouldered my bags, and walked.

The ponderous pace of traffic slackened. Astonishment jammed the stream. Rich people forced down the squeaky windows of Rolls or Bentley to crane at the sight of someone taking a walk. I waved. "Allez-vous comme moi?" I asked sweetly: goin' my way? The windows squeaked up. The seal-mobiles slithered away.

The sun was white in a sky of implacable blue. I sweated, and shifted the load: bag, coat, purse. I wished I were wearing the vacuuming shirt instead of the elbowless sweater. I stopped in a shop and bought a bar of Lindt bittersweet chocolate. There'd be no free chowder from a kindly trucker today. The chocolate cost almost double what it would have in altruistic Paris. In addition, the shop sold plates, stamps, coins, ashtrays, cigarette lighters, cigarette cases, placemats, cocktail napkins, backscratchers, hotplates, light-switch covers, scarves, sunglasses, and money clips all stamped with the smiling countenance of Princess Grace, née Kelly, Philadelphia's own. Who bought these souvenirs? I pictured a lackey kneeling on the sidewalk, holding up a tray to the window of a Rolls, as the billionaire enthroned on the back seat perused the selection of Princess Grace cufflinks. I almost bought a backscratcher for Randy, but it cost five dollars. A five-dollar joke wasn't funny.

Nibbling chocolate already soft from the heat, I slogged uphill. I cursed the suede boots smothering my toes and

ankles. My only other shoes were high heels to go with the
dress, and tennies. I didn't have the guts to unpack my
bag on the sidewalk and put on tennis shoes.

The sidewalk rose to a landscaped plateau. The grass in
its circles and triangles was cropped like the nape of a
West Point cadet. Palms and eucalyptus trees imitated sen-
tries. Hedges pretended to be wrought-iron fences. Flower-
beds pretended to be moats. The zoological masquerade
was enhanced by a reverent hush and a smell of perfume,
fertilizer, Scotch, and money. In the midst of this elaborate
park, clicking with the sounds of clippers, rose a palace. I
approached, expecting to be seized by troops in tall hats
with chin straps and high black boots, toy soldiers come to
life. But the only guard at the door of the house of Rainier
was an old man in unconvincing livery. He looked like a
Rent-a-Cop.

I said, en français, "Is this the palace?"

The impervious mask of the doorman never cracked.
"Non, mademoiselle," he said, "c'est le casino."

The casino! Who had designed it—Victor Herbert? I
decided to go in. I could spare a few francs for the slot
machine. Besides, I was dying to know if the matches and
glasses and cocktail napkins and tables and chairs and
towels in the ladies' room were decaled with Princess
Grace. But the doorman barred my way.

"Je regret, mademoiselle," he said, pointing to my jeans.

"But I'm an American," I said in English. How could I
cut through Grace's yard without taking a shot at a booth
in Grace's carnival?

To pacify me, he gave me a pamphlet—probably a tract
against the evils of gambling—and pointed beyond the
terrace, across the incredible drop and sweep of white cliffs
and bright blue sea to a shrimp-pink box on the opposite
bank of the harbor. "C'est le palais de Rainier," he said.

"That pink thing?" I said. It looked like the new dorm
on campus. Grace was a fool. She should have made whoever held the franchise on the gambling den swap quarters.

Barred from instant riches, I took up my bag, which felt
like a kingsize mattress by now, and walked. At the swell
of another hill, the sidewalk was flanked on the right by a
chest-high wall. I rested the bag on the wall and looked
over the edge. Far below, tennis courts of red clay were
set in a Kelly-green lawn. Half a dozen supple dolls in

brilliant white were tripping and gamboling after a swarm of balls. Doll gods in blue sat on high steel chairs. They seemed to be lifeguards, prepared to dive in and rescue a player who'd gotten beyond his depth.

A man in a tennis sweater leaned on the wall beside me. He was too pretty to be real. I suspected that he was a model, hired by the king to decorate the route to Menton. He wasn't local—he was under sixty. The handsome plant regarded me and smiled. I could almost read the print of the advertisement across his chest.

"Bonjour," he said. Noting my luggage, he added in French, "Where are you going?"

"To Italy," I said, "but I have to walk. No one will give me a ride."

"I have my car," he said, pointing to a snappy red sportscar at the curb. "I will take you to the border at Menton."

"Merci bien!" I said.

In the car, I kept sneaking looks at his profile. He was the prettiest man I'd ever seen. You could clap a wig on a face like that and cast it opposite Robert Redford. On the other hand, Jean-Paul had been gorgeous too. Who said "All good looks are a snare"? I was acutely aware that I'd been traveling bathless for two days and sweating all morning. I hadn't washed my hair since Paris, and it felt like the windshield of a car that had driven the length of Mexico.

This man probably didn't sweat at all; he didn't seem to have pores. He was asking me the usual questions: where was I from, where was I going, wasn't I glad to escape from materialistic America, what did I think of (unassuming, simple) Monaco? I was tired of being A. I wanted to be Q for a change. I asked him what he did, exactly, allowing him leeway to answer in terms of occupation or pastime. He shrugged. Like most pretty people, he wasn't the Personality Kid.

Turning off the intracity highway, he nosed the little red car along a leafy avenue. In the sun-veined deeps beyond the screens of foliage, I caught flashes of white or dark stone, of the manor houses of fiefs. We seemed to be taking the scenic route. "The Advertisement" must be desperate for diversion. I sagged against the seat and rolled my head.

It felt wonderful to be out of the sun, to let my sticky feet dangle.

The pretty one put out a manicured, sun-browned hand and stroked my hair. "Ces sont jolies, les cheveux," he said: pretty hair.

I didn't even tense. "You must be kidding," I said.

"Comment?" he said, settling his hand on my denim thigh. A cloud of dust arose. I giggled. Encouraged, he slid his fingers downward inside the curve of my thigh. More dust. "Non," I said, removing the hand, which was gritty now. "Non non."

"Mais pourquoi pas?" he wheedled, "pourquoi pas, chérie?": why not?

"Pourquoi?" I said: *why?*

He zipped back to Main Street and kicked me out at the first red light. I hoped the old lady who paid for his next manicure had awful breath.

Marching across the entire expanse of Monaco sounds like more effort than it is, since the country is roughly the size of Shaker Heights. But anyone who's ever been arrested for walking barefoot in Shaker Heights, as I have, knows what it's like to haul a canvas pack through Monaco. I was back in France, and then at the French-Italian border, by early afternoon. But I was thoroughly disheartened.

Mind Your Bag

The French guards waved me through. I was too grubby to excite their interest. The Italian guards exploded in a passionate babble as I plodded toward their booth. I set down my bag. They grinned. "Passaportay, per favoray, signorina," sang out the one who was eating salami. I dug my passport out of the bottom of my purse, filling my left hand and elbow with money, chocolate, an orange, Dan's letter, my address book—containing the addresses of Emparo, Dee, and Dan, which might come in handy, and of Denny and Clive, which would not—the journal my parents had sent me for Christmas, with its reproachful white pages; a picture of Anouk and me that Dee had snapped in the park. Good old Anouk must be froncing her sourcils at lunch right now. . . .

The guard shifted his sausage to his left hand, wiped his right on his pants, and took my passport. His eyes never left my breasts. His pal, who'd been reading a comic book as he waved cars through, sang out, "Buon giorno, bella signorina!" I smiled faintly and said, "Buon giorno." Grinning, he gave my whole body an intense examination. "Would you like me to turn around?" I said.

"Non capisco," he said: I don't get you. He shrugged. In body language, the shrug was an international cliché. But an Italian shrug took twice as much time, and five times as many muscles, as a French shrug. "C'est un joli jour," I said: nice day, ain't it? The guards looked at each other and shrugged. Back to Square One—the mute or the dolt, pick a role.

The salami man handed me back my passport. The cover smelled like salami. He took a chaw from his sausage and a gnaw from the loaf of bread crumbling across a log book on the counter of the booth. He demanded something in Italian.

"Non capisco," I said. I shrugged. Mine was more gymnastic than a French shrug, but less abandoned than an

Italian shrug, with an Ohio "That's the breaks" accent. The comic reader laughed. The salami man asked me in tumbling and hopping mime how much money I had. He thought I was a vagrant. No wonder—I looked like I'd rolled off a freight. I held out the roll of francs. He eyed it, took it, counted it. Nodding severely, he handed it back. Now the money smelled like salami. The guards waved me through. When I looked back, they were leaning out of the booth, watching my ass.

I changed the odoriferous francs into lire at a trailer parked by the road. Recalling the warnings of Emparo and Dee, I took the lire and wadded it up in two rolls. I tucked a roll in either front pocket of my jeans. In case I fell in with lusty, romantic, salami-scented thieves, I thought it would be wise to spread the wealth.

I stuck out my thumb.

All the cars that puttered past me toward the highway were stuffed with people, the windows that faced me increasingly filled, as the car neared my post, with delighted and curious faces. Young men and old men, fat ageless women, numberless children, bulgy or stringy old ladies, dogs . . . "tout le monde," as we say in France, "the whole world" was entering Italy, and all in one car. But the cars kept coming. I was amazed that so many Italians drove 1956 Pontiac sedans. (I knew the model from outerspace flicks of the middle fifties, the golden age of cheapies.) Watching the passage of round-shouldered cars, crammed with heads caroming and bobbing like molecules in steam, I wondered if I'd have to walk across Italy too, or ride in someone's trunk. Even the humped roofs were lashed with creosote baskets. Where had they been, these Italians with empty baskets, where were they going? Would some adventurous paisan be willing to let an American signorina ride in the basket mounted on his Pontiac, like a maharajah precariously perched atop an elephant?

A sky-blue Volkswagen van was parked by the side of the road near the money changer's trailer. The man and woman sharing the front seat were big and blond, and the sticker on the rear door was a "D," for "Deutschland": they were German. They had been consulting a map and drinking orange pop. Now they observed me with interest. As the van's motor started, I rolled my head, allowing my body to droop. I was fairing the Waif.

The man called, in French, "Where are you going?"

I snapped to. "Florence, finalement," I said.

"We are taking the coastal route, going very slowly," he said, speaking French more lentement than I did. "But you are welcome to ride with us."

It was the leisurely tour with the Deutsch or the elephant ride. "Thank you!" I said. The German couple shifted their belongings in the back of the van to make me a space on the mattress. I slung my bag and purse and coat in a corner. "It is so good to sit!" I remarked inanely. They smiled. I couldn't get over how large and fair and calm they were, after the French. They were on holiday, taking two weeks to roam the coast of Italy. We laughed about the fact that none of us spoke Italian. The man spoke some English; we veered between English and French as the car poked along in the single lane of a road bottled up with basket-laden cars and trucks. The van rolled forward a few feet, and stopped, and rolled again, and stopped. The road plunged down a hill and into a tunnel. Beyond the tunnel, we could see the road as it sloped and curved to a bridge, and beyond the bridge, the dark, splayed stacks of buildings of the town. The whole route was strung with the motionless beads of cars.

"I wonder what all these big baskets are for," I said.

"We have asked the border patrol," said the man in English. "This is the market day in the town there. All these"—he flicked a pale hand at the chain of cars—"are Italians who live at Menton. They come to buy in the market."

Why would an Italian live in France? Perhaps, like the Spanish maids of Paris, Italians could earn higher wages in France than they could at home. Living in Menton, just across the border, they could pile in the Pontiac, change their French-gotten francs into lire, and spend them foolishly back in the old home town. It was just my luck to hitch into Italy the one day in the week when the entire Italian ghetto of Menton was on wheels, converging on Ventimiglia to blitz the banana stands.

The German pointed off to the left, where we could see the broad stretch of a highway, traversed by tiny bullets of cars. "That is the autostrada," he said. "We are not using it. You have to pay . . ."

"Tolls?"

"Tolls," he nodded. "In Germany the highways are excellent, and they are free."

German superhighways . . . Adolph had had some ideas about that. Didn't you have to be blue-eyed and blond to steer your German-made car through the entrance gate? My host and hostess qualified—they could have been Siegfried and Sieglinde—but they would have had to ditch me on the asphalt island of a comfort station. Marooned for my brown hair and freckles. No Irish Need Apply.

The work ethic nibbled at my entrails. I should have been out there on the autostrada, waving my thumb at Italians bound for Florence or Bust. I was wasting hours of road time, sacked out in the van, which crept along in ceremonial procession like a float in the Columbus Day parade. I gave the work ethic some chocolate to keep it quiet.

Many links up in the metal necklace, someone honked a horn.

Honking, under the circumstances, was spitting into a hurricane. The hurricane's response was annihilating. Everybody honked. Up and down the widing chain of cars, frenetic, impeded Italians honked, bellowed, pounded on their steering wheels, violated the air with the sweeping obscenities of gestures, threw open their doors, leaped from their cars and ran up and down the center line of the road, roaring abuse at abusive drivers in the stalled lane, and at drivers in the opposite lane of traffic who didn't even swerve to keep from creaming a countryman.

My German friends loved it. They laughed, leaned forward, pointed out particularly antic specimens of outraged Latino. The big blond man got into the spirit and gave his horn a few shy toots, as the woman laughed indulgently: what the hell, it's our vacation. At once, the man yanked his hand away from the horn. "Polizei," he said, pointing to a cop car cruising down the center line, scraping fenders in either lane and reaping furious comment from the crowd, now united in impotent wrath against the cops, the government, the world, and God.

The tempest waxed and waned as the line of cars nudged forward. We reached the fortress wall of delapidated blackened brick tenements that bound off the outskirts of the market town. The German woman pointed to the heaped dunes of bottles, orange peels, grape stems, eggshells, rusted cans, cheese rinds, sausage casings, greasy papers, oddly modern plastic bags, and similar offal beneath the windows of the courtyard of the nearest building. As we watched, two hands and a pail appeared in a fourth-story window, and a wash of slops descended. Overhead, a network of clothesline bounced with flapping garments, as agitated in the breeze as the drivers who had burst from their cars and capered in the road.

The Germans murmured and laughed. The man turned to me. "Now we are in Italy," he said. "That is the difference between Italians and French. Italians put their garbage and their underclothes out in the street."

The van rolled and stopped.

Our section of the parade had attained the center of town. Cars were turning off down cramped alleys to park, heedless of cars already installed or of cars ramming in behind them. Parking, like driving, was fender to fender. When the baskets were loaded and the sun was flushed with red, like the little blood oranges in the stalls, and one by one, these madmen tried to retrieve their wheels . . . the honking and roaring and ripping and chopping the air with fevered fingers would swell, unabated, till night and the summons of imminent dinner enforced a peace.

The work ethic's gnawing would not be silenced. I put the bribery chocolate back in my purse. In English, I said carefully, "I think I am going to get out here and go over to the autostrada. Otherwise, I will never get to Florence before it gets dark." I had been lucky en route to Nice. I hadn't had to hitch the final lap in the dark. I was afraid to hitch at night.

The Germans looked surprised and amused. "Yes?" said the man. Fruitlessly, I pulled at the stiff metal handle of the door. The woman leaned over the seat, and thrust down the handle with one firm yank. I got my coat and bag. "Thank you very much," I said. "I hope you have a nice vacation. Auf Wiedersehen!"

They smiled serenely. "Good luck," the man said.

Ventimiglia on market day! Under the almost turquoise sky, hemmed in by the crumbling dark facades of buildings rearing up from the broken stones of the street like mountains thrust up out of the plain . . . the length and breadth of the town, the main street and side streets, every space but the car-crammed alleys was packed with wooden stalls, peeping out from under the jungle profusion of the harvest:

vegetables, green and red and yellow, corn, pea pods, peppers, seven kinds of beans, fluted gourds and rounded tubes of squash, sheafs of carrots, ivory globes of onions, somber purple cabbage, forests of wet lush spinach, frills of dark-green and ice-green and ruby-veined lettuce, tumbling and hurtling over each other, bursting with pliant freshness. Pyramids of green and yellow apples, firm brown pears, red-tinged oranges, teepees of fat, smug bananas threatened to dislodge and avalanche the town with heavy sweetness. Chickens squawking and pecking through the slats of crates were suddenly inverted, protesting with frantic beating wings, and hoisted aloft by their legs to be poked and squeezed. And everywhere were people, hordes of people, a Mardi Gras mass and press of people, chattering, carping, comparing prices, calling up to windows and down to the street, smacking children, drinking coffee elbow-to-elbow, buying and selling ice cream and beer, directing fishmongers digging for crabs in crushed ice, thrusting their piled baskets high above the heads of the crowd, jubilant even in the throes of indignation with the challenge of selecting and bargaining for the very best that was offered by the overwhelming richness of the banquet.

I crossed the street to the swarming curb as the line of cars began to move. I set down the canvas bag on the sidewalk and started to put on my coat. With disquiet, I realized that something was missing, something was wrong. What was it? . . .

My purse was gone.

I searched the sidewalk trampled by oblivious Italian feet. I clutched myself in a panic. I whirled around, staring at the end of my spine as if the purse might be dangling there behind me. I ran among the cars now rolling forward up the street, peering under the moving wheels. Horns brayed. "Oh, shut up!" I said. Where the hell was my purse? I must have left it in the Germans' van. Grabbing my coat in one hand and the canvas bag in the other, I ran.

Traffic was moving freely now. I could glimpse the squared roof of blue above the bumpy sequence of hoods and fenders. As I ran, the distance between the van and me increased. The bag bumped my shoulder, weighing me down. I flung it to the sidewalk and the coat along with it, and ran. "They can have those," I thought, "just let me get my passport and my airline ticket back!" My money was in two fat bunches in my pockets, but everything I owned that identified me as me was in that purse. The van had turned off the main route into a side street. My lungs ached, my ears pounded, my ribs and stomach were torn with the pain of running. I could just see the license plate of the van: 302 DAD. If I couldn't catch them, I'd have to go to the police and initiate a dragnet. How could I talk Italian cops into tracking down a German van when I didn't speak Italian? "Please, God," I prayed, "please let me catch them!"

The corner: I took it at a broken gallop. Up the hill, the light turned red. The van stopped. "Thank you!" I yelled, gasping. Skinny kids prodded their pear-shaped mothers, telling them to watch. Involved in bananas and cabbages, the women glanced up without interest. I gained the van just as the light changed. I pounded on the door.

The big blond man rolled down the window. "What is the matter?" he said.

"My bag . . ." I said, trying to breathe, "leather bag . . . I left it . . ."

He pulled the van over. The woman opened the back door and helped me push aside the blankets and bags on the mattress. We searched. My purse wasn't there.

Dazed, I thanked them. Their smiles were softened by concern. My bewilderment had broken through the locked wrists of their shared complacency. "It's okay, it must have fallen into the street, I'll go find it," I said rapidly, "thank you, goodbye!"

Retracing my route, I found the bag and coat on the corner where I'd flung them down. When I reached what seemed to be the spot where I'd climbed down from the van, I hunted up and down the street, obstructing the concourse of vendors and buyers. "Permesso," people said, thrusting me out of their paths with impersonal hands, "scusi . . . permesso . . ."

Then, like an unexpected gift of flowers, the German man appeared. He was at once a vision and a bulwark, solid, fair, and friendly in the multitude of little dark strangers. He helped me hunt. His tenacious decency was steadying in its familiar reluctance. Poor man! He wanted to be tooling down the coast at his holiday leisure, and instead he was ensnared in my idiotic self-incurred catastrophe. Finally we admitted to each other what we each had suspected all along—the purse was gone. The German found a cop. Smartly belted up in black, the cop looked like the chief engineer of a coup in some banana republic. He didn't speak English, German, or French. The German conveyed my predicament with shy, inhibited motions, like a recluse who'd been rooted out and made to play Charades. The dictator got the picture. "Passaportay," he demanded.

"No passaportay," I said.

He marched me off to the station. I waved goodbye to my friend. The cop set a brisk pace; I had to trot to keep up. Intrigued by the intervention of the law, shoppers prodded each other as we passed, the striding, starched policeman and the sniveling hippie. No doubt the bookies were taking bets on the grounds of my arrest.

The floors in the police station were brown linoleum, and smelled like the oil soap they'd made us use to clean our desks at school. Delivered into the hands of authority, I felt the mingled awe and guilt and relief I'd felt at school when I'd been sent to the principal's office. Wrath would rain upon me, but ultimately justice would be served and right restored.

The cop at the desk was rumpled and wrinkled. Worry trudged in unbroken lines from his eyebrows to his scalp. As the dictator told him my problem, he put down his crossword puzzle and looked depressed. "No passaportay," they kept saying, shaking their heads with a chilling finality, like relatives at the bier. More cops came in. None of them spoke English or French. They argued. The argument accelerated, primed with pantomime, pumped up with shouts. I felt like a car in a traffic collision, deserted, shattered and steaming, in the intersection, while witnesses and drivers disputed the blame. I sat at the center of the passionate, incomprehensible debate, and cried.

"You're twenty-one years old! Stop crying!" I sneered at myself. But my plight was hopeless. I'd never get home to America without an airline ticket. Without a passport, I couldn't leave the country. If no one showed up who spoke English or French, I might eke out the rest of my wretched life in the Ventimiglia police station, washing the floors with oil soap, subsisting on antidyspeptic mints and paper cups of coffee, till I'd learned enough Italian from crossword puzzles to plead my case.

A stocky little man in a brown suit and yellow shirt

entered. His waxy skull floated on a level with my nose. At his entrance, there was an instant's silence. Then the participants swiveled and the argument redoubled, the semaphores and rippling, gushing syllables now directed at the spry little man with the baby's skull. Beaming, he spread his arms and calmed the torrents of debate. Smiling beautifully, he gave me his arm. Sniveling, I took it. He escorted me into an office where the plastered walls, the papers stacked and strewn across the desk, the magazines on a table, the framed citations and clippings, the photographs of family groups, faces tiny and blurred in the photographer's attempt to squeeze thirty faces into the camera's eye, were all tinted the dry ivory color of antique newsprint. The little man lowered me into a chair. He perched on the edge of his desk. He looked so much like Anouk that I wanted to shove one arm at his chest to keep him from falling. He offered me a cigarette, some wine. I shook my head.

In French, he asked me what had happened.

In French, I had hysterics.

I hadn't known I had the vocabulary in me. "Lent-a-ment, *s'il* vous plâit, madama-*zail*-a," the little man kept saying in his syncopated French.

The office door opened and my German friend was ushered in. He gave me a haggard smile. Some vacation! I worshipped him. He towered over the bald dwarf on the desk like a fair-haired monolith. In plodding, one-key French, he meted out an explanation.

The little man assured us that we were not at fault. Doubtless the purse had been stolen the instant I'd stepped from the van. On market day, Ventimiglia was full of (lusty, romantic) thieves. The passport would be sold on a more lucrative market—the black one. As for the airline ticket, he thought I might be able to replace it. "Go to Genova, to the consulate," he told me. "The Americans will give you another passport."

"How long will that take?" the German asked.

The little Italian extended and flourished his arms, as if he were throwing confetti. "Half an hour," he said.

The German and I exchanged hopeful, dubious glances. We liked the dwarf, but we didn't believe him. He summoned the rumpled crossword puzzle fan and gave me a hastily typed report, with official stamp, stating where and when I had lost what, and how. "You go to the consulate," he told me. "That is to help Americans." Beaming, he made a little joke. "That is why you pay your taxes!"

The German looked shocked. One did not joke about taxes in the fatherland. Steadfast as ever, he took me to the van where his wife was waiting, tranquilly reading a guidebook on Italy. They drove me to the autostrada. I felt stripped and dishonored without my passport. Climbing out, I said, "Thank you so much." They gave me guilty smiles. Clearly, they believed that they should drive me to Genova. The German work ethic worked overtime. "Don't derange yourselves," I said earnestly, "everything will be fine. I'll get a ride very fast"—vite! vite!—"on the autostrada. I'll have another passport by tonight. You've been very very nice. Thank you! Goodbye!" I scampered in front of a truck to the southbound side of the autostrada. I waved to the Germans across the road. They waved. The van didn't move.

Under a sign which said, NO AUTOSTOP, I stuck out my thumb. I had competition. A boy and girl, bedraggled in army surplus and laden like mules with packs and sleeping bags and strapped-on pans stood some yards closer to the entering lane of traffic. They kept squatting in turn to rest, one clutching the other's arm for balance and sinking unsteadily under the back-bending weight. Rising was even more tricky; the planted partner needed a pulley to haul the sunken one erect. They must have been futilely reaching out to drivers for hours. Two teenaged boys were sprawled on the grass between the couple and me, jerking their thumbs at cars. There wasn't much traffic. Everyone was out picking pockets. At last an enormous truck rumbled upon us. The couple lifted drooping arms. The boys leaped up and wildly flagged the driver. Last in line, I put out my thumb, searching the glass for the face, the eyes. The driver stuck his head out the window. "Sola?" he said.

"Huh?" I said. "Oh, solo! Sì, sì, solo mio!"

He waved me into the truck. I felt remorse for the weary packmule who'd lost out because she was half of a team. But she got affection. I got a ride. Life was a great equalizer. I looked across the autostrada. As the truck began to gather speed, the blue van eased off the berm and onto the road. My German friends had waited to resume their journey till they'd seen me safely off.

No Tickee, No Washee

Everybody sing: "We're off to see the Consul . . ."

The truck driver's name was Gino. He spoke a little French, and Italian sounded enough like French that I could get his drift. We discussed the sexual revolution, politics, inflation, the beauty of the verdant, hilly countryside, my sex life, Gino's sex life, their possible concurrence, my objections. The conversation had an inevitable cyclic pattern: from sex to sex. But Gino was a philosopher. He had a wife in Genova and eight kids, and an "amie" in Sicily. He loved them all and showed me all their pictures. He gave me chewing gum and advised me, "Don't ever take a piece of candy from a man unless he eats one first." He held up a hand to prevent me from putting the gum in my mouth till he'd started chewing his own.

Gino dropped me off right in the center of town, on a bridge with an overlook of factory chimneys spewing black and yellow smoke. "Ciao!" he called after me. "Okay, good luck!"

I went straight for the first pensione sign I saw, and asked for a room. The woman at the desk spoke French. She looked French: pinched nose, inquisitive bird-brown eyes. Was there a strong hot shower? and would I have to pay for it? I asked. No no no, madama-*zail*-a, she said, the shower is right in here and you can use it any time, regardez! She threw open the door to a mammoth, white-tiled, sparkling chamber with a monstrous tub. It looked like Napoleon's tomb. I'd have to cross the lobby in my nightie with my hair in a towel. I didn't care. "I'll take it," I said.

She smiled metallically, as if she had a mouthful of iron filings. "Passportay, s'il vous plaît," she said.

"No passportay," I said.

"No chambre," she said: no room.

I explained my misfortune and produced my Ventimiglia document with official stamp. She read it, shook her head and clucked—her sympathy had the substance of tin foil—and said, "No passaportay, no chambre." In English: "No tickee, no washee."

I got excited. I brandished my document. Signora Tin Foil was firm.

"What will I do?" I fairly shrieked. "I have to sleep, don't I?"

At last she gave me a form to take to the cops. If they signed it, and stamped it with an official stamp, I could have the room. But I would have to pay in advance.

"In a pig's eye," I said. I was fed up with lusty romantic Italians. In French, I said, "I'll pay when I have the paper from your police."

"Faites vite, madama-*zail*-a" said the tin foil lady: make it snappy. She gave me directions to the headquarters of the carabinieri. I set off, toting my bag, since I didn't trust her not to sell it. It looked like I'd be seeing a lot of official Italy: The Form and File Card Tour.

It was after six o'clock. The sky was deep purple, with here and there a small cloud of pillowed pink. In the park of the public square, little girls in dark, austere Catholic school uniforms sat in the grass. Old men in soft hats wandered among the pigeons, eating ice cream from fluted paper cups. "Gelati," the ice cream vendor called, scooping up spheres of brown and pink and yellow, each mound staked with a long, thin wafer, like a flag. Soldiers in brown, fitted jackets and flat hats were everywhere, making eyes at girls with full breasts and tight skirts and long, wavy, blue-black hair. Italian women looked eminently fertile compared to the narrow-hipped females of France. Even the teenaged signorinas exuded a womanly pleasure in the roundness of their hips. Camouflaged in wool and dust, lumbered with a grease-stained bag, I wanted to apologize for taking up space. Bodies hurtled past me, bumping my bag. Each impact left me feeling bruised and disoriented. "Scusi," I kept saying to shoulders and backs. I had to ask directions twice. Both of the middle-aged, harried-looking women I stopped spoke only Italian. They pointed and pantomimed the route, carving the air with crisscrossed roads that vanished as they turned away.

The carabinieri building was a vast inflated cube of dark stone. The cavernous hall I entered was silent and empty, with only a massive desk set like a boulder in the center of the marble plain. INFORMAZIONE said a metal plate wired to a basket of pink and blue forms. Speaking into the pencil sharpener, I said, "Where is everybody?" There wasn't even a bench to sleep on, in case nobody came to sign my paper. In a corridor, I found a water fountain, which was somehow reassuring, an artifact of contemporary life. My ears pricked up at the cadences of argument. I tracked the sound.

A six-sided verbal war was raging in a dim chamber bulging with Italians, all wearing checked suits. Were these cops? Was a checked suit the Italian version of the FBI trenchcoat? No one paid any attention to my entrance. After a lengthy wait, I took the only chair. I observed the manual ebb and flow of discussion, noting the personal fillips of each man's rhetorical style. I sighed.

All at once the argument departed, a mass of clashing checks and churning arms and rippling syllables, tripping and hopping down the hall, like a paramecium working up a vaudeville act. The lone remaining cop in his funereal black uniform emerged from the shadows. He signed and stamped the tin foil lady's form.

I searched through the dark streets, emptying in the flurried gaiety of family dinners, and found the pensione. I paid the unfamiliar clerk, a stoop-shouldered, daunted-looking man who had the pitted, waxy skin of one who sleeps when the sun is out. I'd bought a roll of bread and some cheese and a bottle of chianti at a groceria. I planned to drink half the bottle with dinner, take a boiling hour-long bath, and drink the other half. While I ate my bread and cheese, I skimmed through an Italian fashion magazine I'd swiped from the lobby. I learned that "della" probably meant "of," and "a sinistra," "on the left." Taking a slug of coarse red wine from the straw-cradled bottle, I told myself, "You always had a flair for languages." Then I got into my nightie and took up soap, shampoo, and Isadora Duncan's *My Life,* and wrapped them in my towel. No greater luxury exists than reading a really terrific book in the tub. I stalked across the lobby, as the night clerk stroked me with his clammy gaze. Resting the bundle on the stool by the side of the cold, curving sleigh of the bathtub, I shucked my nightgown and turned on the hot water tap.

Nothing happened.

I stood on the rim of the tub and examined the water heater, a white metal bulge in the wall. Its cord was only a few inches long, and the plug hung useless, three feet from the socket.

Cursing, I put on my nightgown and went to ask the clerk for an extension cord. He gave me a hermit's memory of a smile and showed me, his whitish fingers simulating the hands of a clock, that I would have to wait thirty minutes for the water to heat. "Bene," I said: swell. I took my bundle back to my room. I read about Isadora in Greece and drank chianti, waiting an hour for extra-steamy water. I went back to the lobby, stepping carefully over the swimming flowers in the linoleum. Exhaustion and chianti had all but crossed my eyes.

"Bagno caldo?" I said to the clerk, having looked up the phrase for "hot bath" in the "Handy Phrases" section of *The Book.*

"Sì," the clerk whispered. What was this place, a sanatorium? He took up a pencil and wrote with his fishy fingers on an envelope: "400 L."

"No," I said, "the signora said no." The tin lady had told me I could take a bath. She hadn't said a bath would cost me four hundred lire.

"Sì," the hermit whispered, "bagno è quattrocento lire."

We argued, he in Italian in whispers, I in my nightie in English. I pounded on the counter. He called the tin foil lady on the phone and had her confirm the news. A hot bath in Napoleon's tomb would cost me four hundred lire. Bath equals fifty cents.

I stomped back across the dancing plastic flowers to my room. Drunk, disorderly, and dirty, I went to bed.

I dreamed that I was sleeping on a train, with a great clanking iron wheel just beneath my head. I woke in the dark to a pounding, pumping noise that shook the bed. Nauseated, terrified, I realized that the blackness was thick and acrid with the fumes of gasoline. I snapped on the light and opened the door to the hall.

Directly across from my room was the open door to a closet. Inside the closet, the hermit clerk was pumping gasoline from a metal tank into a pail. When he saw me, he jumped, his stringy, wasted body wavering in a shudder. His teeth began to chatter. I watched them jump and heard the little clicking sounds they made as they touched. I'd never seen teeth chatter. It came to me that in my rancor over the bath, I hadn't tried to speak to him in French. "Parlez-vous français?" I said. He nodded. He looked scared. I wondered if he were stealing gasoline from the landlady. Probably he drank it, on ice. I said, en français, "Is this going to continue all night?" The trembling man shook his head no. "Bien," I said, closing the door.

The night was silent. But the room was filled with fumes. I was afraid to go to sleep. If I died of asphyxiation in Genova without a passport, the tin foil lady and the hermit would have me buried in a potter's field behind the railroad station, with six cops in checked suits to carry the cardboard box. I opened the window. The pillow was a plush log, like the arm of a chair. I pushed it away and encountered my jeans, with all my money in the pockets. I had put them under my pillow for safekeeping. I had been robbed of my identity. Money was all I had left.

In the morning, I went back to the police station. Sunshine sliced across the marble floor through the fortress slits of windows. A cop was eating a pastry and manning the INFORMAZIONE desk. The pink and blue forms in the basket were sprinkled with powdered sugar. He sent me up some stairs and down a corridor to the BUREAU D'ÉTRANGERS.

Behind the glass door, a plump man in an oddly stark navy pin-striped suit was playing with his swivel chair, swinging from side to side in a creaky, metronomic rhythm. When he saw me, he adopted a grave expression, cocking his head to one side, as if he were testing and adjusting the joints of the chair. He bounced up out of his ratcheting seat to greet me. His jolly anxious face was furrowed with laughter and apprehension.

"Signorina," he sang with the caressing welcome of yearning fulfilled. He took my bag and tenderly placed it on a bench. He detached the paper bag from my fingers and laid it sideways on his desk, saying, "Let me take your breakfast."

"It's my lunch," I said, hoping the chianti bottle wouldn't uncork. It was actually leftover dinner.

"I already know of your problem," he said, taking my hands in his. He looked into my face with kind, worried eyes. "The police at Ventimiglia have had no word of your passport. I am afraid it is gone."

I sniffled. He was so nice.

"Today you must go to the consulate."

I started to cry, again. I'd cried so much in the last eighteen hours, my nose was sore from blowing. "Oh no!" I blubbered. "I can't go to the consulate here! I have to go to Florence!"

"Ah, Feer-*en*-zay, che bella!" the man said, beaming.

"No, Florence," I said.

"Sì, Firenze *is* Florence. In Italia"—he shrugged, as if asking my indulgence for a hidebound local custom—"we say 'Firenze.' "

"I have to go there today," I said. "Right away, this morning." The previous night had instilled me with a loathing for Genova that bordered on mania. If I didn't escape within the hour, I would start to glibber and twitch and have to be restrained with plastic cords.

"Friends are expecting you?" he said, patting my hands. I wished my hands were clean.

"No," I said. I blurted, "I don't want to spend my whole vacation in a place I never heard of!"

He was hurt. "But all Americans know of Genova," he assured me. "Genova is the birthplace of Christopher Columbus!"

I didn't care if Amerigo Vespucci ran the laundromat. "I can't spend another night here! I want to go to Florence!"

Seeing that I was a hopeless neurotic, he patted my cheek, his plump face puckered with good will. "Wait," he said, "don't upset you, wait." He dialed a number on the telephone and gave me the receiver. "Your consulate," he said.

The party on the line was female. From her grasp of consulate procedures, she seemed to be the cleaning woman, who was amusing herself by playing with the switchboard. After all, it was Saturday morning. But she was sympathetic. She asked me to spell my name. As I began, the helpful man beside me held up the paper from the

Ventimiglia police, so I could look at my name in print,
as a guide.

After an emotional exchange, we agreed that I would
go to the consulate in Firenze to apply for another passport. The Genova consulate would alert the Firenze
consulate. The Genova police would notify the Firenze
police, and the Ventimiglia police, of my arrival in Firenze.
I would have to go to the police as soon as I hit Firenze—
pronto! pronto!—to register. My every movement within
the borders of Italy would be chartered by two govern-
ments. I felt like a Mafia hitman on parole.

After I hung up the phone and blew my nose, the man
patted my cheek again. "You see, it is not so terrible," he
said. "Everyone wants to help you. I want to help you,
little signorina. I want to give you my heart."

"You're very nice," I said tearfully. "I'm sorry I don't
like Genova."

His arms drew scallops in the air. "We say in Italia,
that is why there is dry wine and sweet wine!"

"We say in Ohio, that's why there's chocolate and
vanilla."

We laughed. He kissed me goodbye on both cheeks. He
presented me with my leaking lunch. "Ciao!" he said.
"Italia loves you! Enjoy, signorina, enjoy!"

As the first step toward enjoyment, I decided to spoil
myself and take the train. I didn't feel jolly enough to
converse. On a train, I could sit in a corner and sulk. I
went to the station and bought a ticket to Firenze and
a paper cup of caffé latte, café au lait with cinnamon on
top. I sat on a bench and ate my bread and cheese to pass
the minutes till train time.

The minutes passed into an hour.

The lady beside me, all in red—red dress, red shoes,
red earrings and beads, red polish on her nails, red lips—
kept sighing in a heaving collapse of the pelvis, looking
at her watch, at me, at the strolling, yammering, gesturing,
eating and drinking crowd on the platform, at the empty
track, at the uniformed attendants who turned to peer
down the track whenever we looked at them, to show that
they were on our side, victims of technology and gross
incompetence farther up the line—and proclaiming, "Mama
mia!"

The train barreled in, trying to impress us with efficient

noise to make up for being forty minutes late. The porters
and attendants on the platform shouted and batted their
arms. The conductors and porters and attendants on the
train shouted back. The lady in red gave the ticket taker
hell as she twitched her butt up the stairs. He spread his
hands and rolled his eyes—"Train? Nevah hoid of it"—
and when she turned away, he watched her ass.

"Firenze?" I said as he took my ticket.

"Sì, sì, Firenze," he said.

But the people stuffed in every compartment I passed
kept babbling about "Firenze" and "Roma." Misgivings
bobbed up and would not be suppressed. I grabbed an
attendant. "Firenze?" I said.

The attendant shook his head. "Roma," he said.

"Oh no!" I cried, about to bolt for the exit, though the
train was moving.

"No no, signorina," he said grabbing my arm in turn.
"Americana? Buono. No train for Firenze oggi. Change at
Pisa." He hustled away, exchanging abuse with the passengers expressing their joyous wrath in the next compartment.

Pisa. Change at Pisa. Look for the sign of the Leaning
Tower. All the compartments were full, or full of soldiers
who gave me grins of lascivious welcome and tried to draw
me inside as I passed. At last I found room in a third-class
compartment which had been converted in the space of
five minutes into a flat for a family of six. The mother
spread her huge hips over half a seat meant for three,
balancing—between the mounds of her stomach, her
pendulous breasts and her swollen thighs—the fattest baby
I'd ever seen in my life. His grotesque proportions, his
basset jowls and suet chins, his cantaloupe knees and
knockwurst thighs, were accounted during our journey
by four hours in which he never stopped eating.

Beside this ballooning madonna and child, a sturdy
little girl in kneesocks and ink-black braids was leaning
out the window, singing "Galleria!" whenever we approached a tunnel. Across from her, a skinny boy of about
eleven, with pale hair and glasses, was sunk in a concave
head of disgust in his seat, obviously wishing he were back
in the Engineering Library, brushing up on centrifugal
force, instead of imbedded in the bosom of his low-brow
family. Beside him were two firm-fleshed, lustrous-haired

teenagers, a girl with huge breasts who was chewing gum and reading a comic book full of people kissing and saying, "Amore!" and a boy in a Banlon shirt, who was giving me the glad eye. When his mother frowned at him, he turned and looked out the window in the door to the corridor. But she made him get up and hoist my bag onto the luggage rack above our heads, which was already jammed with plastic bags, all of which proved to contain the family's lunch.

As I squeezed myself into the slot on the seat between the wall and the mother, she asked me something. "Non capisco," I said, smiling. "Inglese," she said, and said something to the teenagers, who laughed. The whole family smiled at me, their eyes friendly and curious. The baby was sucking a lollipop, which his mother held with superhuman patience as he licked it, pushed it away and wailed, stuck it in his hair, grabbed it, dropped it. His mother made the little girl in kneesocks pick it up and take it to the lavatory to rinse it (in a sink flanked by the usual notice, in Italian, French, and English: WATER NOT FOR DRINKING). Meanwhile the mother was conducting a discussion, trying to draw in the older boy. She teased him, poked him, ruffled his hair—which he suffered with impatience—asked his opinions, nodding with respect as he grudgingly gave them. She badgered everyone else, responding to their comments with "Ah, sì?" or sarcastic jokes. At least in this Italian family, the oldest son was the prince—"Himself," as they say in Ireland, or, as we say in Ohio, "King Shit." The rest of the children seemed to accept this disparity. The argument clipped along with easygoing zest, peaking in bursts of laughter. The oldest boy offered me cigarettes and gum. "No, grazie," I said. They all looked at each other and shrugged. "Galleria!" the little girl sang. When we emerged from the tunnel, the mother made the oldest boy and girl take down the bags of lunch.

All the way to Pisa, we ate. I wasn't hungry, and I was ashamed that I'd eaten my shabby lunch on the platform, leaving me nothing to share. No matter; the mother refused to accept my refusal. Stuffing half a banana in the baby's mouth to keep him busy while she dispersed the sandwiches, she sliced hard rolls of bread and tucked in translucent slices of whitish cheese and little discs of

sausage, unwrapped from greasy white paper. She handed
the rolls around, starting with Himself, and coming next
to me. "No, grazie," I said. She shoved the roll in my
hand, saying in Italian, "Take it, take it!" I laughed and
I took it. Everybody chewed. The mother smiled around
at us, her cheeks and chins bouncing as she chewed, the
baby's cheeks bouncing as he gummed his banana, their
various pillows of arms and thighs and bellies jiggling
with the movements of the train. "Buono," I said, waving
the sandwich. "Buono!" said the mother to the munching
kids. They laughed and nodded at me. The guru baby
gummed a roll. After an almost endless procession of rolls
had marched down gullets, we had flat, wide, sugary
cookies—"No, grazie!" "Take it, take it!"—and hard-
boiled eggs and oranges and bananas and chocolate kisses.
When we were finished, I felt like I'd just eaten Christmas
dinner with Dee. We lay back in the seats, belching.

Entertainment in this diesel-driven delicatessen was
provided in the lulls between whooshing, skidding, grinding halts and jerking, clinking, squealing starts at various
stations. In the stationary intervals, indistinguishable herds
of people passed through the corridor in opposite directions. Soldiers, plastic-bag-and-basket-laden women, children clinging to their mothers or ignoring them to demonstrate sophistication, shapeless, ageless women in black
shawls who should have been riding in wooden-wheeled
carts: each entering passenger physically jousted with his
or her counterpart trying to exit, some barreling into the
enemy flank, some meekly scooching through sideways.
The first time the bumping racket announced a stop, I
craned out the window, looking in vain for a sign. Was
this Pisa? I had to change trains at Pisa. I jumped up to
snag the conductor. He didn't appear among the bodies
packing the aisle.

"Pisa?" I demanded of the mother, who was up to her
elbows in bread and bananas.

"Pisa?" she responded, as if "pisa" were an unfamiliar
condiment, like chutney.

"Sì, Mama, *Pisa*," the kids repeated. The anemic whiz
kid in spectacles looked pained. He was so out of place
in that strapping clan glowing with mindless appetite, that
he looked like a changeling. "No Pisa," he informed me
with a patronizing air. His older brother and sister

squelched him. They reassured me: *they* would alert me
when the train reached Pisa. I hope they'd let me know
in time to wade through the smorgasbord and hack my
way to the door.

As a further diversion, the whiz kid and his mother had
an argument over the disposal of the garbage. The mother
had collected the orange and banana peels, the eggshells
and butcher paper, the bread crusts and sausage strings
and candy wrappers, and mashed them into a wad. She
kept trying to give the wad to the boy in the glasses. He
wasn't having any. She shoved it at him; he slapped at
her hands. If he'd been mine I would have thrown him
out the window. Instead, his mother handed off the fifty-
pound baby to the zoftig sister, shoved down the window
—directly beneath a sign which warned, in Italian, French
and English, THROW NOTHING FROM THE TRAIN ON PAIN
OF PROSECUTION—and heaved the wad of garbage into the
rich green country.

At the next station—"Pisa?" "No Pisa, no Pisa!"—
Himself descended to the platform and brought back orange
drink for all of us. Our quarters were invaded by a pretty
Italian girl in black velvet. She refused the mother's offer
of a cookie or an orange drink, eyed the blimplike baby
with repugnance, stonewalled the smitten crown prince,
and generally let us all know that she was slumming. We
had only won her by default—first and second class were
filled. When the mother chucked the orange drink bottles
out the window—there was a sharp crack! as a bottle
struck the track and broke, and the mother winced and
laughed—I thought the girl was going to make a citizen's
arrest. She gave me a look which presumed our shared
disgust. I looked like a bum, but she knew that rich
Americans, like princes in fairy tales, liked to roam the
countryside disguised as paupers, to savor peasant life. In
case I were rich, she didn't want me to think that all
Italians chewed gum, picked their teeth in public, read
"amore" comics, bloated their babies with sugar and
starch, and threw their garbage out of trains.

I gave her a checkmate look of family pride. I was right
at home with these warm, crazy people.

Suddenly she said to me in English, "Italians are not
the only people who throw garbage out of trains."

The seven of us were dumbstruck. The six Italians looked at me. "I'm sure," I said lamely.

"I have traveled extensively by train, throughout Europe. In all countries, it is forbidden to throw the garbage on the track. But only in France is the rule obeyed. That is because in France, no one throws anything away."

I started to laugh, but she continued. "In Spain, they throw everything out the windows, and at the border, when the crowd is rushing through the customs, they throw their suitcases out of the windows and jump out after them. In Switzerland, they bundle up their garbage and wait until the train has crossed the border into Austria, and then they throw it out the window."

I said, "Your English is beautiful."

Expressionless, she said, "In America, no one throws garbage from the windows of trains, because you do not have trains."

"We throw it out of cars," I agreed.

Screeching, chuffing, clanking, humping, vibrating ever more slowly and metallically with every revolution of the wheels, the train was dragged, protesting and resisting, into a station. The girl in velvet got up and walked out, without a word or a smile. The oldest boy leaned around the corner of the doorway to the aisle and watched her ass. Then they turned to me, my buddies, questioning, eager.

I opened my mouth, and closed it. I shrugged.

The mother slapped her forehead and started to laugh. Of course I couldn't tell them what she'd said, I couldn't speak Italian! They should have asked *her* what she was saying, they should have made her interpret for them! That was the gist of the garble the mother launched at her sons and daughters. She poked me, her pumpkin face bursting with bottled-in laughter, and barked out, as if it were the punch line of our favorite joke, "Inglese!" I started to laugh, and she broke into billows of laughter. She drew in the grinning, embarrassed kids, prodding them, tickling them, imitating the high-toned signorina and shaking the carriage walls with the thunderous twitch of her hips, slapping her jelly thighs, whooping, wheezing, gasping out "Inglese!" She loved laughing so much that it was impossible not to join in her laughter. Even the sulky son in spectacles fell. We roared and roistered, tears drip-

ping down our chins, stopping to ease our stomach muscles
and breathe, and catching each other's eyes, breaking out
again in giggles, all the way to Pisa.

When clankings and shufflings signaled the stop at Pisa,
the little girl in braids and the skinny boy in glasses gave
the alarm. "Pisa, Mama!" The oldest boy lifted down my
bag, while the mother stuck cookies in the pockets of my
coat. "Ciao!" everybody sang, "arrivederci!" The mother
issued admonitions and benedictions, while the teenagers
laughed, yanked on her skirt, grinned at me, and shrugged.
"Mama, Inglese," the kid in glasses said.

"Inglese, Inglese," the mother said, sluffing off this trivial
bar to communication. She was a mother; I was a daughter; I would understand. I did. She was saying have fun,
behave yourself, don't take a piece of candy from a man
unless he eats one first, and mind your bag.

"Ciao, goodbye," I said, squeezing into the crush of
bags and bodies in the aisle. Minutes later, wrenched and
pummeled, I tumbled out onto the platform. "Goo'bye,
goo'bye," the little girl called from her window as the
train began to move. I waved goodbye.

The train I took from Pisa to Firenze was so packed
with people that I had to ride on the platform between
two cars. Protection from falling to a pulpy death consisted of a lean-to of corrugated metal partitions, wired
together with cable so that great gaps admitted the hurtling
wind and the green blur of passing country. The metal
sheets were racked with wind; the platform shuddered.
Sparks from the clash of wheel and track shot up through
holes in the deck. I shared this shelter with four other
people: a middle-aged couple, short and rotund, like salt
and pepper shakers, each dressed in brown and burdened
with a wicker suitcase; a small man with a large cigar
which he never removed from his mouth; and a soldier,
seated on his duffle bag. The soldier kept patting his knee
and saying, "Asseyez-vous, signorina." Quickly, he held
up both hands, palms out, to show that he had nothing
up his sleeve. When I got tired of ricocheting off the walls,
I sat. He locked an arm around my waist under my coat—
just to keep me from falling, he assured me in French
and Italian—but his hand kept slipping upward to brush
my breast. "No!" I said, shoving it down and rising, a

living portrait of maiden outrage. "Scusi, scusi, signorina!"
he cried, each time prostrate with grief that I'd taken
offense. His explanation seemed to import that I was so
voluptuous a morsel, he couldn't restrain his virile lust.
Since by this time I looked and smelled like a Little
Leaguer who'd just played a double header, I didn't see
why he bothered. Like all men I'd hitched with, he liked
to, so to speak, keep his hand in. By the time we got to
Firenze I was so bored with both our roles that the soldier accomplished his goal and touched my breast. Stunned
by victory, he kissed my wrist. "Go home and write it in
your diary," I told him.

The train, which was due in Firenze at 3:12, staggered
home at 5:04. When the doors were opened, compressed
mankind burst forth in choked streams, swelling the del-
uge of tourists already swamping the neat small city.

Every cobbled street and cloistered passage, every courtyard and tile-roofed bridge, was glutted with tourists. As
in Ventimiglia on market day, the narrow stone-paved
lanes of the ancient city were clogged with cars stuffed
with tourists, and buses crammed with tourists. Drivers
shrieked and honked at throngs of tourists on foot. Chaos
was embellished by the heedless panache of the tourists
who were Italian. Firenze was the first place I'd seen in
Europe where most of the visitors were natives of the
country. Italian tourists in Italy were not intimidated by
waiters, shopkeepers, taxis and bus drivers, hosts of pensiones or sheriffs of museums. They considered that the
city belonged to them as long as they cared to stay, and
they treated it like home: climbing up onto the statute of
Michelangelo's *David* to pose for pictures; reviling the
chef and the quality of the dinner, even as they scraped
their plates of the last six portions of the house specialty;
launching offensives at landlords over every item on the
bill. But they got away with it. They didn't tip, and they
got the best service. They insulted the merchandise, and
the merchants smiled, bowed, apologized, lowered the
prices and raised the tourists' kiddies to chuck them under
their chins. When American hippies paid for bread and
wine, shopkeepers gave them hard candy instead of lire,
shrugging: sorry, no small change! But a housewife from
Genova or Napoli who'd been handed two lemon drops

instead of five lire would have torn the merchant limb from limb, and gotten off at the trial.

Dropped into the maelstrom of Firenze on a Saturday evening, I bought a city map in a stall at the railroad station. I set off to look for the police station. The cops had a classy clubhouse in Florence, in keeping with the guarded Renaissance beauty of the town—a mansion of dun-colored stone, marked by the purity of plain stone arches. A couple of young cops and soldiers were lounging around a marble-topped table, playing cards and drinking something which they ditched behind a fuchsia plastic wastebasket when they heard me coming. They gave me the glad eye, briefly. One of them signed my paper, looking into my eyes with ironic significance as he stamped the official stamp. As I trundled off across the cool, wide hall, they sang, "Buona sera, signorina," like a barber shop quartet.

Now that I had my sleeping papers, I needed some place to sleep. In view of the glut of transients, I stooped to consult *The Book*. I went to four pensiones that were highly recommended, three that were fondly mentioned, two that were grudgingly noted, and one that was vilified. Then I hunted on my own, shouldering my bag, edging through the hustling streets, strewing my path with "scusis," hauling my boots up every flight of stairs that led to a PENSIONE sign.

Every bed in Frienze was taken. Every lobby was littered with rejects, sitting on their luggage, easing their swollen feet.

Despairing, I stood in the street.

Twilight had deepened. With the ebbing of the sun's heat, a chill had drifted off the river and coated the aged stone walls. Windows were bright with the gloating warmth of lamps. I'd never slept in a doorway. I'd never seen anyone sleep in a doorway, till I'd come to Europe. I climbed the steps to a church and sat on the topmost step.

Watching the tributaries of bodies flow along the stones, I achieved detachment. I'd been in a tighter spot than this, the day I'd let the plane go home without me. I'd been alone and poor and mute, in a city where foreigners are given no quarter, and I'd gotten by. Now I had a second language, and money, and friends in Spain and England, if I could find them. What was I worried about?

I knew what I had to do. I was just putting it off. I had to look in *The Book* and find the address of the student hostel.

Shouldering my bag, which I'd so carefully chosen because it wasn't a backpack, I ventured into hostel territory.

Camp

The Book was vague about the student hostel and how to find it; a bus was referred to. After some earnest but fruitless efforts, I started shouting requests for directions to whole intersections of people. Two little Swiss boys in grey suede shorts and soup bowl haircuts rescued me and put me on the bus. The driver told me when to get off, along with six red backpacks. Khaki equipment might do for campers, but hippies' backpacks were dyed in hunters' colors, as if vagabonds in European cities were in danger of being mistaken for moose, and shot. I trailed behind the backpacks, who walked six abreast like advancing redcoats, blocking the road. Each nylon mound was patched with a red maple leaf on a field of white. I thought the hikers must be a brotherhood sworn to defend the environment till I saw them strewing the gravel path to the hostel with turquoise foil wrappers from chocolate drops. While we were waiting to register, I tapped the hunk of nylon in front of me and asked the freckled female face attached to the front of it what the maple leaf meant. The expanse of freckles folded in descending curves of disgust. "You Americans," said its flat American voice. "It's the bloody Canadian flag. Ever heard of Canada? We've got the same border as you. You bloody Americans think the end of America is the end of the bloody world. You think the world is flat, and after America ends, there's just a cliff and a lot of bloody space!" The face disappeared. The nylon mound presented its square white iris and leafy pupil.

I was tempted to tap the mound again and confront the freckles with the details of my Girl Scout troop excursion to Montreal—one of my mother's Conestoga specials—on which I'd been carsick eight times in seven days. I wanted to tell the freckles, "Not many know Canada as I do."

271

But I was about to know Canada better. The freckles and
I were assigned the top and bottom planks in one of forty
bunkbeds set up in the hall. As if to rub salt in the wound
of her national pride, I got the top bunk and she got the
bottom bunk. She never forgave me for that.

The hostel was a rambling villa built in the eighteenth
century of grey stones loosely cemented together. It looked
like a three-story fireplace. To reach it, we walked up a
sloping gravel path through fields of flowering trees, their
slender trunks obscured with dusk-empurpled blossoms.
Cars and campers lodged beneath the canopies of flowers,
like sleeping metal beasts, and tents and campfires sprouted
in the wildly tangled vines. Close to the house was a formal
garden laced with paths and starred with white stone
benches. Magnolias dropped their creamy petals in the
long grass, and forsythia flamed up yellow against the
dark walls.

The crowd in the lobby, grouped before the registration
desk in lines of the shuffling, the drooping, the crouching
and the collapsed, reminded me of Dan and the Three
Gorillas in the Café St. André-des-Arts, where I'd first
seen them. All of the travelers aspiring to beds for the
night were bent beneath, or clinging to, or sitting on, or
dragging, or kicking, as they moved up in line, the lumpish,
dusty, beloved, and neglected bundles of all they possessed.
One bum staggered under the consolidated poundage of
wardrobes for three different climates; another only carried
an extra pair of jeans to wear while the first pair were
sloshing in the sink. Whatever each of us couldn't do
without was rolled small and shoved in a satchel. Backpacks, knapsacks, bedrolls bound with ropes and leather
thongs and belts, straw and canvas handbags, pillow cases,
airline bags with ripping zippers, bright striped plastic
bags from stores in countries days back, countries now as
mythical again as when they'd been mere names and lists
of chief products and cities in geography books . . . all
were variations on the hobo's bandana and stick, that
enduring symbol of the road's romance, of running away
from home.

Intermingled with the hardcore hardy were bewildered
members of the species "tourist." With hotels overflowing,
tourists who'd left home without intending to leave its
comforts were obliged to seek shelter in the flophouse of

youth. One lady in spike heels, gripping a monogrammed alligator bag, stood stricken in the rubble of her luggage while her husband demanded a private room and tried to pay with Master Charge. "Cash only," said the top dog at the desk, who was called, often with caustic overtones, the warden. He sold the man two hostel memberships, two sheet sleeping bags, and two slots in the coop, at a total cost of thirty-two dollars and forty cents. "This is outrageous!" the man said, scooping out lire like seed. "I'm going straight to the consulate, first thing Monday morning!"

"Men's staircase on the left, women's staircase on the right," said the warden.

Luckily for me, the warden's flunky was assigned to my line. She asked for my hostel membership card. "It was stolen," I lied. I'd never bought one. Staying in a hostel had seemed like defeat—like eating in a mission. I explained the loss of my passport and all my papers. "Do you have a sheet sleeping bag?" she said. "No," I said, "that was stolen too." She shot an apprehensive glance at the warden, who was busy splitting up a honeymoon couple. I looked her in the eye. "I don't know how long I'll have to wait in Italy before I get another passport," I said, "but I haven't got much money. I should really be sleeping on a bench in the yard."

She fiddled with the card I'd signed. "All right," she said, and handed me a folded muslin sheet, sewn to fit around the celibate's mattress on the bed I'd been awarded. "Please be silent about it."

"Thank you," I said. Since she was a human being, I added, "Is it always this crowded on the weekend in Florence, I mean Firenze?"

She looked startled, then gradually, appalled. "But this is the weekend of *Easter*," she said.

Easter. I'd forgotten. No wonder the city was swamped. Latin Catholics celebrated holy days with processions and dances, with fireworks and carnivals, even in Ohio. The greatest day in the year in Little Italy in Cleveland was the festival day of the Feast of the Assumption of the Blessed Virgin Mary into Heaven, called for short—the Feast. Easter must be Firenze's version of the Feast. Even now on the Ponte Vecchio, the ancient stone bridge where Dante had first seen Beatrice, monks and nuns must be setting up the booths for the shooting gallery, the pizza-by-the-slice, and the raffle of the Barcalounger.

The women's dormitory was like a multilingual reform school for hardened cases. There was no heat. The water in the sinks and showers, when there was any water, was cold. The toilets that had seats were clogged and spilling over, and the toilets that had footrests and holes in the floor were sometimes not flushed for hours. The stench from the toilets wafted in a dank and putrid stream down the corridor where we slept, and where the strong of stomach ate their bread and jelly. When driven to use the bathroom, I held my breath as long as I could. Then I gulped air through my mouth.

The inmates were a variegated lot. German schoolgirls on a low-budget tour marched in lockstep out of the bus, each with her single suitcase. Leading the platoon was a woman whose neat brown suit made her look like a female security guard, which was apt. She had eyes that glittered like quartz. She demanded attention and order among her troops by clicking a small metal object, making a cricket sound. Click-click! They marched in single file across the cluttered lobby, stepping over legs and parcels, twenty eyes drilling the fogged eyes of "hippie-type travelers." Click-click! They marched upstairs, twenty feet in oddly frivolous platform shoes hammering down like hobnailed boots. Click-click! They marched down the hall lined with beds, scattering girls in underwear, tromping on folded laundry, honking out their language in shrill, measured beats. Assigned a separate room instead of a section of the public ward, they turned it into a barracks, contriving to render the flat, bunched pads of the mattresses into precisely neat beds for the guard's inspection.

Out on the ward, there were French girls in couturier T-shirts and sleek jeans worn to threads by unknown asses. They blew their skillfully sculpted hair into place every morning with dryers that they carried in Gucci bags. They ate radish sandwiches made with Italian loaves cut in thin slices, as they sat on benches in the garden, reading *Vogue*. There were Israeli girls, who hoarded figs and oranges and complained about oppression of women on the kibbutz. "But the sex was good," they said. There was a Dutch girl who was studying to be a missionary, and three Italian Communists who tried to start political discussions in the bathroom, without success, since none of the visitors to Italy knew who the President of Italy was. There were two girls from South Africa, both of whom were over six feet tall. They never stopped eating. As they were polishing off two quarts of yogurt, a loaf of bread, a pound of cherries, and a chicken, one would remark to the other, "After tea, we'd better go and see about dinner." They were voyaging around the world by freighter. They'd been at sea or in port for thirteen months. They carried backpacks that would have broken the legs of a prospector's mule. They gave us their views on apartheid. "Black and white both are a bloody dull lot," they said, "bugger the whole bleedin' country."

And there were Americans.

The freckles in the bunk below me and her maple leaf brigade made a point of telling everyone they met—before they'd said their names or asked to use the sugar—that they were not American. "I'm Canadian, you know, and so's he, he's Canadian. Not bloody American, Canadian." (The girl with freckles said everything three times, bristling with each repetition, though she hadn't been contradicted.) If a hosteler or a Florentine assumed that an American-looking, American-sounding person hailed from the States, the maligned Canadian flew into a passion, or dug in his boots in determination to separate himself from the image of the greedy, war-mongering, earth-befouling, military-corporate state of America. The easiest way to engage a Canadian in conversation was to say, "I hear American industry is taking over Ottawa." It was like dropping a quarter in a juke box. I could put my feet up and beat time to the cadence of a nationalistic harangue.

The Canadians were boring. Otherwise, I might have hidden behind a maple leaf myself. The Americans in the hostel were divided into blocs. The first faction were wholesome and crass, spreading their maps across the stairwell just as the breakfast gong sounded; stumping upstairs from a full day's hike and offering to lead calisthenics on the lawn. The other faction were dissipated, slumped at tables in the snack bar, greying the air with diminishing tones as they vied for the title of Most World Weary:

"Yeah, I haven't seen a newspaper in a year and a half, I mean all that's got nothing to do with people, with life. . . ."

"Fuermentara, man, that's the place . . . lie on the beach, smoke kif, you get hungry you just dip your hand in the water and pull out a fish . . . you can live on like twelve cents a day. . . ."

"This hostel trip is weird, it's like the first time I've had to pay for a bed since I came over. I mean, the people take me in, everywhere I go . . . they feed me, they tell me about their customs and, you know, folkways, traditions, they sing me their ancient songs and all . . . they like make me their brother, you know? . . ."

"You went to Avignon? . . . Too bad, that's just for tourists now. The really great place is Aix, it's totally unspoiled. . . . Na, it's not worth going now. I mean when *I* was there it was totally unspoiled, but right about when I left it, it was starting to turn. Starting to get *commercial*. And that was like four months ago. By now American Express owns the whole fucking town. . . ."

"Venice? . . . Bad scene, man. Venice is a total rip-off. I mean they have *motorboats* on the canals, it's like Lake Michigan, man. It's the small towns, the hidden villages, that's where life is still lived like it was a thousand years ago . . . I can't give you the name of a village like that, I don't ask *names*, man, *names* are an invention of the system, I don't get sucked in by that . . . and I wouldn't tell you how to find these places anyway, when I find a place that's authentically native, I don't tell *Americans* about it. . . ."

I didn't plan to hang around Americans much. The Dutch missionary had a better sense of humor.

Saturday night, after I'd staked out my bunk, I took my sketch pad downstairs to the snack bar, where Disaffected Youth was gathered, complaining about the prices. I ordered a beer and a hamburger. The bar man was a Scot. A permanent sneer had lodged in the furze that covered his cheeks and chin. He slapped down a paper cup of beer on the puddled surface of the bar. As half the contents of the cup foamed over the rim and into the stagnant stream, bloated flies launched into flight and coasted down in groggy spirals. The bar man slung a cellophane-wrapped discus into the microwave. When the burger had been sterilized, if not heated, he dropped it on a paper plate the size of a coaster, and assessed me twice what I'd paid for the bed.

"You're kidding," I said.

"Take it or leave it," he said.

"I've already left the beer on the bar," I said.

He shrugged. A Scottish shrug is a twitch.

I couldn't face the four-mile walk to town to seek a plate of pasta, on Holy Saturday night, when everyone else was either in church or playing high-stake bingo on the Ponte Vecchio. "Put a head on this beer," I said with the flinty aplomb I'd acquired in Paree. The furze-face nearly registered surprise, but he mastered his impulse and gave my cup another blat of suds. I plunked down a sheaf of hundred-lire notes in the puddle of beer. He did the same with the paper plate, which disintegrated like Kleenex under the hose. "I can see we're going to be pals," I said.

Holding the burger by the fluted corner of its envelope, and tucking the sketch pad under one arm, I carried the drizzling beer to a table. The snack bar had the same ambience as the cafeteria in my high school, where at any hour, disgruntled adolescents could be found, smoking, eating microwave burgers from a vending machine, and cranking out tales of disillusionment which explained why they weren't in class. I sat in a corner, back to the wall, sketch pad at the ready like a six-gun, to defend me from inane conversation. The hamburger tasted like warm, pliant styrofoam, but the beer impressed me. The bar man must be a chemical genius—he had invented a beer that was three-quarters foam, and tasted flat. I yearned for the bar of chocolate or the orange in my long-lost purse. Tomorrow, I'd have to forage for breakfast in town.

The rank stench from the lavatory had driven me out of the dorm. But the talk within earshot was almost as lethal. The World Weary Ones were conducting a purge. An American "hippie-type traveler" who still had a shine of innocence sat in their midst, as if at the feet of tribal chiefs, while they made him present his credentials. During the trial, the judges drank the candidate's chianti.

"How long you been over?"

"Six weeks."

Silence.

"Well, I mean, it's almost two months, actually, I mean, based on when I started *out*, but I figure I'll be here a year, years, I mean, why go home?"

"You still call it home? I mean, you think of America

as home?"—sadder and wiser smile—"I can't believe I ever lived there. It's like a dream, like a nightmare."

"Oh, yeah, well, it's habit, you know, I mean, I know what you mean, what do I have to say to those people any more, you know? I mean I haven't written to my folks since I left because like . . . *what could they understand?*"

"Money, man. That's what they understand. That's all the whole fucking country understands. America! Your old man—and your old lady—and your uncles and aunts, your fucking grandmother, man"—(the candidate winced)—"are like everybody else in that country—they can't grasp that we don't *want* their fucking money, we don't *need* their fucking money, we are *free* of it, dig?"

"Oh, God, yeah, that's exactly right, that's exactly why I don't want any money from my old man, I mean you know what he does to get it? He owns a factory that makes parts for tanks! That's blood money, baby—I even told him that, I said, 'I don't want your blood money!' "

Silence.

"You blew it."

"What? . . . what? . . . what do you mean?"

"You just . . . you just don't get it, man. You haven't got the picture. *That* money, you *take* it, you take it *all* if you can get it, you remove it from the American market-place, the American capitalistic cycle—that way you undercut the system, don't you see that?"

"Oh, right! Right, I dig! Yeah, I should like take the money and get it out of America! And put it to really beautiful and meaningful use, something *constructive*—"

"No, man, no! Blow it! Show your contempt for the system it came from! Blow it on a Cadillac, and then set fire to the Cadillac! You want to make a gesture, a symbol that says, 'Up yours, America!' Blow it on porn movies, man!"

"Porn movies! Wow! Like buy up all the porn movies in America and show them free in all the ghettoes! That would show my father!"

Fairing the dedicated artiste, I gazed at a page of the sketch pad and doodled. I was thinking of the Captain and his destitute crew, padding their underfed bodies against the all-piercing cold, jouncing mindless and wretched over the Seine in their splintering barge, like cats in an orange crate set adrift to drown. At least when they played Poverty, they played it for real.

When the purge was over, and the victim was writhing in abasement, cleansed of his bourgeois taint, the gurus and gurettes surveyed the bleachers for another prospect. The wholesome contingent were out in the yard, roping the meek of all nations into frisbee. I was the only freelance American in the room. I concentrated fiercely on my pencil point. It broke. Cursing, I caught the bleary eye of a boy who was draining the victim's bottle of wine. I'd noticed the boy before because he wore a sombrero. Minus sombrero, he would have blended completely into the wall. He gave me the old-timer's gaze of rueful wisdom, which, combined with sombrero, made him look like Walter Brennan.

"How long you been over?" he said.

"Over what?" I said.

Dim as he was, he sensed that I wasn't applying to join. He left me alone. The bar man broke up the love feast at 10:45. "It's time. Sod off," he said. El Sombrero and the rest of the die-hards drifted out to the lawn to smoke dope and fool around in the bushes. As I folded my sketch pad and stalked out under the Scot's corroded eye, the lights went out. Curfew had rung its silent knell. In darkness, I groped for the bannister. If the warden caught me skulking around after curfew, he might heave me into solitary. (If I'd really believed that, I would have burst into song.)

I reached the upstairs hall where my bunk was hidden. Groping along that cold, lightless, fetid-smelling corridor, I could have been treading a walkway in a sewer. The darkness stirred with the rhythmic, moaning unselfconscious breathing of sleepers. When I found my bunk by counting the front posts of beds—I was Number 32—there were eight hulks hunkered on it, playing a card game called "Pig" by flashlight. They were drinking Spanish beer and socking each other at intervals. "Excuse me," I said, "but I think that's my bed."

White light knifed my eyes. The hulks gave forth with raucous "haw haw haws." "Bugger off," said several beefy Nordamericanos.

"Get the hell off my bed," I said.

A ghoulish moonface, luminescent and cratered with shadows, hovered in the upward beam of a flashlight. The moon had freckles. Its mouth, beneath a shadow mustache, moved. "That's the American who didn't know what a maple leaf was," said the freckles. I recognized my bunkmate. Why weren't they having this party on *her* bed?

"You know what you can do with the maple leaf," I said. "Get off my bed before I throw you off."

Since there were eight of them, each one made in the image of an orangutan, mine was not a threat—it was a kamikaze pledge. The freckles and another hulk heaved themselves over the side of the bunk and crashed to the floor like twin pianos dropped by a crane. They backed me against the wall. Flashlight beams from the bunk bobbed over our faces. Theirs were belligerent. Both of the muggers were female, but they looked like they'd trained for the backpack by lifting weights. I was beginning to think that every citizen of Canada ate six raw eggs and jogged five miles each morning, hoping to go the distance with the U.S.A.

The freckles gave me a shove. "You've got a lot of nerve, Yank," she said. "You've got a lot of nerve."

"Two down, one to go," I said.

"What's that?"

"You only said it twice. You have to say it one more time."

She shoved me. My spine smacked the wall. "You trying to be cute?"

"No, it's too dark to be cute. Quit shoving me. Look, if you want to play 'Pig,' that's your business, but play it somewhere else. I want to go to sleep. I've been through a lot the last two days—"

"Is that so?" said the block of muscle backing up the freckles. "Well, isn't that just too bad."

The hulks on the bunk said, "Awwwwww . . ." In the faint arc of backwash from the flashlights, I could see the silhouettes of heads and humped shoulders. They looked like apes on a ledge.

"This is ridiculous," I said. "You can't push me around —I'm a woman."

"Girls can beat up other girls. All's fair," said the freckles.

"Don't they teach you to fight in the States?" said a hulk with a pebbly basso. Some of the hulks were male—I had known by the randy pitch of their laughter.

"America is a civilized country," I said, losing my head.

"HAW HAW HAW" resounded through the corridor, shaking the beds with animal mirth. "Civilized! What about Viet Nam?"

The black tidal murmur of the world of sleepers outside our sphere of angry light was broken with shouts of "Shut yer yap!" "Sortez! Allez en bas!" "Stupidischer Americanische!" and similar insults and protests in a dozen tongues. The sentiments were given clout by the deep rough timbres of the voices. There wasn't a single soprano note.

"Wait a minute," I said. "Where am I?"

"Where do you think you are?" said the freckles. "You're in the bloody hostel, where they shouldn't even let Americans in, a hostel is for students and people who can't pay, not for Americans whose pockets are full of other countries' money—"

"Is that your bed?" I said, pointing to the bottom bunk. Someone on flashlight duty swung a beam to spill across the bed. The swaying pool of light gave a porthole view of a mattress, a pair of muddy boots, and a jockstrap.

"Of course it isn't, you bloody ass. My bed's in the woman's section, right under yours."

"Oh, good grief," I said. Thrusting my shoulder into hers, knocking her bulk off balance, I ran. "Hey!" she yelled, giving chase. The other musclemaid joined her. I could hear the pounding of their four hooves, as if I were being pursued by a bull. The apes in the bleachers cheered them on. "Cat fight! . . . Cat fight! . . . Give her a lesson! . . . Good work, Flo! . . . You don't mind if we drink your beer, do you? . . . Don't bother with her, she's too small! . . . Bring her back, I think I love her! . . . Throw her downstairs, Flo, see if she'll bounce! . . ."

The dormitory was roused. I ran blind, left hand trailing the wall like a stick along a fence, but I kept bashing full tilt into men who'd gotten out of bed, and loomed invisible and threatening in the dark, like rocks in an unmarked channel. "Oof!" they said. "Sorry," I said. Some of the "oofs" were oddly highpitched. The mandatory darkness made for heavy traffic between the men's and women's sections. A dorm with broken toilets, overbooked and underheated—what a place to get your nooky. "C'est une femme," said a voice quite close. My thigh brushed an outstretched arm, and its hand grasped at my hip and slipped

282   PART FOUR   *The Free Spirit*

away as I ran. Excited voices clamored around me, more
men jumping into the aisle between the wall and the wall
of beds. I smacked into a body like a pillar of flesh. Hands
fastened on my arm and back. Warm breath stirred my
scalp. My nose was pressed to his lifting throat as he cried
out, exultant. I raked the bone of his naked leg with the
edge of my boot. He yelled. As his fingers loosened, I
wrenched away, and ran.

I gained the stairs.

Below, in the center of the lobby floor between the facing
tiers of stairs, there was a fire burning. Dark figures formed
a collapsed ring around a camper's portable stove. Four fat
candles were planted in pools of wax on the marble floor,
one at each corner of the stove. Dull yellow light from four
flames flicked the foreheads and cheeks of faces in the ring,
and sent black clouds of shadows jiggling over the plaster
walls. Tongues of light licked the edges of the steps as I
bounded down toward the campsite, the maids of the
maple leaf hot on my heels. The staircase shook with the
banging of boots and the slapping of naked feet. The stairwell rang with the rallying cries of the polyglot stampede.
Nightlife was scant around the bunkhouse—the menfolks
were ripe for a riot. Where the hell was the warden? He
must lock us in for the night and repair to his centrally
heated villa, bought with our grubby gold.

As I galloped into the circle of light, I saw that the
campers were having a marshmallow roast. I wouldn't have
believed it if I hadn't recognized the fire-glowing faces of
El Sombrero Blando and the snack bar savants. Americans
—God love 'em, they make themselves at home! Lodged in
an eighteenth-century house with Italian marble floors,
they had responded by staging a marshmallow roast. I
could have killed them.

We thundered into camp like a cossack charge. Campers
scrambled. A scuffle ensued: campers were passing the
joint back and forth like the ball in "Hot Potato," with the
same intent, each player trying to save his hide and screw
his neighbor. They thought we were the law. Only imbe-
cilic paranoia, fed by dope and marshmallows, could render me and my giddy posse into narcs and feds. Americans
scattered, some through the door to the lawn, some up the
females' staircase. Naked or half-dressed Swedes and Japanese and assorted Latins and Anglo-Saxons joyfully pursued

them. It was a free-for-all "Kick the Can" at the General Assembly picnic. In front by a nose, I sprinted up the stairs and down the cold, foul alley of the bed-lined hall, one hand trailing the wall, the other arm crooked in a shield against the blackness. I was aiming for Number 32, but I didn't take time to count the posts. At the least, we were facing one hell of a panty raid.

The light went on.

My eyes slammed shut against its white assault. I shielded them with both hands and cracked them open.

Behind me, naked raiders stumbled and squinted, laughter trapped on their lips. The female Canadian tanks in the vanguard ground to a ponderous halt. Legs and butts of American jeans stuck out from under bunks. Encased in muslin sleeping bags, women moaned, rolled over, blinked, sat up and said, each in her own tongue, "Whazzat?"

Down at the hall's dead end, the German guard, in a nightgown that looked like a uniform, stood with her hand on the light switch.

A still, remote, and awesome figure, she swept the length of the hall with a gaze as impersonal and deadly as machine-gun fire. The barrel of her eyes pointed last at the naked men. If venom were ammo, they would have been blasted to Rome. To a man, they blanched. Leaking scared giggles, they covered their nakedness, clutching at towels and laundry bags whose owners snatched them back. Clustering, bumping, they made a feeble retreat. The Americans slunk out of hiding and shambled out in the raiders' wake.

Four beds from the matron's post, I yanked off my boots and jumped in the sack in my jeans. My vicious bunkmate landed on the plank below me with a force that rattled my teeth.

When all was hushed and rigid, the guard gave her troops the nod.

Click-click! Ten grey flannel nightgowns mounted with ten wax doll heads formed for parade. Each little soldier carried toothbrush in right hand, paste in left. Each wore knitted slippers which muffled the sound of the march. In lockstep, they filed to the bathroom to brush their teeth. Wait till the guard got a look at the bathroom!

Problem: there were ten soldiers and only five sinks. But the matron would have a plan for any contingency. Operation Overshot: I envisioned five short girls, one at each sink, five tall girls placed two steps back and one to the right of the five short girls. Click-click! Short girls wet brushes. Click-click! Tall girls wet brushes as short girls load brushes with paste. Click-click! Tall girls load brushes with paste as short girls brush their teeth. Click-click! Tall girls brush their teeth as short girls bend to spit, once, neatly, into basins. Click-click! Short girls rinse brushes as tall girls bend over short girls' right shoulders and spit, once, neatly, into basins. Click-click! Tall girls rinse brushes as short girls stand at ease. Click-click! Form ranks!

Too bad the matron didn't run the hostel. I would have marched gladly, I told myself, for the sake of sanitation and hearty, wursty meals. I'd have gone straight to the top in the Hitler Youth.

My bunkmate was snoring theatrically, interspersing her snores with dark mumbles which I tried to ignore. Fearful of the matron, she was harmless now, but in the morning in the snack bar, the Yankee commentary might set her fuse alight. She could explode and feed me to the microwave.

I woke at sunrise, so alert that my feet were arched. I tiptoed into the boggy bathroom, scurried around in the dribbly shower—holding my breath against the stink, clenching my very pores against the cold—threw on my jeans, weighted like saddlebags with silver lire, and crept down the staircase. The front door was locked. The warden must have found it open after the rodeo had ended, and locked it to cut down on hanky-panky. Making a circuit of the windows, I found one close enough to a rise of ground for a safe drop, threw out the canvas bag, and let myself out.

The Easter Cuckoo

I walked the four miles into town. In the cobbled courtyard of a piazza, I found an open café. The place looked
expensive. Chairs with backs like wrought-iron flowers and
striped silk seats were set on the stones around tiny round
white-mantled tables, under a sun already sweetly hot.
Waiters passed among the flaking columns of the blackened
stone portico backing the tables, their striped silk vests and
gold bow ties glinting in the shadows. They were old men,
stooped and grizzled. They tottered out among the tables,
wielding in each hand a silver pot, pouring smoky black
and white streams into gilt-edged basins of cups. European
tourists spruced for Easter Sunday were drinking caffè
latte and picking at fluted, toasty-gold pastries stuffed with
yellow custard.

I ordered a caffè latte and a pastry like the one that the
elegant woman at the table on my left was tearing into
bites for her son. The woman's hair was black and sleek in
a low chignon. She wore a grey suit and an ivory silk
blouse with a flowing bow at the neck. The little boy wore
a grey suit with short pants and an ivory silk shirt with a
dark grey tie. His mother spoke to him in Italian, in a rolling mezzo version of Madame's coaxing trill, as she slipped
the sweet morsels of crust and cream into his baby bird
mouth. He gazed at her from under his dark bangs with
round black eyes like her own. Her red lips opened like his
as he took the morsels.

Two Frenchmen sat at the table on my right. They kept
ordering caffè latte refills and pastries, snagging every
waiter who toddled by with new gâteau and demanding
"un comme ça." The Frenchmen were eating so fast and
talking so much that they kept getting custard on the cuffs
of their custommade suits. They didn't even care. "Italians

always eat like this," they kept telling each other en français. When in Rome . . .

What did the scene remind me of? I had a sense of a
cycle completed. I found myself smiling, resting in the
resilient net of the past. Then I remembered the cracked
Kodak print, labeled in my mother's fountain pen script:
Piazza San Marco, Venice, 1951. I saw the sun on the
tables, the background of pigeons and columns, the laughing girls, impossibly young, in their innocent, outdated
frills. "Hi, Mom," I said across the miles and years, "I
guess I'm a gypsy too." I had a flash attack of the homesick blues, which I squelched by recalling Easter in Cleveland, an endless chain of mooshy chocolate marshmallow
eggs. My mother bought boxes and boxes of them. She
thought we loved them. We hated them—they always
looked good, and they always tasted mooshy. To spare her
feelings, we stuck them in the freezer, and when they were
hard, we picked off the chocolate and ate it, peeling the
white rocks bare with our fingernails. The trick was to
peel a whole rock before it softened. My youngest brother
was champ. He could peel a rock in twelve seconds, while
drinking Kool-Aid and watching *I Walked with a Zombie*
on the *Milkman's Matinee.* He used to hide the rocks from
my mother in his Cub Scout hat.

I missed my brothers. But if I went home tomorrow, or
a year, or five years from tomorrow, they would still be
picking chocolate off the frozen marshmallow eggs. I didn't
want to live in marshmallow-egg-land, not yet, not for a
while.

The waiter brought my breakfast. I drank the steaming
liquid, half-rich, half-acrid, mingled in the basin which I
held with both hands, and let the thick heavy custard, cut
with a tang of lemon, melt into bliss on the back of my
tongue. When sunlight coated the courtyard stones the
color of dust, and gabbling throngs in pastel finery ambled
through the fluttering, settling clouds of pigeons, the little
boy whispered in his mother's ear. She helped him down
from his striped silk cushion and led him away from the
tables. There in the piazza, the woman in grey took down
her son's grey pants and watched him pee. Then she buttoned him up again, tucked in his shirt, kissed him, and
led him back to his seat.

The tourists and pigeons were too engrossed in their

separate roles to notice. But the Frenchmen on my right
were entranced. Watching, they ate all the sugar cubes out
of the bowl on their table. I waited for them to get up and
pee in the square. When in Rome . . . Licking cream from
his tie pin, one of the Frenchmen said that they'd better go,
if they wanted to see "le spectacle." In the café, men were
packing up their Sunday papers. Women were fluffing
corsages and gathering bags and gloves. There was a rush
of payment and departure. In the square, pigeon photog-
raphers shouldered their cameras and dragged their ruffled
children toward one alley exit, already jammed with an
immobile crowd. The woman in grey wiped her little boy's
face and hands with a napkin. She picked him up and
carried him across the square, moving along in the current
of the crowd. The Frenchmen, who would probably have
fainted if anyone had bumped them in the Métro in Paris,
plunged blithely into the crush and were lost in the surge
of heads and bodies.

Almost at once, the overflow from the alley spread across
the corner of the square in a seething, bunching, squawking mass. Having joined the mob, people were hemmed in
and squashed by the next wave of bodies. Pushing and
yelling, they stood held-fast, fixed by the pressure of an-
guished numbers, like a painted flood.

What could it be, this Easter morning spectacle? I
wanted to see, but I couldn't face the suffocating impact
of all those bodies. Then I saw some Italian families who'd
been parading in the piazza. They were hurrying off through
another exit. Two of the ancient waiters joined the rene-
gades. These people were natives—they knew the short
cuts. I left the money for my breakfast on the table and
followed them.

The alley was a sunless, cramped, pebble-paved tunnel
between the smooth stone walls of houses, colorless in
shadow. Windows were gaps, as if the single square of
stone that filled each chink had been yanked like a tooth,
with pliers. I could brush both walls with my fingertips as
I slipped down the smooth dry lumps of rocks. The stone
facades seemed to lean inward as they rose, shutting out all
but one long strip of blue. Up ahead where mamas and
papas and children hustled, telling each other to hurry—
pronto! pronto!—more mamas and papas and children
burst forth, laughing, chattering, arguing, kids giving sass

and getting smacked, as if they didn't know they lived in poverty and darkness. A marigold in a flower pot sat like hope on a ledge beside a door.

The dark path led to a tilted square hole, hewn out of stone, white hot with sun, alive with sailing dust. Just as I'd almost reached the exit, I was caught up in a troop of skinny children, alternately marshaled and ignored by their waddling mama. As her only holiday ornament, the mother wore a pink pillbox hat crowned with two floppy tulle-petaled roses, blooming on either side of her pink straw scalp like the ears of Mickey Mouse.

"Mama! Mama! Veronica! Il pesce! Cioccolata!" Cries and confusion went up from the pack of kids. They had the raucous voices of those who have to compete to be heard. The center of the clamor was the smallest child, a little girl with limbs protruding like broken bones from the shapeless lilac mass of an older sister's dress. Stubborn, silent, she was staring at her mother and hugging something to her bunchy cotton chest. "Ai-ee! Veronica!" her mother declared to the strip of sky. She stopped the parade at the mouth of the alley and gave the child an order, flinging out her arm in the direction from which we'd come.

"No," said Veronica, clutching her chest, sharp little face white and set.

Her mother unleashed a roar of gabble, hurling her arms in wrathful frenzy, courting bruised knuckles as she almost smacked the alley walls. The roses on her hat bounced and wiggled. Veronica didn't budge. "No," she said, her voice as fragile and unyielding as her stiffly planted stalks of legs.

"Ai-eeeee!" Her mother swooped at her, wrenching her bony arms from her chest. A smooth brown oval object about ten inches long, like a flat, narrow football, fell to the stones. Veronica started to cry. Still yelling, her mother fumbled in her bosom for a handkerchief and wiped at the brown stains smeared across Veronica's hand-me-down Sunday dress and her poky white arms. The other kids dived for the oval object. One of the bigger boys seized it and held it tenderly, stroking its scalloped carving. It was a molded chocolate fish with one pink candy eye, like an American Easter rabbit. The scales had been smudged by the heat and pressure of the little girl's embrace as she'd trotted behind her brothers and sisters. Another child stooped and picked up some bright-colored pebbles from among the cobbles. The others gathered around the boy who held the fish, touching it with wounded awe. An L-shaped crack had been made in the fish's side, by the little girl's grip or by the fall. The boy poked a finger under the chocolate flap, and the girl who'd scooped up the pebbles tried to push them through the crack. The flap sprang upward as the chocolate broke along the fish's spine.

The boy and girl screamed at each other. The mother screamed at both of them. Everyone screamed at Veronica. She cried, her face rigid, like the chocolate face of the fish. The boy lifted off the broken piece of chocolate. Inside, the fish was filled with jelly beans and tiny foil-wrapped eggs. Some of the foil eggs had fallen out when Veronica had dropped the fish, and her brother and sister had tried to replace them, and done the beautiful fish more harm.

Abruptly, the mother turned on the gang of kids and told them to shut up! leave Veronica alone! She dried the little girl's tears and smoothed her hair and the brown-smeared, blotchy wet front of her dress. Veronica seized her mother's soft, round hips and buried her face in the folds of stomach. The biggest boy was dispatched up the alley to take the treasure home.

How many hours had the mother worked, at what exhausting, grubby task, to buy her kids one Easter gift, a chocolate fish to share? I imagined the mother's bitter pride, the delight of the small ones, the older kids' twinges of understanding of what their mother had given for it. And then the baby, Veronica, couldn't bear to leave the magical chocolate fish at home. She had carried it, hidden against her chest. She'd been discovered. Now the treasure was flawed. I thought of Leah's Christmas, the elevator crammed with presents, the bicyclette now stiffening, unoiled, in a closet. Leah must have gotten an aquarium of chocolate this morning. Chocolate fishes, chocolate marshmallow eggs . . . somehow they were all connected, all those rich and sticky gifts, all that confusion of love.

Arrested by the family group planted in the tunnel's mouth, a small crowd had collected. Indignant at the traffic jam, and then intrigued, they had taken sides, egging on their favorites. Now that a fatalistic peace had descended, the fans were antsy. We could hear the deafening static of thousands of voices, hoarse, shrill, exuberant, competing like those of Veronica's brothers and sisters. When the boy returned, we popped out into the sun-steeped world beyond the portals. It was a world ringed by crumbling stone, lidded with searing blue, and packed like the chocolate fish with the bright eggs of legless, faceless bodies.

Our little party was at once engulfed, lost in the swell and hum, sucked up in the moist hot press and sway of the shifting weights of bodies. Trying to stand apart and watch, I was thrust straight into the crush by the hardnosed advance of another platoon. In a moment, I was bound in by yards, and soon by what seemed to be acres, of people, yelling, waving placards painted with COMUNISTA slogans, tearing down the placards, laughing and hooting, screaming at each other, taking punches—a feat in itself, when they couldn't rare back to take aim—chanting, with childlike impatience, a rhyme that built to a walloping roar as the chant was taken up by a thousand voices, till it was broken off, dropped like a toy that had fallen out of favor. Small, hunched figures bobbed above the sea of heads: children, their faces bright with expectancy, riding the shoulders of fathers or brothers. I thought I saw Veronica's sharp little face across the waves.

All of a sudden the number of bodies in any one space doubled. My arms were pressed against my sides. I couldn't raise them. I ran with the crowd, my feet stilled or driven by the motionless press or the forward or backward or rightward sweep of the pack. I was terrified, and yet exultant. I couldn't question; I needn't think. I had only to stay on my feet, to dance to the will of the mob. It was a master class in going-with-the-flow.

We were in a piazza, irregularly shaped and narrow at the center, like a bow tie. I was enmeshed in the center of the bow tie's knot. Police had set up wooden rails to hold back the crowd, bounding off a lane that ran the length of the piazza from the entrance off to the right, a stone path vanishing under an arch, to a clearing in front of the gleaming, tawny doors of a church. The sheen of the figured bronze panels when the sunlight struck the doors from a certain angle was visionary. Through the fence of wavering heads, I saw the shining doors swing open, dazing the crowd with the radiant shooting rays of refracted sun. Two boys in white lace tunics over black cassocks moved to either side of the wide black hole between the doors.

The crowd bellowed, shoving forward. The black-suited carabinieri shoved them back, waving their clubs dramatically, bellowing silently into the ocean of noise. In the backward and leftward swing of the crowd, I was turned around. For the first time I saw people sitting in tiers, elevated above the mass of frantic, sweaty groundlings. How had they been plucked from the pit? A familiar, dreaded shape engraved itself on my eye . . . a sombrero. There in the topmost row, commanding the vestal view of "le spectacle," El Sombrero Blando and his Gypsies of Drivel were passing binoculars and bottled water, and eating what looked like a chocolate fish. All of the fans in the bleachers except the hostel claque were dressed with fastidious gaiety, the women in silken prints and weights of beads, the men in funeral suits with hats or kerchiefs knotted aroud their scalps to keep off the sun. The Americans looked like squatters. Somewhere in the crowd, displaced Italian ticket holders were embroiled, cursing. Or maybe the Americans had bought their seats. Someone's father had moved another shipment of propeller parts, and come across with a check.

Something was happening in the end zone. A violent ripple urged the crowd forward and right. I faced the cleared lane. Bodies pressed into me, bare skin or flesh beneath fabric hot on mine, sharp bones or cushions of fat fused with my bones and flesh and then gracelessly wrenched away. The smells of sweat and hair oil and cologne and dust rose in a visible shimmer toward the sun. I couldn't see the arch at the right end of the marked lane, but everyone was yelling and those who could free their arms were waving and pointing. In a sudden cessation of pressure, I raised myself on tiptoe. The pressure was at once redoubled. I couldn't get back down. Effortlessly, buoyed up by strangers' hips and shoulders, I danced on point for the next half hour. I felt like the Nymph of Easter, but at least I could see.

Two men marched from beneath the arch. They were dressed in maroon cloaks, puffy berets, velvet breeches, and scarred cuffed leather boots. They carried tattered banners, the faded symbols on the worn cloth solemn with age. They led a procession of paired men in the same maroon dress of medieval guardsmen, each man playing or carrying some tarnished instrument, slender horns curving into morning glory cups, small drums strung in intricate diamonds, dangling from muscular necks. The crowd shushed itself as the band approached. We could hear a brassy clatter which fell short of melody, melancholy, wheezing, sporadically defunct. The costumes of the men were in a similarly invalided state. As they neared the clearing in front of the church, I could see the patches on the scraped nap of the velvet, the replacement berets of black and green, the substituted everyday trousers rolled up to the knee and fastened with pink-headed diaper pins, the hairy, knotty calves and short black socks and workman's Sunday shoes. The double line of men in maroon gave way to a double line of men in black, white plumes gasping last on their black berets. Each man's eyes bored into the thick, glistening neck of the man preceding him, as if the neck were a music stand and the notes were inked on the skin. Sweat plastered hair on foreheads and necks; sweat trickled down past ears and into collarbones, and drenched the tunics under the velvet cloaks. We in the crowd dressed for summer were weakened by the sun. The men of Firenze, stifling in velvet, must have had to summon up all their religious pride and masculine fervor not to faint.

After the guardsmen came dark-eyed boys in cassocks and white lace tunics, singing a hymn which could have been the tune that the band was playing. Sweet soprano crowned the chords, flickered here and there with a treacherous baritone shadow. The little boys weren't as tough as the guardsmen. For every boy whose eyes were clapped on his forerunner's neck, there were three who were grinning at their buddies in the crowd, giggling with their partners at faulty notes, giving supercilious looks to girls, and maintaining, throughout their frittering, the stream of unearthly music.

The choirboys ushered in a string of priests, their ivory silk robes filigreed with gold. The last in line bore the crucifix, a golden sunburst mounted at the crossing of the golden bars. In the center of the sun's heavy, grainy-gold rays, a circle of glass preserved the small white disc, the resurrected Lord. The priests were singing in fervid, monotonous baritone and bass. Their chant set the pace for their measured stepping. Sweat gushed down their sun-burned faces, darkening the necks of their ivory robes.

As the priest with the crucifix cleared the arch, a voice behind me rose above the murmur. "Okay, Dorothy, now try to get a clear shot of the oxcart and the dove. The dove, that's the ticket, that's what you want to watch for."

"What does the dove mean, hon? I know they told us, but there's so much to remember—" A flurry of elbows in my kidneys accompanied jockeying for a camera angle.

The man said patiently, "That's your tradition, the dove part is the whole meat of the thing. If the dove flies *toward* the altar, that means God'll bless the wine crop. Good weather, good wine, see? If it *lands* on the altar, that's the payoff. But it might fly right in the opposite direction, that's where your gamble comes in, that means it could go either way, no go, bad wine. That's what makes a horse race."

Ah ha! "Le spectacle" was building to a splashy finish. No wonder the city had turned out to watch! Four guardsmen emerged from the pool of shade beneath the arc of stone. Older and smaller than the bandsmen, they were swathed in black and yellow stripes. They looked like bees who were dressed to escort the Pope. Instead, they escorted four white oxen, each beast crowned with a flower wreath, so that its ears were framed in a jiggling pink and yellow nimbus.

The crowd went bananas: cheering, whistling, leaping, clapping, throwing flowers and palms and money and anything else they had at hand. The mass was pummeled by clashing surges of force. Someone stepped on my foot and rested. "Watch it!" I said. "Permesso!" The words were only mouthings in the expanding funnel of noise. The flower-twined harness strained and shook as the oxen hauled at the cart behind them. It was a plain wooden cart, beneath its baroque, fantastic burden: an enormous white tower, curlicued and sculpted, a cross between a wedding cake and a cuckoo clock. As the honor guard and oxen plodded toward the church, I saw small sticks tied all over the tower. I didn't see the dove. Cuckoolike, he was hiding inside.

The oxcart came to rest in front of the open doors of the church. The two bands, ranged around the square, left off their brassy wheezing. The choirboys and priests had vanished into the church. The crowd contained its frenzy, which gradually tapered to a speculative hum. The moment of revelation was at hand. The state of the wine crop rested on the whim of a small white bird. I had to admire the Italians for the flair with which they gambled, combining Easter with Ground Hog Day. What if the dove decided to dump on the wine crop? Quel disaster!— as if the angel had rolled away the stone from the tomb and Jesus had come out and seen his shadow and gone back inside till spring. No doubt a lot of lire—molto! molto!—was up for grabs in side bets. The four old beemen had taken up long lighted tapers. Now they applied them to the sticks that were fastened all over the cuckoo clock.

The sticks exploded in fizzling, crackling sparks. What class! a touch of the Fourth of July! As the fireworks set off an ear-numbing cheer from the mob, the little door in the rococo tower flew open. A white bird whose stiff wings might mean that it was paralyzed with fear from the noise sailed straight from the cuckoo clock into the black square between the lustrous doors. The crowd went berserk, every throat open and trumpeting, every arm flailing at the heavens, every foot stomping adjacent toes in a frenzy of approval. In the universal tribal dance, I freed my right arm—the left was hugging my coat and bag—and waved it, yelling, "All right!" the American equivalent of "Bravo!" Someone ravaged my hip. "Scusi," said a voice. It seemed like excessive courtesy, saying "Excuse me" in a stampede. "Permesso," I said. "BRA-VO!"

But I did have a question. Who won? We didn't know which way the dove had flown. Except for the priests and choirboys, we were all outside the church. Cheering, I waited for the priest to appear and give thumbs up or thumbs down.

But nothing happened. Evidently satisfied, the sunstruck and spectacle-replete aficionados began to disperse. Guardsmen stripped off their strangling cloaks and tunics and sat on the littered stones, pouring water over their heads from plastic buckets toted by choirboys. The old men dismantled their beesuits. They sat in a row in the bleachers, four tough old birds in their undershirts, sunburned, sinewy, grimed with sweat, passing a bottle of wine.

A woman in a lime-green pantsuit stood near me, taking pictures of the oxen, which were engorging hay at one end and letting it out at the other. "Don't take the picture now, for chrissake," said her husband. He was a bald man in a jacket striped in cantaloupe and white. It looked like an awning over a golf cart. Easter Sunday in Italy was a great day for stripes, like St. Patrick's Day for the wearin' o' the green.

"I'm just taking the front part, hon," said the woman, "they look so dear in those bridesmaid wreaths."

I knew their voices. They'd been discussing the dove in the crowd behind me. "Excuse me," I said, "did you happen to hear which way the dove flew?"

The man perked up at the sound of my sloppy consonants. "You're from the Midwest, aren't you?"

"Cleveland," I said.

"Cleveland! No kidding!" They beamed at me. "We're from Pennsylvania. Pymatuning, Pennsylvania."

"Happy Easter," I said. "Do you happen to know which way the dove flew? I mean, did he land on the altar or what?"

"On the altar, didn't he, hon?" said the woman.

"Sure," said the man. "Always lands on the altar. It's rigged. They do it with wires. They're clever, these people, give 'em that. You think they haven't got two brains to rub together, but some of 'em are goddamn shrewd. They do this religious stuff for the tourists, can't let 'em down, so they wire the dove."

He had said "tourists" with a dismissive flap of his beetle-ringed hand. His wife shook her head, smiling: those poor gullible tourists, always being taken in! These people didn't see themselves as tourists either. Tourists, like witches, couldn't see themselves in mirrors.

"Oh, I want a sno-cone," said the woman as a man wheeled up his cart, with its clinking cargo of bottles of varicolored syrups. "I want a lemon sno-cone, Carl."

"Your wish is my command, my lady," said the man, hauling out a roll of lire the size of a roll of toilet paper. He handed the bug-eyed vendor a note. "Make it duo," he said.

My tongue was sticking to the roof of my mouth. I reached for my pocket. "What about you, young lady? On me. What's your pleasure?" said the man.

I had lime. I hadn't had a sno-cone since my mother's last Conestoga tour of Cedar Point. The blues nudged my throat again, in between the collarbones. To quash them, I lingered with Carl and Dorothy, looking at their slides of Rome and of their daughter's wedding. "That's the Coliseum. I couldn't get it all in," said Dorothy, handing me a tinted patch of gel. Squinting, I made out something that looked like a crumbling dam.

"I'll tell you, Kerry, Rome is a hell of an impressive place," said Carl. "All that antiquity . . . it just bowled us over, didn't it, Dorothy?"

"This is Sue-Ann in her going-away dress, and that's Bob," said Dorothy. I squinted at the faces in the gel. They squinted back. They must have gone away on a very sunny day. "She's pretty," I said.

"We're real proud of that girl," said Carl, patting Dorothy's head. The sprayed meringue of her gilded hair-do flattened and sprang back, unsquashable. Dorothy smiled up at him. "Now don't go all teary," he said.

They took me to lunch. They insisted. We ate in a restaurant near the Ponte Vecchio, which was less a bridge than a street across water, lined on either side with tiny houses propped on stilts, and blighted with the usual junk shops and postcard stands. Carl bought a leather wallet engraved with the meeting of Dante and Beatrice. The restaurant was called, of course, Il Inferno, but the American menu, printed in red and coated with wax, was as good as a sign: IL RIP-OFF. I was afraid to look at the prices, since I felt guilty already. I was dancing on a wire suspended between the masochistic work ethic I'd refined in France, and the take-it-and-smirk philosophy of El Sombrero Blando and his ilk. I ordered, with my right or price eye closed, a hamburger. Dorothy and Carl had prime rib, which arrived on the plates in a stringy, depleted state, as if the bull had been run at Pamplona and never recovered. "Italians don't know beef," said Carl. "First thing I'm gonna have when we get back to the States is a big fat juicy sirloin steak." My hamburger was packed in shredded bitter lettuce, compressed by a genuine American all-cotton bun. Carl poked at the garnish on his plate, which looked like pickled okra. "What the hell is this?" he said.

"You don't have to eat it, hon," said Dorothy. "Just leave it on your plate."

We went to the Uffizi Gallery. Carl wouldn't let me pay my way in, or buy them caffè latte later in the afternoon. "Wouldn't hear of it, Missy," he said. "Sometime someone'll do the same for Sue-Ann." It seemed unlikely that Sue-Ann would ever wander lonely as a cloud in Florence, too poor to pay for a private bed, wearing a vented sweater that smelled of baby powder. "You're too nice," I said. They beamed. I couldn't see the pictures on the walls of the Uffizi, which seemed to be holding a cocktail party for all of northern Italy. I trailed Dorothy among the elbows as she told me the story of Bob and Sue-Ann's courtship. They'd been going steady since seventh grade. "That's how long I've had this sweater," I said. "Why you poor little thing," said Dorothy.

When I left them at their American-style hotel, they gave me their address. "Now you come see us if you're ever in Pennsylvania," said Dorothy. "I will," I said. "We'll give you a real live hamburger!" said Carl. "Ground round, one quarter-pound, no fat!"

I crossed the Ponte Vecchio and strolled along the quai, gazing across the brown waters of the Arno to the golden stone houses and rusty tile roofs and domes and spires of the town. I basked in a mellow evening light that reflected an inner glow. What nice people, what nice Americans! Carl and Dorothy gave me hope—not for the spoilers in the hostel or the certifiable whackos like Duse, but for the corny, kindly folks like Grace Pitasky. Grace and whichever survivor of the Rat Hunt she chose for her consort might grow up to be Dorothy and Carl. For the first time, I wished I could be that simple. Who could say if Dorothy and Carl wore blinders, or if they looked straight into the heart?

Mist was creeping up the mud bank toward the town. Once again, I stood on the border of day, looking into the night without a haven. Instead of chumming around with Pennsylvanians, I should have been stumping hotels, trying to bribe my way into a bed. I'd better count my money.

I reached into the right-hand pocket of my jeans, and kept reaching. The pocket was empty.

With a sickening drop, I was plunged back into the

crowd—into the dust and sun, the sea of heads, the press of flesh. I was yelling "Bravo!" in a torrent of bravos, and flinging my arm above my head in a wind-tossed forest of arms. A body was slamming into my right hip with specially brutal force. A voice was mumbling, "Scusi." "Permesso," I was saying, not glancing at the face. "Permesso . . ."

This time I didn't cry. I sat on the wall of the quai and counted my money. The thief had missed the lump of lire on the left. I had ninety-seven dollars left.

Tomorrow I would go to the consulate and throw myself on the consul's mercy. He would rush me another passport to get me off his hands. He would get an economic hammerlock on some airline executive and force the airline to issue me another ticket. As soon as I had a ticket and a passport, I would go home. Freedom was too much for me. I couldn't handle it. I didn't deserve it. Italy would be better off without another moron American dilettante on the loose.

When I could face it, I picked up my bag and started the four-mile hike to the hostel.

Holding in Rome

The hostel was locked up tight when I got there. Jumping, I couldn't touch the ledge of the only open window. I slept on a bench in the garden. The air smelled of grass and earth, and of flowers open to the moist night. The bench was hard, like the bunk I'd slept on the night before. I took my nightgown out of my bag and wadded it into a pillow. I hadn't slept outside since I was in high school, when Randy and I had gone with a bunch of our friends to a rundown cottage on the lake. Everyone had borrowed or brought a false I.D., so we could sneak into bars in Geneva, the neighboring carny town. One night when the cottage was overrun with sozzle-headed boys ensnared in some fumescent dump, Randy and I had gotten bored with the stick-shift dialogue and headed for the beach. We'd sat digging our toes in the dark cool sand, listening to the rufflets of the tide. We'd talked about life. After a while, we'd lain down and watched the stars. Now in Firenze, I turned on the slab of damp cement and let the dark glittering bowl of the sky descend and surround me. Same sky, same stars as on that night on the shores of a lake three thousand miles away.

Good ole Randy. It would be neat to see her. April in Cleveland . . . I wondered if it were snowing. You never knew with Ohio. My family would be glad to have me home. My father would laugh like hell at the tale of the Easter cuckoo clock. My mother would break out the chocolate marshmallow eggs, and the bottle of Setzubal, a Spanish liqueur which we drank at family fetes. Randy would be there, and Great-Uncle Al and his girl friend, and Aunt Martha, and maybe even Grace, if I drove to the west side to pick her up. Grace had never been east of downtown. We'd sit around the dining room table till midnight, while I told tales of my wanderings, editing where needed. They'd tell me all their news. I'd been gone since November; something must have happened in Cleveland. And in the morning—not the first day home, but the second or third day—I'd go and look for a job. I wouldn't take a stopgap job like coding; I'd wait for a job I could live with, a job I could like—a grownup's job. It wouldn't be so bad, going home . . .

I remember thinking before I went to sleep that the stars were as big and as thickly sprinkled as the chocolate chips in really good ice cream.

When the hostel opened up to birdsong, I went inside and waited till the three Italian Communists came downstairs. Then I asked the most broachable one, Camilla, if she'd make a phone call for me. If I had to fight with a pay phone and an operator, both Italian, before I'd had my breakfast, I knew I wouldn't make it through the day. Camilla called the consulate, berating every flunky who stood between her and competence. She got the consul's secretary, who, we agreed, would know more than the consul. "Crisp" was the word for the secretary. She'd heard of my problem—she lived at her desk—and she said, in an accent which managed to be both clipped and Italian, "I can do nothing for you. You must go to Rome."

"Now hold it," I said. "In Ventimiglia, they told me Genova. In Genova, they told me Firenze. I haven't got the money to go traipsing off to Rome. All I want to do is get home."

"That is why you must go to Rome, to the embassy," said the frosty voice. "They have the power to issue you a special passport quickly. The consul has not the power."

"Why in hell didn't they tell me that in Genova and Ventimiglia," I said. "I wouldn't have come to Firenze and got my pocket picked!" The trio of Communists, hovering, slipped each other ironic smiles: il governamento, la burocrazia, mama mia!

"Because they do not know the procedure in those places," said the voice, dropping a note of contempt.

"Look," I said, "will you call the embassy and tell *them* the procedure, so when I get there, they'll know what to do with me?"

"Yes, I will tell them. But one cannot promise that they will remember my call. They are Italians."

She broke the connection. Here was a woman who was not, as we say in Ohio, "happy in her work."

Happily, Camilla and her cohorts were driving to Rome right after breakfast. They offered to take me, if I'd share the cost of gas. "That would be wonderful!" I said. How much could gas cost, split four ways? And then, there'd be all those free pamphlets.

Breakfast in the hostel snack bar was American cereal, the tasteless, brannish kind, served in little boxes—"en cardboard," as we say in France—with bluish milk. We drank some coffee, another of the bar man's chemical coups: it tasted like pencil shavings, and it was green. "Do you make this from an old Scottish recipe?" I asked him.

"Take it or leave it," he said.

The ride to Rome was uneventful. Camilla's fellow travelers were named Teresa—they had agreed to share a name. They let me ride in front, but I had to hold the goat. I'd never met a goat before, or held one on the front seat of a Fiat. This was a charming goat, small and black, also named Teresa. (How had Camilla escaped? She must be a Troskyite.) The goat was trained to pee in a box beneath the dashboard. When she got skittish, every ten minutes or so, Teresa the driver would tell me to dump Teresa the goat in her box so she could pee. But Teresa the goat was too nervous to pee, perhaps because she'd noticed that Teresa the driver steered with her face turned over her shoulder, exchanging dialectic with Teresa in the back seat. Camilla looked out the window.

We took back roads through hills of the greenest, lushest grass I'd ever seen, grass so deeply green that the roots of the bunching spears were black where they clung in earth. Dusty white villages wound up the slopes to the church that crowned each peak. We drove past fields and vineyards buttery with sun, past the greyish haze of olive groves. Under a trellis interwoven with honeysuckle vines, an old man in a vest was dozing in a weathered cane chair. With an unconscious hand, he stroked the white cat sleeping across his knees. I found myself stroking the silken ears of Teresa, the little black goat.

We stopped to eat our bread and cheese in a cemetery. Buttercups made spongy yellow cushions for the fallen stones. The oldest date I could trace with my fingers was

1457. "1457 . . . America hadn't been discovered yet," I said. Camilla smiled. "Yes, you are very young," she said. "That is why you have hope." She shrugged. "In Italia, our sewers were built before the fall of Rome."

Teresa the driver let me out in front of the railroad station in Rome. Teresa in the back seat had figured up my bill. "Really?" I said, staggered. "Petrol is much more expensive in our country than in yours," she said. "Also, there was the lunch." She showed me the paper listing the cost of the food and the gasoline. She had divided the total in half. "Um . . ." I said, inwardly cringing, ". . . um . . . am I . . . you know . . . paying half? And you three are, like . . . splitting the other half?"

Teresa the driver joined forces with Teresa the bill collector. "We are Communists," she said. Communists, of course: sharing bread and cheese and goats and names and half the cost of a journey, and gouging the capitalist for the other half. There was a moral purity about this point of view that I couldn't dispute, except to holler, "Rip-off!"

I looked at Camilla. She looked out the window. I paid. If there were three Teresas on that journey, there was also more than one goat.

I went to the informazione center in the station and got a map, directions to the embassy, and a list of pensiones. The disastrous effects of trying to do everything myself had humbled me. I didn't have to run around like a chicken with its head off either. The map was headed in heavy black letters, NUOVA PIANTA DI ROMA. It was as big as a tablecloth. I blocked two lanes of traffic on the sidewalk as I held the map open, both arms outstretched, and followed my nose along the yellow strips of streets around the station. I'd better stake a claim on a bed before I stormed the embassy.

I found Signora Antonielli's pensione up three flights of a staircase hidden in the courtyard of a tenement. The building loomed over a shabby busy street. The windows of the flanking stores were sparsely filled with wares: a barrel of apples, pimply naked chickens, tinny watches and rings. The window of the hardware store featured an espresso machine and a drying rack. Only the groceria window had a bounteous display. Sausages and hams and smooth white tubes of cheese, bound in quarters with string, dangled over eight wicker baskets, each basket filled with a different shape and thickness of homemade pasta—fluted shells, rippled bands, green sticks and brown sticks, macaroni curls. There was a stand-up coffee bar where several women in ratty men's sweaters and worn print dresses that flapped around their calves were drinking espresso and talking to a sorry-looking waiter. There was a laundromat, with turquoise machines as big as the houses perched on the Ponte Vecchio. Hunting for Stairway B, I had to ask directions of the ladies in the laundromat. Four of them looked at my piece of paper. Six of them walked me to the alley connecting the courtyard to the street. The courtyard was ringed with the backsides of buildings, brick smeared black with soot behind the heavy bars of fire escapes, and canopied with sheets and diapers flopping like fish in a net of clothesline rope.

Signora Antonielli was a tiny lady with a wizened face and sparkly hazel eyes. She wore a wig at all times, the kind that looks like doll's hair, made of coarse, shiny threads visibly sewn to a net; the mesh center parting came just to my chin. The color of the wig was an unlikely auburn. The style was "upward mobile ethnic," combining pompadour with flip, with an emphasis on regimentation and bounce. There was a feisty resilience about the wig that suited the signora. As she showed me to my room, chattering about her previous American guests, all close friends of Sergio Franchi and Frank Sinatra, she interspersed her monologue in English with Italian rejoinders to a basso counterpoint that issued from the back of the house. From the muffled vowels and punctured rhythms of the disembodied voice, I guessed that the man was in the kitchen, arguing with his mouth full. The signora kept stopping short—I nearly fell over her—to hurl hoarse dissent down the hall. Once we'd gained the bedroom, she smiled hugely, patted the cheery red-flowered bedspread, took off a slipper to wriggle her toes in the fleecy pink rug, showed me the closet—four shelves, ten hangers— where I could stow my dress, gave me a towel and a bar of soap the size of a Scrabble tile. All the while, the chomping and the commentary flowed from the kitchen. The signora kept her end up with sardonic laughter, muttering, and violent twitches. As she opened the window to show me the view—a closeup of a gargantuan night-

gown cavorting on a clothesline—the volume of the man's
voice rose, but the speaker switched. He was sitting at the
kitchen table, next to an open window. Most of the windows opening onto the courtyard were kitchen windows;
each framed a family around a table, arguing and eating,
sometimes over the audible buzz of a television. Signora
Antonielli leaned out of her window and hollered, the
whole upper half of her little body extended over the
sill. I stood behind her, poised to grab her ankles if she
toppled. The man leaned out and hollered back, the napkin tucked in the front of his undershirt waving like a
banner. Various heads popped out of sundry kitchens and
contributed remarks, making a choral effect. Never a boring afternoon on Stairway B.

The United States embassy was in the plummy district
near the Spanish Steps. Apart from the flag implanted in
the landscaped garden, and the eagle spreading its gilded
wings across the wall of the consul's fourth assistant's
office, I could have been in Mussolini's guesthouse. Marble
was the keynote. It was all rich for the blood of a tax-
payer, even one who'd gotten all her taxes back. Half of
my tax return belonged to a crooked Italian now. Somehow that gave me the right to feel abused. The woman
who attended to my problem—the consul's fourth assistant's understudy—was very efficient, very polite, very
American, and very sorry. I had no identification. She
would have to clear me with the State Department before
she could grant me another passport. Clearance would take
two weeks.

"I can't stay in Italy for two more weeks!" I said. "All
I have is eighty dollars! Maybe you've been taken in by
The Book. Eighty dollars won't last me a week in Rome."

"I understand that the student hostel is very cheap—"
she began.

I said, "Have you ever had a citizen set herself on fire
on the embassy steps?"

"In cases of emergency, we can wire the State Department and request a wired reply. You might have a passport in four days. But you will have to pay for the wire.
It costs ten dollars."

Ten dollars for a wire to the State Department, and
another ten for the passport, and a fee for new pictures
. . . I raised my voice.

"I am a United States citizen," I said. "I pay taxes. My father pays taxes. My Great-Uncle Al pays taxes. My Aunt Martha pays taxes. The United States government can damn well give us back ten dollars for a telegram, so I can get home!"

Daunted, or else hungry—it was after six—the functionary conceded that the government, in cases of extremity—which I took to mean, when pushed—could pay the cost of wiring itself a question and an answer. "Good. Do that," I said.

The clerk said that four days was the minimum of time it would take to hear from Washington. Four days could stretch to a week. Tomorrow, I'd go to the airline office and try to get another ticket home. If they wouldn't give me one, I'd have to wire my father for plane fare. After four months at hard labor just to prove my independence, I'd have to join the ranks of her AmEx hippies. It didn't seem fair. Meanwhile, I couldn't afford to fritter away another lire. The cheery room off Stairway B was four bucks a night—more than double the hostel fee. Tomorrow, I would swallow hard, and cherche the hostel.

To celebrate the onset of bankruptcy, I went to a storefront ristorante and ordered the most I could get for two dollars—two pastas, spaghetti alla bolognese and tortellini napolitano. Starting tomorrow, I knew I'd be hungry till I got back to the States. I wanted to go for bulk. The bread was free, and after I ordered, the waitress brought me a glass of wine on the house. The staff turned out to watch me eat: the waitress, the bus boy, the chef, the cashier, the dishwasher. All of them had the same face. I ate everything, scraping the plates with the bread. The bus boy was crushed when I passed up dessert. I think he'd put money on it.

Staggering up Stairway B, I got a good look at Signora Antonielli's parlor, which had been a blur in the hoopla of welcome. The walls on two sides were blotted out by huge oil portraits of Pope John XXIII and John F. Kennedy, rendered in a multi-tinted style reminiscent of paint-by-the-numbers kits. The flesh tones of the skin were overlaid with streaks of brown and loops of orange, for "shading." Both subjects were gazing raptly toward the open window —as if they perceived the utopian future, flickering over the wide screen of the X-L nightgown dangling just outside. Limp brown palm fronds draped the billboards. The room was chockablock with tables cluttered with objects: photographs of slick-haired little boys in sailor collars and little girls in bridal veils, all with unfocused caramel eyes, all bathed in a soft brown glow; plastic ferns in dimestore vases; little pottery nuns playing baseball; a tiny gold-sequined high-heeled shoe, filled with toothpicks; an ash-tray ringed with china squirrels and deer and rabbits, filing behind a St. Francis laden with birds. The object that gave me pause was a Kennedy half-dollar, mounted on a square of blue velvet and covered with a plastic shield.

Sounds of confrontation and rejoicing emanated from the kitchen. It was depressing, being alone in someone else's house. I had to invade the signora's party to ask if I could take a shower. I hadn't had a hot shower since Paris; I would pay any price for steam. I poked my head into the kitchen, saying. "Scusi, signora . . ." I couldn't find my hostess in the multitude of acrobatic arms that was a dozen Italians talking. I recognized some of the laundromat ladies, and the man who'd leaned out of the window in his undershirt. Now he was wearing a red-and-green figured shirt and a bright red tie. The table was covered with plates of little pastries and espresso cups. The laundromat ladies saw me and set up a cry: "Ehe, Aurelia! . . . Signorina Americana!"

The red cemented ridges of the wig popped up near my belt. Was she shrinking? No, she was picking up crumbs off the floor, at the same time flailing her arms and dropping the crumbs again as she made her points in the twelve-way conversation. When she saw me, she bobbed up, gave me a hug, sat me down, fed me three pastries, poured me a cup of "American coffee"—good ole Paris Nescafé—introduced me to her friends, dismissed her husband, nameless, and asked me if I knew Frank Sinatra.

"No, I'm sorry," I said. "Do you suppose I could take a shower? I'll pay for it."

The neighbors set up a clamor of laughter and sympathetic moans: poor little Signorina Americana, she wants to take a shower! The signora took the coffee cup out of my hand. She marched me out of the kitchen as the neighbors called farewells and blessings. With flourishes, she threw open the door of the bathroom, a glorious pink and blue domain with a tropical motif. Plastic lavender flowers burst out of the toilet tank, spewed from the towel rack, swung in blue nets from the ceiling. "Help yourself!" the signora cried. "All is for you! No charge! Only do not take all the hot water—I have four Swedes this week! They are such lovers of steam!"

Half an hour later, I hacked my way out of the plastic jungle. I was so thoroughly steamed I was puffy. Conserving some steam for the Swedes, I had shut off the water at intervals and sat on the edge of the tub, dripping and soapy. I sagged with contentment. The loss and frustration of the last three days was swept down the drain with the stink and the dust. I was happy. I put on my nightgown—how lovely to wear a nightgown! how lovely to sleep in a bed!—and wandered down the hall to my room, wet hair swathed in a towel. I passed the four Swedes, who recognized and returned my steamed-out smile. I climbed into bed—dolce! dolce!—and fell asleep with the light on.

In the morning, I told the signora that I would have to leave.

"You did not like the shower?" she asked.

I explained about the passport, the cuckoo thief, the stretching of the overstretched budget, the bottom-line hostel fee. "You wait," she said. She hollered over her shoulder, "Angelina!"

A plump little woman whose body seemed to be made up of round, distinct sections, like meatballs, came galloping down the hall from the kitchen. She carried a scrub brush. The hem of her faded brown dress was soaked and matted with wet black dust. She was smiling anxiously, eager to please. The top of her head came just to my nose, which gave her four inches over the auburn wig. Signora Antonielli took the little woman aside. They conferred. I could see the little woman's head of wiry curls bouncing up and down, sì sì and back and forth, no no. Then, beaming, they turned to me.

"This is Angelina, my maid," said the signora. We nodded, exchanging anxious grins. "She lives upstairs. She will give you a room in her house for eight hundred lire."

Eight hundred lire: a dollar. Less than the hostel. "Oh, are you *sure?*" I said. The curly head bounced to the right as Angelina smiled down at her boss and awaited translation of this question.

"Yes, yes, it is arranged," said the voice beneath the wig.

"She has an extra room, and this is what you should pay her. You see, it is not as nice as here. She will show you where to go."

I thanked the signora and shook her hand, promising to send her a dozen Kennedy half-dollars when I got back to America. "Sure, sure," she said, having heard such promises before. "That's okay, ciao."

Angelina led me up another three flights. Her apartment was the same size and shape as Signora Antonielli's, but the pictures on the parlor walls were magazine pages taped over seams in the plaster. Flakes of plaster hung like frozen snow from the ceilings. There were tarry gaps in the linoleum. The only piece of bric-a-brac was a pottery nun with a jagged white scar instead of a catcher's mitt. It was an employer's castaway, the equivalent of Mouse's shrunken cashmere sweater. I wondered how much the nice signora paid her smiling maid. At the moment, Angelina was looking deeply anxious. She was afraid I'd feel I'd come down in the world when I'd moved up three flights. I wished I could tell her how much I felt at home in the servants' quarters. I smiled and bobbed and said, "Bene, molto bene."

A gorgeous glow spread across her little meatball cheeks. With pride, she showed me my room. The floor was bare, and the spread on the bed was thin cotton, much-mended. But the room was very clean, and twice as big as my room downstairs. "Molto bene," I said.

Angelina had three kids, two boys and a girl, and a husband. All of them showed up for midday dinner as I was going out. The kids broke off an argument to stare at me with three tiers of black, startled eyes. I didn't look like any young woman they knew, and I didn't live like one. Angelina's husband was a solid, worn-looking man, his sweat-stained workshirt rolled above the furry muscles of his arms. He nodded, shy and friendly, above his plate of soup. I smiled and bobbed and nodded.

As I went out through the kitchen, both boys grabbed for the loaf of bread in the center of the flowered oilcloth. Their mother slapped at their hands. In the jostling, the fat loaf fell to the floor.

"Ai-ee!" said Angelina, smacking the kid she could reach. She stooped and seized the loaf. Straightening up, she kissed it. She shoved it at the two boys. The little one kissed the bread too. Then she saw me watching, and she and the husband looked ashamed; I would think they were peasants.

I couldn't express how I felt, so I smiled and smiled, and I went out.

I was prepared to stoke the fires of righteousness again for the folks in the airline office. But the man at the counter disarmed me. He had flaxen ringlets and translucent skin, and he couldn't look me in the eye. What seemed to intimidate him most was my boots, which I'd worn to counter my freckles, lest the airline think I was easy to bully. I found myself speaking to the shrinking youth in tones of soft encouragement. Once he understood my problem, he expressed surprise that I'd encountered thieves in his country. Perhaps he'd been reared in a monastery? He pushed a lot of buttons on a sleek machine. We watched it percolate and grind out tape. "No one has used the ticket," the youth said, reading the tape. "It is unlikely that anyone will. When you have a passport, come back to this office and we will give you another ticket. But if anyone uses the original ticket within a year, you will have to reimburse the airline for it."

"I'll chance it," I said.

He made a reservation for me on the two o'clock flight out of Luxembourg, the following Monday, six days away.

I felt quite jolly as I left the office. I didn't have to appeal to my father. I had my own way home. And I didn't have to take it yet; I had a cosy place to stay, and just enough money to savor six days' grace before Ohio closed in. See Rome and die!

I started to walk, eating an apple, the staple of cheapie diets.

"Buon giorno, bella signorina!"

"Non capisco," I said, walking faster.

"Oho, you are American!" the voice crowed gleefully. "I have cousins in Buff-a-lo!"

"Non capisco," I said, "allez, laissez-moi tranquille!" Let him think I was French. No one could faire the snob like the French.

"Fran-say! For-mee-*doo*-blay! Madama-*zail*-a est *bail*-a!" The voice was overjoyed. Rats!

"Non! Non capisco!" Recklessly, I cried "Vamoose!" I didn't look around. The voice seemed to issue from the small of my back. Either he was a midget or he was walking on his knees, zooming in on the center of my attractions.

"Ehe! Señorita! Come esta usted?"

The mask of El Rocko cracked—I laughed, and bit my cheek. I was almost running down the sidewalk, dodging in and out of groups of tourists taking pictures and natives advising the tourists on angles and shots. The voice clung, insistent. "Maria! . . . Consuela! . . . Conchita! . . . Rosa! . . ."

I couldn't shake him. In desperation, I whirled and threw my apple core. It smacked the hollow chest of a toothless old man. Startled, the old man giggled.

"Ehe, bellissima! Over here!"

I looked down and left. Romeo was hooded in globular plastic, neon-striped in red, white, and lime, the colors of the Italian flag. He wore a black leather jacket and straddled a motorcycle. (Later, I saw that his jacket was embroidered across the back in wobbly yellow: KISS ME, I'M ITALIAN. Mario confessed that the jacket had been the gift of an Americana—young, like me, but not as bella— who'd mailed it to him after she'd gone back to Jersey City.) Under the blue-tinted eyeshield, his face was all grin. "You can' fool Mario, bella," said the gleeful voice. "You Americana!"

So I let him show me Rome.

Rome from a motorcycle: fenders, grills, quacking horns, exhaust pipes, purple shrieking faces, headlights, nauseating fumes, frantic fists, wounded cries . . . There was no end to the drama of it—every moment, a brush with death. I turned it into a contest. Which of the drivers could come the closest to wiping us out? Driving was brutal and brainless, each driver bent on his destination, dedicated to himself, wholly unable to comprehend that all other drivers would not clear a path for him. Patterns were kaleidoscopic, shifting, snarling, smoothing out, all in the course of a minute. Jams were frequent and cathartic. Drivers hurtled out of their cars and pounded on the hoods of cars that blocked their way. Cars rushed into an open space, no matter how that space in turn was blocked, or where the channel led. Violently critical of other drivers' foibles, he kept lifting both hands off the grips to chop one elbow in obscene salute; Mario was ruthless in his disregard for life—his, mine, everybody's. When the road was blocked, he shot his cycle onto sidewalks, driving pedestrians into the doorways of stores. "I'm terribly sorry," I kept calling over my shoulder into the wind. Near murders were doubly embarrassing because of all the witnesses. People in Rome stood around on corners, waiting for something to happen. The major occupation was minding other people's business: watching, making comments, horning in and giving advice, scorning opposing counsel, arguing, roping in reinforcements. A minor mishap could spark a debate that lasted two hours and engrossed the whole block. Witnesses, friends of witnesses, passersby, drivers, pedestrians, black-suited cops—everybody hollered, jumped up and down, beat their heads with their fists. Mario kept up with all of them, ramming the cycle into parked cars as he catapulted off the seat and into the furor. When the jam broke up and the round was over, Mario and I zipped off, and the witnesses went to have coffee.

The Coliseum, like the Arc de Triomphe in Paris, was smack in the center of a vast, unmarked suicide circle of cars whizzing out of and into major routes to the city. From the astounded fury and elaborate maneuvering with which uprushing speedhounds swerved around it and plunged on, cursing, the ancient monument seemed to be an awkward highway marker, dropped in the road in the night. The suicide circle was further obstructed by ice cream men with their carts and patrons, tourists in and out of buses, horse-drawn carriages, picturesque with fragrant markers and halos of flies. Mario executed a slalom run among the piles of dung, and parked in the center of a convocation of nuns. When I could walk, he escorted me into the shell of blasted stone.

The Coliseum scared me.

Parts of the stone floor had crumbled away, revealing the honeycomb of cells beneath—cells where the Christians and the lions had been penned to wait. I could see myself sitting on a stone bench in one of those dark, airless cells, listening to the cheering that shook the stone above my head, the floor of the arena; cheering that blotted out the sound of my own prayers and the prayers of my hidden companions. I listened to the cheering and breathed the cat house odor from the lion pens.

"Fifty thousand people," said Mario, with a sweep of

arms worthy of Caesar. "And the whole crowd could empty in ten minoot. Is achievement!" He slipped an arm around my waist.

"Doesn't it make you angry?" I said.

"Angry?" He frowned and fiddled with the buckle on my belt. I removed his hand.

"Yes!" I said. "Angry at all those Hollywood martyr movies—like *The Robe!* All that phony baloney glory, the clouds of light and the Mormon Tabernacle Choir when the Christians go to their happy deaths—I mean they never showed you it was *real*. It happened here, in this building, over and over—people went out to get eaten by lions, and other people watched!"

"Ah; Sì! The lions!" I was talking so fast that poor Mario couldn't keep up. But he caught the key word: lions. "Sì, was terrible. Violence, much violence!" He tried to console me by tugging my zipper. On cue, we were engulfed by nuns.

Back on the cycle, we made a rocky circuit of the Forum, so I could get a grasp of its scope. Then Mario parked in the same spot, riffling the veils of the same, now departing, nuns. At a cavalry gallop, we crossed the suicide circle and entered the Forum.

Have you ever had the feeling that you've lived somewhere before?

The Forum covered blocks and was ringed by highways. Trucks rumbled just beyond the walls. Japanese tourists shackled with cameras hogged the steps of temples; mounting, clustering, smiling, descending, passing off cameras, adjusting lenses, clicking shutters, mounting, posing. None of it mattered.

The Forum was a magic place, green and wild, all knee-high grass, soaring shards of grey-white columns, brick walls falling to rubble in tangles of ivy, arbors of lilacs drooping over the fragments of temples. Cats ambled among the ruins, shabby grey cats coursing through the small red flowers; sleek white cats sleeping curled in the grass, like pieces of tumbled stone. Soldiers in two and fours, like overgrown Boy Scouts in their flat berets and brown uniforms, strolled up to every girl and asked her name. Defeated, they sat in the grass in the sun, lonely, idle, watching the bees in the purple clover blossoms. Families picknicked on the remnants of stone walls built before the birth of Christ. Kids climbed the trees and rested in the crooks of green branches. A little boy of about three years old ran hooting with laughter through the long grass, almost disappearing in the high, wild strands.

"Yes, this is it," I said.

"Sì, the Forum," said Mario. We were sitting on a fallen column in a field of grass and red and yellow flowers.

"No, I mean . . . this is it. This is where I want to live."

"In Italia?" said Mario with delight.

"In the Forum. I want to rent that little temple, the one that looks like a tool shed."

Mario thought I was kidding. I wasn't. When I'd seen the Place des Vosges by moonlight with Dan, I'd felt a sense of affirmation. That was the kind of place I'd wanted in Europe; that was how France was supposed to look. I wanted to go away again, and know that there would be that stillness, that crystallized beauty, that world unstruck by time. The Place des Vosges was perfect. But the Forum was cozy. I felt at home. I knew at that moment, sitting on a column that had rested in the same spot for two thousand years, that I would be at peace if I could stay forever within those walls, running barefoot in the high grass, rubbing my face in the lilac blossoms, resting my cheek on the chipped, fluted pillars of the little temple, nodding to the cats. I would live on bread and cheese and apples and chianti, stepping out on Sundays for the carbohydrate special at the little ristorante. I would let visitors into my Forum, but only if they promised to respect its serenity. I had found my spiritual home.

Mario felt at home in the Forum too. He wanted to neck. He was Roman. Necking in the Forum was the same to him as necking on the grounds of the Garfield Monument was to me or Randy. I was very happy. I knew I would come back the next day, alone. So we necked. Mario was one terrific kisser.

Rome was one terrific city. In the days that followed, I became certain of what I'd discovered that first hour I'd wandered with Mario in the Forum—Rome was what I'd wanted when I'd set out to leave home. It wasn't like I'd thought Rome would be: it wasn't brown. My images of Rome had come from Caesar movies, where the whole city was pillars and chariot races. There was a lot of dust in *Ben Hur*. But Rome wasn't dusty—it was green. There were parks everywhere, taking up blocks in the center of town that would have been parking lots in the U.S.A. And the parks in Rome weren't organized, like the parks in Paris with their hedge-and-gravel-bordered plots for carousels, puppet stalls, waffle-vendors, pony rides; their signs, forbidding sitting on the grass; their segregated benches where the rich mamas sat with rich mamas, and au pairs sat with other au pairs. The parks in Rome were wild and lush, the deep green of overgrown grass pungent with damp beneath thick-trunked ancient trees. Pairs of lovers embraced in the soft moss, twiddling buttercups under each others' chins. Solitary lovers roamed, gazing up into the branches, easing their pain with the tender pallor of the undersides of leaves. Gazing at the trees, I kept walking into chunks of Roman walls, which emerged from the high grass unremarked and ivy green, like tree stumps.

The parks of Rome would have been perfect if it weren't for the wolves. But somehow I didn't mind the Italian wolves as much as the ones in France. Italians didn't wait till I had passed them, and hiss, like leaky radiators. They didn't hunch behind trees with their flies unzipped. They looked me straight in the eye and grinned and said, "Good morning, bella!" I liked the direct approach. Italian people flirted like they breathed and ate ziti and drank chianti and drove their blunt-nosed cars—with passion and humor and manic zest. They made me laugh. I loved them. I loved their tough courage and their humorous despair. I loved the way they dived headlong at life. Within my County Kerry exterior, I had a heart that beat with an Umbrian rhythm.

And Saturday, I had to go home.

Shipwrecked

Mario gave me a ride to the autostrada on the outskirts of Rome. He kissed me goodbye. That took up ten minutes of road time, but it was a fine Italian send-off. He thought I was crazy to leave. "But the Forum! Your little house!" he kept saying. "Tortellini napolitano! The bread! The vino! The people of Rome, so full of laughing and tears!" He knew all the buttons to push. "I know, I know," I said sadly. "But I'll come back!" He shook his head. Friday night he took me to the Fountain of Trevi. Poor old Rome—every lovely spot was screened with celuloid. I kept hearing the Hollywood Strings, sliding down the opening bars of (beat) "Three coins in the foun . . . tain . . ." Mario showed me the ropes: turn around three times, stand with your back to the fountain, close your eyes, and throw a lira over your shoulder. If it lands in the fountain, you'll return to Rome.

"Oh, like the dove and the wine crop," I said.

Like the wired dove, the fountain was rigged. It was as big as a baseball diamond. Chances that I wouldn't return to Rome were scant. When my lire plopped into the water, Mario swept me into an embrace that was ninety-proof garlic—we'd both had spaghetti al pesto for lunch. "It is a sign!" he cried. "You cannot go back to O-hee-ho! I will get you work in Roma. My cousin seeks a bella signorina to help him sell his leather goods. He has the shop on la Piazza di Spagna. You could working there."

I was tempted. But the bit was in my teeth; the pace of the trek was set. I had settled into the rhythm of the journey. I had the ticket, the passport, the plane reservation. I'd wired my parents. I'd sent a postcard to Dan, c/o American Express, Madrid, telling him that the Whirlwind Tour, Phase II, had been postponed. "Look me up in Ohio," I'd written, "if you keep moving long enough,

315

you'll pass through Cleveland." I'd even sent a postcard to Anouk. Maybe Madame would save it for her, so she could read it when she grew up. I hadn't been able to write something simple and real and loving, in French, that I'd want her mother and father to read. So I'd printed, "Dear Anouk, Visit this place some day. You will like it. Love, Kerry." The postcard showed the little doll-house temple in the Forum.

Oh, I didn't want to go! I'd hugged Signora Antonielli, and Angelina—Angelina, who'd chased her family out of their own house on Friday night, so I could wash my hair. Angelina's apartment didn't have a bathroom, and the water in the kitchen sink was cold. Angelina had sent her kids and her husband into the streets, so they wouldn't invade the kitchen. She'd heated two enormous kettles of water on the stove, and brought me a chair to kneel on at the sink, and a saucepan to rinse with, and towels. I'd kept saying, "Thank you, thank you . . ." and she'd kept bobbing and smiling. . . . This morning I'd hugged her and kissed her cheek, and shaken hands with her husband and children, and said goodbye to the laundromat ladies. "I will come back," I'd kept promising all of them, promising myself. "Capisco!" they'd said, bobbing and smiling: sure, okay, ciao. "Arrivederci!"

"Arrivederci, carissima," said Mario tearfully. "Kerry" was "carissima" now. I liked it better. Carissima: dear. "Send me a cartay postalay!"

"I will!" I hugged him. Crying, waving, blowing kisses, brushing death, Mario slammed his cycle into a six-lane charge of metal jaws.

I stuck out my thumb.

I'd written the route in my sketch book: up through Italy and Switzerland to Luxembourg, sticking to the main routes, taking the efficient rides, the trucks blitzing over the continent on deadlines, not the seers of sights. The plane left Luxembourg at 2 P.M. on Monday. Saturday night, I should couche in Milano; Sunday night, however late, in Luxembourg. Pleasure was over. Getting back to Cleveland was a job.

The painted flat of the far horizon was broken by a double flash of sunlight on chrome. Two cars were approaching, snout to snout. If both of the drivers were Latin men, they'd fracture us all in their race to assist me. I braced myself to leap for the sewage ditch. Then the oncoming cars took shape, and shrunk. The smoking beasts of motorcycles snuffled up the road.

At first I thought Mario was back with a friend. As the cycles drew up in a hail of gravel, I saw that the riders were faceless in goggles and ruthless in black. They were cops.

The cycles circled me clockwise and counterclockwise, sputtering smoke. I coughed. Fifty yards beyond them, I could see the white square of the back of the sign that Mario and I had shot past, Mario laughing and pointing: NO AUTOSTOP. I smiled. They might be cops, but they were also Italians. The eggshells under the goggles didn't crack. They might be Italians, but they were also cops. Most of the cops I'd seen in Firenze and Roma had looked like they were bored with the game. I'd seen soldiers on sentry duty at the Victor Emmanuel monument sitting on the steps, like little kids stuck in the outfield when no one was hitting past the pitcher's mound. But these cops were playing in the major leagues, the highways, and this morning they were playing for the pennant. The spokesman tried me in Italian first. Then he said, "Americana? Sì. What are you doing on the highway?"

"Uh . . . autostopping," I said, all but hanging my head.

"Sì. Do you know it is illegal to autostop on the highway in this country?"

"Uh . . ."

They demanded my passport. I felt a little thrill at being able to produce one. The second cop leaned over the first cop's shoulder to look at my passport picture, as if it were a *Playboy* centerfold. The goggled eggshells lifted and leveled. I reproduced the desperate smile of the girl in the picture. The eggshells nodded. The first cop gave me back my passport. I stuck it in my pocket, and safety-pinned the pocket closed. The second cop took my canvas bag. The first cop slung one leg across his cycle. He jerked his thumb at the leather cushion behind him.

I was barely astraddle the rear wheel when he bolted. I clung to his waist as the wind pushed my face, and rested my cheek on his black leather back, briefly regretting the loss of the wiggly motto: KISS ME, I'M ITALIAN. I could embroider the jackets of the whole police force, if I went to jail. I closed my eyes. I wasn't even worried.

Worrying had peaked and played itself out in three days, when I'd lost my identity and my money. Maybe my arrest was fate. God wanted me in Italy, even if it had to be in jail.

But the cops dropped me off on a dirt road, meandering between an olive grove and a field of tumbled grass. I could see a farm in the sun-hazed distance, with a tidy barn like a wooden toy. I had no idea where I was. But the only wheeled object likely to creak up this road was a donkey cart. "Stay off the autostrada," said the first cop as the second cop gave me back my bag. "Yes, sir," I said. They blasted off, revving, rumbling away and vanishing in sync, trailing identical plumes of exhaust and dust.

I sat on my bag and ate a yellow apple. I watched a string of blackbirds flap across the blank grey sky. It looked like rain.

Down the gullyed road, I caught the glimmer of metal. A car was coming. I jumped up and stuck out my thumb and smiled with all my bunny teeth. This might be the first voiture to pass this way since the tanks had departed. Unless its driver were making familiar, sinister motions under a raincoat spread across his lap, I'd have to take my chances.

Looming out of the pastoral backdrop, the car assumed a strange shape, or series of shapes. The base of the apparition was the dusty purple color of a grape and the shape of a pear. Two thin black wands protruded horizontally from either side of the upper bulb of the pear. Atop the upper bulb, symmetrical with the wands, were a pair of wedge-shaped silver wings, crowned with a silver dome. The whole scene was straight from a horror movie: the hitchhiker, stranded on a country road, a stranger to the place and its inhabitants, the only witness to the manifestation of an interplanetry presence.

The Martians had stopped in the road. A cheery voice tootled, "Viens donc, chérie!": come on! I could hardly believe it. The words were French, and the cheery voice was female.

The pear in the mitre had resolved itself into a Volkswagen with the hull of a boat inverted and lashed to its roof. The hull protruded for several feet behind and in front of the car. Oppressed by a silver aluminum cloud, the purple VW moved within the boat's perpetual shadow.

The car's interior was dark, like a house with the blinds drawn. The car was towing a second silver hull, this one righted, floating on a black metal trailer. The masts and tightly furled sails of both boats were tied to the bottom of the trailer. I didn't know where I was, but I knew I wasn't near the coast. The people in the purple pear might be more eccentric than Martians. I got in.

The driver was a middle-aged woman, bony, with a leathery tan and white hair in a Birdseye Kid bob. She was wearing a shapeless wraparound cotton print garment, known in Ohio as a swirl, and a Ronald Colman sweater—a tweedy cardigan with pockets, a belt, and a rolled collar tapering to lapels—and red tennis shoes. She was the least French-looking person I had ever seen, in or out of France. She was speaking the least French-sounding French I'd ever heard. The front seat of the car was filled with glass jars and bottles, which she shoved to the floor and tossed in the back to allow me to sit. I held my canvas bag on my lap, my feet on a heap of glass. If we stopped abruptly, my ankles would be amputated in the crash—a niggling inconvenience compared to the havoc wrought by the tendency of moving boats to remain in motion.

The lady with the red tennies patted my knee and gave me a piece of buttered bread with one lone anchovy stretched across its surface, like a bathing beauty on a raft. It was hard to believe the lady was French. She was blithely unbowed by her accent and accoutrements—housedress, tennies, jars and bottles, boats . . . eh bien alors! so what?

The back seat coughed.

The driver laughed and turned around, without removing her foot from the accelerator. She didn't pay much mind to the road. Collision wasn't imminent, since ours was the only vehicle for miles. But if we veered to the left, we might hit a tree. I concentrated on my hors d'oeuvres. The driver introduced the cougher, who must have been ducking pitched bottles as I'd entered. "C'est François!" the lady announced. "Il est magicien, vraiment magicien aux bateaux!": François was a boat magician.

François nodded, smiling. He was an ageless, elfish chap with a pug nose and tight, fair curls. What did a boat magician do? Did he make them disappear? Or did he do an act on board, pulling a mackerel out of a hat, sawing carp in half? . . .

"Et moi, je suis Constance!" She glanced at the road just long enough to see that it was there. She explained that she lived in Avignon with her husband Jean-Pierre. She and François had been visiting friends in Perugia and Rome, and had bought two sailboats in Piombino. Now they were en route to a regatta in Nice, to give the boats their maiden dunk. But they were worried about the rising wind. As she spoke, Constance had to pitch her voice above the creaking of the boats, one bobbing and louring above us, one swaying and bouncing behind. "Et toi, chérie, où vas-tu?"

"Luxembourg—" I began.

"Mais chérie, *pourquoi?*" Constance was mystified. With Italy and France to play around in, why would anyone go to Luxembourg? I told her I had to catch a plane; I was going home.

"Mais c'est terrible!" she cried: I must on no account go home. How could I want to go home?

"Je suis fatigué," I said, sounding feeble even to myself: I'm *tired*. Constance exchanged a look of consternation with François in the back seat. How could I be tired? the look said, Constance had never been tired in her life! I explained that I'd spent the winter in Paris—"Quel bonheur!" what bliss!—babysitting for French enfantes—"Quelle horreur!": what horror! She demanded the sordid details. Poor Constance! When she put that quarter in the slot, she hit the jackpot. I regaled her with tales of the whims of Mouse and slices of life with Leah. Constance was a wonderful audience—clucking, hissing, exclaiming, "Insupportable!" There was no one so bourgeoise, she assured me, nodding emphatically as if at the cows we were passing, as a nouvelle riche Parisian woman. Constance was astounded when I said I was American.

"But I thought you was French!" she cried, thus proving that she didn't hear American French any better than she spoke French English. She must be myopic too. One glance should have told her that I wasn't French; that if I'd ever been French, they'd revoked my passport for criminal grooming. She wasn't French or English; she didn't sound Italian or Spanish or German; her accent was across-the-boards garble. She continued, "But you are very little for an American! Americans are all stupendous big! François, elle est americaine, tu écoute? C'est incroyable! But, my dear, I lived in America for two years in 1957. In Tallahassee, tu connais?"

I could very well connais that in Tallahassee, 1957 had seemed like two years. In Cleveland, February seemed like a year and a half.

"Florida, chérie, the South—au bord de la mer, François, by the sea, mais pas comme le sud de la France quand même!" she tootled with laughter and slapped my knee—"a fierce cry from Nice, ma chère, Tallahassee est comme a nightmare, vraiment, les gens, the natives, quelle horreur!"

Constance's husband Jean-Pierre was a painter. They had gone to Tallahassee because he had had an urge to paint alligators. "Magnificent creatures, chérie, but com-pletements magnifique! Très intelligent, tu sais, très agréeable, hideous of course but that is why they good pets, they work so hard to be charming. . . . I bred them, I kept what you call a kennel? Oui? . . . but I had too much success! I made the market a déluge! Le pauvre Jean had *no* success, he could not sell his alligator paintings, the natives of Tallahassee were lost, vraiment lost, they said, 'Can't yew paint somethin pooty, haow baout a sunsit?'"

I laughed. I asked how many languages she spoke besides English, French, and Tallahassee.

"Alors!" she cried, slapping her forehead. She frowned. "Il y a Grecque, Greek, you comprehend . . . a little Russian, some Polish . . . Rumanian, that is my strong, Jean et moi was guides in a factory in Timisoara in 1968— triste, c'était triste, my dear, un tel depressing time, I assure you—those poor stark people, they have nothing, rien du tout! . . . they offer you hundreds of dollars for Elvis Presley records—but Jean wanted to paint the life of the factory, tu connais? . . . man against the stupendous pipes! L'homme contre la mécanique, François!"

I looked over the seat at François. His pug nose was pressed against the grit-dimmed glass of the rear window. He was watching the quivering hulls of the boats as they strained at their bonds and bobbed on the rising swells of wind. In a light, grainy tenor he murmured, "Constance, je crois . . ."

"I have a how you say, a smattering? . . . voilà! je fais bien! a smattering of Dutch, and of course some African dialects—I was born in Libya—but beaucoup de my tribal tongues are pas pratique maintenant—the poor dears are interdit de visiter, one can't get in to see them, they live like nuns. My passports are Libyan and Greek, because of my father, and French, bien sûr, because of Jean-Pierre . . . aussi I have a Viennese letter of safe conduct from that affair in Denmark in forty-two, I keep it pour nostalgie, tu sais . . ."

"Constance . . ."

"Jean and I have been at Avignon seven months, he is painting the bridge. Tu connais, 'le pont d'Avignon'?" Waggling a finger, she sang, "Sur le pont . . . d'Avignon . . . on y danse, on y danse . . ." Breaking off, she added, "Le pauvre Jean can sell ten millions paintings of 'le pont d'Avignon,' American tourists will buy tout, vraiment tout, the bathrooms of Tallahassee will be déluged with prints of the bridge. I tell Jean, 'Chéri, paint a petit alligator in the waters, who will see—' "

"Constance." François raised his sand-in-the-gearshift tenor over the raucous squeaking and groaning of the boat above our heads. Through the windshield, I could see the meadows billowing beyond the road, the rich green grass laid flat and whipped upward in scythelike sweeps of wind. The trees writhed, new buds stripped from the tortured branches, tumbled, flung to the grass. "Constance, c'est un problème . . ."

"Comment, chéri? . . . Mon Dieu!!! Qu'est-ce que c'est?"

The object snaking across the windshield was an end of rope. The oval pool of darkness in which we had moved for the last hour had vanished. I could see the sky again—grey, opaque, laced with vaporous, hurried streams of cloud.

Constance leaped out of her seat and into the road so fast, she left the motor running. She stood facing us, her head cut off by the roof of the car, her tough, bangled hands on her hips. The flowered cotton swathing her lean torso snapped in the wind. "Merde," said the torso. François and I piled out.

Goaded by the uproarious wind, the vessel had torn itself loose from its mooring. Sailing briefly and joyously into a field, it was rolling and bounding along like a spar in a rough high tide.

Constance and François gave chase. I shut off the ignition

and put the keys in my pocket before I ran after them.
Constance was vaulting through the hay-high grass. Halfway to the boat, she halted, teetering, flailing her arms for
balance as she twisted around. She waved me back. She
cupped her mouth with her hands and screamed into the
wind. I heard: ". . . reste-là, chérie . . . keep watch, tu
sais . . . let not other fly away . . . *attention au vent!*"

Attention au vent: watch out for wind.

I picked my way out of the meadow, pulling the flapping
tails of my coat closed around me. The warmth of the
day had gone with the sun. I wondered what time it was.
Rome to Milano, I'd figured, was ten to twelve hours on the
road. The wind was sharply cold. The boat on the trailer
was almost free of its bonds; it reared and bucked with
every buffet of wind. I tried to tighten the ropes, but someone who knew his knots—François, the boat magician—
would have to undo them and batten down the whole craft
more securely. The wind attacked. The boat cavorted. How
could I keep it from blowing away?

Voilà! I climbed aboard.

After a Paris winter on the empty icebox cure, I'd
weighed, on Mouse's scale, forty-six kilos—a hundred and
three pounds, ten less than when I'd left home. A week in
the land of lasagna had added leverage to my ass, but I
still wasn't much of an anchor. I willed myself heavy,
clinging to the rail as the wind tried to pluck me away.
Strands of hair cracked my face and flickered in my eyes.
I shifted to the plank seat. Dead weight was heavier than
conscious weight, as I recalled from Alfred Hitchcock re-
runs, but I was afraid to go limp and lose my grip for
fear the wind would snatch me up like dandelion fluff. I
lay down in the bottom of the boat.

It started to rain.

I could see nothing but sky, an endless span of mottled
grey and white, shooting into my eyes in a hundred billion
droplets, grey and fine. My metal cradle bucked and
rocked. I swayed and rattled. I could believe myself shipwrecked, adrift and abandoned. But I was aware of a
bouncy lightness about my heart. An effervescent sense
of well-being bubbled up in my chest and flowed through
my body. I found myself grinning. This pure, silly happi-
ness must be what a "free spirit" meant. I could cope

with anything. I needed nothing. Shipwrecked on a high-way outside of Rome? Eh bien alors!: so what?

Now I'm ready to travel, I thought, now that I'm going home!

I pulled myself up to peer over the side, to see how the elf and the madwoman faired with the runaway. The flying vessel had lodged against a tree, not quite upside down, the swelling curve of the hull exposed, like a small silver blimp that had crashed in a field. Constance and François were pushing and hauling, but the boat was too heavy or too firmly stuck to budge. The erratic wind and uncertain footing made their task more difficult. As I watched, Constance stood on the hull and kicked it. She stomped her tennies, haranguing the wind with her fists. Then she opened her arms to embrace the elements—the wind, the dense insistent rain—and she laughed. She waved to François, pointing to a spot some yards away. François tramped off. He poked around in the tall weeds, hunting. Then he stooped and gathered up a mighty stone. I could have used it for weight in the boat. He tottered back to the beached ship, the boulder in his arms. Constance seized it, raised it over her head—in my eyes, she had assumed the dimensions of a bust on Rushmore—and dashed the boulder down on the hull. When the boulder rolled into the grass, a hole appeared in the silver sphere. François hoisted his arm in a gesture of "Bravo!" "Bra-*vo!*" I yelled to the wind. Constance held up the hem of her swirl on either side, and curtseyed.

She joined me on the bounding main as François made the craft secure. Her hair, like mine, was slicked flat on her scalp by the rain. But she was exuberant. "Tu as compris?" she cried, giving me the one-armed hug of a comrade. "L'assurance? insurance? . . . there must have serious damages, or no, you don't collect, mais pas du tout! It is, on dit . . . the fine print, tu connais?"

"Voilà," I agreed, having learned the fine points of fine print at Occidental Insurance. As we in Coding used to put it, "Many collide, but few collect."

The craft trussed, François assisted us over the side. "C'est ça!" said Constance, landing buoyant as a gymnast in her tennies. "Now we must go to the next town and call the insurance! Mais toi, chérie . . . what does one do with you? Where do you go today?"

"Well, Milano, I hope," I said. Milano sounded boring.

"Bon! I will take you to the autostrada—you can make charming smiles for the trucks, you will be in Milano in time for tea!"

François faired the sport and stayed to guard the salvage till Constance returned with the cops and the fine print merchants. With luck, she would bemuse the entire Italian highway patrol till a trucker had whisked me away. If that team of hard-boiled cyclists found me soliciting on the autostrada a second time in one morning . . . my ass, as we say in Ohio, would be grass. We towed the carrier off the road and unhitched it from the car. The rain was still falling in sepia sheets—we could have been in Paris. Constance gave François a tarp to put over his head. He stuck out an arm from his cave and waved as we peeled away. "Courage, mon vieux!" Constance cried to him, "je vais faire tout de suite!"

Detached from its double load, the Volkswagen clipped along. En route to Viterbo, the nearest town, Constance gave me an Italiano itinerary. She had forgotten that I was leaving Italy. I didn't interrupt her. It was fun to hear about my soulmate country from someone who loved it as much as I did and knew it well. "You *must* go to Venice! Ai-ee, Venezia! Che bella, bella città! You must see its treasures before they are complements décimes, in ten more years elle n'est pas là! Venice will be gone, all gone! They are selling la toute ville piece by piece to Arabs. Ma chère, c'est impératif, they *must*—sì non, all must be drowned in the waters. Mais oui, it has happened some years since, many many paintings rompues dans le déluge . . . ah, chérie, to see Italia for the first time, I have envy of you! But the men! les hommes! Mon Dieu, one cannot discourage them, useless to try! Mais les Italiens sont *mer-veill-eux,* they live the life intensely, tu connais, to the full—"

"Capisco," I said.

"—but they have no morals, pas du tout. Tant pis! They steal."

"Voilà."

We laughed.

". . . Ah, Venezia . . . when I was a girl . . . les cafés . . . the dancing on the piazza in the evenings . . . c'est là where I fell in love, chérie, the great, great love of my life . . ." Dreamily, she stared at the windshield. The road was obliterated by rain. The windshield wiper on the left was broken. Under the fainting stroke of the right-hand wiper, only a small fan-shaped peephole appeared and vanished, in the splashing grey tide on the glass.

"With Jean-Pierre?" I said.

"Comment?" she murmured, smiling.

"You fell in love with Jean-Pierre in Venice?"

". . . Oh! . . . oh non non non, chérie! . . ." She laughed and pinched my cheek. "Mon amour, c'est le voyage . . . travel, adventure, liberté . . . a life which embraces the best, le mieux, from all parts of the world, the most of most . . . that is the greatest romance!"

"That's how I want to live," I said. "Screw Ohio."

When we reached the autostrada, Constance insisted on driving down the entrance ramp and pulling off to the side of the road. "Here they will see you!" she said. As I opened the door of the car, the force of the torrent redoubled. "But chérie, you will get wet!" cried Constance, as if she'd just noticed the rain. Both of us were drenched. My jeans clung, nastily wet, to my legs. "Where is your macintosh?"

"My which?"

"The how you call, sleek-air? Wetcoat, tu compris? You have no wetcoat?"

"Oh, oh no, I just have this regular coat—"

"Mais c'est kismet, tu sais! I have a wetcoat perfect suited for the adventure, which will fit you but exactly, comme on dit 'made to order.' " Constance rooted around among the bottles in the back seat and untangled a heap of crushed canvas, the bright orange color of highway markers. "Voilà! It is a Norwegian sailor's coat, it is made for standing up to the tempest, I wore it in the hurricane in Tallahassee and I was all comfy cozy, vraiment! But put it, put it, try for the size, chérie!"

She clambered out of the car and stood in the downpour on the berm, as Latino demons of the road swooshed past us, spraying us with rocks and water. To keep me from getting wet, Constance was going to get us killed. I put on the raincoat. It must have been loose on Constance, who was at least a head taller than me. Its folds hung around me without taking form from my body. I seemed to be clamped inside an orange canvas telephone booth. The hem hovered just at my ankles. The bulky cuffs of the sleeves hid my fingers. The hood was better than blinders. Constance pulled the drawstring on the hood. The canvas puckered into a circle framing my eyes and nose. Backing up into the road to admire me, she clapped her hands and laughed.

"It's me, huh?" I said.

"Chérie, c'est parfait! In this wetcoat you will triumph over all weathers! You will have great autostop success!"

It didn't seem likely that any Italian would come to a screeching halt in a rainstorm to pick up a five-foot-three-inch, bright orange monolith-with-thumb. But I said, "Merci bien, Constance—it'll really be a big help. And thank you for the ride! I had a wonderful time!"

She kissed me on both orange canvas cheeks and once on the nose, for luck. Half in and half out of the car, she scribbled an address on a wet scrap of paper. She stuck the paper in the coat's snap-flap pocket. "This is Jean et moi, you must come to Avignon and rendre une visite, it is une telle ville, very small but completemente exquisite! The city of the bridge, tu connais?" Rain dripping down our noses, we sang, "Sur le pont . . . d'Avignon . . . on y danse, on y danse . . ."

"I will come," I said. "Not this trip, but the next one!"

"Très bien, parfait! Come whenever you are in France, ma petite! They say in Tallahassee, 'Y'all drop by!'"

The purple pear puttered off, cutting in front of a shiny red Volvo. Horns brayed like maddened cattle. The drivers of the Volvo and the three cars tearing in a teeth-on-ankle chain behind it rolled down their windows and screamed invective into the tempest. The Volkswagen sailed on, oblivious, single wiper waving.

Warm inside my canvas tent, smiling invisibly into my canvas muzzle, I stuck out my thumb. While I waited for some Italian whacko to stop just to see what I was, I contemplated a budget. I would get a waitress job—Randy had worked in a Dog n' Suds where tips were good and they let you eat the ice cream—and live at home and never spend money. Europe stories ought to buy my beer all summer—till I'd saved enough to hit the road. And this time I would do it right! I would join the Y and take Italian lessons. I would write to Dee . . . maybe she'd like to show me London. It rained a lot in London. My

Constance wetcoat would come in handy. And Dan, of course, I'd write to Dan, to tell him to keep in touch. I'd send him a postcard of the Garfield Monument, Cleveland's reply to Napoleon's Tomb. "Let me know where you are in the fall," I'd say.

I might turn up anywhere.

Mary Gallagher is an actress, playwright and novelist. She began her acting career at the Cleveland Playhouse and is presently a member of the actors' co-op Orphans of the Storm. Her first full-length play, Fly Away Home, *was produced in 1977 in San Francisco and her most recent play,* Father Dreams, *will be produced by Theatre Matrix in New York City.* Spend It Foolishly *is her first published novel.*